All at once their bedroom closed in around her...

Cole's presence was everywhere all at once. The slow creaking sound of the wood on rusting hinges heightened her anticipation and when the door opened completely, he took his first step inside the room. Abby felt her knees go weak.

His large masculine form framed the doorway. The only sounds she could hear now were the echo of his worn leather boots on the hard wooden floor and the delicious pounding of her heart. Cole's face, soot stained and weary, had been carved to perfection with deep contours and planes that defined his chiseled features. The brown bared skin of his chest glimmered with sweat in the lantern's light.

He tossed his hat onto the bed and started toward her. He ran his fingers through his still damp hair, stopping mere inches away. Abby could all but taste the sweat emanating from his taut body.

"Fire's out," he rasped, his voice husky and dry as he reached up to touch her face.

The tingling in her belly told her it was only just beginning.

the Rancher

REDBOURNE SERIES BOOK ONE
COLE'S STORY

KELLI ANN MORGAN

inspire books

Inspire Books
A Division of Inspire Creative Services
937 West 1350 North, Clinton, Utah 84015, USA

THE RANCHER

An Inspire Book published by arrangement with the author

First Inspire Books paperback edition August 2012

ISBN-13: 978-1-939049-00-1
ISBN-10: 1-939049-00-8

Printed in the United States of America

PRAISE FOR THE RANCHER BY READERS

"An amazing book! I read it in 2 days!! I was envious of the relationship between the main characters. A must read!! This book has everything you could want in a good read!!"

—*Nicole Campbell*

"It is hard to find romance novels that capture your heart, leave you longing for the sequel, and are clean enough you can recommend them to your mother! *The Rancher* does all that and more. You won't be disappointed."

—*Camy Albrecht*

"Fabulous book. A must read!! My favorite thing about this book is it kept my attention the whole time. I could not put it down. All the characters were fun and it was easy to picture what was taking place in the story. Love the chemistry of the main characters!! Can't wait for the second installment. Thanks, Kelli Ann for sharing your talent."

—*Angela Jacob*

"Intrigue. Mystery. Romance. A real page-turner."

—*Cheri Buys*

"Kelli Ann Morgan is a bright and gifted writer. She inspires, amazes, and motivates her readers. I highly recommend reading this brilliant piece of love and hope."

—*Susie Dawson*

"I totally enjoyed reading and look forward to many more. *The Rancher* is a well-written, well-researched book. It is very romantic, without being overly graphic, and will appeal to a wide variety of readers."

—*Rocky Palmer*

ACKNOWLEDGEMENTS

This journey, while it is far from over, has been one of the most incredible of my life. I am so grateful to those who have helped me along the way...

To all of my young childhood friends whose encouragement fueled my passion.

To Peter Gacioch (1973 – 1990) who, as a little seventh grade boy, believed that a little seventh grade girl would one day become a published author and wasn't afraid to say so. You'll never know what that meant to me, Pete.

To Mrs. Marcusen, my ninth grade English teacher, who understood my dream, had faith in my abilities, and opened doors for me to learn and develop my craft.

To my dad, Rocky Palmer, who got me started reading romance novels in the first place, and my mom, Carolyn Palmer, for always encouraging my creativity and humoring my visions of grandeur.

To my sisters, Kathy and Cheri, for believing in me, cheering me on, and for being faithful readers. To my brothers, Steven and Brandon, just because. And to Grandma Peggy for never giving up hope that someday I would make it.

To Sarah Jarman for volunteering for the task of being my first beta reader and to all of my other wonderful volunteer beta readers who were an invaluable part in making this dream a reality. Thank you for your excitement and honesty. You know who you are.

To LL Muir for showing me that nothing happens without a little risk, for paving the way before, and being there to encourage, push, and remind me of the reasons I write to begin with. You have been an inspiration and lifeline.

To URWA for teaching me the rules—even though I sometimes break them, and for all of the wonderful writers with whom I have the opportunity to rub elbows and learn from on a regular basis. I can't tell you how much your support, courage, knowledge, and dedication have helped me through the years.

To my wonderful characters who just can't stay out of my head and who talk to me even when it's not convenient, I couldn't have done this without you.

To my little Noah, who has put up with his mama only being available to play for a few hours a day and who makes me feel like I am the most talented woman in the world—imitation really is the best form of flattery.

And lastly to my wonderful, creative, talented, and supportive husband, Grant, who has spent countless hours with me talking through plotlines, proofreading, making dinner, doing laundry, and whatever else it has taken to make sure I could have the time to write, edit, design, format, and whatever else it has been needed to get me to this point. And for loving me amidst the chaos that is my busy life.

To Grant, the incredible and handsome hero in my own love story, and to Noah, my little hero in the making. I love you!

CHAPTER ONE

Colorado, Spring 1876

"You can't just ride into town in your mother's wedding dress, Abby, and expect some man to marry you." An incredulous snort accompanied Lily's proclamation.

Abigail McCallister jerked her head toward her best friend and frowned. She hit her gloves against her denims, pulled her hat a little lower on her head, and wiped her wrist across her chin, wet with perspiration.

"Well, it's true." Lily stepped up onto the wide bottom plank of the fence separating the two women.

Abby noted how Lily's raven curls, pulled up onto her head, contrasted dramatically with the spring yellow of her dress. She mused at the huge dissimilarity between the two of them. Best friends all their lives, nothing in common. Lily, as usual, was gussied up in a fancy dress and would be attending the Patterson's tea party this afternoon. Abby looked down at her own clothes, faded denims and work boots. The last event she'd attended, other than standing at the back of church most Sundays, was her mother's funeral.

She tilted her head enough to see Lily out of the corner of her eye.

Nothing alike, she determined.

Abby leaned against the fence where her friend had perched. Avoiding Lily's eyes, she crossed her legs at the ankle and folded her arms. With one deep breath she inhaled the fresh spring air.

She loved mornings on the ranch. The sun had just risen over the countryside, framed by snow-capped mountain peaks. It appeared as if an artist's brush had swept pink and orange hues across an otherwise cloudless sky.

"True or not, it has to work." Abby flipped her hand at a buzzing sound in her ear. "My pa's not used to losing bets. If I don't find my own husband by the time the stage leaves on Friday, I have to be on it."

"What about Alaric?" Lily's question was simple enough, but Abby had not wanted to think about the boy who'd walked away from her nearly six years ago. His tall blond image had haunted her dreams for far too long. It was time to let it go, but the familiar knot in her stomach returned in protest.

"His promise expired a long time ago," Abby said, blowing a lock of hair from her face. Normally, her curls stayed tucked up under the faded brown leather hat, but today, one stubborn strand fell in disarray at her temple. She folded it behind her ear for the third time this morning.

"You don't think he'll come and whisk you away on his noble white steed?" Lily asked with dramatic flair.

"He said two years, Lily. It's been almost six. He's not coming." She hoped her tone would end this line of conversation.

It did. But Abby didn't know if she liked the new topic any better and she turned on the fence to watch the horses in the corral.

"I can't remember the last time you put on a proper dress. I'll bet most of the men in this town don't even remember you're a girl." Lily held on to the top fence plank and leaned back, her face aglow in the morning light.

Abby dropped her head with an exasperated sigh.

Snapping her head up quickly, as if she'd just had a sudden thought, Lily leaned in close to Abby's ear and whispered, "Except for maybe Jeremiah Carson," she giggled.

Abby's gaze shot up.

"If you're so set on getting a husband," Lily said more

loudly with teasing laughter in her voice, "why don't you just ask him?".

A cloud of dust appeared a short distance down the road, rescuing Abby from a reply. Three horsemen approached. She hoped they had the new stallion in tow. Abby pushed away from the fence, scurried to the gate, and swung it open wide, allowing the riders unrestricted entrance.

"Your pa's gonna whip you good if he sees you in them men's britches again." The gruff old hand dismounted, shaking his head and muttering under his breath.

Abby reached up to grab the front of her hat and tilted her chin downward to hide the smile that threatened. When he pulled the new horse around into Abby's view, her breath caught in her throat and she could contain it no longer. Excitement welled inside of her until she could hardly breathe.

"Oh, Caleb," she exclaimed, rubbing the horse's neck and leaning into his long, slender nose, "he's beautiful!"

Pulling away from the stallion she took in the horse's strong features and ran her hand down the front of his nose. She bent toward him and blew into his face. The horse shook his head and whinnied in approval.

"What's his na..," she spun around, the words on her tongue, but stopped short when four faces, laced with quizzical expressions, stared back at her, "...name?" she finished.

"What in tarnation are you doing there, girly?" Caleb had taken off his hat and scratched his head.

Abby looked into the faces of each of her observers with furrowed brows. The tall redheaded boy, Davey, was new to the ranch and his freckled mouth hung wide open. Jim, one of the older hands at the SilverHawk, stood a might shorter than her own five feet five inches. His nose scrunched above a burley orange mustache, his eyes bulging heavily from their sockets. And then she glanced at Lily, whose eyebrows arched higher than Abby had ever seen them.

She looked back at the horse and realized they didn't know about the new technique she'd learned from their previous foreman. "I overheard Jesse say that blowing gently into his face is the quickest way to teach him my scent."

Each of their faces relaxed in understanding. All except for Caleb, who harrumphed. Jesse had been killed in a bar room fight just a few weeks ago.

"Well, get on with ya then." Caleb returned his hat to its place on top of his slick graying head. "He'll be needin' a good brushin' and feedin' before ya do any work with 'im." He waited long enough for Abby to nod, then turned his paint gelding around and led him to the bunkhouse.

Abby smiled to herself. She was grateful that the horse didn't seem to be skittish or ornery. They'd been careful to take all the mares out to the pasture to run and play while the new stallion was introduced to the ranch.

Abby reached down and gathered the horse's reins in her hand. She leaned into him, nuzzling her cheek into his, and wrapped an arm under his neck in a welcoming embrace. "Chester," she said, hugging the willing horse close to her. "We'll call you Chester."

"You sure do have a way with horses, Abby." Lily came from behind and linked her yellow satin covered arm with hers.

Abby tried to pull away, worried about dirtying Lily's dress, but her friend held firm. Abby smiled. With the reins still in her free hand, she led Chester into the stable, where a fresh stall awaited the newest addition to the SilverHawk ranch.

"It was my mother's dream." She pulled her arm from Lily's to open the stall door and guide the beautiful stallion inside. "To breed and train horses, I mean," she continued once the horse was settled.

"We all know how much she loved this ranch. Do you still think about her a lot?" Lily took the brush box off the metal post in the wall and handed it to Abby, who set it on the floor next to Chester.

"I know it's silly. It was a long time ago, but this…" Abby looked out into the yard and around the ranch, "this was all she ever wanted." Abby moved across the stable and loaded a tin bucket with oats. She handed it to Lily, who stared at her in disbelief.

"And what, exactly, am I supposed to do with this?" Lily asked with an upturned nose.

Picking up a larger bucket near the stall door, Abby smirked at her inexperienced friend. "Feed him, silly. I'm going out to pump some water for the trough."

Abby had only gotten a few feet from the stable when a hair-raising scream reverberated off the walls of the stable and into the courtyard. Abby dropped her stick and both water pails, running back toward the stable.

Lily, crouched into the corner of the stall, had terror etched across her face. She held the bucket of oats up to her chin, her eyes open wide and wet. Chester's nostrils flared and he snorted heavily with apprehension.

Before Abby could see what had evoked such fear in her friend and had riled the horse, she heard it. Only one creature sounded like an innocent baby's toy before lunging with its deadly strike.

She snapped her head toward the sound and was greeted by a coiled rattlesnake flicking its forked tongue in the air, seemingly focused on the whimpering woman in the stall. Slowly, Abby reached inside the stable door to the wall where her papa's old Winchester rested. She removed it slowly from the sturdy nail bracket, careful and steady.

Boom. The shot shook the rafters and all of the horses, within the close confines of the stable, snorted and reared, pawing at the air. Within moments men's voices sounded from every direction.

Abby reached down, the rifle in one hand, and picked up the now headless serpent. The width of its body required the use of both hands. Abby laid the Winchester on the worktable and moved to the open doorway. A half a dozen men ran toward her, mostly coming from the bunkhouse and the barn.

"Miss Abby?" Davey was the first at the door, bent over, hands on his knees, attempting to catch his breath. He raised his head to look at her, his breaths coming in ragged heaves. "Is everything..." he swallowed, "all right?"

Abby shifted with the weight of the snake. The buttons of

the tail rattled together in reaction. Davey's eyes opened wide. He jerked up, board straight, and took one slow step backward. Without warning, Bert, another young hand, plowed into him from behind, and they sprawled forward toward Abby and the dead rattler.

Abby dropped her shoulder as they came at her and the two men fell to the stable floor, scrambling against each other for their footings. Abby stepped over them and out into the courtyard.

A short, curt whistle stopped the rest of the frenzy. "Everything is fine," she bellowed. Holding up the snake's lifeless body for all to see, she attempted to reassure them. "It was just a rattler."

"Yeah, one with seven buttons on its tail." Davey emerged from under Abby's arm, just below the snake's once formidable rattle. A low breathy whistle of his own followed his appraisal.

The other men, satisfied all was well, returned to their various chores about the ranch.

Abby smiled. Davey looked down at the snake and then back at Abby. She swore it was admiration playing with the freckles on his face. He tipped his hat, turned, and walked away, grabbing a reluctant Bert by the arm as he left.

Lily cleared her throat. "Well, that was unpleasant." She stood up and brushed the skirt of her dress. One hand moved to the back of her head, primping the loose tendrils at her nape. "Tell me again why on earth you like this type of work."

Abby tossed the snake toward the muck pile and opened her mouth to respond.

"Now, that's good eatin'." Caleb spoke before she could. "I'd wager near four feet of prime meat."

Lily nearly choked. "Excuse me. You are going to eat," she looked toward the dead serpent, "that?"

Caleb used the handle of his shovel to pick up the snake carcass. "Why, sure, missy. Haven't had Rattlesnake stew since ol' Broots left us to cook for the Graysons' last year." He hung it over a hook near the door.

Abby rolled her eyes. Satisfied Lily was fine, she walked

into the stall where Chester now appeared unaffected by the potentially perilous display. She roamed her hands over his flanks and up his neck, rubbing as she went.

Looking down into the freshly laid bedding, Abby noticed a small, torn piece of black cloth protruding from the straw at the edge of the stall. She patted Chester on the side of his neck and reached down to pick it up.

"What is it?" Lily asked.

Abby pulled at the cloth and freed a large black linen knapsack. She couldn't think of a reason as to why it would be in the stall or where it had come from. She had prepared the room herself just a little over a half an hour ago and had not seen anyone else enter since she'd spread the straw on the floor. Something didn't feel right, but she dismissed the feeling as nerves from killing the snake.

"Nothin'." Abby shoved the cloth into her back pocket.

Content all had returned to normal, Abby grabbed the bucket of oats from the spot Lily had dropped it and handed it to Caleb, who leaned against the stable entrance, picking at his teeth with a piece of straw. He took the bucket without a word and pushed himself away from the door.

Abby returned outside for the water pails she'd left in the courtyard.

Lily followed.

After she retrieved her pole and pails, she walked with a determined pace toward the water wagon. Something still just didn't sit right. She'd killed her fair share of snakes before, but she'd never seen a rattler on the ranch. They were too far away from the hills.

"Are you all right?" Lily broke into her thoughts.

Abby looked back at her friend, who struggled to catch up, her heeled shoes no match for the gravel and dirt that made up the courtyard.

What is wrong with you Abby McCallister? She took a deep breath and slowed enough for Lily to walk companionably next to her.

"My mama sure loved this place, you know?" Abby forced

her thoughts in a different direction. "It's because of her that McCallister stock is the most requested in the territory. She sure knew her horses."

They reached the water wagon and Abby turned the spigot to fill the oversized pails. She leaned her backside against the base.

"I know you miss her and all, Abs, but..." Lily paused lowering her eyes away from Abby, "...she's still alive," she reached out a hand and placed it over Abby's heart, "in here. You don't have to be exactly like her to keep her memory alive."

"She was different than most mothers, I know that. But she taught me how to ride, how to respect and handle hors—"

"No one is saying your ma wasn't a great woman, Abs. In fact, I am very thankful right now for the skills she taught you. They just saved my life," Lily exclaimed, her hand raised across her heart.

The door to the main house opened. Her father's broad shoulders filled the entry. Abby noted how the white flecks in his hair aged him somewhat and she was saddened to think of all he had endured over the last several years without her mother.

"It's my pa you should thank for that one."

Her father motioned for Caleb to join him on the porch. Abby watched the tense body language between the two men as they spoke. When her father looked up and caught her eyes he held her stare for a moment then turned inside, slamming the door behind him.

"Uh, Abby? The water." Lily nudged her toward the overflowing pail.

She quickly switched the full bucket with the empty and was more careful to watch as the second one filled. Her father was still angry. This was the most troubled she had seen him in a long time, but she wouldn't give in. Couldn't give in to what he wanted from her.

"What exactly happened between you two last night?" Lily asked.

Abby did not appreciate how in tune Lily could be sometimes.

"And don't say 'nothing' because I know better," Lily continued, moving her hands to her hips.

Abby turned away from her, but could still feel her friend's eyes boring holes into the back of her head.

"He just told me it's time to get married, is all." She closed the spigot and picked up the second pail, placing it on the elevated shelf to the left of the wooden faucet.

"He thinks I'll have a better chance at landing a man in Denver society with my aunt Iris than I do here. She's supposed to teach me to be more refined or something." Abby slid her carrying pole into the handles of the full water buckets.

"So, why his sudden change? Hasn't he always said that no man is good enough for his little rancher girl? Not even the ever-so-perfect Mr. Alaric Johansson?" Lily tilted her head and batted her eyelashes.

Abby's feelings for the young boy she'd believed she'd loved had died a long time ago. It had been ages since she'd thought about him. Lily just wanted her to be happy, but she just couldn't understand that the land made her happy. The horses. The ranch.

"I don't know what happened, but Papa's been actin' all strange like for the past few weeks." Abby positioned herself under the pole, attempting to balance the water evenly on her shoulders.

She remembered the day, just after her ma died, when her father had defended her to Mrs. Patterson, the store keeper. He'd said any man worth a grain of salt could see she was worth her weight in gold and if the fine and well-to-do Alaric Johansson couldn't see it, he wasn't worthy of her. He'd told the nosy busybody that a truly worthy man would recognize her value straight away and wouldn't make a lady wait, not even one day. His little rancher girl deserved only the best.

So, why *had* he changed his mind now?

"I don't know," she repeated. Her words no more than a whisper this time. Abby pushed her legs into a standing position, the weight of the pails throwing her balance off slightly. She wavered.

Lily ducked her head under the pole and rested it against her shoulders and together they heaved the buckets toward the stable.

"Suddenly, he's decided that working on a ranch is not fit for a lady and he wants something better for me." Abby's hands wrapped more tightly around the pole. She shook her head and took a deep breath, hoping it would clear her thoughts and help her to focus on the task at hand. It didn't work.

"I love ranching and he knows it. He's the one who taught me how to ride and shoot better than anyone else in the territory... including him. No, the SilverHawk was my mother's dream and I am not about to back away from it."

When they finally reached the stable, they nearly dropped the buckets. Abby had forgotten how heavy they could be when full.

"Here, let us get those." Jim and Bert stood on either side of them and removed the buckets from the pole and dumped them into Chester's in-stall trough.

Abby was grateful for the help, but thought it odd. The hired hands rarely stepped up to help with her chores. They each bowed awkwardly and smiled before leaving. She glanced over at Lily who had a mile-wide smile plastered on her face. She looked back to the hands and it dawned on her. They weren't helping with her chores, they were trying to impress Lily.

Abby snorted as she took the brush off its hook on the wall.

"So, are you really going to do it, then?" Lily asked casually as she sat down on a small wooden stool near the stable doors.

"Do what?" Abby swung the stall door wide and walked into Chester's stall to brush him. When Lily didn't respond immediately, Abby glanced up.

Clay McCallister stood in the entrance of the stable. Abby stopped brushing, but didn't move. She remembered a time when her father had been larger than life to her. It hadn't been that long ago. Something had changed in the last little while and she didn't know how to reach him, to make him understand that she couldn't bear to leave him or the ranch.

They had just purchased a new herd of cattle and a few more prize horses from someone down in Texas. The last thing on her mind had been getting married. She turned back to Chester and continued brushing his mane.

"I heard about the incident with a rattler this morning." The brusqueness in his voice hurt, but Abby was determined to appear unaffected.

"Yep."

"They said you got it in one shot."

Was that pride in his voice?

"It was close range." Abby shrugged her shoulders to brush off the possible compliment. She was grateful her back faced her father. She didn't want him to see that she was pleased by his words.

Silence.

"What is this?" Clay demanded, pulling the black knapsack from her back pocket.

She spun around, but almost wished she hadn't. The pride she'd sensed in her father just moments ago had transformed into anger, even fear. She'd almost forgotten about the rag. Clay held it up to her face. She didn't take her eyes off his, but pursed her lips and shrugged.

His eyes turned hard and distant. "Where did you get this?" The material all but disappeared in his balled fists.

"I found it," Abby's head pulled backward. She blinked hard at his sudden abruptness, "under the straw, here in Chester's stall. I thought maybe one of the hand—"

"The stage leaves at three o'clock on Friday," her father interrupted. "Be on it." He turned away from her, nodded to Lily on his way out the door and strode with determined step toward the bunkhouse.

He paused and glanced back over his shoulder. "The new foreman will be here on Saturday morning to help with the new stallion. Feed the horse and brush him, but don't ride or start working with him, ya hear?" Without waiting for her response he turned and picked up his stride.

Lily's face had a look of pity, mixed with sad surrender.

Abby's mind raced. "I still have two days to find a husband," she shouted after him and then nodded to Lily.

Clay stopped, still as stone, his head fixed forward.

"I don't know what's going on with you, Papa, but I'm gonna win our little wager and find myself a husband."

He started walking away again, the first few steps slow, then much faster.

"This horse. The new herd. And a place of my own." Her voice got louder with each phrase. "On the ranch!" she practically screamed at her father's retreating form.

Abby's short fingernails bit into the flesh of her hands and she stomped her feet, her body shaking all over.

Lily stepped in front of her, blocking Clay McCallister's back from his daughter's view. "What do we need to do?"

CHAPTER TWO

Two Weeks Earlier, Kansas

"You can't go on livin' like this, Cole." Raine threw his leg over the saddle of his bay roan and dismounted.

Cole looked past his eldest brother and squinted his eyes at the horizon.

"Marty," he called out to a gangly cowpoke sloshing a cup of water down his throat, "looks like there's a fence down on the property border over on the north side." Cole flicked his chin toward the far end of the pasture.

The dark-headed flank rider lowered the tin ladle from his cracking lips and wiped his newly wet mouth with the back of his hand.

"Take a couple of men over there and get it up before we lose half this herd to the Marcusen's." Cole removed his rawhide gloves, tight from sweat, and hit them against his hand.

"Sure thing, Boss," Marty responded before escaping into the small group of men who had just returned from the drive.

The air had not yet settled from the dust of thousands of steer and horse hooves trampling over the dirt road and onto the green pastures of Redbourne land. *Another successful cattle drive, complete.*

"Cole," Raine attempted once again, his voice low and resolute.

Cole glanced up at his brother and, without further acknowledgement, walked right past him toward the ranch house. With each quickened step, his determination grew and his stride elongated.

Raine was right behind him. His strong hand gripped Cole's upper arm and squeezed.

"Alaric's dead," Raine said in a quiet, but firm tone. "It's been nearly a year, but it's still eating at you."

Cole froze. The familiar pang stabbed him in the chest. He shook his arm free from his brother's grasp and turned to face him head on. "Leave Alaric out of this, Raine," he countered with clear deliberation. His jaw flexed and his teeth crushed together with intensity.

"You can't keep blaming yourself for what happened." Raine's defensive stance exuded his many years of experience apprehending outlaws. "The men can hardly stand to be around you anymore," he pushed a little further. "It used to be that you cared about what you were doing. Cared about the men you did it with."

Cole's eyes stung from the last two sleepless nights on the trail. His ears were hot and his hands ached from gripping the reins of the gelding he'd chosen for the trip. His attitude matched. Hot and aching.

"If they don't like the way I run things, well, then they can find another rancher to work for." Cole rubbed his neck and arched his back, his shoulders working to meet in the middle.

Raine opened his mouth to speak, but Cole cut in before the words could sound.

"Look Raine, I've been gone for nearly three months. I'm tired and sore. We lost a hundred head or so, and two of the hired hands quit before we even reached the Texas border. Can we not do this right now?" Cole shoved his gloves into his back pocket and walked into the house.

"Welcome home, little brother," Cole thought he'd heard Raine call after him.

The smell of rolls baking in the late afternoon wafted through the corridor in a trail of welcoming fog. Cole followed his nose down the hallway. One foot inside his mother's kitchen and he was pulled into a vast array of heavenly aromas battling for his attention. Fresh homemade stew bubbled on the stove. Two rather large chickens turned on the spit in the oversized adobe fireplace. And, three warm baked cobblers sat on the windowsill, a seductive haze rising from their golden crusts as they cooled. It certainly was a welcome sight after the long drive with only Griff's cookin' to sustain a man.

Cole breathed deeply before crossing the newly swept wooden floor into the study. He removed his hat and tossed it into his father's oversized mahogany chair. Moving to the desk he opened the top right hand drawer. A brown leather bound ledger rested at the top, veiling a locked black metal box from immediate view. Reaching in, he pulled both items from their resting place and set them on top of the desk. He placed his hand inside his vest and retrieved a long, discolored envelope from the inner pocket.

"The herd looks good."

Cole glanced up from his task to see his father standing casually in the doorway. Jameson Redbourne had a commanding presence. Standing six feet two inches, he and Cole measured equal, but something in the way his father carried himself filled the room. He lifted one foot to rest on the edge of a wooden table, his arm propped on his bent leg, his hat in hand.

"Lost near sixty at Red River and another thirty, or so, at Doan's Pass." The hardness in Cole's voice surprised even him. He averted his father's searching eyes and focused on the lockbox. He pulled the money Tag had given him and placed it in the metal container, careful to record the numbers accordingly in the ledger.

"It happens."

"Not to me." Cole's jaw ached from grinding his teeth. He had never lost this many cattle in one drive and it ate at him.

"How's your brother?" Jameson interrupted his self-criticism.

"Tag's fine." Cole traced multiple times over the numbers he had written, the current entry now much darker than the last. "Brenna's having another baby and little Jamie says he misses his poppa." He tried to appear casual.

A deep hearty laugh erupted from Jameson's throat. Surprised, Cole dared look up for a fleeting moment. His father took great pride in his grandchildren and he loved being called Poppa. His dimples carved happiness into his face, a trait Cole saw in his own reflection—the dimples anyway. When Jameson lowered his eyes to focus on his son and his lips returned to a simple smile, experience told Cole there was something else on his father's mind.

"How many horses did you pick up from Taggert on this last drive?" Jameson asked.

"Twenty-eight." Cole had handpicked each of the horses from Tag's herd. "Most are Morgans, but there are some Kentuckys and Appaloosas among the bunch."

"How many can be bred?"

"Nine stallions. Seven studs. The rest have been gelded, but are of the highest quality work and trail horses." Cole was anxious to be on his way. The final leg of the drive to the Colorado territory would be short in comparison to the trek from Texas, but with prairie wolves stalking the herd, Cole wanted to get on the trail as soon as possible.

Cole could feel his father's eyes tracing every movement he made.

"So, McCallister wants me to be the foreman on his ranch there in Silver Falls." Cole hated small talk, but he was tired and not at all sure he wanted to have a real conversation with the man next to him. Jameson had a tendency to get a little personal and he didn't want to talk about what ailed him.

"What about you?" His father asked, his voice laced with concern.

"What about me?" Cole asked, careful not to roll his eyes. He slammed the black box into the drawer and threw the ledger over it. His tone played at the verge of disrespect and he immediately regretted speaking the words aloud. He remembered well the time his father had overheard him speak disrespectfully to his mother and never wanted to repeat the experience.

If Jameson was perturbed by his son, he hid it well. However, there was something brimming just beneath the surface in his father's eyes. Hurt? Anger? Disappointment? Pity?

"I'm told you drove the team pretty hard." Jameson walked over to the desk and set his hat at the corner.

"Raine needs to keep his mouth shut."

"Wasn't Raine."

Cole wrapped his fingers around a stone paperweight at the edge of the desk and gripped it until his knuckles whitened. His other hand, balled into a fist, strained equally as hard against the desk top.

"I know the Chisholm is overrun and there's not lot of grazing left, but cutting your own trail? Crossing the Red in a rainstorm, especially two men down?"

Cole dropped his head.

Jameson placed an open hand on Cole's stooped back. "I don't have to tell you how dangerous that can be, son."

"The Griffin Trail is not exactly new." Cole pounded the rock against the thick stack of papers it held. His father's hand fell to his side.

"Some of the men say as long as you are Trail Boss, they won't ride."

"So, we'll find new men." Cole released his grasp on the rock and massaged his now aching fingers.

"That's not the point, Cole, and you know it."

Cole stood straight and faced his father squarely. The two men locked stares.

"Now we'll need a setting for twelve." A woman's voice carried through the kitchen and into the study, interrupting their brief standoff.

Cole was the first to break away. He ducked around his father to stand in the shadows of the study door where he could observe the scene in the other room.

While his mother was a great cook, Cole could only remember twice before when his mother had taken control in the kitchen. Once, when she'd haphazardly invited two of his brothers' new brides to dinner while Lottie, the family cook, had gone to visit her dying mother in Baltimore, and the second time when Granddad Redbourne showed up unannounced.

"Lottie, put the eggs on to boil," his mother delegated with authority no one questioned. The gray-haired Mexican woman, however, did not look at all like she appreciated her kitchen being usurped. Her hands were on her hips and if her eyes rolled any farther back into her head, they would disappear completely.

"And Hannah dear, will you go down and retrieve two jars of peaches from the cellar?" Cole mused at how his mother's voice turned soft and coaxing when she addressed her daughter.

"I'll do that." A male baritone voice interjected when Hannah pushed away from the table, revealing her round, protruding belly.

"Hannah and Eli are here?" Cole turned to his father, speaking in an accusatorily incredulous whisper.

Jameson cleared his throat. He picked his hat up off the desk and walked toward Cole. "Prepare yourself," he warned, both eyebrows raised as he brushed past him. "We'll finish this conversation later."

Trouble was coming and Cole wasn't sure he wanted to be there to greet it.

The sound of the back door clacking against its wooden frame as Eli left for the cellar was Cole's cue. He spoke a silent prayer and stepped out from the darkened study into the now busy kitchen.

"Cole," his little sister squealed.

Hannah waddled over to him and lifted her nose, waiting for him to brush his own nose back and forth across hers. They had done the ritual since they were children, but now it seemed outgrown. Cole hadn't seen her since their fight the day Alaric died. Their relationship wasn't the same. He didn't know if it ever would be.

Hannah stood a good foot shorter than he. When he grasped her by the shoulders and gently set her away from him, without even so much as a smile, her lips pursed together in an injured pout. Tears formed at the corners of her eyes.

"Hannah," he greeted her with a stiff nod of his head.

She looked around the room from their father to Raine to their mother and back at Cole. Then, she picked up the hem of her dress and ran out the back door, her blond curls bobbing behind her.

Damn.

"Cole Alexander Redbourne. You'll go apologize to your sister," his mother chastised, wiping her hands on her favorite white broadcloth apron, "but, first you come over here and kiss your mother."

Cole dutifully embraced Leah Redbourne and bent low to place a kiss on the side of her face. She squeezed him tighter.

"It's good to have you home, son," she whispered into his ear, patting him on the back.

Cole closed his eyes, tightened his hold around her motherly frame, and lifted her a foot off the ground, enticing a giggle from her lips.

When she released him, she turned him by his shoulders and swatted his rear end. "Now, git. That was no way to greet your sister."

A scowl formed as he tramped to the doorway.

"Cole," his mother called after him.

He paused and slowly turned to look at her, unsmiling.

"Wash up before supper, son." She grinned at him in a way that confirmed she was up to something.

His groan was covered up by the sound of the opening door.

"And shave," she added.

The door slammed shut behind him.

"Shave?" Cole took one large step off the back porch, running his hand over his now full beard and mustache. The trail had been long and arduous, but a large majority of the cattle still had to be transported to the McCallister ranch in Colorado. Whatever his mother had planned, he would only be home another week or so. He could endure. He hoped.

The sound of ducks quacking drew Cole to the pond behind the ranch house. When he rounded the corner, he spotted the large maple tree that had been the staple for enjoyment at the Redbourne ranch for all eight children. There he saw Hannah, sitting on the swing that dangled from one of the lower, sturdier branches. She stared out across the pond, one arm clutched around the side rope, her head resting against it.

Cole moved closer, but he wasn't ready to face Hannah. Not quite yet. He sat down some distance behind the swing and quietly nestled himself into the tall grasses growing there.

His forearms rested around his knees, his hands woven together in front of him. He gazed out over the deep blue of the water reflecting the hues from the sky.

A family of ducks, a mother and five little ducklings, waddled down the bank and into the water where they glided toward the other side, blissfully unaware of the turmoil wrenching Cole's mind and heart. The gentle lowing of cattle and the sweet song of a lark laid background to the stillness of the meadow surrounding them.

He sat, legs bent in front of him. His mind, unable to settle into the quiet serenity the land offered, screamed with impatience. He reached into his pocket and pulled out a carefully folded picture he'd torn from one of Brenna's magazines on his visit to Tag's ranch in Texas.

His fingers gently caressed the illustration of a homestead in the center of a flourishing valley. Towering mountains outlined the image and a herd of horses dotted the land. The artist had depicted Cole's dream with clarity and vision. *Soon*, he told himself. *I'll have enough for it, soon.* He gingerly refolded the paper and placed it back into his inside pocket.

"You've changed big brother," Hannah said after a while, pulling him away from his thoughts. She did not turn around, but, somehow she'd sensed his presence. There was no tearful catch in her voice, just sadness.

Cole pushed himself up from the ground and removed his hat. "I'm sorry, Hannah." His voice still sounded harsh, forced.

She didn't turn around. Didn't speak.

Cole cleared his throat. "It was not my intention to be rude or to hurt you," he said, rotating the brim of his hat around in his hands. Turning away from her, he paused, opening his mouth to say more. When the words didn't come, he closed it again, put his Stetson back on his head and trudged back toward the house.

Cole walked up the stairs of the homestead and into his room. Everything was just as he'd left it, except for the mirrored oak washstand. The water basin had been filled and his shaving utensils and scissors had been set out evenly on the side support boards. A fresh towel hung over the mirror post.

Cole removed his shirt and threw it onto his oversized oak bed. He pulled his suspenders down off his shoulders, picked up the grooming scissors, and began to clip away at his newly grown whiskers.

Small streaks of lather spotted his face once it was shaved to the skin. He bent over the water basin to wet his neck, cheeks, and chin, and then he wiped them clean. Reaching for the towel, he took it from its perch and patted his face dry.

Cole stood straight. Laying the damp cloth across the spindled post of the washstand, he glanced into the mirror. He opened his mouth and rubbed his face, turning it from side to side, making sure he had gotten everything.

A glint of silver at the corner of the basin caught his attention. It was Alaric's makeshift ring, bent out of a horseshoe nail. It represented his reason for taking the job as Trail Boss for the Colorado run and served as his constant reminder of what had been lost.

She'll be there...waiting for me. Cole heard Alaric's voice in his head, like he had so many times before. He reached down to the trinket and swept it up into his hand.

"I know," he said with a loud voice, willing the rest of Alaric's plea to stop echoing through his mind. His teeth clenched together. The ridges of the horseshoe ring cut into his palm before he opened his hand again.

"I know," he said more quietly, re-closing his fingers,

almost reverently over the ring. He tucked it into a small pocket at the front of his britches.

A splash of blue against his brown bedcover caught his attention. He crossed the room to find a cerulean linen shirt, a brown leather vest, and his russet colored hat already laid out for him. The colors reminded him of the vivid sky in his last painting.

He placed the hat low onto his head and grabbed the shirt and vest from the bed on his way out the door. Sliding his arms through the sleeves of the shirt and his vest in hand, he took the stairs two at a time.

To his surprise, the Dawson twins, Arena and Aurora, and MaryBeth Hutchinson stood at the bottom of the stairs, gawking up at him. He stopped mid stride, almost losing his balance.

When Arena and Aurora both put their hands up to their mouths and giggled, everyone else in the sitting room turned around to gawk at him.

As he glanced over the small crowd, he caught the one stare he'd hoped to avoid. MaryBeth's. She threw him an appraising glance. The tip of her tongue touched the edge of her front teeth. Cole took a deep breath and groaned. It had been a long time and he had no desire to repeat the past.

Mother, he screamed in his mind. Growling to himself, he forced some semblance of a smile.

Fully aware of his state of undress, he kept his face stoic and plodded down each of the remaining stairs, his shirt open and his suspenders dangling at his sides.

When he reached the bottom step, he tipped his hat. "Ladies," he said aloud with false politeness before darting past them and into the kitchen.

"That was quite an entrance," Raine mocked, closely following behind him. "MaryBeth sure looked pleased."

"Did you know they were coming?" Cole turned on his brother, eyes squinted in speculation.

"Come on, Charcoal." His brother sat down in the chair nearest the door and leaned back onto the back legs. He placed one booted foot across the arm of the chair next to him, and the other rested against the rod at the bottom of his chair. "You just turned twenty-five. What did you think would happen when you got home?"

"Granddad's will," he said with exasperation. It came out more of a statement than a question. Cole pumped a glass of water and stood with his back against the sink. "I should've known." Bringing the glass to his lips he pondered his situation. He'd forgotten all about it, since he had no desire to comply with its stipulations.

The money from his inheritance would give him the start he needed for his own place, but he didn't think marrying MaryBeth Hutchinson or any of the other available girls in town would be worth the trouble. He just wanted to be left alone to build and run his own ranch.

The front two legs of Raine's chair returned to the floor with a thud, bringing Cole back to the immediate present. "You don't seem the least bit disturbed that mother has invited *three* young, eligible ladies to dinner." Cole raised one eyebrow at his brother.

"Already got my inheritance," Raine laughed. "They're not here for me. Though, I wouldn't mind a courtin' that Arena Dawson. Have you ever seen eyes that blue?"

Cole hadn't noticed. "Come to think of it, why three? Is Rafe in town?"

"Mama just wants you to have more to choose from, little brother."

Cole wanted to wipe away the grin that spread across his brother's face.

Girlish laughter and heavy footsteps in the hallway extracted an inward groan from Cole. He pitched his glass to slide across the countertop and buttoned his shirt. He had just managed to tuck it in before the parade of guests entered the room.

"Ladies," Leah Redbourne purred as she ran her hand across Cole's back. "Cole is only home for a couple of days and I thought it would be nice if you all had the opportunity to become better acquainted."

Raine grinned from ear to ear, obviously enjoying every moment of Cole's discomfort. Cole's fist curled at his side, ready to strike Raine at any moment.

"And, as I am sure you already know," his mother placed her other hand on Raine's back, "this is my eldest son, Raine. He's living here and also unattached."

Raine's smile dropped. Cole unclenched his fist with a smirk.

Getting married was the last thing Cole wanted to worry about and the thought of his mother arranging this dinner, simply to encourage him to meet the requirements of the will, made his stomach churn and his head hurt.

MaryBeth Hutchinson took the seat in between him and Raine. Her strong floral scent, once irresistible to him, now infused aversely with the delicious culinary aromas that had permeated the kitchen moments earlier.

She reached under the table and placed her hand on his leg, just above the knee. When he turned to look at her she batted her eyelashes in coquettish fashion. He forced a half smile. *There has to be another way.*

CHAPTER THREE

Colorado, Thursday

"You've been staring at that box forever, Abby. Open it."

Abby sat on the floor with her legs curled behind her. Her fingers glided across the beautiful engraving on the front of her mother's dark walnut chest. Lily was right.

Abby fondled the long, slender key in her lap. She hadn't opened it since her mother had passed away, nearly six years ago. She glanced at Lily, who sat on the edge of Abby's four poster bed, her arm wrapped around its wooden post. She offered a nod of encouragement.

Abby lifted the key and placed it into the metal adorned opening just below the lid. She turned it.

Click.

All she had to do was lift the top. She took a deep breath and exhaled slowly. A soft creak accompanied the lid as it opened. Abby lifted herself onto her knees and rested the lid against the footboard of her bed. Both young women peered over the top and with reverence looked down into the chest.

A pungent cedar aroma escaped into the air, mixing with the lilac scent of Abby's freshly washed hair—some concoction Lily had demanded she use. Abby closed her eyes to the familiar fragrance, reveling in the memory of her mother pulling her denim patchwork quilt from the chest and wrapping it around Abby's shoulders as she read to her.

At the sound of Lily clearing her throat, Abby reached into

the box and pulled out a mass of soft silk and lace, the color of buttercream. Abby held the dress up to her bosom and spread the bottom of it out around her.

Lily moved to the other side of the room and stopped when she reached the bottom hem of the fine material.

"It's hard to believe your mama ever wore something so..." Lily bit her lip, "...so, beautiful."

"It is exquisite isn't it?" Abby caressed the delicate fabric with awe.

"Abby, are you sure you know what you're doing?" Lily fingered the lace, shaking her head.

Abby stood, draping the creamy layers over her forearm, and moved to the full-length mirror in the corner of the room. After removing an old hat and a pair of worn trousers from the scroll-like posts holding the mirror together, she held the bridal gown up to her less than feminine appearance and frowned. The intricate wooden carvings that surrounded the mirrored glass created a stunning frame for her otherwise disheveled reflection.

"Put it on," Lily encouraged, her amber eyes alight.

Abby froze, reluctant to even hope her plan might work. It had been so long since she'd worn something so beautiful. She'd always wished that one day she would get hitched and have a family, but somewhere along the road, she'd stopped believing it would ever happen. She'd accepted that a long time ago and had been content living on the ranch with her father and the horses. Now, things were different. She lifted her chin. She had to try.

Lily hurried across the room, took the dress from Abby, and laid it across the bed while Abby began discarding her clothes.

"Maybe there are some bloomers and a corset in the chest, too." Lily raised her eyebrows and half smiled as she peered over the wooden coffer. After a few moments, she squealed with excitement. To Abby's dismay, she must have found what she'd been looking for. She pulled out a pair of bloomers, a corset, pantalets, and a chemise. A soft smile appeared on Lily's lips. She gave one slow nod.

Abby groaned.

After she'd donned the appropriate undergarments, she stepped into the dress and held her breath while Lily fastened the back. Lily turned her to face the full-length mirror in the corner of her room. She opened one eye and then the other.

Nothing spectacular happened. She hadn't been suddenly transformed into a vision of beauty or status. Her same old reflection stared back at her, only this reflection wore a pretty dress. Abby's shoulders slumped.

Lily stepped forward and pinched Abby's cheeks and brushed a group of unruly tendrils from her eyes.

"They just have to see who I see," Lily coaxed. "And I see a very talented young lady with spirit and gumption."

Abby smiled then shrugged. She moved away from the mirror and toward the worn chaise in the opposite corner of the room. "There's not much use in trying to be somebody I'm not, but I can't go to Denver. The only horses there are hooked up to fancy carriages on paved roads."

Lily laughed and joined her on the chaise.

"I went to see Jeremiah Carson last night." Abby smirked at the look of shock that spread across Lily's face.

"You did not." Lily slipped her shoes back onto her feet while Abby stood to remove the dress and return it to the hope chest.

Abby had wanted to share the information with her friend earlier about her encounter with young Mr. Carson, but the memory of it still smarted.

"He told me it was inappropriate for the woman to do the asking and it was just like me to think I could do a man's job," Abby said matter-of-factly.

Lily's jaw hung wide open.

After she'd donned her work shirt and britches, she grabbed her wide brimmed hat and smashed it onto her head. Her father's old work coat lay haphazardly over the footstool and Abby swept it up and flung it over her arm. This time of year still held a certain chill.

"He told me he's always been a little sweet on me, but..." Abby pulled her chin into her chest and with a deep voice attempted to imitate the man, "...I don't want to marry a ranch hand. Once you decide to act like a woman, then maybe I'll court ya."

Seeing the stricken look on Lily's face, Abby's smile fell, but then, without warning, they both burst into laughter. They walked out her bedroom door and across the living area of the house to the yard.

Once outside, Lily turned to Abby. "He said he's sweet on you?" Lily asked, unbelief dripping from her words.

"He even kissed me once."

Abby laughed at the shocked abhorrence that distorted Lily's face.

"What?" she asked in a gasp. "Jeremiah Carson, kissed you?"

"Just a few months back. We were by that big oak tree just outside of town." Abby hung her coat over a nail protruding from the wall in the barn.

"How was it?" Lily asked eagerly. Then, her bottom lip protruded slightly. "Why didn't you tell me?"

"I was embarrassed," Abby stated flatly, pulling her saddle tack from the closet. "It wasn't at all how I remembered kissing to be and besides, who would have believed me?" Abby looked at her friend and blushed.

Pushing the thought of Alaric's sweet kisses out of her mind was more of a difficult task than she had anticipated. It had been over five years since he'd kissed her goodbye with the promise of returning to marry her and she could still feel the featherlike touch of his lips on hers. She'd believed he loved her, even if she wasn't traditional wife material. *Foolish girl.*

"I would have believed you." Lily sat on the small wooden stool, her fisted hands holding up her chin, hanging on every word as if it was the most fascinating story ever told. "What happened?"

Shaking her head free from dusty thoughts of her young love, she continued. "I think he'd just had another fight with his pa or something, 'cause he was pretty riled. He said he would feel better if he had somebody to talk to, so I tethered Outback, one of the new geldings, to a lower branch and sat down next to him under the tree."

Abby could see a sparkle in Lily's eye and she hated to continue the disappointing story. *Why couldn't I just keep my big mouth shut?*

A small collection of horses grazed in the field just beyond the stables. Abby whistled—two short, one long—and her beautiful white mount perked her head up and trotted over to the fence.

"You can't just stop there, Abby. I have to know how the story ends." Lily stood up and followed her into the yard.

Abby opened the gate between the pasture and the corral.

"Hello, old girl. You ready?" She ran her hand down the length of the mare and then stepped around her to close the gate. Bella had been her mother's favorite mare and was one of the only things she had left that had belonged to her. She snuggled her face into the horse's neck.

"Abby," Lily said with mock scolding.

"There's really not much more to tell. He kissed me. It was awful. Not at all like what I had expected. After a few minutes," Abby shrugged, "the Spencer boys walked by. They'd seen us kissing and just stood there, mouths gaping.

"When Benjamin had collected his wits, he reached down and picked Jeremiah up by the scruff of his neck. At first I thought he might hit him." Abby walked into the barn and picked up her saddle, Lily just two steps behind her. When she turned around, she nearly ran into her friend.

"Did he? Punch Jeremiah, I mean," Lily asked.

Abby threw the saddle up over her horse. "Nope," she said as she fastened the straps. "Jeremiah just threw his head back and laughed, put his arm around Ben's shoulders, and all four of them turned around and walked away." She faced Lily now, her hands resting casually on her hips.

"Where is that blasted bucket of bolts?" Abby looked about the room, but couldn't find her objective.

"And they just left you standing there? Alone by the tree?"

"It was a long time ago." Abby walked over to the dresser that had been converted into a giant tool box, and opened one of the top drawers. "He really hasn't changed all that much. Our parents may have liked the idea of us combining our properties and becoming family and all, but I think I'll take my chances in town."

Abby pushed aside an assortment of nuts and bolts and tiny little odds and ends until she found what she'd been looking for. "Perfect," she said, holding up a thin, perfectly round, banded ring. "Time to get hitched."

Kansas, One Week Earlier

"I wanted to talk to you a bit before you leave this morning, son." A small cloud of white smoky vapor accompanied Jameson Redbourne's breath in the still of the morning. He reached down to pick up a nail and handed it to Cole.

The sun had just risen over the hills and morning light spilled into the stable. Cole looked up from the horse's hoof he was re-shoeing and took the nail from his father's outstretched hand. He put it into place and pounded it securely into the target.

"I know which route to take," Cole said, his jaw tight as he tested the stability of the shoe. He dropped the gelding's foot and looked up at his father. After he led the gelding back to the other cattle horses and turned him loose in the smaller corral, Cole leaned up against the round pen fence with his forearms and placed one foot on the bottom plank.

"I'm taking the job with McCallister. I notified him last week," Cole announced casually, knowing his parents would both disagree with his decision.

After weeks of deliberation, Cole had decided taking the

foreman job at the SilverHawk ranch in Silver Falls would be the only way he could make good on his promise to Alaric. Someone there had to know the girl. The inscription on the ring said, "Abby," but Cole now wished he'd had the foresight to ask her last name.

"Come with me, son." Jameson patted Cole on the shoulder and motioned for him to follow.

Cole pushed himself away from the fence. A morning chill swept across his face. He pulled his wool lined jacket closer around his neck and tugged his hat lower on his head.

"I have a proposition for you, but first, there's something you need to know," Jameson said as he hopped up onto the homestead's front porch steps.

Cole groaned, but still followed his father across the kitchen and into the study. His mother had been quite upset when Cole told her he had no interest in getting married anytime soon and he didn't want to have to have the same discussion with his father.

In contrast to the brisk spring morning, his father's den was warm from the pot belly stove roaring to life in the corner. The musky scent of burning pine wood permeated the room. Cole sat down in the overstuffed chair across his father's desk. He let his jacket fall open as he slouched into the back cushions.

"So, we hadn't seen MaryBeth around here in a while. Are you going to be seeing anymore of Miss Hutchinson?"

Cole tilted his head backward, eyes closed, and took a deep breath. "Not if I can help it."

A loud guffaw burst out of a now amused Jameson. "Your mother just wants you to be happy, Cole."

"Why does everyone think they know what'll make me happy? That I need their help? I just want to be left alone." Cole stood to leave. "I'm not going to marry some girl just because Granddad believed any man over twenty-five and not married was a nuisance to society. No pittance is worth that kind of trouble."

The back door opened and a short gust of wind blustered

through the room. "Oh, it's no pittance, little brother." Raine stepped into the study, shaking off the cold and rubbing his hands together. He put them up to his mouth and blew into them.

Cole looked from Raine back to his father. "Not you too?"

"Don't look at me." Jameson held both hands up in a surrendering gesture. "I just want to let you know what you're up against."

Cole dropped back down in the chair, his gaze still shifting between his father and eldest brother. "I don't need it. Nor do I want it," Cole stated flatly.

"Maybe not. But you do want a ranch of your own and I'm gonna tell you how to get it."

Cole had become obsessed with ranching and driving cattle. The harder he worked, the less time he had to think about what had been lost. Cole's jaw clenched. He should have been the one who died at the bottom of that ravine. Not Alaric.

"Nothing seems to bring you joy anymore. Not us. Not God. If you keep driving yourself the way you are driving your men, you're gonna drop and not be able to pull yourself up again."

"That's not what Alaric would have wanted," Raine interjected.

"Leave him out of this." Cole shot a quelling look at his brother.

"Your mother and I have seen what Alaric's death has done to you."

"We all have," Raine said.

Jameson cleared his throat. "And now, it's time to stop wallowing in self-loathing and guilt and start thinking about someone besides yourself."

Cole pushed himself up, out of the chair. "I am *not* getting married."

"Sit down!" Jameson boomed, rising to his feet, arms pressing against his desktop, his eyes not wavering from Cole's. "And, I'd advise you to watch your tone here, young man. You've got people who care about you and are trying to help.

Don't make an old man come whoop some sense into that thick skull of yours."

Cole took a deep breath. He knew everything his father spoke was true. He'd been selfish to think that closing himself off from his family and depriving himself of happiness wouldn't affect those closest to him. His shoulders slumped slightly.

"Yes, sir." Cole couldn't remember the last time he'd seen his father so forceful. He slowly returned to his seat.

"We changed the ownership of the land in Silver Falls, Colorado into your name. Wife or not. We were waiting to tell you until you returned from this last drive." Jameson reached into the slender drawer in the middle of his desk and withdrew a leather bound folder. He pushed it across the top to rest directly in front of Cole.

Cole glanced down at the rawhide packet. He was speechless.

"Wait. We have land in Silver Falls?"

"Open it," his father urged.

Cole slid his hands over the soft leather and untied the thin straps that held it together. Inside, he found a yellowed document—his Granddad's deed and will for the Colorado property. He read—

I, William Joshua Deardon, declare on this twelfth day of May, Eighteen Hundred and Thirty-Two, before the eyes of the undersigned notary, that the name listed herein is to be hereafter, a recognized guardian and heir of the property surrounding and including the city of Silver Falls, Colorado, as mapped out in this document. The guardian will have undisputed authority and responsibility over the protection of said property and all decisions concerning the land and its uses, until the time he meets his demise. This name may only be changed by the undersigned and/or current guardian.

There were multiple lines listed at the bottom, each with a name and a corresponding signature. Granddad Deardon's name was first. His mother, Leah Deardon Redbourne, second.

And now, his name, Cole Alexander Redbourne, was written in big black lettering.

"Now, all you have to do is sign the document to make it official." Jameson sat back in his chair looking very pleased with himself. "You may choose your beneficiary now or wait until a later date. You'll just need to file it with the registrar's office in Denver once you've decided."

Cole stared at his father. He didn't know what to say.

"A local banker has been collecting all of the mortgage payments from the townsfolk and store proprietors. He's been depositing the money into a branch of the Deardon Trust in Silver Falls. You'll have what you need."

"How did you know I was gonna stay in Silver Falls?" Cole had specifically asked his father if he could take the lead on the cattle drive to Silver Falls and to one certain Clayton McCallister. Alaric's grandparents had lived there and that is where his friend had fallen for a young girl named Abby. It had been just over a year since Alaric died and Cole felt that the time had come to see his promise through.

"I'm looking for a Mr. Cole Alexander Redbourne, please," the gangly man announced, looking down his nose through round wire spectacles.

"You found 'im." Cole tilted his hat backward and wiped the sweat from his neck. He scooped a ladle full of water from the bucket at the top of the well and placed it in a short tin cup.

"At last." The man's heels clicked together and he bent forward slightly, his head and chin tilted up. "Mr. Redbourne, my name is Charleton Tacy. I wonder if I might have a moment of your time."

"What can I do for you, Mr. Tacy? I've got a lot of work to finish up before we head out in the morning." Cole brought the cup to his lips and started to drink.

"Oh, I'm so pleased I caught up with you. I represent Mr.

Alaric Kurtis Johansson, sir." Mr. Tacy reached down and picked up a small, dusty, black case and held it in front of him.

Cole choked on the water in his mouth and he spit it out, spraying the unsuspecting Mr. Tacy in the process. The man pulled a limp handkerchief from the pocket in his brown twill suit coat and dabbed at his face.

"I guess you haven't been expecting me?" he asked, wiping the splattered water droplets from his glasses.

"No, sir. Alaric's dead."

"Precisely. Might we go inside?"

Cole turned and walked toward the house without another word. When he reached the door, he looked back to find that the odd man had not followed. "You comin'?"

While Mr. Tacy scurried to the front door, Cole glanced out into the corral where his father and Raine were working with one of the new horses. He caught Raine's eye and motioned for him to come inside with a jerk of his head.

Mr. Tacy tipped his bowler hat as he slid past Cole into the house.

Cole was now accustomed to the wide eyed looks he received whenever he and his brothers stood together in a room. The same look appeared on Mr. Tacy's face when Raine and his father joined them in the parlor.

After some brief introductions, Cole asked again, "Now, what can I do for you?"

Mr. Tacy removed his hat and set it on the edge of the small round table. He reached down into his bag and retrieved a sealed manila envelope. He set it down on the table in front of him.

"Let me express to you our condolences. My firm has worked with the Johansson family for a very long time and we are deeply sorry for your loss." He folded his hands in front of him, resting his forearms on the table, closed his eyes, and nodded.

Raine, Jameson, and Cole all stared expectantly at the messenger.

"Yes, well, on to business. A few days before young Alaric

passed away he came into our office and added a beneficiary to his will. That beneficiary, Mr. Redbourne," he looked at Cole, "is you." Mr. Tacy pushed the envelope toward a disbelieving Cole.

Cole laughed darkly. "Are you trying to tell me that, what...?" He shot a glance at his brother and father, then shifted in his seat.

"What exactly *are* you trying to tell me, Mr. Tacy?" Cole asked, his eyes squinting in apprehension.

"If you will just open the folder." The man nodded at the thick package now in front of Cole.

Cole looked down at the oversized envelope. His mouth went dry. Alaric's name jumped at him from the unopened packet. He ran his forefinger and thumb across the corners of his mouth before he reached out to pick it up. Carefully, he opened the flap and pulled out a familiar looking folded leather binder and carefully relieved its contents.

This document was nearly identical to the property deed and will he had just received from his father.

"Do you know what this is?" Cole searched Jameson's face for any hint of recognition. He looked at Raine who shrugged.

Cole's eyes jumped to the bottom of the page where the names were listed—Friedrich Kurtis Johansson, Alaric Kurtis Johansson, and Cole Alexander Redbourne. Cole was grateful he was sitting down because he was sure he would have fallen over.

This folder included a will and map of the property lines as well as the claim title for a silver mine.

"I don't want it." Cole tossed the parchment down onto the table, stood up, and started to pace the small parlor area. He felt like a cougar trapped in a hole.

"It wasn't your fault, son," his father spoke quietly.

"Will everyone stop saying that?" It came out louder than he had anticipated. After seeing the frightened look on Mr. Tacy's face, he resumed his pacing. "You don't understand. It *was* my fault," he said a in a lower tone, glancing at his brother. "If I had just gotten to him sooner, he would still be alive."

"Please. Is there a problem?"

"Yes. Get someone else to take it." Cole pounded his fist on the deed, shaking the table and startling Mr. Tacy into hiccups. A small torn piece of paper fluttered into the air from the force.

"What's this?" Raine asked as he picked up the note.

"I don't deserve to live on that land, let alone own it. It's Alaric's. It should be his."

Cole couldn't think straight. His head started spinning and he could only think about getting out of the house and into the fresh air. Hot waves consumed him. Sweat dampened the hair at the back of his neck. He couldn't breathe.

He shoved past everyone and once outside the door, he stood gasping for the air that taunted his lungs with fulfillment. He bent over, holding himself up with his hands on his knees. The pungent aroma of fresh cut grass greeted him in the open air and he breathed deeply, each breath a little easier than the one before. He prayed to rid himself of the powerful emotions riding dangerously close to the surface.

"Let someone else do it," he muttered to himself. The harsh clod of feet on the front porch steps triggered him upright. He didn't want to talk about it anymore and with one determined step started toward the corral.

"Hang on there, little brother." Raine was right behind him, like always.

"What do you want, Raine?" Cole's voice was hard as steel. He yanked at the saddle resting on his tack horse. It lifted mere inches from the wooden form, the back end not budging from its secured structure. Cole ground his teeth together. One of the straps was still attached to the timber underbelly. He pulled the buckle back and the pin sliced at his fore knuckle. A forceful groan of frustration sounded deep in his throat and he quickly drew his finger into his mouth, sucking at the blood that appeared there.

"Cole," Raine started again.

Cole grabbed a hold of the saddle once again and yanked, this time it came off freely. He pushed past Raine toward the remuda for a fresh mount.

"I don't believe Alaric's death was an accident." Raine's words all came out in a rush.

Cole stopped, still as stone. Slowly, he pivoted on one foot until he stood square to Raine. His fists twitched and his grip tightened on his rigid leather tack. "What did you say?" Cole asked, sure he'd misheard.

"I don't believe Alaric's death was an accident," Raine repeated slowly, emphasizing each word.

The pounding in Cole's head sped in wild rhythm. He threw his saddle to the ground and jumped over it toward Raine. His fingers curled in a death grip around the loose material at the front of Raine's shirt and he hurled his brother up against the side of the tack shed. One moment his fist was cocked, ready to strike, and the next he found himself with his hands behind his back, his arms locked awkwardly in Raine's upward hold.

How many times had his brother William told him he was careless when he was angry? Control the emotion, control the fight. Cole tugged his arms, attempting to loosen Raine's grasp on him, but to no avail.

"You weren't the only one who lost someone when Alaric died." Raine wrenched Cole's arms so tight his shoulder blades nearly touched. "He was like a brother to all of us."

Cole backed hard into his unsuspecting brother, bending at his waist. He heaved his brother over his back and head. Raine landed flat on his back. Now, William would have been proud of that.

Cole's success was short lived when Raine grabbed his ankles and tugged, pulling him onto the ground next to him. Cole had the wind knocked out of him. Without time to react, Raine rolled Cole over onto his belly, straddled him, and held his hands together just below his belt and against his back. His face rubbed into the dirt, but he was just too tired to fight anymore.

"Look at this." Raine released his hold on Cole and rolled sideways to sit next to Cole. Forearms resting on his knees he held the small ripped parchment up for Cole to see.

Cole turned his head and pulled himself into a seated position, brushing the dust from the front of his shirt.

"Tacy said Alaric was in a hurry when he wrote this, but left strict instructions to have it delivered to you if anything happened to him."

The handwriting was familiar. Alaric's.

Be careful, my friend. They will stop at nothing to get what they want. My granddad is dead because he wouldn't give in and now I feel them watching me. You are the only one I trust to keep it safe. To keep her safe.

Cole read the words aloud, but it took some time before their meaning sunk in. His heart thumped against his chest in heavy, solid beats.

"I guess we're staying in Silver Falls?" Raine's voice blended into the background of Cole's racing thoughts.

With his arm resting on his knee, he reread the note, unable to peel his eyes away from the realization of what it meant.

Alaric's death wasn't an accident. *Not an accident.*

Cole fell backward onto his back, his knees still bent, and he stared intently at the cloud filled sky. His wrist dropped at his side, note still in hand. He closed his eyes.

Not an accident. He repeated again in his mind. He didn't have to open his eyes to know when Raine laid down next to him. They sat in silence for a while. Cole raised the note and opened his eyes to look it over again. He sat up straight when he noticed something written on the backside of the paper. A single word.

"McCallister," he read aloud. "I guess it's a good thing I'll be taking that job after all."

CHAPTER FOUR

Colorado, Friday

Abby watched from her bedroom window and waited until her father and his horse finally disappeared over the far ridge of the sun soaked hillside. Friday had come all too soon, but Lily had come early to help her get ready and to offer moral support. Abby was unaccustomed to letting her hair hang in curls, but she trusted Lily to make her into a presentable female. She could hardly believe her reflection. She was almost...pretty. Abby took a deep breath and headed for the door.

Most of the hired hands would be out with her father fixing the broken dam at the far end of the property and repairing a few fences that had been ruined during the last windstorm. However, there would be at least one hand who would have been left behind to make the run into town for the weekly supplies.

She couldn't risk anyone discovering her plan before she'd had a chance to carry it through. She'd lose their wager for sure and she'd have no choice but to leave for Denver this afternoon. That was not an option. Today she would find a man to marry. Somehow.

Pulling her father's large coat around her shoulders she hoped to avoid Martha or any of the hands. They would surely start asking questions if they saw the frills beneath the coat.

"Abby," Lily whispered, "I can't ride like this." She pointed to the trim, bustled waistline and tapered skirt of her dress.

Abby took a hold of Lily's hand and dragged her across the courtyard toward the barn. The cows would have already been milked early this morning and none of the horses were scheduled to be bred today. The barn should be mostly empty, other than the cows, a few chickens, and a dozen or so horses.

Abby heaved open the unpainted double doors. "Come on," she motioned to Lily. "We'll have to hitch a ride on the wagon."

When they reached the oversized stall where the wagon was kept, it was gone. Abby opened the doors on the opposite side of the barn and was pleased to see it had already been hitched with a fresh team of horses.

"This is gonna be easier than I thought." Abby heaved up the skirts of her dress high enough to place one heavily booted foot on the step plank at the side of the buckboard.

Davey poked his head up from the opposite side of the wagon.

"Oh. Hi, Abby," he said casually.

Abby dropped her foot to the ground in an instant, haphazardly shoving her skirts downward, and smiled sheepishly at the gangly red-headed hired hand. So, Davey was the lucky hand to have been chosen to stay behind and make the run to town.

Glancing from Abby to Lily, Davey stretched his neck forward and swallowed. He licked his hand and ran it over the stubborn cowlick at his temple. "Miss Lily, I didn't know you was here." His face changed three different shades of pink as he spoke, his freckles becoming more pronounced. "Um...What are you..." he looked at Abby, "...ladies doing out here?" He cleared his throat and moved the hammer he held from one hand to the other.

"Davey," she tried to cover the surprise in her voice as she looked around the barn, thinking of what to say, "I, we," she corrected, "have to make a trip into town today to...uh, pick up a few things, and uh, I didn't want Lily here to have to ride horseback in her pretty new dress."

As if on cue, Lily bowed her head demurely and smiled, glancing up coyly through lowered lashes.

"It's a mighty perty dress, Miss Lily." Davey dropped the hammer.

Lily placed her hand over her mouth quaintly and giggled.

When the young Davey vanished behind the wagon to retrieve the fallen tool, Lily pulled a sour face at Abby, her normally beautiful features contorted.

Davey's disorderly red hair leapt, before once again settling on his head, as he reappeared over the edge of the wagon. He placed the hammer in a box in the back of the buckboard and walked around to the front of the horses. Pulling an oily black rag from his pocket he wiped his dirty hands.

"Just finished oilin' the back wheel. Been givin' us problems for a while." He jutted his head toward the rear wheel against the back wall.

Abby rolled her eyes at the toothy grin that, in the last few minutes, had become a permanent fixture on Davey's face. What Lily could do to some of these men.

"So," she rocked back and forth on her heels, "I guess she's ready then?" Abby started to lift up her skirts enough to reach the loading board.

"Sorry, Abby. Can't have the wagon today."

Abby paused, her skirt layers around her knees, turned a fixed stare on the scrawny little string of a man standing in the way of her brilliant plan. With a look she was sure undid all of Lily's hard work with her this morning, she walked toward him with strong, focused steps, until her chin nearly ran into his chest.

Davey took a step backward. "You're in luck though," a nervous laugh accompanied his words. "I'm on my way into town right now. That's why I was a fixin' the wheel," he darted a glance at Lily, who stood with her hands wrapped neatly in front of her, still smiling in his direction, "I'd be happy to take ya," he finished with a look of utter triumph on his face.

Abby grunted. Maybe this would work after all.

"I'll just saddle Bella. No need to be cramped on that little old seat." Abby walked toward the stall where her mother's beautiful white mare resided. "How ya doin', ol' girl?"

As if in response the Thoroughbred lifted her head and whinnied. Abby clenched her hands together to stop them from shaking. "I'm doing the right thing," she whispered under her breath.

Once saddled, she hiked the dress up enough she could mount without a problem. She dropped the heavy layers down around her, the bottom of the dress not able to reach her calves and feet. Inappropriate she knew, but, she rationalized, at this point it could only help. She shrugged her shoulders and nudged the horse outside of the barn toward the awaiting wagon. "We ready?"

"You owe me," Abby caught Lily's mouthed words as she sat in extreme proximity to the gawky ranch hand.

"Thank you," she mouthed back.

Davey jumped down from the seat and closed the barn doors. He started climbing back up onto the buckboard when he hopped back off and ran to the house and in through the kitchen doors. When he returned, he had a list in his hand.

"Martha woulda had my hide if I'd forgotten her lard and such." Davey looked down over the list before sticking it safely into his shirt pocket.

Abby was grateful for the slower pace the wagon provided on the drive into town. She needed time to calm her nerves. Every few minutes she would glance up and see Lily's tolerating smile bestowed on the red-headed boy at her side, or she would catch her friend's pleading glance at her for an end to the torment.

Silver Falls bustled with folks in town for the day. The first weekend of the month was usually the busiest. Farmers and ranchers who could not spare the time away from their own places often sent their sons or hired help to pick up supplies. Abby looked about and was pleased to see more than a handful of eligible men roaming the streets today.

She dismounted and tied Bella to a tree just beyond the church house. Davey pulled the wagon up to the front of the new telegraph office, which was still a novelty in town. Abby watched as he held a hand up to Lily, helping her down from the high perch of the buckboard. Once on the ground with stable footing, Lily offered a short curtsy, her head bowed. Then, she whipped around to face Abby. Her shoulders squared, and she leaned forward slightly as she made her way to where Abby stood. As she got closer, her eyes narrowed into slits and her lips pursed together.

"Abby McCallister," Lily spoke firmly, "if you ever leave me alone with a hopeful gentleman suitor from your ranch again, I'll...I'll..." She never finished her sentence. A huge bubble of laughter exploded out of her mouth.

Abby watched in amazement. She had never seen Lily act anything but the lady in public, and she had lost count of how many times Lily had told her that laughing loudly, especially in front of the townspeople, was certainly not lady-like.

With her faced flushed and her eyes aglow, Lily placed her hands on her hips and calmed herself. Her lips twitched a few times before she gave one small shake of her head and was finished with her outburst. Abby, amused at all the stares they were receiving, couldn't help a twitch of her own.

Lily linked her arm through Abby's and they walked toward the church.

"Abby, you are my best friend in the whole world. Are you sure you know what you are doing?"

"What other choice do I have?"

Lily opened her mouth to respond when a fight broke out over by the mercantile, between what looked to be the three youngest Spencer boys. Lily's attention was pulled from Abby and focused on the direction of the ruckus.

"Will they ever grow up?" Lily asked with disgust.

Abby couldn't think about that right now. Dragonflies had set up home in her belly and were all a flutter. She took one step forward, then another as she started her walk across the dusty road, toward the church steps, her chosen podium for her announcement.

"Benjamin's no better at twenty-two than Thomas at

sixteen," she said without looking back at Lily. Ben was Jeremiah's best friend and Abby did not want to revisit her most recent visit with the latter.

"Abby, have you really thought this through?" Lily caught up with her and whispered in her ear. "You could end up marrying anyone. It could be one of those Spencer boys," she said flickering her wrist in the direction of the disturbance, "or even worse yet, their drunken father. Or... even that old, dirty miner. What's his name?" Lily searched the ground, looking wildly about as they continued slowly toward the chapel.

"Oh, Lily." Abby tried to hide the impatience in her voice.

A gust of wind pushed Abby's hat forward on her head. She used one hand to hold it in place and the other to gather the hem of her dress.

"Matthew, that's it. That's his name." Lily clapped, then pushed her blowing hair out of her face as she looked in the direction of the mercantile, where the old man loaded a wagon full of mining supplies. She scrunched up her nose before turning back to Abby.

"Matthew is a kind old man who is still in love with the memory of his dead wife. He'd no sooner marry me than stop searching for gold."

They reached the stairs.

"Lily," Abby turned to look her straight in the eye. I *am* going to do this. I have to." She sat down on the bottom step to calm her racing heart.

"Okay, then. What do you want me to do?"

"Just watch for my father. If I don't have a prospective groom within the hour...well, just watch for him."

Abby closed her eyes and said a quick prayer. She needed all the help she could get and wanted to make sure the Lord was with her. *And, please,* she pleaded silently, *don't let him be a Spencer.*

Abby stood up at the base of the steps gathering courage for what she was about to do. She'd much rather be driving a fence post, even shoveling manure, than swallowing her pride and asking for just any man to be her husband.

There has to be another way. The thought had crossed her mind more than once today.

A dark haired man, whom she'd never seen around town before, stood across the street, arms folded and resting against the low hanging branch of an old oak tree, staring at her. There was something in the way he watched her that made her feel empowered and she mustered enough courage to take the first step up. Her legs nearly betrayed her when she took on the second step. She wished there was a railing to grab onto. The last thing she needed was to fall on her face. She'd lose for sure. She clung to the fact that women were sparse out here and she may get someone logical enough to appreciate her skills as a rancher. She stood up a little taller and took the next step.

When she reached the top, she slowly turned around to look at the bustling crowd. A few people darted a glance in her direction, but most were going hastily about their own business. Abby tightened her grip around the fastenings of her father's coat.

The early afternoon still had a chill and by the look of the sky, a storm would soon be rolling in. She secured the thick coat more closely around her neck. Tipping her head forward, she reached up and pulled her low riding hat from off her head. She tousled her hair, running her fingers through its length to free the hair tucked up underneath and shook them loose. After all, if she wanted a husband, she guessed she'd better look at least a little female.

"Take off the coat," Lily coaxed quietly from below.

Abby had taken comfort in the bulky covering. Her fingers shook as she touched the collar. She started to pull it open when she caught the eye of the stranger across the way. It was as if he dared her to remove it in front of the whole town and she wasn't ready for that yet.

"I noticed a few of the Grayson's hands in the barbershop. The more you have to choose from, the better." Lily sighed and then smiled as she headed across the street.

No fear, she kept telling herself, but realized she'd rather be facing another rattler or even a bear than standing here exposed to the entire town. She dropped her hands away from the coat.

Time to get on with it.

Two fingers moved naturally to her mouth and with one loud whistle she had the attention of most of the passersby between the church and the mercantile.

Abby's heart began to race when she saw her stranger push himself away from the strapping post and situate himself at the back of the growing and curious crowd. He stared at her, his eyes dark and unsettling, amusement only a glimmer on his face. Her hands fidgeted at her sides and she cleared her throat. When the stranger tilted his head and cocked an eyebrow in what seemed a blatant challenge to speak her peace, she suddenly felt up to whatever new adventure awaited her. Starting today.

Colorado, Two Days Earlier

"We've been on your land for the last couple of hours." Raine pulled up alongside Cole. "That pasture fence there looks a might on the weathered side, but daylight'll be gone soon. Best get 'em corralled up for the night."

Cole had driven the crew hard from sun up to sun down and to his dismay, the sun was once again setting just over the mountains to the west.

The two brothers rode the perimeter of the enclosed field. Two sections of the fence had fallen completely and would need fixing, but it'd serve their purposes for now. They'd mend what they could in what little light was left and build camp just outside the weak sections of the enclosure.

Cole whistled and waved his arm in a circular motion above his head, telling the other drovers to round the cattle up and lead them into the small fenced pasture. He snorted at the ruddy dilapidated barn and adjoining lean-to.

Cattle drives were especially dangerous at night and where

Cole normally would have pushed through for another couple of hours, he did not want anything to go wrong this close to his final destination. It still hadn't sunk in completely. This was *his* land. It would be the best place to stop and regroup. If McCallister had anything to do with Alaric's death, he would know soon enough. But only if he had the man's trust first. He was supposed to deliver the herd and report to the SilverHawk on Saturday. That would give him two days to make a few repairs and scout out the town beforehand.

His father had been pleased when Cole had finally accepted his new role as guardian and had agreed to live on the land. However, after Mr. Tacy left and the two boys had shown Jameson the note Alaric left, Jameson's joy had been short-lived.

"Now, don't go and do anything rash son," his father had said, "Just because McCallister's name is written on the back of the note, does not mean he had anything to do with Alaric's death."

But his counsel hadn't resonated with Cole. He would find out exactly what had happened to his friend, even if it got him killed in the process.

"There are two sections of fence down on the south side, boss, but the herd should be good for the night. The round pen is in pretty good condition and we're corralling the horses there now."

"Thanks, Marty. We're going to settle here for a couple of days and then we'll push on to the McCallister stead to deliver the herd on Saturday morning." He hated holding onto the cattle for longer than necessary, but he wanted to be prepared when he met his new employer for the first time.

The flank rider stared at him a moment, a confused expression pinching his features. He recovered quickly and tipped his hat. "Yes, boss." Marty jerked his horse around to go tell the others.

"He's probably afraid you'll change your mind." Raine laughed and clapped his brother on the shoulder.

Two weeks on the cattle trail earned his team this short

rest. Patience had never been one of Cole's stronger virtues, however, it was time to get some rest to prepare for the days ahead. It wouldn't do anybody any good to start the charade sleep deprived.

"Tomorrow, my friend," Cole spoke to the wind, hoping Alaric could hear. "Tomorrow, I'll find your girl and set things right. However many tomorrows that may take."

Colorado, Friday

Cole stood, stretching muscles used extensively over the last few months. He had become accustomed to sleeping on the hard ground, but somehow doing so on property he could call his own invigorated him. His tall, black Arabian stallion nickered at him and Cole took a deep breath.

"Can you smell that, Mav?" He asked his horse, his trusted friend. The fresh scent of the morning dew still lingered on the brush. The murmur of hundreds of cattle, interspersed with an occasional whinny, set a wistful background in Cole's mind for the picture of his dream, his ranch. He planned to ride the land, to familiarize himself with every inch of his soil, but that would have to wait until he'd delivered the herd.

He draped his saddle over one of the fence posts in the round pen, which creaked in objection. He'd risen early in attempt to familiarize himself with the immediate vicinity. Along with Raine, he rode out a mile or two round about the area, surveying the surroundings and gazing over the luscious green hills dotted with new spring growth. Jagged, purple mountains encircled the fertile green of the valley. Deep blue ripples of water, crested in white caps, crashed over clusters of angled rocks as they raced down the winding riverbed. The winter must have brought a lot of snow to these parts. The spring runoff was more than he'd expected. He patted his vest pocket. *Here it is*, he thought, his mind retracing the picture under his fingertips.

The outer fences had all been mended and the lean-to, resting against the barn, had been cleaned. Raine had insisted on transporting an old coal stove for warmth from the barn into the make-shift building and constructing frames for their bedrolls. Although Raine liked ranching, it had been a long time since he'd had to sleep on the ground. It didn't seem to suit him.

One of the steers had collapsed from exhaustion yesterday and Cole had helped Cook dress him for jerky and hide. Some of the meat now hung from the short rafters in a sectioned off area of the lean-to and the rest, along with the hide was draped from a support beam in the barn. Bales of straw were stacked at the entrance of the barn and fresh hay lined the first stall.

This morning's ride had proved to be fruitful. Although, he and Raine had not yet discovered the entrance to the mine, they had spotted a small farmhouse not far off. When they'd inquired of the farmer, he'd agreed to sell them straw, hay, some fruit jerky, and two flattened mattress beds. The mattresses would have to be re-stuffed, but Cole was pleased with their find.

The only thing still left to do, was to check out the town. According to the will, Cole owned the town of Silver Falls and most everything in it, as well as a good chunk of the surrounding land.

Once the horses were saddled, the two brothers headed out. They moved at a steady pace, approaching the outskirts of town within the hour. They pulled into Silver Falls, past the confectioners shop and looked around. People bustled about.

Raine dismounted in front of the Sheriff's office and Cole followed suit. A mass of people huddled together and were shouting out in excitement near the town livery. Raine finished tying his horse to the wooden rail and turned to Cole. "Looks like trouble. I'm going to go and see what all the fuss is about."

Cole nodded. If anyone could stop trouble it was Raine. He knew Raine was content working alongside him, but watching him make his way through the crowd to the center of the action, Cole again wondered why he'd never pursued his love of the law. Heaven knew he was better with a gun than anyone Cole had ever met and his sense of justice was unparalleled.

"Either of you strangers lookin' to get yerself a wife?" Cole looked up to see a small, round, balding man walking out of the barbershop chuckling.

"Not today." Cole stared at the man, whose unruly moustache still had crumbs from his breakfast. "Maybe not ever."

What an odd question, he thought, patting Maverick on his side. Surely, his mother hadn't...

He shook his head as he started walking away, but stopped at the thought. Turning back over his shoulder, he found the man still staring after him with ruddy cheeks and a wide toothy grin, shooing him forward.

She wouldn't.

Cole moved into the crowd to find Raine. It didn't take long. Raine was in the center pulling apart two men actively engaged in fisticuffs. Cole caught his eye. Raine jerked his chin upward in two abrupt movements toward the quaint, white structure that appeared to serve as the church. Cole worked his way through the whispering assembly of onlookers as they migrated toward the center of town.

As he neared the church the smell of fresh paint lingered in the air and Cole guessed the building had just received a fresh coat.

One of the branches of an oak tree at the back of the church yard protruded just above his head and he raised his arms to lean against it. He froze when a woman, draped in an old woolen army coat, caught his stare. When she made eye contact, he could not bring himself to look away.

She smiled in his direction before turning to climb the steps. At the top of the church steps, she slowly turned around and looked warily out at the town, assessing something. She bowed her head to remove her black Stetson. Loose curls, the color of wheat with rich auburn sun kisses, fell down around her shoulders as she roughly shook her head from side to side.

He was intrigued. She pulled her coat tighter around her neck, her fiery tresses spilling over her shoulders in direct contrast with the green wool. Her lips were full and inviting and Cole found himself unable to take his eyes off her. He stood mesmerized, taken in by the passionate flair he saw in her eyes. From this distance he could not distinguish their exact color, but found himself wanting to know. A small unexpected smile touched his lips as a long whistle, loud enough to put any trail boss to shame, shot out from between her fingers. He unwittingly took a step toward her.

CHAPTER FIVE

Just as Abby was about to run down the church steps and away from so many inquisitive eyes, the dark-haired stranger smiled awkwardly, once again challenging her to state her purpose. A small crowd had gathered around her and she spotted at least seven marriageable age men. She swallowed the lump in her throat and smiled as demurely as she could.

"Now that I've got all yer attention, I guess I should tell you why I'm here." She felt nervous for the first time in a long time and didn't like the feeling one bit.

"All of you," she paused, glancing at the town's newest visitor, then corrected, "Well, *most* all of you know me, and you know my ranch."

"McCallister's sellin' their ranch," a young cowboy yelled out to his friends over near the saloon.

"Marcus Dingle," Abby chastised, "we are doing no such thing."

Her words were barely audible above the murmur of the quickly growing crowd and the hoots and hollering from the tussle happening next door. "If you'll just listen for a moment."

"What ya doin', Abby?" a voice called out from somewhere in the crowd.

"Why, it's not proper to have a young lady act like—"

"What young lady?" Someone else yelled out before the woman could finish.

"Why ya wearin' that getup, Abby? Ain't never seen ya in a dress before."

Abby blushed.

Laughter exploded through the crowd and the sudden roar of conversation made it nearly impossible for Abby to continue.

She couldn't tell which comment came from where and she realized she wouldn't accomplish her task if she didn't focus crowd's attention. She pulled out the small pistol she'd hidden in the folds of her dress and aimed it directly above her. When she fired, the crowd fell silent.

"Now, that's better." Abby tucked the gun back into her skirt. She tried to think of how Lily would act in this situation. She looked around for her friend, but she'd disappeared. Abby placed her hands together in front of her and pushed her shoulders forward, tilting her head slightly to one side as she'd seen Lily do before.

"Gentlemen," Abby began again, "well, except for those two of course," smiling sheepishly, she pointed to the two Spencer boys now being held at their necks by a different newcomer. The crowd laughed as the boys kicked and squirmed in the man's grasp. Silver Falls didn't get many strangers and she guessed these two had come together.

"The SilverHawk is a large spread with plenty of work to be done. Some of the finest horses in the territory have been bred out of our ranch and many more will come." She dared a glance at the stranger standing just a few heads back, and took heart at the intrigue dancing about his features. Her throat, suddenly dry, struggled with the words she must force out.

"I need a good Christian man who will take a more...," she paused glancing over the men in the crowd trying to anticipate their reaction, "...active role on my ranch."

A low, long whistle came from the crowd.

"What exactly are ya talking about, Miss Abby?" an older man wearing a faded plaid shirt under dull red suspenders called up to her. She smiled at him with what she hoped was an endearing curve of her lips.

"I'm gettin' to that Matthew," she stopped, took a deep breath, and exhaled slowly. Returning a smile to her face, she pulled her shoulders back and straightened her spine, focusing on the few she thought acceptable choices. "I need a man with some experience breeding horses and running a ranch." She swallowed.

"I thought *you* was the one that did all them things at SilverHawk," Benjamin Spencer called out, still in the clutches of the second stranger. Laughter erupted from the group and he plastered a satisfied grin across his face.

Abby gulped back her nervous giggle when the second stranger kneed Ben in his hind end. His face scrunched up with mock indignation.

"What I mean to say, is that I am offering to share my stakes in the SilverHawk ranch with the man who'll be...my husband," she breathed out the last with resignation of her dignity.

"When did you get yourself hitched, Abby?"

Abby grunted in frustration. "It's the husband part that I still need, Marcus. Today." She was sure her racing heart indicated she was dying.

A loud guffaw came from the front row. Abby blinked when she saw Jeremiah Carson actually laughing at her. "You just couldn't leave well enough alone could ya, Abby? No man's gonna marry a girl like you. Not until you decide to be what a wife should."

"And just what is that, Mr. Carson?"

"A woman. Hell, Abby, you can't even wear a dress without coverin' it up with a man's coat. If you want to get yourself a husband, you need to be Miss McCallister," Jeremiah squawked at her. "Show a feminine interest once in a while. A man wants a woman he'd be proud to have on his arm. He doesn't want to have to compete with her newest stud horse."

Abashed by his mocking she looked for the stranger who had unknowingly given her the courage to speak it aloud. When her eyes found his, she smiled uneasily in his direction. His expression had changed, however. It was no longer full of lighthearted interest, but had altered into something closer to anger, leaving her confused and frustrated. His brows were creased into a solitary line and the smile was gone from his face.

She watched with disappointment and embarrassment as he turned on his heel and strode away. He was a stranger to her. She didn't know him. So, why should his opinion matter to her? Taking a deep breath, she regained her composure. She stood up straighter before attempting to respond to Jeremiah's cruel banter. Her mind, however, would not release the image of the stranger's dark brooding eyes and she forced her gaze away from his retreating back.

Earl took a step forward and opened his mouth to speak. Abby closed her eyes. Of all the Spencer's, Benjamin would certainly be the best, but...

"Where I come from, that is no way to treat a lady." The second stranger appeared suddenly to defend her honor. He had relinquished his hold on the Spencer boys and stood in open challenge to Jeremiah.

Abby's gaze moved from Ben, to the stranger, and then to Jeremiah.

"Here neither, friend," Jeremiah replied. "So, when you find one, I'll treat her all respectable like."

One moment Jeremiah stood there, his head thrown back and laughing, and the next he lay flat on the ground, one arm thrown above his head and the corner of his mouth bleeding.

"I am not your friend."

Abby looked at the man standing in front of her. She warmed to him immediately, however, her gaze inadvertently followed searched the crowd for the first. There was something about him that drew her attention.

"You all right, ma'am?" The stranger asked.

Abby couldn't think what to say, so she nodded. The stranger mirrored her action. The two Spencer boys he'd held stood hovering over their friend. The man resumed his grip on their necks and carted them back toward the Sheriff's office.

"Ain't too smart are ya, boys?"

Cole felt as if he'd been kicked in the gut when her words triggered the sickly realization of her identity. The name, the hair, the town--not only was she McCallister's daughter, she was Alaric's Abby and she stood there proposing marriage to anyone who'd take her. He didn't know if he was more angry at her for putting herself in such a compromising position or the men who mocked her.

Apprehension, anger, and relief all danced with one another inside of him. He swallowed the knot that had begun to form in his throat. Turning abruptly he stalked back to the horses in front of the sheriff's office.

She'll be there...waiting for me, he heard the same plea in his mind that had haunted him for months. *Please go to her, tell her I didn't forget. Tell her...I loved her.* Alaric's last words prickled heavily at Cole's conscience.

Alaric had believed this Abby from his youth would always wait for him--no matter how long it took to return. He hadn't been to Silver Falls in five years or more and yet he'd still believed she'd wait. He wished Alaric were standing in front of him because for the first time since he'd died, Cole wanted to punch him for being so blind.

Raine was behind Cole in an instant, both the fighting boys still within his clutch. "They were stupid enough to stick around even after I hit the insolent pup back there."

"Lucky for you," Cole stated with facetious disdain toward the two youth.

"Where's the sheriff? Raine called to the barber who had just stepped out onto the lifted porch.

"Ain't none."

Cursing under his breath, Raine looked from one boy to the other and with a few short words whispered sharply in their ears, he let them go with a push. Both of them ran down the street, not once looking back, and disappeared into the fields surrounding the town.

Grumbling to himself, Cole fidgeted around in his saddle bag to find the small token representing Alaric's affection for the girl. He looked up when he heard a hearty chuckle. The same balding man stood like a pompous old bear watching the scene playing out before him.

"Not gonna change your mind now are you, son? She may not be feminine and all, and she's real tough around the edges, but you have to give it to her. She has a lot of spunk and plenty of curves to keep a man satisfied."

With a low growl in his throat Cole stared at the man menacingly with one brow raised. The smile on the man's face faded almost instantly and any further hint at humor restrained itself from sounding.

Things had just become very complicated. Cole had never imagined Alaric's Abby would turn out to be McCallister's only daughter. He would have to resort to more drastic measures than he had originally intended to discover the truth and fulfill his promise to his friend. Cole finished fastening the latch on his bag and turned back toward the crowd. Taking a deep breath, he let it out slowly. Time to be charming.

Cole could feel Raine's eyes on him, but he said nothing. He took a step toward the church.

She'll be there waiting for me, he echoed his friends empty promise in his mind. "Well," he said aloud as he picked up his pace, "she wasn't waiting for you, friend."

"You can't be serious about this, Abby," her blond heckler said, pulling himself up from the ground.

"Jeremiah," she started. Her face flushed at using such informality in public. She smoothed an invisible crease from the coat covering her dress. Her voice lowered. "Mr. Carson, I believe you had your chance yesterday when I spoke to you at your ranch. If I'm not what you want in a wife, then fine, move aside and let me find someone who thinks my ranch, or at least my latest stud, is worth the price." The crowd laughed. Heat rose in her cheeks. They burned even hotter when she recalled her earlier encounter with the young man, whose eyes now bored holes into her the size of two-bits.

"Not like this, Abby. What are you doing?" Jeremiah spoke through gritted teeth.

Abby pulled away from his wolf-like expression. "I'm glad I've seen you for who you are, Mr. Carson. I wouldn't marry you now to save me. Feminine or not."

"We were making progress. It's always been understood between our families. You can't do this. You'll ruin everything," he barely whispered. He stepped forward taking her possessively by the arm and tried to pull her down the steps. As Abby resisted him, his fingers clamped tighter, like iron grips pressing into her flesh.

"Jeremiah. Please." Twisting, she pulled herself back, away from his grasp, she had only compromised one step.

"You're not doing this, Abby." Jeremiah spit the words before grinding his teeth together.

"I feel bad for you, Mr. Carson. It seems you are not my husband, nor will you be, therefore I can do whatever I have a mind to." Abby felt her voice rising louder with each word. "I plan on having a husband when I go home tonight."

"And you'll have one," a deep baritone voice called out from the back of the group.

A hush fell over the crowd. All eyes turned to the stranger who made his way back toward her. Abby, appalled her conversation with Jeremiah had been witnessed by the large group, silently cursed herself for letting her emotions show.

The swarm of onlookers parted and when she saw the face of the dark-haired stranger re-emerge from the crowd she felt her heart skip a beat. Everyone stared, watching his lithe movements with interest as he approached the steps. His faded denims were snug around his thighs and his white shirt was open slightly at the neck with a soft brown leather vest hanging in worn disarray. His dark features were chiseled and even with the small scar just above his eyebrow, to Abby he was physical perfection.

He extended her his bronzed right hand--palm up, his left still clenched into a fist. She looked around at the familiar faces she had grown up loving, each one a friend or acquaintance. She had known what to expect from all of them, but from this stranger she drew a complete blank.

Abby almost glanced behind her to make sure the stranger was not looking at someone else. His lips were formed into a straight line slightly curving at the edges. His gaze intensified, one eyebrow cocked. Something stirring within the depths of his dark walnut brown eyes captivated her and she risked another glance at his patiently extended hand.

The stranger, the one who had stopped the fight between the Spencer brothers and who had punched Jeremiah in the face, stepped forward and placed his hand on her stranger's shoulder. "Cole?" he questioned in a low voice that resonated in the silence.

Abby had never seen the likes of these men before. The second was taller than the first with even darker hair. Both strangers had the same basic build and Abby guessed them brothers. She was amazed at the strength that emanated from each of them. She would swear she'd seen moose smaller in size.

"We'll discuss it later, Raine." Cole spoke without turning around. The finality in his voice took her by surprise and she felt a twinge of fear at his command. Raine's jaw tensed and his blue eyes narrowed. He glanced at Abby, lingering only a moment before taking one step backward. His rigid stance, however, betrayed his objection.

Cole cocked a dark eyebrow. His hand clenched then opened as he extended it once again to Abby, nodding for her to take it. The intensity in his face almost frightened her, yet something in the way he carried himself, something in his manner drew her in.

She stood brimming with curiosity at the appearance of this mysterious outsider now offering to be a part of her life. Her hand twitched and she started to raise it toward his, her eyes unwavering.

"Now wait a minute, Abby," Jeremiah protested. "You're not just going to up and marry some stranger who just rode into town. We've known each other near our whole lives and everyone has expected us to get hitched someday."

The spell was broken and Abby rested her hand once again at her side.

"As the *lady* said," Raine spoke as he moved one step to the left, blocking Jeremiah from her view, "you had your chance yesterday, *Mr. Carson*." He spoke the man's name with slow precision.

Abby gasped incredulously. She had never seen nor heard anyone speak that way to Jeremiah Carson and her appreciation for this other stranger, Raine, deepened. She glanced back to Cole, his dark eyes still fastened on her, and with a slight upturn of her mouth she took a step forward.

Abby skittered down the remaining steps and leaned toward him. She spoke so softly he had to bend his head to hear her. "This is a lifetime commitment. There'll be no going back. Are you prepared for that?"

"Are you?"

Abby had not taken the time to consider her own question. Looking up at the very handsome man who had consented to marry her, she thought if he would be half as nice a husband as he was to look at, she would be the most blessed woman in the territory. She stood so close to him now she could feel the heat radiating from his body and it left her heady. She took a very small step backward attempting to clear her head.

"Are you wanted?" she asked, avoiding his direct gaze.

"Just by my mother, ma'am." The corners of his mouth twitched.

Abby forced herself not to smile, but felt herself relax a little at his attempted humor. Her eyes squinted at him and she met his open stare, waiting for the real answer.

"No, ma'am." His voice was slow and steady. Any hint of a smile was gone.

Abby let out the breath she didn't realize she'd been holding.

"Are you familiar and experienced with ranch work?"

Cole closed his eyes and took a deep breath. "Yes, ma'am,"

his frozen smile returned to his face.

"Christian? Kind? Good?" Each one word question had received a curt nod from Cole except the last which altered something in his brooding smoky eyes and his smile warmed a little under its influence.

"I try," he spoke almost playfully.

She swallowed. Cole stared down at her expectantly. She imagined how her father would react and the stubborn set to her jaw returned.

Satisfied with his answers, she searched his face, not knowing what she looked for. He shifted uncomfortably under her gaze.

"Do you ever smile, Cole? Really smile? The kind that touches your eyes?" she leaned into him and asked in a whisper.

"Of course, I smile," he answered gruffly.

"Show me, then." Taunting a man was not her strong suit, but Abby found herself enjoying the intimate exchange.

He blinked. Then stared. "Do you want a husband or not?"

Abby thought for a moment, staring hard into his eyes. There was sadness there and once she realized that, she understood him better. She found herself wanting to be his reason to smile and couldn't explain the peace she felt when the answer to his question touched her lips.

"Yes."

She laughed nervously when she slid her hand into his much larger one. She was unprepared for the sensations his touch sent spiraling through each of her limbs and torso. That touch evoked a tingling sensation that began in the tips of her toes and reached the top of her head with lightning speed. She smiled up at him, her heart thundering within her chest.

"Yes. I will marry you."

Abby caught sight of Davey who had apparently finished loading the supplies from the mercantile. His mouth gaped open and he jumped up onto the buckboard and tore out of town like fire licked at his heels. Her father would know within the hour what she was doing. She just hoped it would be too late for him to do anything about it.

Abby looked back at her prospective husband. She had known her determination would take her home with a man, but she had never imagined the exhilaration she would feel at such a handsome prospect. She closed her eyes tight and then opened them to make sure she was not dreaming. A fresh wave of self-consciousness hit. She had grown up in this small town and any other man there would know what he was getting.

She in turn knew nothing of Cole or his family. This was all happening so fast.

"Where can we find the preacher?" Cole's voice resonated across the murmuring crowd.

"Haven't seen 'im in weeks," the old miner volunteered. "He lives up the side of that there mount'n, behind the old church. Might try for 'im there."

Cole looked to where Matthew pointed behind the chapel. He and Raine whispered something to each other, too quietly for her to hear.

Abby hadn't thought about the preacher being out of town and she cursed herself for her lapse in preparation. He just *had* to be there.

Movement just to the left of Cole's shoulder caught Abby's eye. Lily's father, Henry Campbell, had just stumbled out of the saloon. Lily held him up, bowing under the strain of his weight. She helped him into the back of their wagon. Once he was settled, Jed, the Campbell's foreman, drove away.

When Abby met her friend's eye, Lily broke into a run down the old wooden walkway toward her. Abby retracted her hand, less than gracefully, from Cole's grasp and started forward, hoping it didn't mean trouble.

"Are you all right?" Abby asked, concerned.

Lily nodded. "You?"

"I did it Lily. I'm getting married."

Lily's eyes widened and her jaw dropped slightly. "Please tell me it's not Matthew."

Abby dropped one of Lily's hands and pulled her friend excitedly by the other along the boardwalk and onto the dirt road toward the two tall strangers whose eyes had followed her with scarcely concealed interest. She stopped short as she saw the silent exchange between the two men. The majestic countenance of their lean forms and broad shoulders was a sight to behold and she soaked it in, self-consciously biting the inside of her lip. She squeezed Lily's hand even tighter and pulled her alongside the two newest brothers in town.

"Lily, this is Mr. Cole...uh," Abby searched Cole's face for a moment, heat rising in her cheeks. She didn't even know his surname.

"Redbourne," Raine provided, tipping his hat toward the ladies. He pushed his way past Cole, his eyes never leaving Lily's face. "Good afternoon, ma'am." His voice was like honey and his grin wide. "I am Raine Redbourne and this is my little brother Cole."

CHAPTER SIX

Cole pulled his gaze away from Abby's eyes, which he now noted were the color of raw emeralds, to see Raine once again laying on the charm. Cole glanced at Abby's friend and she appeared mesmerized, as the women usually did when one of his siblings was present.

"There is only time for one wedding today, brother, and we already have a lot to do." Cole clapped Raine on the back.

Raine threw his head back and laughed. Lily looked slightly disconcerted. Her cheeks flushed a soft pink.

"Well, ma'am, it would be my pleasure to escort you to *the* wedding." Raine extended his bent arm in Lily's direction. With a meaningful glance at Abby, Lily took Raine's arm and they walked toward the church.

"I'll go find the preacher." Cole felt his gut tighten, the same way it always did when he closed an important deal. He turned to walk away, but stopped when the soft weight of Abby's hand grasped his forearm. He stopped and turned to face her. Her hand remained steady against his skin. He met her questioning gaze with uncomfortable silence.

"I don't know anything about you," she said quietly.

Was there a question hiding somewhere in her words?

"I thought you wanted a husband. By tonight. And so, here I am." He was unable to meet her eyes completely. Her touch stirred something within him. Something he hadn't felt in a long time. He didn't want to feel anything, but did not move.

"I know." She removed her hand self-consciously, leaving

a vacant feeling in its place. "I just wondered... I mean, why you volunteered. Surely, you can have any woman you want." She searched his face, her eyes petitioning answers.

Cole was taken aback by the plainness of her words. If she really knew the truth, she would be running back to the blond oaf in the crowd. However, he was not prepared to justify his actions and would not do so--even to himself. "It's getting late. We better find that preacher or there will not *be* any wedding."

Her reluctant smile sent a surge of guilt through his veins. Stepping off the boardwalk, he tipped his hat and backed away before Abby could say another word. "I'll meet you in the church in one hour," he managed before he'd turned around completely.

You're playing with fire, Cole. His conscience would not leave him alone as he walked across the street. He knew he was in uncharted territory, but something inside drove him forward. *Marriage?* he asked himself as he walked toward the church. *What the hell am I doing?*

"Marriage? To a complete stranger?" Abby spoke aloud as she sat on the edge of the boardwalk in front of the mercantile. Her elbow rested on her knees and her hands were gathered into fists under her chin. "What am I doing?" She felt numb all over. She wondered how her father would react. Surely, he would be in town within the hour. Abby just hoped that Cole returned with the preacher before then.

A gust of wind picked up the loose tendrils of her hair and blew them in every direction until she was sure she looked like the neighbor's rag doll. What a sight she would be. She tried to smooth down some of the flailing curls with the palm of her hand.

Lily had excused herself to attend to some details with an upcoming tea and Abby'd had no desire to sit and listen to all the gossip the young ladies in town would surely provide.

Gossip was a big part of a small town like Silver Falls, and like it or not, Abby was sure her little stunt would make her the center of it today.

Abby stood up and stepped onto the boardwalk and began to walk, trying to keep herself from going stir crazy with nothing else to do while she waited. Most of those who'd witnessed her moment of insanity still stood around in clustered crowds, whispering. She noticed a group of older ladies as she rounded the corner near the hotel. She froze when she overheard them buzzing wildly about today's wedding. They hadn't seen her.

"I would have never thought it," said Ms. Gillespie, an old spinster woman in glasses, whose face was pinched so tightly in disapproval, Abby thought she must have just eaten a bad batch of horehound. "Of course, with a mother like Clara McCallister it's no wonder the girl has never learned to be a lady." Her orange hair, pulled tightly into a bun, was accented perfectly by the simple brown dress she wore.

Abby ground her teeth together. They hadn't understood her mother like she had.

"I wonder if Clay knows what his daughter is up to." The large peacock feather in Mrs. Dalton's hat tousled about in the breeze.

"Of course, he does. A shotgun wedding if I've ever seen one."

Abby didn't see who'd made the last comment, but at the several tsking sounds that came from the group, Abby lowered her head. She should have suspected people would believe the worst.

Not wanting the women to know she'd been affected by their words or that she'd even heard them, she lifted her head high and stepped into sight, effectively cutting through the surreptitious entourage of simple gossip surrounding her. As she passed them, some threw out their own words of ancient wisdom and others scolded her for being so brash and indiscreet.

Abby was surprised to see Mrs. Hutchinson among these

ladies. The old milliner did not usually associate with the
gossipers in town. A true lady of class, her hair was always in a
perfect coiffeur, forever adorned in a stylish new hat, and she
carried a dainty black parasol at all times. There was something
real in her eyes that made others feel comfortable around her.
Like she'd experienced loss and understood.

When Abby realized Mrs. Hutchinson watched her, she
quickly turned away only to have the recent widow take her by
the elbow and guide her away from the crowd, toward her
shop.

"Come with me, dear. There is something I think you
should have on your wedding day." Mrs. Hutchinson put her
arm around Abby's shoulders, encompassing her under a shawl,
and escorted her around through the back doors of her small
millinery business.

Abby had never cared much for the fancier parts of town.
She'd always preferred to stay at the ranch, despite her mother's
objections, and on the rare occasions that she did come, she
stuck to the church and the mercantile.

Mrs. Hutchinson's little shop was nothing like what Abby
had expected. Had she not seen the outside, she would believe
she was in a quaint English cottage.

"Sophie, get some shortbread and punch for the girl and
I'll require a spot of tea." Mrs. Hutchinson called to a small girl,
of no more than thirteen, sitting in the corner chair, reading the
latest *Harper's Bazar* fashion magazine. "And please get my
cherish box from the dresser and bring it to me."

"Yes, mum." The young girl stood and rushed behind a
curtain, laying the magazine open on the floor.

Abby realized the kind, eccentric, old woman wanted to
help her get ready for her impromptu wedding.

Mrs. Hutchinson set her black umbrella in the corner.

"Tell me, dear, why on earth would a pretty young thing
like you want to throw yourself into the arms of just any young
man? We always thought you would marry that young, good-
looking Carson boy. Jeremiah, I believe is his name. Why not
just marry him?" She removed her shawl and gently laid it

across the top of the charming woven couch.

Abby had always considered herself to be plain and was surprised at Mrs. Hutchinson's compliment. Jeremiah had, on occasion, told her she was pretty in her own way, but she had known she would never be as pretty as *he* was.

She pulled herself from her thoughts and realized Mrs. Hutchinson awaited a reply. None came. How could she tell the woman that she had practically thrown herself at Jeremiah's mercy the day before and he had rejected her, laughed at her impulsiveness, and had ridiculed her in front of the town.

"You weren't there, were you?"

"Where, dear?" Mrs. Hutchinson eyed her with interest.

"At the church..." Abby couldn't bring herself to say it. "Never mind. It's not important."

Jeremiah didn't care about her. He never had. Abby understood that, but had been willing to overlook that for her home. When she'd told him about her bet with her father, his lip had turned up into a scowl and he'd told her that living in society for a time would help her to become the kind of lady he wanted for a wife. *No wife of mine is going to be out working on a ranch with the men. It just isn't right,* he'd said.

Abby replaced the unpleasant memory with the look on Cole's face as he stood there, a perfect stranger, offering her his hand. Her lips unwittingly curved into a smile.

"Please excuse me, Mrs. Hutchinson," Abby said, realizing that the woman was expectant of further explanation, "was there something you needed from me?"

The elder woman smiled.

"I saw the looks on those women's faces when I passed them. Most of them must believe I am tainted in some way to have acted so rashly. Why are *you* trying to help? You hardly know me."

Motioning for Abby to sit in front of an intricately carved dressing table, Mrs. Hutchinson removed her gloves and picked up a beautiful ivory handled brush. She began to stroke Abby's tangled curls with gentle ease.

"Because dear, I recognize the makings of a good match

when I see one. Although, I must warn you that marriage isn't always easy. Oh, it can be wonderful to the right man of course, but just the same, there are adjustments that must be made...compromises."

Abby was silent.

"How long have you known that young man?"

"Not long." Surely the older woman had heard all the gossip. She had to have known they'd only just met.

"You are a very lucky girl to be marrying into the Redbourne family, you know?" Mrs. Hutchison spoke as she fussed with Abby's hair.

Abby twisted in her seat and immediately regretted it as her locks were still entwined in the bristles of Mrs. Hutchinson's brush. She returned to her face forward position.

"How did you know he was a—"

"A Redbourne, dear?"

Abby nodded.

"Your refreshments, mum." Sophie set down a silver tray on the small end table next to the vanity.

"Thank you, child. And my box?"

"Right away, mum." Sophie disappeared again behind the curtain.

"You know them? The Redbournes?" Abby prodded, unable to keep the excitement from her voice. Something in the woman's reflection betrayed a deep hurt, sadness of some kind. It was then Abby remembered it had only been a few months since the widow had lost her husband.

"Forgive me. I'm sorry for your recent loss," Abby said with a twinge of guilt.

Mrs. Hutchinson gathered another section of her hair and continued brushing. "I saw the way that young man looked at you before," she said, effectively changing the subject. "There was fire in his eyes and when you announced you needed a husband, well..." she paused and clicked her tongue, "the look on his face became masked. Unreadable. It could have been jealousy maybe or fury? Disbelief? You must be a very special girl indeed to incite such emotion in a man."

"He doesn't even know me," Abby admitted.

"He looks just like his father did at that age."

"You *do* know him. His family? His father?" Abby didn't realize how much she needed to find some connection to the man she was about to give her life to.

"It was a long time ago. I will tell you about it someday." Mrs. Hutchinson patiently turned Abby back around and began pinning her hair. She looked into the mirror, into Abby's searching face and offered a reassuring smile. "If he is anything like his father, he is a good man. But remember, even good men make bad decisions from time to time."

"What do you mean?"

"Never you mind. I'm just an old woman rambling on. He will love you. And, in time, you will grow to love him—the man, not just the idea of him."

Abby's whole body seemed to relax at her words and she turned to face Mrs. Hutchinson, who added some finishing touches to her new coiffeur. "He is handsome, isn't he?"

"Yes, dear. Just like his father."

Abby pinched her cheeks, her spirits noticeably uplifted. Ms. Hutchinson handed her a small plate with a shortbread cookie and fruit tart. Abby noticed a small ornate box lying to the side of the vanity and wondered when Sophie had brought it in. Mrs. Hutchinson followed her gaze and caressed the top of the box.

"I've held onto this for far too long now. It is time to pass it on to a real Redbourne bride."

When she opened the box, Abby stared at a beautiful silver hair comb. It was exquisite in design and had a singular rich, deep red jewel at the ridge.

"Garnet," Mrs. Hutchinson said as she grazed the gem with her fingertips.

"What do you mean by *a real* Redbourne bride?" Abby's curiosity was at the brink of turmoil.

Mrs. Hutchinson removed the comb from the box and placed it securely at the crown of Abby's head.

"That is a story for another day, my dear."

Abby opened her mouth in protest, but the grandfather clock chimed two o'clock. She would already be late.

"Thank you." Abby reached out and squeezed Mrs. Hutchinson's hand, which rested on the closed wooden box.

Ms. Hutchinson smiled warmly and gently caressed Abby's cheek.

"I think I will stay here, my dear. You don't mind going back to the church unaccompanied, do you? An old woman like me can only handle so much excitement in one day."

Abby nodded. "Thank you."

"Hold up there, Charcoal." Raine matched his resolute speed and caught up to him in no time. "What has come over you?"

Cole didn't turn around.

"What do you want, Raine?" Cole was not in the mood for one of his big brother lectures and he continued his strict pace up the hill.

"What do I want? What the hell has gotten into you?" Raine tugged on his arm, effectively turning him about face. The rocks under Cole's feet gave way and threw him off balance. He nearly fell forward into Raine.

Regaining his footing, Cole glowered at his brother, his fists tightened at his sides.

"Nothing." Cole's teeth clenched tightly and he breathed heavily through his nose.

"Is it Granddad's will? I thought you didn't care about the money." Raine baited him and he knew it.

Cole didn't respond. He could feel the heat rising in his face.

"Please, tell me you didn't agree to marry her because she's McCallister's daughter. It won't solve anything."

"Go back, Raine. Shouldn't you be charming the knickers off Abby's friend, Lily?"

Raine's fist slammed Cole in the mouth, just to the side of his chin, sending him sprawling onto his backside. Cole propped himself up onto one elbow and opened his mouth, trying to stretch his throbbing jaw. He'd never been able to master the block of a left hook.

"Damn it, Cole." Raine shook his hand and walked in a short circle. "When did you become so bitter?"

"She's Alaric's girl, Raine." Cole slumped back onto the ground, relief washing over him at the admission. "He'd planned to come back here and marry her."

"You mean Abby is...?"

"The one and only."

A loud guffaw burst from an otherwise solemn Raine. "So, it wasn't just some momentary lack of judgment that threw you at her feet. You're taking his place." Raine reached his hand out to a prostrate Cole.

"I didn't intend on marrying the girl." Cole took Raine's offered hand and sat up. "I was just supposed to give her this and tell her he loved her. I swore I would protect her. To make sure she was all right." Cole reached into his vest pocket and retrieved the bent horseshoe nail. He held it aloft in his hand. "How the hell was I supposed to do all that if she was somebody else's wife?" The calm in his voice hinted of exasperation and he knew it. He held the small trinket between his thumbs and forefingers.

"This might complicate the job with McCallister."

Cole nodded. "Can we talk about it later? I have a preacher to find and a woman to marry." He pushed himself up off the ground, once again picking up the course he'd left off with more determination in his step.

He left the dusty road behind to follow a small trail, carved by much use, through the tall, grassy hillside meadow. His destination in sight, he stomped over the new morning glory and blue flax flowers that had crept onto the path. The small wooden cabin was set high above the city of Silver Falls. Back home the preacher had lived in a small room behind the church and Cole wondered why this parson had chosen to live so far away from his congregation.

The clouds were playing hide and seek with the sun and the wind vexed the trees with its force. Cole looked up into the sky. A storm was brewing.

He arrived at the front door to the cabin. The windows were off their hinges and an odd stench came from the space below the door. Cole lifted his fist to knock, but froze before it touched the gnarled wood, and he dropped it to his side. He turned back to look at Raine, who'd always been there for him and had taught him a lot over the years. Not quite as forcefully in the past, but he'd learned a lot from his oldest brother.

Concern etched Raine's brow.

"I really don't care about the money." Cole couldn't quite meet his brother's eyes because he knew what he would find there.

"Then, why now? Why this girl? Alaric would never expect you to marry her out of guilt."

"Alaric loved her, Raine and if it weren't for me they could have been together now."

"Loved her?" Raine snorted. "Maybe. And every other pretty gal between here and Abilene."

Cole's stance became rigid. Alaric had loved women. And he'd never wanted for female attentions. Cole couldn't deny that, but every time he'd talked about Abby, how different she was from all of the others, Cole had known she was special to him.

"I'm not sure Alaric knew what it meant to love a woman," Raine said. "Lily told me he left her here, waiting, nearly six years ago. He didn't love her. He loved the idea of her. When Sarah and I fell in love, I didn't want to be a single day away from her."

Cole's jaw flexed. "Alaric wasn't you." He lifted his hand once again to the door.

"Are you sure about this, Charcoal?"

"No."

Raine placed his hand on Cole's shoulder and both men turned to sit on the stone slates that created a makeshift porch.

Cole lowered his head into his hands, his elbows resting on his knees. He ran his fingers through his hair and then lifted his head to look out at the wildflowers and brush growing in front of the preacher's house. He massaged his fingertips against his temples and forehead before he rested them, linked together, across his spread lap.

"I'm not accustomed to second guessing myself," Cole stated flatly.

"When Sarah died, I thought my life was over. I imagine I felt much the same way you do now, and I started to mistrust my instincts."

"How did you get over it?" Cole asked. He had only been fourteen when Sarah died. He remembered one night in particular, almost a year later, when he'd walked into his house and had found his eldest brother crying at the kitchen table. He'd become himself again after that night.

Raine looked out over the valley. "I heard Sarah's voice in my head telling me to get over myself. That I had grieved long enough and I needed to move on and live a good life. I can't explain it, Charcoal, but I had to learn to trust myself again. And in time, I figured out what she'd meant. Life is a gift."

Cole focused his attention on a spatter of red paintbrush decorating the hill. What Raine said made sense, and the first step in learning to trust himself again was to follow through with what he'd started. "I'm rea..."

"You chaps just hold it right there."

Cole looked up to the end of a rifle barrel peering at them from around the corner of the house.

"Mr. Daniels?" Cole asked.

"Who's asking, please?" The Brit asked without moving his eye from the sights.

Cole and Raine stood up together, very slowly, both with their palms flat and up in front of them.

"You don't know us. We're new in town, but you might know my betrothed, Abby McCallister."

He didn't move.

"Look, we don't want any trouble. We're just looking for

the good reverend."

The man took a step forward. A twig snapped beneath his feet, startling a group of birds perched in the trees. They scattered in all directions. The gun fired. Air grazed Cole's jaw as the bullet whirred by, missing him by mere inches.

Cole instinctively reached for his gun, but Raine had already disarmed the man and had him face first up against the trunk of a tree, his arm twisted behind his back.

"You okay?" Raine asked, out of breath.

Cole nodded.

"I don't think he is, though." Cole pointed at the trapped man.

Sweat trailed from his forehead, down his nose, until it mixed the blood at the corner of his mouth.

"You can let him go."

Raine released his grasp on the man and took two steps back, the rifle in one hand and his raised pistol in the other.

"Sorry about that," he said. "Didn't mean for it to go off then, did I?"

"You Daniels?" Cole asked.

The man shook his head and wiped the blood from his mouth. Then, he hunched over and braced himself up with his hands on his knees. "Name's Harris." He stood up and offered his hand.

Neither Raine, nor Cole moved to take it.

Harris looked at his hand and then wiped it on his trousers. "Well, then. What did you want Mr. Daniel's for? He's away for a time. I'm the new associate pastor here. Haven't even met my congregation yet."

His smiled looked rehearsed.

"Well, Mr. Harris, why the gun?"

"Daniel's said there had been some trouble. You know, collectors taking more than their share, breaking things," he pointed at the windows, "and the like. I thought you might be one of them and honestly, I don't have much to give."

"Well, preacher, we'll be needing you to come into town with us. I'm getting married and your services are required."

"Now? I'm sorry, who are you exactly?"

Despite the fact that the Brit had nearly killed him, Cole didn't think he proposed further threat and took a step toward him, his hand extended.

"I am Cole Redbourne, and this is Raine."

Harris's face turned ash white. "Redbourne?" He reluctantly took Cole's hand with a short, awkward laugh, then removed a rag from his pocket and wiped the sweat from his brow. "I'm sorry, my dear man, but I won't be able to perform any ceremonies at this time. I do apologize. Wait for Reverend Daniels to return. He should be back in a fortnight and has much more experience in these matters."

"As long as you'll come, I don't care how inexperienced you are."

Harris swallowed. "Do I have a choice?"

"Yes," Raine said. "Come willingly or go to jail for attempted murder."

"Just let me grab my bible."

"We'll wait," Raine said.

The preacher pushed open the door to the little house and closed it behind him. Raine stayed put, but nodded for Cole to head around back. Cole quickly moved behind the cabin and leaned up against the stone wall just to the side of an open window. Sure enough, within moments a small knapsack hit the ground, followed by the preacher climbing through the window. When both feet hit the ground, Cole cleared his throat.

Harris shook his head. "Which way?"

Cole pointed back toward the front of the house.

"Are you *sure* you know what you're doin'?" Raine asked as they started back down the hill.

"Nope." Cole picked up a small pebble and studied it for a moment before tossing it into the brush. No matter the reasons at this point, within the hour Abigail McCallister would be his bride. He'd contemplate the repercussions later.

CHAPTER SEVEN

Abby hurried down the stairs and onto the boardwalk toward the church. She knew her father had probably heard about her impetuous decision by now and she wanted to make sure he would not make it into town before the groom could say, 'I do.'

She'd watched Davey fight the crowd and head for the buckboard as soon as he'd heard what she planned to do. He'd ridden out to the SilverHawk, she was sure to tell her father, but it was a good hour ride to the ranch and another hour back. They had plenty of time. As long as they hurried along.

Lily.

She glimpsed her friend walk into the chapel with Cole's brother. Nobody would be watching out for Clay. Abby picked up the hem of her dress and without another thought jumped onto the dusty street--stealing for the church.

At the back of the chapel, she peered in to find, what Abby was sure was, the entire town of Silver Falls waiting in the pews. She was sure the gossip in town would never die after this. She spotted Lily sitting near the front, laughing at something Raine had said. Abby searched for a way to get her attention without drawing it to back to herself. One of the eight Simpson boys was about to run past her, leading a rambunctious cluster of youngsters. She reached out and grabbed him by the arm.

"Hey, watcha gotta go and do that fer? I was winnin'." The small boy stared up at her indignantly.

Abby reached into her shoe and pulled out two bits, laying it on display in her palm for the boy to look at.

"This will be yours if you get Miss Lily to come out without anyone else knowing I'm here."

The boy's eyes widened and he grabbed the two bits from her hand as he ran inside. He tugged on Lily's dress. When she looked over at him, Abby quelled a smile as she watched the youngster pull Lily so close to his mouth that it was obvious he had taken his responsibility seriously. When he pulled away from her, Lily looked up, but straight ahead, avoiding the back of the church.

Abby backed herself against the white wooden planks of the rear entrance to the church.

The young Simpson kid ran off in a near skip, calling back to her. "Thanks, Miss Abby," he said as he ran to catch up with his friends.

She watched him for a moment, holes in the knees of his trousers and hair badly in need of a cut. She wondered how the Simpson's had been able to provide for eight small children after his crop had been ruined by thugs. Yet each of them still wore smiles on their faces and stayed away from the kind of trouble one might expect them to find—unlike the Spencer boys.

Abby rested her back and open palms against the newly painted wood and closed her eyes, willing her heart to stop pounding so violently.

"Ah," Lily exclaimed, her mouth opened wide. "Your hair is lovely. How—"

"I'll tell you later." Abby flapped her hand dismissively. "Mr. Redbourne?"

"Mr. Redbourne is such a gentleman," Lily said in a gleeful whisper as she grabbed a hold of Abby's arm. "I think he's wonderful."

Abby's eyes flashed open. "Lily!" her voice was a mixture of panic and relief. Then, her face fell and her expression became serious. "Wait. How do you know he's wonderful? You've only just met him."

"I know, but those deep blue eyes and his..."

"Wait, Cole has brown eyes."

"Oh," Lily put her hand up to her mouth and twittered. "I wasn't talking about *your* Mr. Redbourne."

"You've only just met him," Abby repeated her cautionary warning.

"Well, you've just met his brother and that's not stopping you from *marrying* the man!" Lily folded her arms across her chest for emphasis. "Where have you been anyway? Cole has been in the church for nearly forty-five minutes waiting for you."

Abby didn't know what to say. She peered around the corner of the open door and peered in at her impromptu groom.

Lily dropped her hands to her sides, "I know. I'm just not sure how to react. You told me this is what you wanted. Have you changed your mind?"

"No. It's just that...I thought I would at least know the man I would share my life with. I thought I would marry someone I grew up with or at least someone I've spent more than five minutes with. I know nothing about Cole Redbourne. And well, he's just not..."

"Who? Alaric? The man's had a long time to come for you, Abby. You haven't received any correspondence in years. Do you really think he remembers a promise you both made six years ago? You were only sixteen." The question hung in the air like cotton on a tree. "Besides, I thought you were over him."

"I thought so too."

Abby straightened her shoulders and stood upright. "Half the girls in this town were married by the time they were sixteen, but you're right. Alaric was my past. Cole is my future. I don't know what's the matter with me. At least I'll be able to stay at the ranch."

"Raine," Lily covered her mouth, "I mean, Mr. Redbourne told me his brother is a good man."

"What else is he going to say about his own brother?" Abby half smiled.

"He did say that some people just took their sense of duty too far, whatever that means. He also said that once Cole has made up his mind about something, being dragged by a herd of wild mustangs couldn't make him change it."

"Great. I'm just going trade one foul tempered man for another."

Lily tried to hide her smile, but Abby could not help hers. "So, I guess I got myself a groom." She glanced out the door into the darkening sky. "Did my groom find the preacher? These clouds have been threatening havoc for the last hour and unless we get on with it, we're going to have a long, wet ride home."

Looking skyward Lily's eyes opened wide with apprehension, as if she hadn't noticed the black clouds quickly rolling in overhead.

"Yes," Lily gasped, "and who is he? I've never seen the likes of him before. I had no idea Reverend Daniels had left."

Abby shrugged.

"Well, he doesn't at all look like any preacher I've ever seen. If the man would just quit dabbing his forehead with his handkerchief and put a smile on his face he might actually be handsome—but not as handsome as either of these Redbournes, of course." Lily looked at Abby and blushed. With another quick peek into the church Lily stated, "It almost looks like wild horses dragged *him* here." Both women giggled.

"Oh, my bouquet. I left it on the horse."

"Trust me. I don't think he'll notice."

"But I will." Abby had one foot outside the church. "This may not be the event I always thought my wedding would be, but I at least want to *feel* like a real bride. This morning I picked the first spring flowers that had blossomed near the ranch and I think they will look lovely with my mother's dress. Besides, the rings are in my saddle bags. I'll be right back," she added hurriedly at the disapproving look on Lily's face.

"Okay, but hurry. By the way, Abby," she said before Abby made it two strides. "Your hair really does look beautiful."

Abby stepped back into the church. A few minutes to tell

Lily about the hat shop wouldn't hurt.

"It was Mrs. Hutchinson. I had no idea she was such a nice lady. I always thought she was a bit…odd. She's usually so quiet and keeps to herself."

"Well, she certainly outdid herself today. You look lovely. Cole will be blown away. I could have never done something like that." Lily reached up to touch a perfect curl.

Abby twirled around, feeling almost girlish. "She gave me this comb and said it had been made for a Redbourne bride and it's time someone wore it."

"Does she know the Redbournes?" Lily asked with interest.

"I think she knew them a long time ago and by the way she spoke, I think she was going to marry one. She was so mysterious about it. But I am happy to have something to wear that was meant to be in his family. It makes it all seem so much more…real." Abby shrugged her shoulders tight into ears as a crack of lightning split the sky. The two young women exchanged glances.

"Go!" Lily commanded before Abby could say another word.

Abby walked down the steps, slower than usual despite herself. "I'll just make him wait a moment longer," she whispered to the quiet breeze.

Bella was tied up to the apple tree over next to the sheriff's office and when Abby approached the old mare, she was greeted with dancing feet and flaring nostrils.

"I know a storm's coming girl. I won't be long." Abby rubbed the white horse's neck on both sides and kissed the side of her nose, hugging her close. Then she reached for her saddle bag and delved inside, searching for the tiny trinket that would symbolize her commitment to a complete stranger. She caught glimpse of her freshly picked flower bouquet dangling from Bella's reins.

One drop. Two. Then the sky broke, sending buckets of rain swiftly to the ground. She quickly unlashed the flowers from the reins, placed the stems in her mouth, and grabbed ahold of the hem of her dress to keep it off the freshly muddied ground. With the ring clutched tightly in her hand, she gathered her dress out of the mud and ran.

Cole stood at the front of the chapel waiting for Abby. He pulled his pocket watch from his trousers. An hour and a half had passed since he'd last spoken with her. He had fired ranch hands for less timeliness.

The blustery weather had taken a turn for the worse. With thunder rolling loudly overhead, Cole felt his impatience grow. He'd known the woman for all part of a day and she was already getting under his skin.

Where is she?

Another crack of thunder came as if in response to Cole's silent question. His freshly shaven face stung and the starched collar he wore irritated his neck. Miss Lily returned to her seat next to his brother and whispered something in Raine's ear.

Cole flexed his still aching jaw, his back teeth grinding against one another.

Raine nodded reassuringly, but Cole could not stop caressing the makeshift ring emanating heat from his pocket.

A hush fell upon the congregation, followed by sporadic gasps. Cole turned to find Abby marching up the aisle, mud drenched and determined.

Lily covered her mouth in horror, but despite himself, Cole had a hard time veiling the laughter that threatened to overpower his rigid expression at the sight of her hair dripping thickly with mire down her face and neck onto her once white dress.

When Abby reached the front of the chapel, she stared straight ahead, unwavering. Cole shifted to face the pastor, but spoke sideways, barely above a whisper. "You look lovely, Miss McCallister. It is so gracious of you to join us. Nice boots."

Her look of utter annoyance and overt warning quelled his facetious attempt at voicing humor. He turned back to the

preacher, a smirk still plastered on his face, and motioned for
the ceremony to begin.

Cole took in a deep breath and let it out again. *It's for Alaric*,
he reminded himself. Still unconvinced his motives were pure,
he refused to recognize the alternative.

"Please, uh, take each other by the hand," the sweating
reverend began.

When Abby rested her cracking, mud covered hand in
Cole's clean open palm, the new reverend let out a small uneasy
chuckle.

Abby's shoulders straightened.

Cole thought he should be irritated, but couldn't help his
amusement at the woman, unlike any other he'd ever known,
who'd walked into the chapel, head held high, with every inch
of her draped in a brown, muddy mess. He kept his face stoic
and locked his eyes on the preacher.

While the top of her hand was encased in dried, peeling
clay, her palm was still sticky with mud. Cole couldn't help
himself. He squeezed her hand tightly, squishing the tacky
substance between both of their fingers.

He dared glance down. A bubble of laughter started
somewhere deep inside him and welled up until he could barely
contain it. Abby whipped her hand from his and spun to face
the rest of the congregation. She scanned the chapel.

Cole also turned to look out into the faces of those
attending the improvised ceremony. Lily sat at the edge of her
pew bench, ready to pounce on the first reprobate to laugh.
However, Cole knew that if Abby even glanced at Raine's
reddened face, all would be lost.

The flowers in Abby's hand lay limp at her side, soggy and
dripping puddles onto the chapel floor. She fought with a
sodden lock of hair that kept falling into her eyes.

Cole stepped down in front of her and placed his hands on
her arms. He reached up to wipe away the stray wisp of hair
that had once again fallen onto her forehead and he placed it
tenderly behind her ear before returning his hand to her arm.

She bit her lower lip.

"Are you sure this is what you want?" he asked, the laughter all but gone from his face. Whether he'd asked for her benefit, or his, he was unsure.

Abby's focus strayed from the congregation until it found him. Cole gazed into eyes the color of an English hillside after a storm. Their brilliance even more defined with the mud smudged over the rest of her face. His amusement faded and was replaced with awe.

"Look at me." Her shoulders dropped as she spoke.

"I am."

This was the first falter in her self-confidence Cole had witnessed. It endeared her to him...a little.

"What you see here, Mr. Redbourne, is what you get. Are you sure this is what *you* want?" She took a step back.

He dropped his hands.

"I don't need anyone's pity," she said as she lifted her chin.

Cole faced a decision right now that would affect the rest of his life. How many times had he heard his mother say that happiness is a choice? How many times had his brothers pounded into him the notion that strength and honor come from within? While he knew he would need a constant reminder, the time had come to stop making excuses.

Cole met her stare with one raised brow. "Nobody's offering it."

"I'm hardly a fit bride." Her arms bent at the elbow as she raised her hands waist high in display. "Who am I foolin'?" She dropped her hands. "I'm no beauty and I haven't yet cooked a meal on my own that didn't burn and, well..." she looked at him straight in the eye, "I ride well. I shoot well. I'd sooner wear britches than a dress. Now's your chance to run, Mr. Redbourne. 'Cause if you don't, you're stuck with me. Britches and all."

Cole held up one finger and then turned on his heel and ran down the steps at the front of the chapel, through the gasps and chatter of the congregation, and out the front door into the downpour of the storm. He didn't know what drove him, but he stood in the pouring rain, allowing it to drench his clothes through, to wash away his pain.

He took a step of the porch and into a mud puddle, which splattered mud droplets up the thigh of his pants. He bent over and picked up a handful of the gushing mire and proceeded to wipe it across on his face and down his shirt covered chest, arms, and hands. When he felt good and dirty he turned to go back into the church.

"What the hell?" Raine stared at him, mouth gaping, an incredulous catch in his voice.

Cole looked down at his muddied attire and shrugged. It felt good, liberating almost.

When Abby had looked down at her soiled dress and offered him a way out, all he'd been able to see was a strong woman, with courage to spare, dripping mud all over the church floor.

He smiled at what her reaction might be to his newfound insanity. He hoped she would feel more comfortable this way. It had been a long time since he'd done something for someone else and it felt great.

"You comin'?" Cole called back to Raine as he took the church steps two at a time and ran back into the chapel.

He slowed his pace as he reached the front pew. He walked right past a stunned Abby and whispered, "Ready?"

It was the last thing Cole had expected. Abby began laughing. Not just a small, ladylike laugh, but a deep, meaningful, belly laugh. The tension, the apprehension, and self-depreciation were gone from her face.

She turned away from his gaze to face the preacher. Her hand extended, she waited with a smile on her face for him to take it.

Cole found himself, for the first time since Alaric's accident, wanting to laugh. Wanting to feel. Something in the way Abby looked at him made him feel as if he could conquer the world. He slid his hand into hers and squeezed. Alaric had said she was different from all the others and Cole realized he would have the rest of his life to discover all the things that made her special.

Abby glanced in his direction and the smile in her eyes renewed him. Instead of thinking of all the reasons he shouldn't marry her, all of the reasons he didn't deserve this chance at happiness, he held her hand firmly and thought of the one reason right now he should. He had hope.

Mr. Harris cleared his throat and rummaged through his little leather bound book. When it looked as if he'd found the right page, the pastor dabbed at his forehead with an already damp handkerchief and began the ceremony.

Cole was not ready for the moment when the preacher's words pronounced them man and wife. He had, with relentless fervor, rehearsed this scene in his mind many times within the last hour. But now, he realized he was still unprepared for the finality of his actions.

"Oh, um...a ring?" The reverend said, more to himself than to the couple.

"I have a ring," Cole told the reverend.

Abby's surprise was evident.

Cole's conscience played with him as he debated how the ring would affect her. Would she regret marrying him?

"You do?" she asked in disbelief. She unclenched her own fist to reveal a simple, mud covered band. She placed it in his palm, closed his fingers over it, and smiled.

Cole reached into his pocket and pulled out Alaric's makeshift horseshoe nail ring and held it up in front of them.

"My Abby girl, forever." He quoted the amateur inscription he'd read so many times over the last year. He slid it onto her finger, but hadn't anticipated that it would be too big.

She took a step back, letting the ring fall off into her other opened palm. With a glance at Cole, she slowly picked up the small token representing Alaric's affection.

Cole did not take his eyes off her.

She looked from the ring to Cole, her eyes questioning. Her chest began to rise and fall in an exaggerated motion and the rapid increase in her breathing quickened Cole's pulse.

"You may now kiss..." The preacher announced with forced enthusiasm.

Cole looked at him in surprise. He had briefly forgotten about this tradition in his anticipation of giving Abby the ring.

"...the bride," the preacher finished without his previous zeal.

Abby's head was bent forward. She stared at the ring now held firm between her thumb and index finger, her expression distant. He placed his forefinger under her chin and lifted her face to him. With one hand resting along her jaw-line, his thumb brushed across her pouted lips. He suddenly yearned to know how they would taste and slowly bent his head to offer a momentary kiss.

Cole pulled back just enough to look into her face, noting the saltiness of her mouth. A soft mouth he ached to kiss again. His hands framed her face and he waited for some response. As if she had sensed his inquiry, her eyes fluttered open and her questioning gaze penetrated his soul.

"Mrs. Redbourne?" He searched her face unsure of the meaning of the wet pools accumulating in her eyes. "Abby?"

She looked away, closing her eyes. A single tear cascaded down her reddened cheeks and across her full lips, which now folded together to capture the rolling droplet before they opened again a minute bit. She brought her fingertips up to her mouth, gently caressing the exact spot his lips had touched hers.

"But, how did you..." her first question faded. Then, with a small jerk of her head, clarity seemed to make its way into her mind. "Exactly who are you, Mr. Redbourne?"

A plethora of answers danced into his mind, but none seemed the right thing to say. He glanced at the preacher and then down at the floor before once again meeting her questioning gaze. "Your husband," were the only two words that would come.

She pulled her hand from his as if he'd burned her. "This is Alaric's ring." She held the trinket up, inches from his face. "Why do *you* have it?" she asked.

"Can we have this conversation elsewhere?" He couldn't help the edge that had crept into his voice.

"Where is Alaric?" she demanded.

"You tell me, Abby. What happened to Alaric?" All lightheartedness had disappeared. Cole knew it was unfair to throw his pent up anger at Abby, but the familiar nagging suspicions that surrounded her name resurfaced with her accusatory tone. 'McCallister,' Alaric had written on that note and somehow he had to find the connection.

The sparks that surrounded the new couple were only augmented by the electricity of the ominous storm building in strength outside the church.

Cole, acutely aware of the curious townsfolk, quickly replayed their exchange. He could not force himself to tell her the truth, here, in front of all these people. He didn't want to see the hurt now reflected in her eyes, where moments ago they were full of laughter and trust. He had sworn to protect her, but now he wondered if the protection she needed was from him. He could not, would not will the words to come.

Without warning Abby hit him across the face. He closed his eyes. His neck jerked backward. His jaw clenched. She sure didn't hit like a girl. His hand rubbed the offending section, but he stood his ground.

Cole opened his eyes in time to see the flicker of regret in her face before her expression turned cold.

"Stay away from me, Cole Redbourne. I never want to see the likes of you again." Abby backed away from him, not taking her eyes off of his face. Then, with a quick glance at the preacher added, "husband or not."

The fire he saw in her eyes warmed him. *Give it time*, he told himself. He longed to reach out to her, to tell her the truth. To tell her he'd sworn to protect her. He was not accustomed to waiting for what he wanted, but this seemed a fit penance for the cavalier approach he'd taken. Whoever killed Alaric was in Silver Falls, he knew it and he would protect Abby at all costs, whether or not she wanted or needed him.

When her foot reached the top of the petite staircase to the left of the chapel, she held up the ring and threw it at him, then turned on her heel and ran down the aisle toward the rear of the church. As she reached the large brown doors she pivoted, daring him with her narrowed eyes and firm set to her jaw, to follow.

Cole clenched his teeth--flexing the muscles in his now stinging cheek. She met his eyes with mute pain and stubborn defiance. Turning, she threw open the doors and before Cole could blink, she had disappeared into the growing darkness of the stormy day.

Lightning illuminated the now open doorway outside the chapel. The closely following roar of thunder incited Cole to action. He bent down to retrieve the nail ring, jumped over the railing of the elevated platform at the front of the church, and raced toward the exit. As he ran down the aisle, the blond man Abby had called Jeremiah Carson stepped out in front of him, blocking his way.

"Let her be. This marriage charade of yours will not last," Jeremiah mocked.

"You had your chance, Carson. Get out of my way." Cole moved to get past him.

"This isn't over, Redbourne."

"Yes, it is."

Cole paused only long enough to introduce his fist to the unsuspecting man's face, sending him sprawling to the floor. Stepping over his fallen form Cole did not look back, his eyes affixed to the place where his bride had left the church.

Greeted by another crack of lightning, a dark figure appeared in the doorway. Cole tried to move around him, but the man stood firm, as immoveable as a stone statue.

"You the groom?" the man asked a growingly impatient Cole.

"Yes. Now, if you wi—"

Cole had been unprepared for the fist that connected with his jaw. Stumbling, he caught himself on the back of the last pew and in moments Raine was by his side, fists raised, daring the man to strike again.

"What is with the people in this town?" Cole muttered under his breath, having been hit for the third time today. He straightened, wiping the blood from the corner of his mouth. His neck felt hot, his collar stifling. Unaccustomed to being blindsided, he wanted answers, but they would have to wait. He shook Raine away from his arm and took, what he hoped would be, an intimidating step forward.

"If you will excuse me," he spoke through clenched teeth to the ominous man blocking his way. His mind raced. Abby was now his wife and he had to find her. Storms were dangerous, especially with the amount of lightning that cracked the sky.

"Did you really think I would be happy about my daughter marrying some fortune hunting stranger, a blackguard at best?" Undeterred, the man took a step toward him and Raine. "You may be married in name, but I'll see to it that your sham of a marriage is annulled without so much as a simple kiss."

"Too late."

The man growled deep in his throat.

Cole was ready to push through the man with as much force as necessary, but stopped cold as grim realization hit. This man was Clayton McCallister and Abby was his daughter. Gingerly caressing his swollen jaw, he tried to take another step forward, but Raine held him back and stepped up in his place. Cole's eyes narrowed. Was this the man responsible for Alaric's death?

"Until that blasted lawyer of ours gets back into town, you'll be stayin' at my ranch all right and earning your keep just like the rest. My new ranch foreman is a real workhorse by reputation." He eyed Cole in particular, with disdain.

"This *foreman* of yours, you say he has a *reputation* for being a real workhorse? Have you never met him?" Raine asked curiously.

"Sure is. And he comes from a very respected family--just the kind of person my daughter should have married. And no, I don't need to meet him to know Cole Redbourne is a man of caliber."

A smirk crossed Raine's face and he extended his hand as he always did. "Mr. McCallister, I am Raine Redbourne and this," he said moving aside and pointing behind him, "is my little brother. Cole."

Clay McCallister looked from Raine to Cole and back again. Seeming to recognize his obvious mistake, he reached reluctantly toward Raine's extended hand, his face scarlet.

"Call me, Clay," he said to Raine with a firm grip. Then, turning to Cole, he announced, "You're fired."

CHAPTER EIGHT

Cole stopped short just outside the church as a wagon trekked past him, splashing in its wake. He watched as the would-be tracks quickly vanished in the profusion of water that had fallen within such a short time. He glanced up, looking in every direction. He was unfamiliar with this town and had no idea which Abby may have gone.

With water trickling off the edge of his wide brimmed hat, he looked up into the sky. "Nice, Redbourne. You'd better hope she's not gone far," he chastised under his breath.

At the pressure on his arm, Cole turned to find Abby's raven-haired friend standing behind him, accompanied by Raine. A handful of onlookers gathered together behind them, huddled beneath the wooden awning that extended from the church.

"Abby's gone, Mr. Redbourne." Lily spoke in rushed and breathless tones. She blinked away the turrets of rain that slashed at her face.

"What do you mean, she's gone?" Cole demanded.

"She said she needed to be alone." Her voice got louder as she competed with the increasing strength of the storm. "I think she may have gone to the old tree at the bend in Silver Creek."

The name sounded familiar.

Lowering her head, Lily walked closer and motioned for him to lean down so she could whisper something in his ear. When he complied, she lifted herself onto her toes for better reach. Her words, though spoken softly, cut him.

"When you gave her Alaric's ring, she felt his rejection more strongly than if he'd said it to her face. She said Jeremiah Carson was right about everything he said to her this morning, that she wasn't lady enough for even Alaric to want her. To love her." Lily's heels dropped back to the ground and she took one small step away from him. "Do you understand?" she practically screamed against the wind.

Cole's jaw tightened. He hadn't thought about that particular reaction and he had a mind to march back into the church and punch Jeremiah Carson in the face once more for good measure.

"I'm sorry, Mr. Redbourne, but—"

"It's Cole," he ground out angrily, which he immediately regretted. "The name is Cole." He ran his fingers through his hair with quick, abrupt movements. For the first time in a long time Cole wanted to be there for someone. He'd screwed up. He had to find her.

"Cole." Raine held a warning in his voice.

"Excuse me, ma'am." Cole nodded his head in apology. "The bend at Silver Creek, just where is that?" Action was the only way to stop the onslaught of sadness, fear, guilt, and anger that now plagued him.

"Cole—"

"The creek?" Cole asked again, not wanting to waste another moment while Abby was out in this storm.

"The old oak is just north of the old Johansson barn. I can take you there," Lily volunteered.

"I know the place." He looked away from Lily and met Raine's eyes. "If I'm not back by dusk..."

Raine moved to his side and rested a reassuring hand on Cole's shoulder. He nodded in silent understanding.

Cole took one step forward and then turned back again, meeting Raine's eyes once more. "The herd needs to be delivered today."

"Go!" Raine commanded.

Cole ran to the livery where he'd taken his sleek black-

brown stallion to give him a good brushing and some fresh
water before the ceremony. He mounted the horse inside his
stall and rubbed his neck encouragingly. "Come on Mav, we've
got a wife to roundup." Following a high whistle both rider and
horse whisked past the open doors and disappeared into the
tempestuous darkness.

With the fierce wind whipping her long wet tresses into her
face, Abby soon regretted her hasty retreat. All she'd been able
to think of when she saw that ring was Alaric and all the time it
had taken to stop hoping and get on with her life. He'd
promised, but it had been years. Too many. It was irrational.
No one in town, besides Lily, even knew about the ring. But
she knew, and her heart was breaking. Even as the rain slashed
at her face, blurring her vision, she could only focus on the tree
where childhood dreams had been born and a new love created.
She pushed herself forward as the intensity of the storm
increased. She would not cry. She'd done enough of that over
the last couple of years.

"Come on, girl. It's not much farther." She prodded her
mother's horse forward.

A bolt of lightning danced across the sky and Bella reared.
'Whoa, girl. It's okay." The horse only took a moment to settle
with the soft caresses and gentle coaxing from her mistress, but
the electricity in the air remained menacing. When Abby looked
up, she saw the old tree, outlined in the night, beckoning her,
calling her, offering her shelter from the storm. Wearily she
dismounted.

Her eyes closed for a moment, remembering her way to
the tree down the familiar pathway she'd used many times in
the past. Their tree. The path, well-worn and wet, stood as yet
another monument of memories of her youth. As she walked
toward the enormous trunk, Abby was careful to avoid the
banks of the creek that would now be slick with mud from the

overflow of the small stream.

When she reached the old oak, she ran her hand over the familiar words carved so long ago, now channeling rivulets of water. "Two hearts as one," she read the words aloud. The linked hearts were fading as the tree grew, but the memories attached to them were not.

Abby allowed herself to reminisce as she looked up into the towering gnarled branches and spotted the same crook in which she and Alaric had spent many a summer afternoon building the platform and tree house.

Exhausted and shivering, she removed the wire frame molding her dress in fashion. Setting it aside, she painstakingly pulled herself up through the tree limbs, settling herself into the auspicious groove. It was surprisingly dry and she looked upward remembering the hours it had taken them to build the little wooden lookout platform and tree house. She gave a silent prayer of thanks it would offer her some shelter now.

Abby closed her eyes trying to shun the feelings of embarrassment and regret and instead embrace understanding.

Why didn't he come?

The image of Alaric at the blacksmith shop in town, bending that nail into a ring, was embedded into her mind as vividly as the day it had happened. Knowing the hours he must have spent trying to carve the words into the metal of something so small brought a smile to her lips. Abby girl. That had been Alaric's name for her.

He'd been her first and only love. Now, she was married to a stranger, but handsome as he was, she wanted answers.

"Papa was right," she spoke aloud to herself. "I am too impetuous and now I'm stuck."

Not as perfect as I'd hoped. "He may not have lied outright, but he hid the truth." *Why? What could he possibly want from me?*

She tried to rid her mind of the deep voice that even now penetrated her thoughts. She remembered the looks on the faces of everyone at their wedding when Cole came bounding back into the church covered in mud.

Her mind engaged in battle between the two men who

occupied her thoughts. Alaric's promises had filled her with hope for a future that now could never be. And Cole.

He jumped in the mire, for me.

A fresh chill sent shivers down her spine. The rain finally abated and the moon peeked out from behind an onslaught of blackened clouds. She knew she should be heading back. Her father would be worried and she now had to face her...husband. That thought stung like a slap in the face. Why would Alaric do this to her? Why would he send someone else? She wasn't sure she even wanted the answers.

"Why now?" she screamed into the cold.

Abby looked up into the night sky. She hugged her knees more tightly into her body. There was still a ranch to be run, horses to breed, and fences to be mended. Papa couldn't send her away now. She'd won. She'd found a husband. So, why didn't winning feel as good as she'd thought it would?

Her thoughts turned to the man she had just given up her life for, the man with whom she had promised before God to love.

"Please, Father," she pleaded, "tell me what you expect me to do now."

Pieces of her conversation with Mrs. Hutchinson flooded her mind. "If he is anything like his father, he is a good man," she'd said. "But remember, even good men make bad decisions from time to time."

"Ab...by?"

Her name drifted on the wind, muted and low.

She strained he ears to the sound. Her mind must be playing with her.

"Abby McCallister?"

She heard her name again, but this time is was more distinct. She sat up, trying to focus her attention to the noise. However, the sound that greeted her was all too familiar and not at all welcome.

A lone timber wolf called out in the night, howling in the stillness between downpours. Although she was accustomed to the melodious call of the wild, tonight it sounded a little too close for her comfort. She felt the folds of her dress for her pistol and realized she had left it in the hidden pocket inside her father's old coat. She'd been in such a hurry when she left the church, she'd neglected to grab the coat and now she cursed herself for thinking like a female.

"Ab...by?"

There it was again, the beckoning voice getting louder, stronger.

Someone approached on horseback and she strained her eyes to see. The large, angular silhouette in the distance became more defined and visible as it got closer.

"Cole?" she whispered with unexpected hope to the night. He would take her home to SilverHawk, to the safety of her own room, her own bed.

Their bed. Startled at the thought, she fought a whole new set of fears that threatened to waylay her.

She forced the thought from her head. Her arms crossed her chest and her hands frantically rubbed her upper arms and shoulders as she tried to generate some warmth.

A gunshot split the night and Abby bolted upright.

"Abby? Abby McCallister Redbourne can you hear me?" his voice became more insistent, urgent.

Abby McCallister Redbourne. That was different.

"I'm here. In the tree." The wind all but muted her response.

Cole came into full view a short distance from where she now stood. "Listen to me, Abby. Stay where you are no matter what happens. Do you understand me?"

His horse seemed restless, swerving left and then right, but not moving forward.

"Why? What's wrong?"

Bella snorted and started to prance about excitedly below. Abby leaned forward to look over the crude railing of the tree hut.

"Do you understand?" His voice was more urgent this time.

Abby felt her irritation growing and she took two steps to

the other side of the railing to get a better look at her darkened surroundings. A low deep snarl came from beneath her and just a few paces away she saw two glowing, yellow eyes skulking at the base of the tree, glinting in the moonlight.

"No. Get away from here." She desperately looked about for something that would deter or frighten the ominous mountain lion that crouched low on the ground, ready to pounce. Abby was thankful she was up in the tree, but had heard plenty of stories about the enormous cat's ability to climb. A dead branch lay brittle, just out of her reach.

"If I could just..." She swung her legs over the railing and reached for the branch, her nails just able to scratch at the knotted wood. Securing a place for her foot, she inched herself higher on the supporting bough. Again she reached for the impromptu weapon. Her fingertips grazed the sharp grooves of the branch and she extended her arm even farther until her hand was securely wrapped around its thickness.

Crack.

The tip of the large bough on which she stood gave way and she felt her footings relent beneath her. As she grasped for anything within reach to support her, the branch broke and the ground started to come up quickly to meet her. A new wave of fear washed over her.

She stopped abruptly. A lower level branch had caught the excess material of her gown at the waist and left her dangling in midair.

The lion, crouching back on his haunches, his tail twitching and ears laid back, began pumping his hind legs gently up and down. With his head and body low to the ground he opened his mouth in a frightening roar, revealing a copse of sharp yellowed teeth and a curled tongue. Abby looked around at her immediate surroundings for anything that would give her leverage against the predatory animal.

Bella's scream sounded in her ears and Abby watched anxiously as her trusted horse reared below her. Her front legs scraped the air until one connected with the mountain cat, sending it sprawling backward.

Snap.

Her wooden rescuer faltered. A fearful shriek escaped her lips, but was brought short as her arm hooked painfully onto another protruding branch. She reached for the limb with her free hand and kicked out in a desperate attempt to gain her footing. The branch, wet from the rain, became harder to hold on to. She prayed silently the mountain lion had run away.

A lone shot fired, creating a moment's peace in a scene of chaos. Abby glanced up, relived to see Cole, rifle in hand, riding quickly toward her.

A ferocious roar echoed in Abby's ears and she looked down as the mountain lion jumped from his crouched position at her horse. "No," she screamed wildly, desperately trying to dissuade the aggressor, she reached down gingerly and removed one of her work boots and threw it at the animal. Her fingers slipped.

Abby shrieked and shut her eyes. Before she hit the ground, arms, as hard as rock, enveloped her about the waist, pulling her from the air and onto a moving horse in one large protective motion. The wind was knocked from her chest and she felt like a rag doll being tossed about. When she gained her breath, she opened her eyes to see her rescuer. Cole.

He pulled her in front of him, facing him, but did not release his grasp on her waist. He pulled her tight into him.

"Hold on," came his abrupt command.

Bella's fierce scream at her attacker focused Abby's thoughts. She lifted her head above Cole's shoulder to see the mountain lion savagely assaulting her beloved companion.

"Stop," she shouted at Cole. "Please stop." She pounded at his chest. The thought of losing something else tonight was too much to bear, but she knew hysterics would not convince him to turn back. Calming herself with a deep breath, she reached to his clean shaven face, placing a hand on each side, and pulled his face about to look at her. In a much softer voice she pleaded, "Please, Mr. Redbourne, I can't let Bella die—not like this."

With one smooth movement he dislodged his rifle from its

holster and pulled his horse about. A single shot echoed in the night. Bella fell forward atop the cat. Stricken with horror Abby pushed against him.

"You've killed her!" She tried to get off the horse, but Cole held her still.

"Stay," he ordered once again.

Cole dismounted, gun still in hand, and strode toward the brutal scene. Another shot rang out and Abby closed her eyes to the tears that once again threatened to come and she fell forward over the ridden-worn saddle. She could hear Cole speaking in hushed tones.

Her head throbbed, she was cold, and she would now have to go home and face her father with news of her mother's beloved mare. She wondered how she would tell her father Bella was gone. How she would tell him it was all her fault and he'd been right all along. She should've agreed to leave for Denver. Bella wouldn't be dead.

"Tell me Lord, what do I do next? Please give me the strength to endure and the wisdom to act accordingly," she quoted a sermon Reverend Daniels had offered last month.

A quiet nicker carried through the breeze and she abruptly pulled herself upward to see Bella limping toward her, Cole leading her back. Abby's eyes darted from the feline carcass that now lay in a motionless heap at the base of the tree, to the bloody gashes in the mare's front leg and chest, then to Cole.

She could not help but to appreciate the wide expanse of his chest as it strained against the white collared shirt he wore. His tall muscular frame would normally have intimidated her, but tonight she appreciated the strength of this man she did not yet know. She was thankful for his self-assurance and accurate aim and grateful for the time they would have to get to know each other as they worked the ranch.

"This belong to you?" He averted her appraising glance and held out a drenched and shredded boot, nodding at her bare foot.

She felt the heat rise in her cheeks as she reached for the boot.

Cole wrapped the reins of the mare around the saddle horn of his horse.

Abby's focus returned to Bella. She pulled on the old work boot, though a chunk was missing from the top, exposing her flesh on the top of her foot, and deep gouges nearly divided the sole in half, making it all but worthless. Ignoring Cole's raised eyebrow, she swung herself down from the saddle.

Carefully, she began caressing the mare's uninjured flank, gently working her way over the horse. When she reached the open wound on the horse's chest and front forearm, Abby saw the deep slashes that had scraped away Bella's muscular flesh. She felt a fresh rush of warm tears brimming in gratitude the horse was still alive, but she refused to let them spill. She reached up and put her arms around the horse's neck and laid her head against the mare, blinking away any evidence of tears.

"She's favoring her leg, Abby. It may be broken and her chest has been torn in several places. It's just not right to make her suffer." The use of her first name felt natural and oddly intimate.

Cole stood directly behind her. She could feel his nearness. Her heart began to beat wildly. Fully understanding the meaning of his words, she pushed her face away from the horse, but did not remove either hand from the mare.

"I am grateful for all you have done here, Mr. Redbourne, but I assure you, Bella will be all right. She's a fighter." Abby stood to her full height and when she spun around to face Cole, she realized she barely met his shoulder.

"Doc Knight is the best in the territory," she continued, trying to convince herself. She lifted her chin a little, "And it just so happens, he is doing some work for my father at my ranch...our ranch," she corrected quietly, looking down at her hands, now covered in blood.

Cole studied her for a moment. Shaking his head, he removed his jacket, took the suspenders off of his shoulders and began unbuttoning his shirt.

"What are you doing? It is freezing out here," she protested.

As he began tearing at the fabric, she realized he intended to try to help Bella. Once the shirt had been torn into haphazard strips, he reached for a thick branch that had fallen in the storm. Kneeling down near Bella's damaged front leg and with remarkable calm and skill, Cole picked up one of the tree house's floor boards that had come loose in her fall to splint the horse's leg and began to bandage the open wounds.

She watched, mesmerized as he worked, and was a little unnerved at the sight of his bare shoulders and back. Fascinated, she watched his muscles strain against his skin, undulating with every movement. He moved to the uninjured leg and placed a bandage tightly around the thigh and knee areas for support. The strain that would be caused to her good leg by the faulty appendage might prove to be too much. Abby was impressed by his apparent knowledge of horses. Maybe this deal would work out after all.

Without looking at her, Cole swung onto his horse and pulled his suspenders up over his shoulders. He reached down for her--extending his hand.

"There is a small lean-to just through that thicket and an empty worn down barn where she will be safe. I am sure the owner won't mind if we borrow them for the night," he said as he wrapped his hand around her wrist and braced his forearm against hers.

Her pulse quickened as she pulled up behind him. "I'm afraid I don't know the new owners here. I've been told they are very wealthy and have purchased a great deal of the land in the territory, but they keep mostly to themselves. No one has met them yet. I don't know how they would feel if..."

"It's cold and wet." Cole turned in the saddle and wrapped his jacket around her shoulders. "It'll do for now. Your horse won't live through the night Abby, especially if we force her to make the trip all the way back to the SilverHawk tonight. Maverick here certainly cannot carry the both of us and pull her along behind.

"I'll walk," she quickly offered.

"It's no use, Abby. This is the best we can do under the

circumstances. I think with the splint she'll be able to support herself as far as that barn."

Abby couldn't argue. The cuts on Bella's foreleg and chest were very serious and she did not want to risk doing any further damage. She nodded her head and although he could not see her, he must have known she'd relent because he clicked his tongue and his horse began to move forward.

"Wait," she spoke into his ear. "If it's really not that far, I'd like to walk alongside her."

Cole looked down at her foot, nearly bare because of a now useless boot.

"Fine," she spat and thrust her hands around his waist in defeat. Resting her face against his bare shoulder she watched Bella struggling to keep up. Even at this slow pace, she stumbled, faltering with each step on her damaged leg.

"Thank you," she whispered and she snuggled even further into the added warmth Cole's jacket provided.

Lord, help me be strong.

CHAPTER NINE

Cole could barely make out the odd shape of the lean-to jutting away from the side of the barn. Grateful he and Raine had taken the time to clean the small one-room shack, he prodded Maverick forward slow and steady.

He'd had no idea how long he would have to stay at the McCallister place and had wanted to make sure he was prepared for the worst. The miniature cabin-like structure should have served solely as a bunkhouse for the two brothers while the farm house was built. But somehow, it didn't seem fitting for a wedding night.

Expecting cool evenings, the small pot-bellied stove had been fixed against the center back wall of the small room. Having Abby's wet body pressed so closely against him was taking its toll on his inner strength and he was grateful she would now have something other than his body to make her warm.

Focus, Cole, he chastised, reminding himself that feeling protective was only natural. She *was* a woman after all and he was attracted to her without a doubt. But how could he ever love a woman whose father had killed his best friend? Then it dawned on him. She was a McCallister too. Could she have had something to do with it? He dismissed the idea, but until he knew for certain, it was better to keep his distance.

Cole looked toward the barn and shook his head. It had not received the same attention. While Raine had stocked it with straw, hay, and a few other supplies, the doors hung

crookedly and the paint was chipped and faded. He dismounted
and with two short strides reached the barn doors.

Any trace of the herd was gone. Marty had already taken
them out to McCallister's place as planned. He'd just been fired
from the SilverHawk as foreman, so he felt no pressure to get
out to their ranch anytime soon. Except Clay would probably
be worried sick about his daughter.

One fat droplet of rain landed on Cole's cheek and he
craned his neck to look at Abby, still leaning against the back of
his shoulders.

She would catch her death if he didn't get her inside soon.
When he brought his horse to a stop, Abby sat upright. Cole
swung down and reached up for her.

Abby unwrapped Bella's reins from the saddle horn and
slid easily from Maverick's back. Cole was prepared for her legs
to buckle once they hit solid ground and stood ready to catch
her if she fell. She wavered slightly, but caught her footings
immediately. Inexplicably disappointed, he ushered the two
horses and Abby inside the barn.

Fresh straw was stacked in one corner and with a pitchfork
Cole placed a layer of bedding in the newly swept stall to create
a comfortable place for the mare to lie down. He directed Abby
to lead Bella into the newly prepared compartment.

He glimpsed a large wooden bucket dangling from one of
the broken stall doors. "Wait here," he commanded in a voice
that dared her to disobey. Seeing no defiance he turned on his
heel and out the door.

If she had just listened to me, he thought, begrudging his trek to
the creek, the rain falling heavily once again. *But why would she?
She doesn't know me or anything about me.*

He filled the bucket to the brim with water from the near
over-flowing creek. Although the rain fell quite dramatically,
the wind had died to a mere breeze and Cole was careful on his
way to the lean-to not to lose any of the water he'd collected.
He would not know the extent of the horse's wounds until they
had been cleaned thoroughly. He poured the water into the
kettle that sat just behind the door and set the bucket aside. He

hoped he would be able to find some wood in the pile dry enough to burn.

God smiled down on him at that moment and within minutes he had a fire roaring. It was getting colder as the evening progressed into night and he put his hands up to the heat emanating from the small stove. He spotted one of his wool lined coats hanging from a nail next to the door and reached up for it. While the lean-to would be toasty, the barn would still be very cold. He pulled it on and stuck his hands in his pockets.

The water began to boil and with a thick cooking pad he reached for the bucket. The steam rising from the wooden container felt good to Cole as he breathed it in. As he moved to the door, bucket in hand, he tripped over the old washtub by the side of Raine's mattress. His balance was thrown off and he worked quickly to restore his footings.

A small splash of water landed at the edge of Raine's mattress and Cole cursed under his breath. Now Abby would have to sleep on his mattress instead of Raine's. At least he was no stranger to sleeping on the hard ground. He walked out the door and kicked it shut behind him.

When Cole made it to the barn, he stood at the entry and watched as Abby crouched down near the pained animal and began humming. She worked carefully to remove Cole's provisional bandages from the chest and damaged limb of her horse. The first had not been bandaged tightly because of its awkward location. The gentleness he saw in her both delighted and impressed him.

Abby's hair was dark and still encrusted with mud, her white dress ruined and dirty. However, the wet garment clung to her, enhancing every curve. Cole nearly dropped the pail and he quickly set it down. He turned around abruptly and walked back out the door.

Cole was used to seeing women in tight corsets whose waists were pinched so tightly he could wrap them in the breadth of one hand. He was grateful she was not one of those women. His desire to pull her close to him and feel her waist and hips beneath his hands enticed him. He knew he needed to redirect his thoughts or this would turn out to be a very long night.

With one last, deep breath of the fresh air tickling his throat, he returned to the barn. Raine's black mending bag sat next to Abby in the straw.

"Lucky," she said without looking up, "whoever owns this place must have had to doctor some horses of his own. This bag has most everything we'll need to patch her up."

"Abby," Cole cleared his throat.

She looked up from her task.

"You are soaked through. There's a fire burning in the lean-to and a dry blanket rolled up in the corner. Go. I will take care of her."

"I won't leave her."

He noted the dark circles now forming under her eyes and the stiffness in her fingers as she worked.

"Now!" His tone left no room for disagreement.

She stood grudgingly, brushing past him, and with an obvious air of defiance, clipped him in the arm with her shoulder.

Cole smirked. The woman certainly had spirit and he had to admire that in her. She was stronger than any woman he'd ever known, except his mother and sister, who also had strength in spades.

Tonight, it would just be him and Abby. Alone in that cozy little room. He knew he should try to get word to Raine, but he refused to leave Abby alone and suspected she would not leave that horse.

He thought how different things would have been had this day gone as planned. After he was able to drag the preacher down the mountain, he and Raine had made a checklist of everything his mother would have made them do.

A stab of guilt hit him when he thought of Leah Redbourne not being able to see him on his wedding day, especially since it was something she so obviously desired for him. But he took comfort in knowing that even though his heart hadn't been in it, he'd tried really hard to make her proud.

He'd rented the nicest room in the only hotel in town and had requested it be filled with as many flowers as one could find on such short notice. He would have rented two rooms, but he didn't want Abby to be the brunt of talk, and he determined he could just sleep in the chaise that typically accompanied those types of rooms.

He'd ordered a hot bath to be brought to the room and since there was no time for a wedding vacation, he had rented a nice little surrey to escort her around town and maybe take her on an afternoon picnic.

Countless times he'd listened to his mother tell each of his brothers prior to their respective wedding dates that it was the groom's responsibility to make a bride feel special. To spoil her.

He'd failed miserably.

Even the weather had been against him and he felt a twinge of remorse as he reflected on the events of the past few hours. He'd make it up to her. Someday.

He glanced back up at the lean-to, watching Abby's retreating figure dart through the rain and waited for her to duck inside before drawing Raine's bag open. He pulled the liniment, laudanum, clean towels and bandages from the bag. His experienced hands worked to cleanse the wounds on Bella's chest and leg. After dousing the wound at her chest in laudanum, he placed a damp dressing over the laceration and expertly tied another bandage around the horse's neck and under her undamaged leg to hold the dressing in place.

Maverick, seeming to feel forgotten, nickered in the background. "We've done it good this time, boy." Cole stood and stretched out the cramped muscles in his back. Grabbing the pitchfork he pulled another cluster of straw into a clean, but empty stall for his own tired horse. Placing the pitchfork aside he reached for the fancy groomer's brush his little sister had given him last year for Christmas and began stroking the animal to both relax himself and the horse.

"I'm a married man, Maverick old friend. She's McCallister's daughter and Alaric's girl. What am I supposed to do with that?"

When he'd finished putting everything away and had assured himself Bella was as relaxed as possible, he leaned his back and shoulder into the doorframe and took a deep breath—the cool night air filling his lungs. Glancing toward the lean-to, he saw the dim firelight illuminating the only window and smiled.

Abby ran to the door of the small lean-to, attempting to protect herself from the rain with her arms crossed above her head like a shield. When she reached the boards that served as a muddy porch she turned back, looking to the barn for a glimpse of her new husband. She dropped her hands, allowing the rain to drip off her forehead and into her face. She smiled.

She entered the cabin-like shack and was surprised at the warmth pending from the small room. The sweet smell of molasses and drying beef greeted her and she thought how wonderful it would be to have some of Martha's slow cooked stew about now.

Abby scanned the room for something she could wear while her clothes dried. She found a blanket in the corner that would serve as her nightdress and quickly began removing her wet things. She undressed to her chemise and hung her dress and undergarments from the low rafters to dry. She looked down at the thin garment that still allowed for some sense of propriety and paused, looking toward the measly window.

Her skin puckered in a chill. Shaking her head and taking a deep breath, she shed the damp chemise, quickly shook open the wool blanket, and wrapped it securely about her shoulders. Its warmth caused Abby to pull it tighter around her shivering form. She closed her eyes and exhaled deeply.

Abby gazed into the pulsing glow of the fire. The small black stove was similar to the one in her father's den back home, just not as big. Cast iron bars lined the door, allowing the warmth to cradle her. She was amazed at the owner's foresight to pump the pipe through a hole in the ceiling. She'd never before seen a lean-to with a stove inside.

Her lips curved upward and she relaxed back against the wall, closing her eyes again and willing herself to breathe. Her thoughts returned invariably to the stranger whose name she now shared.

A raspy grunt sounded somewhere near her feet. Abby's eyes flew open in surprise and her hand instinctively jerked down to her hip for the small pistol she usually kept hidden in the folds of her skirts. All she grasped was the air, her fingers gaining nothing but a stray woolen string from the inside of the coverlet.

She pulled her knees into her chest and narrowed her eyes into the dark. Something scampered across the floor. After the night she'd had, the last thing she needed was to be trapped naked in a small room with another wild critter.

The firelight had grown dim and she could no longer see the corners of the room. Abby was not accustomed to the feelings of vulnerability that washed over her. But lacking clothes and a weapon in the dark with a scavenger of one sort or another certainly brought out some insecurities. When something bushy brushed across her exposed foot, an inadvertent scream escaped her lips and she pulled herself into a standing position, nearly dropping the blanket.

This is ridiculous, she thought. *It's probably just a squirrel.*

She squared her shoulders.

"All right, you blasted varmint, come out and show yerself."

Cole's heart pounded within his chest at the sound of Abby's fearful scream. He pushed himself away from the door, grabbed his rifle, and made a quick dash for the lean-to. He'd left her alone for some time now. Too long he reckoned. They had already encountered enough trouble tonight.

He hadn't seen a mountain lion in a long time and wondered if there were a lot of them out in these parts. He would have to take that into account as he started growing his own herds. He figured the passing of the storm and Abby's horse had drawn the animal out. He hoped nothing else would threaten his new bride tonight, but he had a feeling that his life from this point on would be one new adventure after another.

His hand reached out for the rounded metal bar of the lean-to door and thrust it open, gun pointed inside. Moonlight spilled into the room and there, standing on its back two legs, was a black masked raccoon, gnawing on a slab of peppered jerky. He silently cursed Raine for leaving the drying meat in the low-hanging rafters in the sectioned-off portion of the lean-to.

Somehow, the little fella had found a way in and Cole hoped he hadn't told his friends. The scavenging creature fell forward onto all four feet--the meat clenched securely between his teeth, and ran out the door past a relieved Cole.

The light from the dying fire cast an orange glow around Abby's body. Her bare creamy shoulder peeked above the top of his saddle blanket and her wet hair cascaded down past her collar bone. Cole groaned inwardly. His head fell back and he closed his eyes. *Lord, give me strength.*

"You all right?" Cole's voice broke in boyish fashion and he cleared his throat, uncomfortable at the physical confirmation of his mental distraction.

He forced himself to look at her face. His heart began to pound and he took one step forward into the close quartered room. What was he thinking?

In a moment of desperation, to guide his thoughts down a different path, he dropped to his knee in front of the stove and set a large knotted pine log over the dying embers of the fire.

Once he was sure the fire would last a while, he stood, not realizing how close she stood to him. Her nearness was about his undoing. He looked down into her face, her eyes lustrous from the now roaring flames, her face mere inches from his own. He had to remind himself to breathe, but he could not pull away.

"If you need anything..." Cole wet his bottom lip with his tongue. He lifted his arm and reached behind her, picking up the bedroll from the shelf that hovered just above Raine's bed, "...just holler."

He shouldn't stay. Couldn't. Not yet. He would sleep in the barn to avoid all temptation until the time was right—when he confirmed what he already knew in his heart. Abby had nothing to do with what had happened to Alaric. He would wait until he was prepared to think of a future with the beautiful creature before him. When he could protect her. Teach her. Love her.

"Cole?" she called out to him and with one small phrase demolished his resolve. "Stay with me," she petitioned, unknowing what she asked of him. He watched her hand slip from beneath the coverlet and rest gently on his forearm. "Please stay."

The weariness he saw in her face begged him to offer the reassurance his presence would provide. He dropped the bedroll onto Raine's mattress in defeat and shut the door.

"Get some sleep," he said, turning away from her. His tone had more of an edge than he'd intended. "Abby girl," he added a bit softer—hoping Alaric's name for her would offer the comfort she needed. A hint of a smile traced his lips, his facial muscles getting more exercise in the last few hours than in the last year.

When he heard the creak of the mattress as she sat on the provisional bed, he let out the breath he'd been holding. He turned around and watched as she snuggled down further into her blanket, unknowing it was his mattress on which she now lay her head.

"Why are you here?" Abby asked as she slid her hands under her head, her eyes blinking heavily.

"Because you asked me to stay," his voice held a hint of sarcasm.

"That's not what I meant."

"I know."

"What brought you here to Silver Falls?" Her voice lowered and her words came out more slowly. As if sensing she were falling asleep, she propped herself up onto one elbow and lifted her head, her eyes meeting his.

"Unfinished business." What was he supposed to tell her? He was there to see if she or her father had murdered his best friend?

"So, you've been here before, then?"

Her eyes, alight from the fire, searched his.

"I inherited land around here. Raine and I came to see if it was the right place to start a ranch of my own and build a life."

It was true. The words came easily. He thought about the land that surrounded them at this very moment and something inside of him confirmed that this was the place to create his dream.

Abby's arm relaxed below her head as it sunk further into the mattress. A throaty groan escaped her lips. Her eyes near closed. "What parrrt? Hmmm..."

He gazed mesmerized, as the fire danced with the auburn highlights in her hair that peeked through pockets of mud and grime. In town, when she'd shaken her hair free of her Stetson, he'd been captivated by its color, but now he wondered what her soft tendrils would feel like under his caress when clean, its thickness brushed and radiant, spilling down over her freckled shoulders. Her skin glowed and her lips looked soft and inviting.

"That's nice," she said yawning and closing her eyes completely. Her tongue touched her top lip before she drifted into a much deserved sleep.

With a silent, inward groan, Cole picked up the well-worn bible from the small wooden box behind Raine's mattress. The book fell open and a photograph dropped to the ground.

Leah Redbourne was a beautiful woman and he longed for the days when he used to sit at the foot of his mother's bed and tell her everything that had happened. He caressed the picture with a work roughened hand. She'd sat for this particular photograph the same day Alaric died. Placing it carefully into the back cover of the book, he let the pages open where they would and was comforted by a simple Psalm.

God is our refuge and strength, a very present help in trouble.

He closed the book, holding it close to his chest with one hand, and put the other behind his head as he lay back onto the thin bedroll. With his eyes shut, he willed the memories haunting him to rest and the other thoughts taunting him to subside. He prayed for the morrow to bring fresh hope and renewed strength.

CHAPTER TEN

Saturday

Abby could sense the light trying to penetrate her closed eyelids. Her nostrils flared at the heavenly scent of meat cooking over an open fire. It had been a long time since she'd slept past dawn. A full recollection of yesterday's events sped through her mind and she stretched her legs, relishing the idea of today being able to sleep a moment longer.

Surely by now her father knew about her marriage and would have told the new foreman his services would no longer be needed. When she arrived home with Cole, she'd gloat for a few moments over having won the bet and then she would be able to start working with the new stud, Chester.

Another delicious waft of smoke made it into the tiny room. She allowed herself to imagine Cole standing bare-chested over the flames, his dark hair curling about his face and neck. She thought of the way his muscles had contracted then relaxed each time he'd pitched the straw into Bella's stall. She wondered if he would be as appealing in the daylight when she wasn't freezing or so overly emotional. She sighed softly and snuggled even closer into the blanket she wore.

Loud male voices penetrated her reverie and she sat up with a start. Grabbing the blanket more tightly around her she pulled herself to her feet and pushed away a grayish-brown curtain from the fogged box window. It looked as if Cole's brother had found them and he did not look pleased.

She pulled away from the glass and scanned the room in search of her dress. It suddenly dawned on her that the grey curtain she had pushed aside wasn't a window covering at all, but her mother's dirty and torn wedding dress. She reached upward, her fingers gently caressing the top layer of dingy sheer material and embroidered lace. As easily as she had picked up the fabric, she let it fall. She would not allow herself to sulk over the ruined garment.

Spotting a green button down shirt and folded denims in the far corner of the lean-to, she drew the dress-made curtain back across the window and threw off the blanket, replacing it with her now dried bloomers, chemise, and the male attire. She'd always been more comfortable in britches than anything else, but the feel of the clothing next to her skin, evoked a wicked giggle. The shirt felt like it had be made with two of her in mind and she had to gather the waist of the trousers together in one hand to stop them from falling off. She looked for a strand of rope or something she could use to hold them up, but to no avail.

Her boots. She tossed the blankets about and upturned one of the bedroll mattresses in attempt to find them. At last, she saw them sticking out from behind the potbellied stove. *Cole must've set them there to dry.* For that she was grateful. She sat on the edge of the bed where she slept and pulled them over her bare feet. There was nothing she could do about the boot that had been damaged, but hoped it would serve her long enough to return home.

Tucking a stray lock of hair behind her ear, her grip firm on the material at her waist, she hoped they would not notice her feet. She reached for the door and caught glimpse of her reflection in a broken shaving mirror perched on the wall.

Black smudges lined her face and streaked her hair. Her skin looked pale. Dark circles encased her eyes. She pinched her cheeks and with her chin held high, she walked out into the open and toward the arguing brothers. Cole wore a fresh white shirt, untucked. His suspenders dangling at his sides. Abby felt a pang of disappointment. She wondered if he'd had the clothing with him in his saddle bags or if he'd found the shirt, like she had, somewhere in the lean-to. She made a mental note to repay anything they'd taken.

Her mind changed focus when she heard Raine's impertinent question.

"Why didn't you put the animal down last night?" he demanded.

Cole looked up from the fire and with a cocked eyebrow and a devilish smirk watched her approach—Raine's back still to her.

"Because *I* asked him not to," she answered for him.

She noted the muscles in Cole's jaw tighten as he turned back to the fire.

Raine whirled to face her and removed his hat. "Good morning, ma'am." He smiled, but it did not reach his eyes.

"Excuse me, ma'am, but you do realize the animal is suffering somethin' mighty?"

Abby glanced at the barn.

"The animal, as you put it, has a name," she spat at Raine with force that even surprised her. "How is *Bella* this morning?" she directed her question to Cole, but it was Raine who answered, apparently unaffected by her outburst.

"Laudanum can only go so far, Abby."

She looked back at Cole who stood from his crouched position over the fire and pulled his frying pan back. When he met her gaze, the realization she'd been trying to elude engulfed her.

She tightened her fist around the gathered material at the waist of her new britches and ran for the barn. Bella lay silently in the stall Cole had prepared for her. A quiet nicker called her closer. Carefully, she smoothed her hand across the horse's side and back, wary to avoid the bandages that had been skillfully wrapped around the mare's wounds.

The horse lifted first her head, then her shoulders and Abby found herself filled with a rush of hope and excitement. "Come on, girl. You can do it." She knew if Bella could just pull herself to a standing position, she would be okay. Bella snorted with another attempt to right herself, then collapsed heavily against the straw. Abby watched, stricken, as the white cloth, used to bandage Bella's chest steadily reddened with fresh blood.

"Good try, girl," she patted her side. The hopelessness of the situation drained her heart as quickly as her hope had filled it. "We've had a good run, you and me. Thank you for always protecting me," her mind traced over the countless times over the years the horse had sensed danger and had reacted bravely and in Abby's interest. Just like last night.

Abby had overcome a lot of touchy situations because of the loyalty and wisdom of her companion. "Thank you." She leaned close to Bella's nose and placed her tear-lined lips against horse's face in a tender kiss. "I love you, Bella, my dear friend." With one last caress over the mare she stood and walked to the door of the barn where Raine and Cole stood watching. Waiting.

She would not let them see her tears. "Do what you feel you must." Her words came out harsh and resentful. She wanted to get away from them, needed a moment to prepare.

Cole grabbed a gentle hold of her arm and pulled her back around. Removing a blade from his belt, he reached to a spool of twine hanging on the wall of the barn and cut off a long strand.

"Stay still," he demanded.

With the same precision that had guided his hands the night before, Cole laced the twine through the gaps in the material where suspenders were normally fastened. He pulled the trousers tight about her waist and secured them with a knot. His warm hands brushed her belly and seared her skin through the light muslin of her undergarment. She didn't dare look up at him. Didn't dare meet the steel she felt in his gaze.

"Here put this on."

Abby looked at the dark jacket Cole now held between them and shook her head.

"Woman, you are going to catch your death if you keep running around in the rain and cold." It wasn't the cold that made her shiver. She took his jacket from his hands. With a fleeting glance up at her husband, she walked past both he and his brother, toward the lean-to.

She had barely made it back to the small building when a piercing shot echoed all around her.

Bella was dead.

With her heart pounding fiercely in her chest and a flood of tears stinging her eyes, she grabbed the tattered cloth that had been her mother's dress from the window and began to run.

She needed to get away from this place, to be enveloped in the arms of her father who would tell her everything would be all right, where she would be safe.

Abby ran harder. The feel of the wind in her hair and the morning sun on her face, renewed her as she fled. She fell. Jagged rocks and sticks ripped at her pants and tore into the flesh of her leg. The front portion of her boot ripped completely away from the rest, exposing her toes to the harsh ground. She didn't care.

She heaved herself up and pushed on, the physical release blurring the pain she felt inside. "Goodbye mother," she whispered to the breeze at the regret of losing one of the only things she had left that had belonged to Clara McCallister. With Bella gone and the dress ruined, Abby only had one token left of her mother's. SilverHawk.

"Do you realize her father and half the town, including me, have been out all night looking for her? For you?"

Cole propped his hands up on his freshly used shovel, one knee bent, his booted heel digging into the dirt. It sure took a long time to dig a hole big enough to bury a horse.

"And just what was I supposed to do big brother? Her blasted horse had been torn apart by a mountain lion and the scent of blood would have brought every scavenger for miles in our direction." The sweat from digging a hole, large enough for the horse, beaded down Cole's face. He wiped it away.

"And I'll ask you again, *little* brother," Raine spoke with forced calm, "why didn't you put the animal down last night? And don't tell me it was because you took orders from a woman you've just met. I know you all too well."

"I have my reasons." Cole dug the shovel into the remaining mound of dirt and tossed one last scoop of soil onto the new grave.

Raine bent his head sideways and clenched his jaw. "That's not enough this time, Charcoal."

"What do you want me to say, Raine? That I don't know what's come over me? Well, I don't, okay?" Cole threw his shovel to the ground and walked toward the barn.

Raine caught up to him and placed a hand on the younger man's shoulder, walking alongside him. "I know you, Cole. You've always confided in me, why not now?"

Cole stopped. He couldn't meet his brother's gaze. It was true Raine had always been there for him. He had stuck up for him when confronted with any type of trouble and had listened patiently the one time Cole opened up to him and lamented Alaric's death.

Apparently resigned to the silence, Raine dropped his hand to his side and spoke firmly. "We have to get her back to her father."

"And we will, now that her horse is buried."

"Mama has always trusted me to keep you in line and to watch out for you my *dear, youngest brother.*" Raine took a step toward his mount. "She'll want to know how I could let you marry some woman you've only known for a whole of ten minutes."

Cole snorted.

"Don't forget our purpose here, Cole. This is *your* land and you have a responsibility to those people down there." He swung into the paint's saddle. "I guess I don't know you as well as I thought," he added, low and steady.

Cole somehow found his voice. "She was Alaric's girl,

Raine. I justified my actions as keeping a promise to my best friend to take care of a woman he'd loved." He took a step toward his retreating brother.

"Alaric told me she'd be waiting for him, but when we got to town, there she was, throwing herself to anyone who'd take her. What kind of a person does that?" Cole pondered his own question and before Raine had a chance to respond, he continued.

"She looked so innocent standing there on the church steps. There must be a good reason for her to have done something as drastic as ask for a husband and then marry a stranger." Cole remembered the way her blond hair had tousled around her face and the way her eyes had called out to him. Enticed him. Captivated him, until he found himself wanting to embrace the things he'd vowed never to feel or do again. Hope. Care. Love.

"It's true. While I felt I owed it to Alaric, a small part of me believed if I married her I would be better positioned to get answers out of McCallister. But now, it's something more. I can't explain it."

"It's okay for you to like her. She is your wife after all," Raine chuckled.

"It isn't fair to Abby or to Alaric. What if *she* is the McCallister written on that note?" Even as he said it, he couldn't accept it and he dropped his head.

"You don't believe that for a second, or we wouldn't be here," Raine said, pulling up alongside Cole.

"I'm not capable of giving her the kind of love she deserves," Cole said without looking up.

For the last year Cole had worked very hard to strip himself of all emotion, determined to never feel the kind of pain and guilt that had consumed him when Alaric died.

"It's a little late for that now, isn't it? You are her husband. You've vowed to love her, honor her, and all those other things you promised to do when you married her. Is it fair to Abby for you to turn your back on all that?" Raine leaned forward low on his mount and looked Cole square in the face.

"It's okay for you to be happy, Charcoal."

Cole turned away. "I feel guilty living a life Alaric will never have a chance at. Starting the ranch. Marrying the girl. Owning the land. I don't deserve any of it."

A lone tear escaped his wet lids to trail down Cole's hard planed cheek. He wiped it away before Raine could see. The familiar torment of Alaric's words taunted Cole once again. *Tell her...I loved her. Make sure she's happy. Take care of her, my friend.*

"So, now my little brother, vowed bachelor, is married." Raine's voice was full of wonder.

"But how do I compete with the memory of a dead man?"

"Let's get you two back to the ranch. Somehow, it will work itself out. Hopefully, her father will be waiting there, without a shotgun, and we can get the word around you are both safe."

Cole went to get Abby. Raine was right. If they didn't get back soon, they'd be in a mess. He strode with hurried pace to the small outbuilding. When he did not see Abby inside, his heart lurched. He called out her name. Running to the creek ledge, Cole scanned the bank to see if she sat near the water. Not that lucky.

He ran back up the abrupt hill and over to where Raine still sat on his horse.

"She's gone," he stated emphatically. Without stopping, he walked into the barn to retrieve his saddle and pull Maverick from his stall.

"What do you mean, she's gone?" Raine called after him, eyeing him incredulously.

Cole pulled his horse alongside Raine's. "I mean she is not in the lean-to, she's not down by the creek. She is simply not here." He pulled the cinches tight and threw a blanket roll on the back of his saddle.

"You are going to have your hands full with that one,

Charcoal." Raine pulled his horse's reins to the left, looking back over his shoulder at a bewildered Cole. "We'd better go find her before she gets herself into another mess of trouble."

"I really do not understand women."

"Welcome to manhood, my boy." Raine laughed and they pulled out of camp.

"Let's check that big oak tree at the far edge of the spread. She seems to have some connection to that spot."

Raine nodded and spurred his horse forward.

Abby sat on a large rock some distance from the tree. Her knees were wrapped tightly against her chest within the span of her husband's jacket and she gripped the shell of her wedding dress in her hands.

Her face had begun to chap from the fierce wind that had continuously slapped against her tear stained cheeks for the better part of a day. Her hair whipped violently around her face. She could not bring herself to divert her eyes from the cold, lifeless animal that lay just feet away.

Her mind recounted, with relentless fervor, images from the last few days. She'd killed a rattle snake in the barn, married a complete stranger, been attacked by a mountain lion, and had to put down her mother's horse. *What a week.*

The unmistakable sound of horses approaching caught Abby's attention and she shifted her head to see the two large forms of her new husband and his brother riding toward her.

She couldn't face him. She'd run away. Again. She had never run from any type of fight before she'd met the likes of Cole Redbourne and she did not want to see the disappointment in his eyes when he looked at her.

"Abby?"

She had expected his voice to be harsh and laced with distain, but was unprepared for the concern she heard there.

She knew her eyes would be red and swollen from crying

and she had no desire to offer proof to his certain conclusion—
that she was weak.

"Abby, look at me." Cole had dismounted and now knelt
next to her. He was bent low, the soothing pressure of his
hands stroking her hair.

Somehow, she felt her fears beginning to relent, and
despite her inward struggle to refrain from meeting his gaze,
she succumbed to his gentle coaxing.

Looking up, she found herself immersed in pools of the
most fascinating shades of brown. She mused how they
matched the hue of his stallion, but with flecks of honey. His
dark complexion added a smoky depth to his eyes and she
searched them, unsure of what she would find or exactly what
she was looking for.

"She's okay!" Cole shouted over his shoulder to Raine—
neither removing his hand from the back of her head nor his
eyes from hers. "You ride on ahead," he said, "and let her
father know we're all right."

"It'll be a good two hours to the McCallister place from
here—if you take it easy. I'll let him know you should be there
in time for supper." Raine tipped his hat and pulled his horse
around.

"I'm sorry, Mr. Redbourne," she began, but he placed a
roughened finger over her lips, moved beside her, and
crouched down, leaning against the rock.

"When do you think you will start calling me Cole?" He
tilted his head and brushed away a loose wisp of hair from her
face. "We *are* husband and wife after all."

She stared at him for a long while, amazed she could call
such a man hers. She noted the slight discoloration and
puffiness of his jaw and a stitch of guilt in her gut. She forced a
smile.

"After our first child, maybe? The second?"

He was teasing her, she knew, but heat rose immediately to
her face.

"Cole." She managed a smile.

"Let's get you back to your ranch...Mrs. Redbourne." He

pulled himself into a standing position. Still holding one of her hands, he entwined his smallest finger with hers. The minute gesture caused his jacket to slip away from her legs and feet to reveal a bloody gash in her shin beneath the torn denim pant leg.

When he looked at her questioningly, she shrugged. "I fell."

Understanding registered on his face. With a slight shake to his head he released her hand and walked over to his horse, unlatching one of his saddle bags.

She watched him closely. When he returned to her, he pulled a bottle of liquid and a small silver jar from the black bag, she now recognized as the doctoring kit from the barn. In his other hand he held a clean piece of his torn shirt they'd used for Bella.

Cole reached down to remove her boots. No words were spoken as he pulled off the semblance of a boot that was now in shreds. He doused the rag with water from his canteen and rubbed it against the white poultice from the silver jar. He ripped the pant leg to a point just above the wound to reveal several other small cuts and blotches of bruised skin.

Still, he didn't speak.

He simply washed the torn flesh, his large work-roughened hands wiping away the dirt from her small wounds.

Abby was surprised again by his gentle manner. He was nothing like Jeremiah Carson. She looked skyward. *Thank you.*

Cole saturated the remaining portion of the rag with the substance from the bottle. He first poured fresh water over her leg and then treated her cuts with what smelled like witch hazel. The aching and stinging in her leg began to diminish almost immediately.

"What is it?" she asked, staring at the white mixture.

"Soap," he replied with a hint of a smile, "mixed with a bit of my ma's special ingredient," he finished after a moment.

His precision with Bella told her he was an expert with horses, but she hadn't expected his expertise to extend to taking care of a woman. *Who are you?* she wondered, and for the first time since she met him, she recognized a real desire to know.

Cole finished and returned the contents of the bag to their place. Then with one seamless movement, he pulled Abby up into his arms. Grasping her boots with two fingers he walked to the horse and placed her in the front of the saddle. Swinging up behind her a moment later, he placed the tattered dress in her lap. The awkward quiet of strangers returned as her back pressed intimately against his chest and they began the long journey home.

Cole groaned inwardly as Abby eased back against him. Although she was still tinted in mud and her hair in disarray, the feel of the soft ripe curve of her hip resting under his arm, was nearly his undoing. For the first time, he wondered why the wealthy ranch owner's daughter had sought escape in a stranger's arms. As a stranger's bride.

"Why didn't he come for me?" Her question was quiet, yet full of self-conscious fears.

"They've been out searching all night. I'm sure he's anxiously waiting your return at home." Cole bent his head forward until his mouth touched her hair. He was surprised at his urge to place a gentle kiss on the back of her head in a comforting gesture. He refrained.

"Not my father," she said, dismissing the idea, "Alaric."

Cole was not ready to explain why he was there in Alaric's stead, but he knew she needed to know what had happened.

"Alaric wanted you to know he didn't forget you. He'd loved you for a very long time."

Her silence willed him to continue, but he could not find the words. *It's simple, Cole. Just say it.*

"Alaric is dead, Abby." Her sudden influx of air was the only indication she'd heard him. He unwittingly tightened his arm around her.

They rode in silence for the better part of the trip. Cole

sensed Abby had fallen asleep and was careful to keep her steady in the saddle.

They'd been following the river for the better part of an hour when the SilverHawk came into view. Straining to focus on the sounds that came from the other side of the small thicket to his left, Cole pulled Maverick to a stop. If he didn't know any better, he would say that there were falls just behind the coppice. If that were the case, it would give Abby a chance to at least wash her face and hands before seeing her father. If she were anything like the other women he'd known, she would be grateful for a short respite.

Cole rode some distance along the clusters of trees until he found what looked to be a trail, obscured by overgrown thicket and brush.

"Abby?" he spoke her name against her ear. No movement. "Abby?" he tried again, rubbing his work roughened hands over her arms brusquely.

"Why did we stop?" She sat up straight and looked around. "We're nearly there."

Cole dismounted. He reached for the dense foliage that covered the trail, only to find it moved easily, in one large piece. *What a clever little hiding place*, he thought.

"How did you know?" she asked, staring at him from her perch on his horse.

"Know what?" He walked back and took Maverick's reins, leading him through the small passageway he'd just uncovered.

"About this place," she replied, her voice seemed a mixture of annoyance and awe.

As he walked farther in, he was pleased to see there was a small inlet from the river, with a grassy area near the bank. He could still hear the hollow rush of a waterfall, but could not see it. He pulled the horse about and was happy the ranch was still visible from his position.

Cole reached up for Abby, but was greeted with apprehension. A few moments passed before Abby slid her hand into his and allowed him to help her dismount.

"We're only a few minutes from the ranch," she stated as

she looked from him back to the buildings clearly in view.

She certainly knew her way around the place and Cole imagined how a young girl might have created a sanctuary here, tucked away from the rest of the world.

"I thought you might want to wash some of that grime off your face and relax here a bit in the sun before we meet up with everyone at the ranch."

A large rock conducting water through a small worn hole caught his attention. He pulled the travel blanket and canteen from Maverick's back and walked to the stream. He tossed the blanket onto the grass and knelt down on the bank. Water spilled through the hole in the rock and Cole set his canteen under the small torrent it created.

A fresh water spring, how 'bout that?

Once the lid was back in place, he set it aside while he unfolded the patchwork blanket on the ground and situated himself on the denim squares, allowing the sun to beat down on his face. He leaned back onto his elbows and watched as the water hurried by.

He'd had plenty of time to think on the ride, but wasn't ready to face Clay McCallister again. The first time they'd met had not gone exactly as planned. Being foreman on the SilverHawk would have given him plenty of opportunity to ask questions, but now he wasn't sure if Abby's father would even let him step foot onto the ranch.

Soaking in the sweet smell of a day following the rain, he tilted his head backward to find his new bride.

Abby reached her hand up to her neck and she bit her bottom lip.

Now she's shy?

She took a step forward, but then broke into a dead run toward the river. She tossed his jacket back to him and jumped into the water without hesitation. He shot to his feet, his eyes fixed on the spot where she'd gone in. Half stunned, half amused, he held his breath, waiting for her to emerge. He was about ready to go in after her when out of the corner of his eye he saw movement. She swam just beneath the surface of the water, moving down the left side of a small fork in the river.

He followed her along the water's ridge, but when Abby disappeared completely under a hedge of overgrown branches and bushes hovering just above the river's bend, he barely avoided a protruding tree branch that would have knocked him flat.

"Fool, woman. She'll catch her death for sure," he grumbled. The foliage was so thick it extended across the river and encompassed the length of the clearing.

"Abby?" he yelled, hoping she could hear him. Praying she was all right.

Nothing.

The thicket wall appeared impenetrable. Like the entrance to this little inlet, Cole suspected there was another way through to the other side of the shrubbery wall. An awkwardly angled stick protruded from the far side of the barrier and with one swift tug, a woven doorway of sorts gave way. He pushed his way through.

The captivating sight that greeted him on the other side kindled a fire inside him that both awed and infuriated him.

CHAPTER ELEVEN

Abby's head broke through the surface of the small lagoon and she took in a deep, satisfying breath. She brushed the hair away from her face and looked around, smiling at her hidden sanctuary with its suspended cascades and grassy knolls. She had discovered it as a child and to her knowledge, no one else had ever ventured past the first clearing.

Abby had known the water would still be freezing this time of year from the spring run-off and the chill had already reached her bones. She chastised herself for her impetuousness. The cold water on Abby's skin invigorated her--its icy sting pierced through the cloud of pain she had experienced over the last twenty-four hours.

The grime and dirt that lined her face had only been part of the physical evidence of this week's emotional whirlwind. The rippling river had called out to her, inviting her to the place where she would find a moment's refuge. Once she'd started moving, she could not force herself to stop and before she could rethink the idea, she had jumped into the frigid waters of the creek.

Abby dragged herself up onto the bank, not realizing how heavy the wet denims would be. The twine at her waist held strong, holding the trousers just above her hips. She turned over and lay on her back, willing the sun to warm her. The shrubbery gate would have been a wiser choice, but Cole would have followed and Abby had needed a moment to herself.

After a few minutes, she sat up, pulling her knees into her

chest. Streaks of muddy water dripped from her hair and down onto the green shirt she still wore. She stood up and quickly unbuttoned the garment, tossing it aside as she crawled up the small rock cliffs to the flat ledge behind the smallest of the burbling cascades.

Abby reached both of her hands in a cupping motion into the rush of water that fell into the lake-like pond, not more than a few feet down. As she splashed the crisp water against her face and bare arms, she could feel the streaks of mud washing away. She leaned forward and flipped her hair in front of her, allowing the pressure from the cascade to rinse the mire completely from her mane.

The frigidity of the water overtook her desire to clean up before facing her father. She squeezed the excess water from her hair and pulled away from the falls and moved back out into the sunlight.

Where yesterday had been bleak and stormy, today the sun had come out, playfully dancing with the few clouds that still lingered in the sky. She closed her eyes and lifted her face skyward, basking in its warmth. Her skin still puckered with a chill and her teeth chattered. She wrapped her arms around her front and looked down at the soaked green shirt she had discarded onto the brush. She wished now for something dry to cover herself. Her bodice was soaked through to transparency and Abby was grateful Cole couldn't see her this exposed.

A moment longer, she thought, *and I will return to him.*

Abby turned to face the vision the cascades provided. This was home. Unaccustomed to having so many conflicting emotions vying for her attention, she sat down and lay back again against the grass, thinking of what awaited her in this new future she'd just created.

Facing Clay McCallister might be harder than she'd originally thought and she hoped Cole was up to the challenge.

Married? What will I do next?

The rustle in the branches told Abby Cole had finally come looking for her. When she darted a glance toward the entrance, which was still covered in a disorganized heap of underbrush, she was met with piercing almost black eyes. She leaned up onto her elbows and stared back.

Cole stood in front of the shrubbery gate as still as a stone statue, his face like carved marble. By the stunned look on his face, she suspected he had been standing there longer than she'd suspected. She quickly stood up and pulled the wet green shirt over her shoulders and held the front of it closed.

The wind whistled a vaguely familiar tune and while her arms were now covered in gooseflesh, the relentless pounding of her heart emanated heat from within. Cole's white linen shirt fell open at the top and his tanned flesh peered at her from beneath the cloth. When her gaze returned to his face she noted his appreciative expression had been replaced with one of steel as he peered back at her. Chiseled. Unreadable.

"Why didn't you tell me you wanted to freeze to death? I would have just left you out in the rain last night, hiding in that tree." His voice was cool and steady, his jaw tight.

A cold shiver ran through her. Whether it originated from his penetrating stare or the frigid breeze against her wet skin she did not know.

Cole cleared his throat. "Your father will be expecting us." His tone was gruff and his look stern. He turned away from her and walked back through the foliage gate.

Abby rubbed her arms from the cold, but she could not bring herself to move from her position. She sat there, watching the place where he had appeared in her secret little haven.

"Cole?" She managed his name through chattering teeth and an inexplicably dry mouth.

She didn't know how he got to her so fast, but he was there in an instant. He undid the remaining buttons of his shirt, then removed hers and pulled her hunched frame into the warmth of his bare chest, vigorously rubbing her back and arms.

Abby tilted her head to look up at him and was surprised to find his face so close to hers. His warming motion slowed on her arms and his grip loosened a little. He leaned toward her, his head bending even closer. She was ready for the moment when his mouth would find hers and with parted lips she closed her eyes.

One moment passed. Then two. She opened her eyes. He let go of her and reached down to pick up the wet shirt. He scooped her up into his arms and trenched over the broken twigs and branches through the thicket wall. When they reached the clearing, he set her down on her feet.

"Stay," he ordered.

She had no intention of disobeying.

He returned to her side with a dry white shirt and brown trousers. "At this rate, I'll need a new wardrobe by morning," he said with a hint of laughter in his voice.

He was teasing. At least she hoped he was.

"Thank you," she spoke in a breathless whisper.

They stood there for some time, staring at each other, before Cole cleared his throat, nodded, and turned his back to her, his arm outstretched.

Confused at first, it only took Abby a moment to realize he wanted her wet things. She undressed quickly and handed him the offending garments.

Cole looked at the contents of his hand. "Chemise too."

She felt the blush stain her cheeks, but hastily complied. She tossed her drenched pantaloons and bodice on top of the other clothes draped from his arm.

Apparently satisfied, he returned to his horse, hung the wet clothing over Maverick's rump, and leaned against the saddle with his forearms. At least he was a gentleman.

The crunching of leaves drew both of their attention across the river. A small brown and white rabbit ducked for a hole just in front of a fallen log. The corners of Cole's mouth upturned as he glanced over at her.

Abby liked it when Cole smiled.

"Ready?" he asked. "Your father will be expecting us."

Three packed bags awaited Abby on the steps to the homestead. Her course was slow as she approached the house.

"I ain't never seen your father so fit to be tied." The white haired woman spoke without looking up. "Going off and gettin' yerself married to a perfect stranger." Martha, the family's cook and housekeeper shook her head as she set a hot cobbler on the porch to cool.

"Martha?" Abby touched the woman on the arm.

"Good heavens, child. Your hair is wet and you're a shiverin' like an autumn leaf. Come in and sit by the fire." The concern in Martha's eyes touched her.

Abby glanced at the bags on the steps.

"Had me pack up all yer things." A tsking sound followed her words.

Abby ran past Martha into the house and up the large staircase at the edge of the living area. The door to her room was closed. She stood there, her hand on the door knob, and breathed. Slowly she opened the door to a spacious room void of her personal belongings. The bed was made with clean white sheets and a woven blanket draped across the bottom. The floor had been recently swept and the furniture had all been dusted. The comfort she had believed she'd find in the solace of her bedroom had all but disappeared.

"Father," she screamed. Running down the stairs she first looked in the kitchen, then his study. "Father," she shouted again.

She nearly knocked the housekeeper over as she ran to the front door. "Where is he, Martha?" she asked, her jaw pulsating.

The back door slammed. Its hearty echo sounded throughout the house.

"Martha?" The deep baritone voice called from the back of the kitchen.

"I'd say he's in the kitchen." Martha spoke as she tried to conceal a smirk by rubbing an imaginary smudge off the corner of her mouth.

Abby walked into the kitchen and over to the back door

where Clay McCallister stood, ignoring her completely.

"Father," she pleaded. "Be reasonable."

Clay McCallister looked Abby square in the face and pulled off his brown leather work gloves. "Martha," he called again walking past his only daughter to where the older woman leaned against the open door to the living area.

"Martha," he looked down at her and smiled. "Will you please warm some milk? That colt is not doing well. He won't eat. We'll need to try to feed him again or we'll lose him."

"The colt? Bella's foal? What do you mean you'll need to feed him? He's nearly four months old and been eating on his own for weeks now." Abby grabbed her father's arm from behind and forced him to look at her, to talk to her.

"It was too soon to take Bella away, Abigail," his voice was stern and she hated it when he used her full name. "The colt has not eaten or taken a drink since yesterday morning."

Her father's words lashed at her conscience and she turned away from him.

"Now that she's gone, we won't have the luxury of weaning him slowly. It'll take some drastic measures to salvage the colt."

Abby looked up at her father, surprised he knew about Bella. When he pointed to the window, she saw Cole talking to Raine near the corral and knew all the evening's events had already been discussed without her. Her feelings of relief at not having to tell her father what had happened were overshadowed by indignation at not being included in the conversation.

A strong hand pressed on her shoulder. Her father squeezed gently and his tone calmed.

"I'm glad you're safe, Abby!" She turned into the large man's encircling embrace. The tears fell freely this time, nothing holding back. She snuggled closer, feeling the comfort only her father's arms could offer.

"Okay, let me in on some of that." Martha stood just behind them with one hand on Abby's back. Abby reached her arm out to bring Martha into the bear size hug.

Abby was the first to pull away, wiping the tears from her reddened eyes.

"My things?" She looked at her father questioningly. He led her down the hallway toward the room reserved for special company. When the door swung open she saw all of her things organized and neatly put away.

"I told Martha to pack your clothes and leave them on the steps in your traveling cases. After all, they had to be moved into your new room anyway." Clay paused and brushed a stray strand of hair from her face. "You had to know the worry I went through while you were gone." He put his arm around her shoulders and kissed her on the top of her head. "This will be your home for as long as you need it to be, Abs."

Her eyes fell on a small shaving bin at the far side of the room and a hat hanging on one of the bed posts.

"So, you're not angry?" she asked with hope in her voice.

"Oh, I'm angry all right. Mad enough to spit nails. But that doesn't change the fact that you're my daughter and, well...I love ya." He gave her a big squeeze before turning back for the kitchen.

Abby followed.

"That doesn't mean, however, that I approve of the stunt you pulled. You changed a lot of lives yesterday, little girl."

"I'm not a little girl. I..." Abby's indignant voice trailed as she saw a slender dark haired woman through the window walking toward Cole and Raine at the edge of the corral. Abby moved closer to the window. She watched the interaction with interest and recognized the coquettish smile that now played on the woman's face.

"When did Jenna get back into town?" she asked, fingering the thin window coverings as she watched the woman acting coy with the men outside. Jenna, adorned in a light brown riding skirt, sleek black riding boots and a red button down shirt tucked into the top of her skirt, threw her head back and laughed at something Cole had said. Abby's fingers tightened their grip on the curtains.

A deep rumbling laugh erupted behind her and she spun to

face her father. "Why, if I didn't know any better I would say you are jealous, young lady." The twinkle in his eye as he spoke made Abby's lips twitch slightly into a brief smile.

"Why should I be jealous?" Abby turned back to the window, eying the scene with unmasked disdain. "He is already *my* husband."

When Jenna began laughing and pawing at Cole's chest, Abby could stand it no longer. "Why that little..." She headed for the door.

"Um, Abby? You might want to change out of that getup before greeting your guest." Martha held up one of her bags.

Abby glanced down at her attire. Cole's clothes were a might too big, but she smiled at the thought of talking to Jenna while she wore Cole's shirt.

"Abby?" Martha warned, seeming to have some idea what was on her mind.

Wiping the mischievous grin from her face, she grabbed the bag from Martha, who followed her into her new quarters.

Abby pulled each article of clothing out of the bag to evaluate its impression and tossed them in every direction until she found the perfect outfit. She held up the dark brown riding trousers she'd received just before her mother died.

Martha pulled a cornflower blue shirt from the closet. "I think you would look just lovely in this my dear."

Abby did not waste another moment. She shed Cole's clothes, laid them on the large cushioned chair in the corner of the room and pulled on her own fitted trousers.

"Father will not be happy to see me wearing britches, but drastic times call for drastic measures."

When Abby was finished dressing she looked at her reflection in the mirrored dresser. The outfit was perfect, but her hair, still wet from the falls hung about her face in a limp disorder.

Martha pushed her down onto the vanity stool and began brushing through her hair. She pulled tightly and then tied a matching ribbon high on the back of Abby's head.

"There. A fit bride. Now, go get your man."

Abby hugged the woman before running out into the kitchen. Pausing at the back door, she took a deep breath, smoothed imaginary wrinkles from her pant legs and put a smile on her face.

Just as Abby stepped off the back porch, an untamed stallion in the corral rushed the fence where Jenna stood.

Abby lurched forward, shocked at the animal's behavior and even more so that the fence bowed, but didn't break. However, the force had sent Jenna sprawling forward directly into Cole's unsuspecting arms.

Minx.

A low whistle came from one of the cowboys.

"Maybe you should stay away from fences with mustangs behind them in the future, ma'am or there may not be anyone to catch you," Cole said as he smiled respectfully at the young woman.

"I'm just lucky to have such strong men all around." Her voice was like hot butter...smooth, but greasy, and Abby found herself wanting to punch her old rival in the face.

With as sickeningly sweet a voice as she could muster, Abby broke into the polite exchange. "Why, Jenna. I didn't know you were back in town. I see you've met my husband and brother-in-law."

Cole eyed her appraisingly. Abby warmed under his stare and when she noted that his eyes traveled the length of her, she felt a blush creeping into her already hot cheeks.

"It's nice to meet you, brother-in-law." Jenna spoke in dreamy tones as she pushed herself back into Cole's chest, circling one of his shirt buttons with her long dainty forefinger.

"Actually," Cole took a step toward Abby, "I'm the husband." Cole removed Jenna's hand from his torso and placed a protective arm around Abby's shoulders.

Warmth radiated through Abby's body under his touch.

"Too bad," Jenna said in a haughty drawl, her displeasure obvious.

She didn't remove her eyes from Cole. With one eyebrow cocked she slid her tongue across the front of her teeth before turning her attention to Abby. Her face lost its practiced beauty as she measured her up.

"Well, Abby. It has been a long time. You haven't changed a bit." Jenna's heavy eyelids were dramatically downcast and her nose pointed at the afternoon clouds.

"You haven't changed either, Jenna. Still trying to steal other women's men I see." Abby plastered on her face the most charming smile she could rally.

Cole nearly choked. He dropped his hand to his side and leaned back against the fence.

The artificial smile on Jenna's face turned into a downright frown, transforming her classic features until they took on a feline quality.

"What do you want, Jenna? Besides *my* husband, I mean?"

Jenna's eyes narrowed into slits. "Clay said the filly was ready. I'll need her before the party tonight."

Abby's mind raced for something to retort, but found nothing.

"Ah, Jenna. Come for your filly I guess?" Clay's voice came from behind. Abby stood firm while the woman swept around her and held out her hand demurely to Clay. Together, the two of them walked into the corral discussing horses and the SilverHawk's new breeding program.

Abby spun around at the rich laughter that burst out from Cole. "You're just a little spitfire, aren't ya?" he asked. The gleam in his eye and the contagious curve of his mouth made hers twitch.

Cole, still with a smirk on his face, pushed himself away from the fence post and took one inquiring step toward her. She froze. Her heart began to race, but the smile that had cracked the surface refused to leave. She didn't move. He seemed encouraged and took two more steps forward until he stood mere inches away from her. She swallowed. Abby had to tilt her head upward to see his eyes.

"Come, wife. Or, should I just call you, my little spitfire?" His voice was like velvet as he lowered his head toward her.

CHAPTER TWELVE

"Hmhhmmh."

In the back of his mind Cole heard Raine clearing his throat. He knew he should pull away, but something kept drawing him closer to Abby's supple lips. He'd looked over her and wanted nothing more than to pull the small blue ribbons from her damp hair and wrap his hands in the silken tresses. Her eyes were now closed. His tongue wet his bottom lip in anticipation of the feel of her mouth surrendering to their first real kiss.

"Abby!" Lily ran up the length of the yard with her dress gathered in her hands. "Abby! I just knew you'd be all right. I just knew it."

The spell was broken. Cole took a step backward.

Lily stopped short the moment she saw Raine.

"Ma'am." Raine tipped his hat to the dark-haired beauty.

She grabbed a hold of Abby, her fingers locking like a vice on Abby's arm.

Lily smiled, not taking her eyes off his brother until she spoke.

"Abby, I'm so glad to see these fine gentlemen have taken such good care of you and brought you home all safe and sound."

Abby rolled her eyes.

Cole laughed. *Her timing is impeccable*, he thought to himself. *And, of course, Raine likes her.*

Cole had yet to meet a woman Raine couldn't charm when

he had a mind to. A low growl formulated at the back of Cole's throat. He glanced toward Abby who watched him with interest.

A woman's laughter filled the yard. Cole, Raine, Abby, and Lily all looked up to see Jenna astride a young paint filly, sauntering out of the barn. Clay walked next to her, reins in hand.

"I'm sure my father will fall in love with her. He finds all of your horses to be caliber." Jenna's voice was smooth as honey. "We'll be back later tonight. Save me a dance, old man."

Cole's jaw dropped when Clay's mouth widened into a grin.

Really?

Instinctively, Cole moved closer to Abby and slid his arm around her shoulders, pulling her close to him. Clay handed the reins to the sporty, very feminine rider with a laugh. She pulled the horse forward and stopped in front of the newlywed couple.

"See you tonight, handsome." Jenna leaned forward on the filly and reached out to his face. He caught her hand before she could touch him.

"Miss Grayson," he nodded as he released her hand. Then, with a haughty laugh and a click of her heels she was gone.

Abby's stance was still rigid. Cole hadn't allowed himself any female companionship over the last year, but he'd had enough experience to tell him there was quite a history between the two very different women.

Jenna had a classic beauty she flaunted at every turn. Abby was timeless and innocent. Cole remembered what the balding man in town had said. *She may not be that perty, and she's real tough around the edges, but she has a lot of spunk and plenty of curves to keep a man satisfied.*

"The men around here must be blinder than a ninety-year-old dog," Cole muttered.

"What was that, son?" Clay asked.

"Nothing, sir."

"Don't let her bother you, Abby." Lily tugged on her arm.

"She's still the same old Jenna. She will always lose the battles that matter."

Cole appreciated what a good friend Lily was to Abby, even if she had bad timing. He was grateful she had someone in her life to talk to and confide in. He had never lacked a listening ear with six older brothers and a younger sister, and he wondered at the loneliness Abby must have felt growing up an only child.

"You must come and tell me all about...last night." Lily finished the latter in lower tones, darting a glance at Cole.

He looked at his wife with a raised eyebrow.

Abby went with her friend into the house, turning back to Cole only once with an expression he could not read.

"Come on, Cole. McCallister needs some help in the barn," Raine called over his shoulder.

Cole cast a meaningful glance back at Abby's retreating form as she and Lily disappeared into the house. Realizing for the first time that Abby didn't know she was beautiful, he smiled.

He was relieved their kiss had been interrupted. He didn't think he wanted to share that moment with everyone on the ranch. So, why did he feel so unsettled? He glanced down at his fists which were clenched into tight balls and released them with a slow breath. His sudden direction of thought startled him. *Not relieved*, he decided, *frustrated as hell.*

"You came highly recommended, Redbourne." Cole looked up from the shovel to see Clay McCallister leaning casually against the fenced arena, chewing on a piece of straw. Cole straightened, resting his gloved hands on the top of the shovel's handle.

"And who, may I ask, made the recommendation?" he asked, taking a momentary break from building the dancing platform Clay had requested.

"Doesn't matter. My daughter is involved now and I have a different set of standards where she is concerned."

"Yes, sir. Is there something on your mind?" Cole patted down the dirt against the foundation board then set the shovel aside and grabbed another wooden plank from the pile.

Clay pushed himself away from the fence and reached down to help steady the board while Cole hammered it into place.

"You made an awfully big commitment yesterday, son."

"Yes, sir." Cole reached for another plank. They were gone. He searched the immediate area for a wood stack he could use to pull him away from Clay's interrogation.

Cole knew he should be assuring the man he would love and cherish his daughter forever. That he would make her the happiest woman in the world, but he couldn't voice what he wasn't sure he could offer.

"Are you a man of your word, Mr. Redbourne?" Clay caught his eye and Cole could not pull away from his stare.

"Look Mr. McCallister. I'm not sure what came over me yesterday, but I am a man of my word and I will do my best to take care of your daughter."

Silence passed between the two men, neither willing to relinquish his hold on the other. Cole understood now that Abby didn't really need someone to take care of her. She had her father's affection and by the looks of her surroundings she'd been afforded every comfort.

Heaven knew Abby had a mind of her own, but he found it a refreshing comparison to the stifling submissiveness of most women. She was more like the women in his family. Maybe that is why he was drawn to her.

"As long as we understand each other." Clay, apparently contented with his discovery, now held out a hand to Cole. Grateful the man would not interrogate him further, Cole gripped Clay's hand with strength.

When they released, they both stood and looked at the almost finished platform.

Clay clapped Cole on the back and together they walked to

the shed for the last of the supplies.

"Abby's gonna be real surprised."

"So, you're telling me you were all alone with him all night in a little one room cabin and *nothing* happened?" The excitement in Lily's voice shook Abby from her stunned silence. "You really must tell me everything."

Abby recounted all that had happened, starting at the point when Cole found her in the old oak tree. Lily responded with oohs and ahs in all the right places and Abby found herself more animated than she had been in a long time. When she was finished with her story, both women lay back onto the large bed and sighed.

"You're starting an adventure Abby, that's for sure." Lily giggled. Abby joined.

When the sound of an approaching carriage carried through the open window, Abby sat upright.

"Lily, what party is everyone talking about?" She stood up to peek out through the curtains. "And why are the Patterson's here?"

"Party?" Lily's innocent act was a little too sincere.

Abby narrowed her eyes at her friend.

"Oh..." Lily hesitated for a moment, "just look over at the barn."

Pulling the curtain aside again she looked out. Everything appeared just the same as always as she scanned the yard, but when her gaze made it to the barn, the image of Cole and her father, building a platform of sorts and securing the base with dirt, stunned her. *The party is here?*

Abby had been aware of all the hammering, but for a horse ranch it was not uncommon for fences to be mended, ranch hands to be making repairs on a buckboard or something else that needed fixing and she hadn't given it much thought. She turned back to Lily, who was now propped up on her elbows with a grin spread wide across her face.

"You deserve it, Abs." Lily scrunched her shoulders forward, an impish smile curling her lips.

Abby was astounded. Her father had not attended a single social since her mother's passing and now he was hosting one? It took a moment, but Abby realized her father had gone to great lengths to throw a celebration in honor of her marriage. "The party is…for me and Cole." It was a statement more than a question.

"I guess Mrs. Patterson is here early to help Martha with the food?"

Lily nodded.

Abby couldn't believe this was really happening. She was married to the most handsome man in town and her father seemed to like him. She never would have believed it. Her father liked one of her suitors. Only Cole wasn't her suitor, he was her husband and she guessed there wasn't much else her father could do about that. She laughed.

"Hopefully, he is as good a rancher as he is a charmer. Tomorrow will be back to work, but for now…" She bit her lip. "I'd like to look the part." She turned to Lily and with a strong plea in her voice asked, "Will you help me?"

A knock sounded at the door.

"Miss Abby?" Martha said as she peeked into the room.

"Come in, Martha."

The older woman pushed open the door and walked in, carrying a bustled lavender gown with a rich purple shawl.

"Your father thought you might like something to wear to the party tonight. He had a seamstress working all night to finish this for you."

"Martha, it's exquisite." Abby jumped up and took the beautiful creation from the woman. She put it up against her and began dancing around the room, twirling and moving about while the other two women were laughing at her sudden giddiness.

Martha motioned to someone behind her to come into the room. Abby turned to see the ranch hand Jim's burley frame marching through her door hauling a large wooden wash tub. Bert and Davey followed, heaving buckets of steaming water.

"I thought you might want to clean up proper before we celebrate. They'll finish filling the tub and I want you washed before supper."

"Oh, Martha. You are wonderful! Thank you." Abby laid the dress on the bed and ran to hug the older woman, who blushed under Abby's appraisal.

"All right, now that's enough. If you don't get to washin', we won't get your hair dry in time." Martha set down a new bar of soap on the chair situated a few feet from the tub. Then, she left, leaving the door open a crack behind her.

This would be the first party she'd attended since her mother died over six years ago. Even then, she'd always felt out of place at these kinds of parties. Boys hadn't ever wanted to dance with her and her dance card had always gone unfilled. Sure they wanted to hunt with her or have her train their horses, but whenever she'd worn a dress to town, everyone had just stared.

This time it was different and she felt giddy at the reason for the celebration. She didn't care if anyone stared. Abby looked at Lily when the last bucket was emptied into the steaming tub.

"Don't mind me. Take your bath. I'll go help Martha in the kitchen and then we'll get you all dressed up nice for your party." Lily waved on her way out the door.

Abby ran to her dresser and opened the top drawer. Inside were two small boxes. She pulled out the one stuffed with cotton and layered with golden taffeta. She had purchased the box, just before her mother died, from a peddler who'd told her it would make those around her believe she was a goddess. Ambrosia, food of the gods, he'd called it. If ever she needed to feel like a goddess, it was tonight.

She opened the box and the soft sent of cantaloupe filled her nostrils with sweet remembrance. The last time she'd smelled the aroma was after her parents had stopped off for a few days on their way home from a cattle drive in the small town of Rocky Ford where the melons grew. Her mother's hair had smelled like that for days. Abby relished the heady scent.

She inhaled deeply and then closed the box, pulling it close.

Once the men had finished filling the tub, Abby sprinkled some of the sweet smelling dust into the water. She removed her clothing and allowed it to drop on the floor around her feet. Lifting one leg over the edge of the tub, she tested the water with her toe. It was hotter than she'd anticipated and she smiled in sweet expectation as she submerged herself into the aromatic warmth.

Cole opened the door to his new bedroom. A warm, heavenly aroma floated in the air around him. He cursed, throwing his gloves down on the bed. If that is what she always smelled like, he didn't know how long he could keep his distance.

"Martha, I forgot to grab the soap. Would you mind handing it to me?"

Cole jerked his head around to see a very naked Abby leaning against the back of an oversized wooden tub, a wet cloth covering her face and her hand extended. Her creamy bare shoulders peaked above the bubble-laced water and her fire-blond tresses spilled over the side.

He spotted the soap sitting on chair just beyond the tub's reach and with one stride was there. He picked up the misshapen bar of soap and placed it in her extended hand, backing away the moment his skin came in contact with hers.

"Thank you, Martha. What do you think Cole will be wearing at the party tonight?" she mused aloud.

Cole yanked his eyes away from the vision before him, desperate to keep his wits about him. He was strong, but still a man and there was only so much he could take.

He forced himself to walk away, to move to the other side of the room where his bag of clothes lay in the corner. He'd packed a clean shirt that matched the cerulean blue paint in his artist tack and a pair of black slacks he usually wore for church on Sunday along with a stack of work clothes and he wondered what Abby would be wearing to the party.

He opened his mouth to answer her question, when the door thrust open.

"Abigail, you'll need to have..." Martha flew in through the open doorway in a hurry, carrying a thick cotton towel. She froze the moment she saw him.

Cole cleared his throat.

Abby pulled the cloth from her face and down into the water, over her chest. She sat up straight in the tub, staring at him. Her cheeks, already flushed from the warm water, turned a hotter, darker red.

"I came in to get my clothes for the get-together this evening." Cole picked up his bag and nodded to both women and left the room.

Once outside, he did not stop until he reached the bunkhouse, where he was sure Raine would be changing. *This is going to be a lot harder than I expected,* he groaned.

"The axle's been cut near clean through," Raine said after inspecting the overturned wagon. "And one of the bolts is missing."

Fresh cut wood, boxes of nails, and a large amount of other building supplies now lay strewn about an irrigation ditch and down a small hillside, lining the far side of the property.

"Davey's arm is broken and it seems his shoulder is dislocated. The fall gave him quite a blow to the head, but overall, the boy's lucky to be alive." Clay shook his head in disgust.

Cole looked over the damaged wagon and scattered supplies. He'd just gone to the bunkhouse to dress for the party when the bloodied and staggering Davey had walked in and collapsed on the floor in front of Raine's bunk.

"This wasn't an accident, Clay." Cole looked meaningfully at his new father-in-law. "Has anything like this happened before?"

Clay scratched his chin, brusque with new growth. "This'll be the third mishap in the last month or so. They were far enough separated I didn't want to believe there was a connection."

"Third? Have you told anyone else?" Cole inquired.

Clay shook his head. "It's really the fourth, I guess. Forgot about the rattler Abby shot in the barn the other morning."

Abby shot a rattlesnake? Cole felt a new appreciation for his bride.

"Four incidents within a month? Sounds like somebody's up to no good." Raine stated the obvious.

All three men worked quickly to clean up the mess that had been created in the fall. Cole didn't think the buckboard would be salvageable, but there were a lot of supplies that needed to be gathered and carted back to the ranch.

"With everything that's been going on, I thought it would be safer for Abby if she went away for a while," Clay stood up, took off his hat, and wiped his brow with the red handkerchief he pulled from his pocket.

Cole threw a blanket roll and a sack of wheat into back of the operational buckboard he'd driven from the ranch and stopped to listen.

"I knew she wouldn't go willingly, so I made her a bet. I told her if she didn't have a husband by Friday, I'd ship her off to her Aunt Iris in Denver, to each her how to be a lady and find a proper man."

Clay snorted a breathy laugh. "I needed her to be safe. But then, she up and married you."

Cole lifted his eyebrows at the irony.

Raine pulled his canteen off his horse and walked over to join them.

"Listen, boys, I know my daughter and I didn't want her to get mixed up in this. I used the first excuse I could think of. I want her out of harm's way. The less she knows about all of this, the better. But, as you may have noticed, my daughter has a will of her own. She didn't want to be away from this ranch in Denver or anywhere else—"

"So she—"

"Married you," Clay finished Cole's statement with a chuckle.

Cole took the canteen from Raine, who held it out to him, and glanced from Clay to the mountain ridge that kept the SilverHawk from view. He took a drink of the cool water.

Abby certainly had taken it into her own hands to get what she wanted. He had to admire that. But that didn't explain why she'd had to resort to marrying just anybody.

"What about Carson?" Cole asked as he wiped the excess water from his lips. "He said they were supposed to get married. Something about being expected. Why didn't she just marry him?"

"Besides his obvious gentlemanly ways and kind demeanor, you mean," Raine sardonically whispered next to him.

"I would never have allowed that. Abby may not be the most feminine gal in these parts, but she's the most amazing young woman. She needs a man who'll appreciate her…gifts. I thought she'd found it once, love, a long time ago, but I'd misjudged his character and she paid for it. He up and left for Kansas, breaking her heart in the process. She deserved better."

"You mean, Alaric?" Cole asked as he handed the canteen to Clay.

"She told you about him, eh?" He took a drink. "Well, he left and never came back. Good riddance. It seems men don't take too kindly to women who can shoot or ride better than they can. You best not be leaving her, son. We'll just leave it at that."

The look in Clay's eye pierced through Cole with its somber warning and Cole nodded in affirmation. "Yes, sir!"

"Clay, you said this was the fourth incident," Raine asked, changing the conversation back to the incident at hand.

"That we know of."

"What else has happened?"

Clay sat down on a felled tree stump. Cole and Raine followed suit and found something to sit on as they discussed.

"Well, at first we just thought one of the hands had left the stall unlocked. The new kid, Davey, noticed one of my most prized studs had gotten loose. Luckily, it didn't take Caleb long to find him. He spotted the horse up the ridge a bit and was able to coax him home without any incident." Clay reached down and picked up a small wooden box. Its hinges were bent and broken from the fall, but the rest of the box was still intact.

"When I went out to check the stalls for the other horses, I noticed three more were unlatched and the gate lock to the corral had been broken." Clay carefully lifted the lid off the box and pulled out a velvety black pouch.

He spilled a long silver chain into his hand, followed by a lavender cameo. Intricately carved into its pale skin was an ivory picture of a man and a woman in a passionate embrace.

"It's beautiful. My mother has a collection of unique cameos. I must say though, I have never seen one like this." Raine had always been fascinated by their mother's collection, but Cole had never found use for it.

"And, the first incident?" Cole's question lingered in the air for a few moments.

Clay returned the cameo to its pouch and placed it back in the box.

"It was hand designed by an Italian friend of mine," he ignored Cole's determination to find out what was happening and kept his attention on his conversation with Raine.

"It was supposed to be for Clara, my wife. Paulo sent it to me a long time ago, I just haven't had the heart to retrieve it until now. The Patterson's have been good to hold onto it for me for all these years." He turned to Cole. "I thought it would make a nice weddin' gift for my daughter." He stood up and placed the carved box into one of his saddle bags.

"As for the first incident," Clay cleared his throat and turned to look pointedly at Cole, "my foreman was killed in a drunken brawl a month or so back."

Cole bit his tongue and lowered his glare, feeling the petulant child. "By who?"

"Nobody knows who started it or how it happened. Everybody was fightin'. All my men came home with cuts and bruises, even the gangly Davey got his punches in I'm told. They'd just gotten back from a successful drive to Wyoming and went into town to celebrate." Clay hunkered down and leaned back onto his heels, his thighs straining against his denims as he propped himself up against the side of the grounded wagon.

"He was just a kid. Younger'n you. 'Bout to get himself hitched."

"What makes you think they're all connected?" Raine asked.

"Let me show you something." Clay rocked back onto his feet, upright, and walked back to the rear axle of the wagon.

Cole and Raine followed.

"See this?" he pointed to a small piece of black cloth tied around a spindle on one of the back wheels. "There's been one of these appear after every incident. There was one clenched in Jesse's fist when he went down--Jesse was my foreman. One was tied to the gate. Another folded like a knapsack and peeking through the straw in the barn and this one."

"Have you told the sheriff about any of this?" Raine inquired, crouched down and examining the axel.

"Can't. He now lives at the town cemetery and the new one hasn't arrived yet. He was supposed to arrive on last week's train, but he didn't make it. No one has heard from him."

How convenient that the only lawman in town was dead.

"Why? Why would someone want to cause all this trouble?" Cole asked.

"A few weeks before you showed up, a man came to my door with an offer to buy the place." Clay rested his boot on the spoke of the wagon wheel. "When I kindly refused his not so generous offer, he said he'd be surprised if I hadn't changed my mind in two fortnights and he'd be back."

"Well, I'm guessing you haven't changed your mind." Cole

picked up a spool of chicken wire and threw it into back of the wagon alongside some of the more recoverable replacement fence posts they'd loaded.

"Nope. So, I reckon he'll be back here in a day or two."

"Who was he?" Raine asked.

"We believe he is working for the new owners of the Gnarled Oak." He looked at Cole. "The property surrounding both the north and east sides of mine.

Cole's eyes widened, but he remained silent.

"Friedrich Johansson died a little over a year ago and since then collectors have been showin' up at folk's doorsteps, demandin' payment on their mortgages. There are four of us who own our land outright, so we figured they would try to get us to sell."

That was the last thing Cole had expected to hear. He shook his head.

"This is why I wanted Abby in Denver." Clay threw his hand up in the air and muttered under his breath, kicking at some of the wood planks that could now only be used for firewood.

"It has to be somebody you know, Clay, for them to get this close without being noticed." Cole looked around at the scattered tools and supplies. *But, who?* Cole decided it was time for him to meet the crew.

"If you're still needin' a foreman..." Cole hadn't forgotten he'd been fired.

Clay turned a darker shade of red. He extended his hand to Cole. "Welcome back, son."

Cole nodded, shaking the man's hand firmly.

"We'd best be getting back. The womenfolk'll be a wonderin' where we are and I don't think Martha or my daughter will take too kindly to my detaining the guest of honor."

"Clay, you said the new sheriff is on his way? Well, there's no tellin' how long it'll take him to get here. We'll just have to do what we can in the meantime to figure out what's going on." Raine clapped Cole on his back.

Cole smiled.

"I knew sending for you was the right choice." Clay spoke, approval in his voice. He pulled himself onto his silver mount.

"Why *did* you send for me?" Cole wasn't sure he wanted the answer to his question. "Surely, there are men around here qualified to run your ranch. Abby, even."

"My daughter is the best I've ever seen. A real natural. But I just can't lose her too. Seems running a ranch has become a real dangerous thing lately, and I needed someone with experience, strength, and good instincts."

"How did you find me?" Cole had done a dozen drives or so between Kansas and Texas, but this was his first job that had taken him all the way into Colorado.

"Levi told me you were the best ranchman he had ever seen, with an eye for detail and a gut for the truth about people. He said your awareness and manner with horses was unparalleled and would put others to shame."

"Levi?" Cole asked aloud. He and Raine exchanged glances.

Clay looked a little sheepish.

"He said if I could get you to come on as my foreman, Raine wouldn't be too far behind. And between the two of you, he said we would have this mess resolved in no time." Clay looked around at the scattered mess. Looking over his shoulder he added, "He seemed to think it would be good for the both of you as well."

Raine mounted his paint horse and pulled to Clay's side. "How do you know our brother?"

All of the Redbournes were accustomed to getting what they wanted, but Levi was particularly keen at using his influence over others to get his way.

"We met when I was transporting horses through Cheyenne on the railroad a few years back. He's been a good friend ever since."

Cole ran his hand over the lead horse's back and pulled himself up onto the functioning wagon. "I don't like being played the fool. You should have let on from the beginning what you needed from me."

"Would you have come?"

Clay waited, his arms crossed against his saddle.

Cole didn't have an answer. Truth was, the state he was in, the more dangerous it had promised to be, the more likely he would have been to accept it. He didn't think that would be the wisest thing to tell his new father-in-law just now.

"Did Abby know about this? About me?"

"No, sir. I didn't want her involved in any of it. She did know I'd hired a new foreman, but that's it." Clay looked back over the debris on the hillside. "I'll send Caleb back to collect anything else that may be of value. Martha is not going to be happy that all of the food stuffs are ruined," he said and with his heels prodded his horse ahead.

"Well, it looks like our dear brother got his way," Raine clicked his paint horse forward. Out of kicking distance. "You took the land and the girl. Looks like you'll be getting your inheritance after all."

Cole urged his team of horses up alongside Raine.

"I should have known when he made the special trip home last month he was up to something." Cole could feel his irritation seeping into his words.

His family just couldn't leave well enough alone. They all had to get involved. He used to love that quality about them. Now, that it was directed at him, it just annoyed him.

"I should have known," Cole repeated under his breath.

CHAPTER THIRTEEN

Abby descended the staircase with grace and poise, two things which were not usually among her greatest of assets. Her hair, upswept, only allowed a few stray tendrils to curl about her neck.

She wore the beautiful garnet comb Mrs. Hutchinson had given her. She'd thought she'd lost it when she'd fallen in the mud on the way to the church, but Lily had found it and cleaned it up for her.

The deep red coloring of the stone took on an accentuating shade of purple undertones that added a striking contrast to her lighter dress. She was a Redbourne bride and was glad she had something that had belonged to Cole's family to wear.

The lavender gown her father had purchased was well-fitted, though the neckline lower than was her custom and she clasped her hands in front of her. A darker purple shawl accented her dress, draped behind her and resting across her forearms.

With each step she took, another head turned in her direction until a hush fell across the entire room, all eyes on her. She scanned the area full of well-wishers, looking for her groom. As the guests parted and Abby saw the handsome face of her husband emerge from the crowd, she dropped her hands to her sides and smiled.

He's beautiful, she thought. Then, Mrs. Hutchinson's words came to her mind.

In time, you will grow to love him—the man, not just the idea of him.

Abby wanted to know the man and she realized at that
moment she would have the rest of her life to discover all there
was to know.

Cole's movements were slow and deliberate. She stopped
midway down the steps, her eyes drawn to his slender torso.
She imagined for a moment what it would be like to be really
held in his arms. To be loved by him. She remembered the
strength of him, shirt open and perspiring, and she swallowed
the lump forming in her throat.

Cole held out his hand to her and she glided down the rest
of the staircase until her hand was nestled securely inside of his.
As he guided her across the large room, the guests began
clapping and wishing them well.

Clay met them at the door. "I always knew this day would
come, but I would have never guessed it would be so soon."
Everyone laughed. "Abby, you won your bet, all right."

Abby blushed, then darted a horrified look in Cole's
direction. He hadn't seemed to notice.

"I want you to be happy and this young man has promised
me he will take care of you. Your mother would be proud to
see the young woman you have become." Clay's voice quivered
as he spoke.

Her father held Abby by the shoulders and turned her
around to face the onlookers. He placed a small lavender
cameo, hanging from a silver chain, around her bare neck and
clasped it into place. She put her hand over the trinket and
looked down at the beautiful carving there.

"I love you, papa." She fell into his arms just as she had
always done. He squeezed her once and then pulled her away
from him, guiding her into the arms of the new man in her life.

"Let the dancing begin!" Clay shouted to the expectant
room. Cheers erupted and Cole took Abby by the hand and
tucked it up into the crook of his elbow, leading her through
the open door outside to the newly built dancing platform.

The brisk cool air felt refreshing against her hot skin. As if
on cue, the fiddles started to play and a sudden train of dancers
appeared on the wooden floor.

Two large fire pits had been built on either side of the platform, but Abby wasn't sure she would need them to keep warm.

Cole took her into his arms and whispered, "May I have this dance? And the next one? And the next?"

Her dance card was full. Abby smiled her agreement and raised her hands to meet his. They began the first dance, a waltz. A few measures into the music other couples joined in and soon the dance floor was in full motion.

When the next reel began everyone got involved. Abby was not at all surprised to see Raine and Lily dancing together, laughing and teasing one another. She smiled, in spite of herself. Lily was already like a sister to her.

She should marry Raine. We would be sisters for real, she thought.

"And to what do I owe the pleasure of your smile, m'lady?" Cole teased, speaking in proper British tones.

Abby smiled, feeling the blush creep into her face. She took Cole's hand. He pulled her close.

"They look nice together, don't they? Lily and Raine, I mean," Abby mused while watching the playful couple.

"Don't even think about it," Cole warned good-naturedly.

Cole spun her around the floor until they were dancing just inches away from Raine and Lily. Raine, still with a smile on his face, caught Cole's eye and tilted his head toward the refreshment table.

Abby did not miss the exchange. When Cole's smile faltered, she followed the direction his eyes had taken to see Jeremiah Carson standing menacingly near the platform steps in the midst of a group of men.

Jeremiah's voice had already begun to carry over the bustle of guests and he was speaking in slurred sentences. Drunk. Determined to hide her annoyance at his rude behavior, she turned back to Cole.

His face dripped with disdain.

"What's wrong?" Abby demanded of her husband.

Cole's smile returned strong as he turned back to face her. "Nothing. I think I'm just starting to get a little winded. Would you like some lemonade?"

Abby nodded, but still felt something was very wrong.
Raine and Cole excused themselves to retrieve the ladies'
drinks.

"What's going on?" Lily asked.

Abby shrugged. Lily laced her arm with Abby's and both
women walked to the edge of the dance floor where they had a
good view of the refreshment table below. Raine and Cole were
collecting glasses of lemonade while deep in strained
conversation, all amusement gone from their faces.

Abby leaned forward trying to hear what Cole was saying,
but the laughter and music was too loud to hear the exchange
being held in hushed tones.

"Lily dear," Mrs. Patterson, the owner of the mercantile,
said as she pushed past Abby with the new preacher in tow.
"Have you met our delightful Mr. Harris? He's single, you
know?" The robust woman leaned in toward Lily and cupped
one hand above her mouth as if she were passing along a great
secret. Not letting go of the poor preacher's arm, Mrs.
Patterson said, in a whisper loud enough for those on the other
side of the barn to hear, "And don't you just think he is so
handsome?"

The preacher's blond hair was combed neatly back and the
spark behind his green eyes startled Abby. She wondered for a
moment about this new reverend. No one had heard anything
about him or had even met him until the wedding. Martha had
told Abby that even Mrs. Patterson, who knew the details of
everyone's lives, was having a hard time discovering anything
about the man.

"It's a pleasure to officially meet you, Reverend." Lily held
out her hand for him.

"The pleasure is all mine, Miss...?" He bowed slightly, but
did not take his eyes off Lily. His thick British accent and
impeccable manners endeared him to her, a little.

Abby rolled her eyes.

"Campbell," Lily provided.

He bent his head forward in acknowledgement. "And good

evening to you, *Mrs*. Redbourne." He bent his head again, this time toward Abby. "Congratulations again on your marriage."

With a brief smile, his attentions quickly returned back to Lily and he extended her his hand.

"Is this dance spoken for, Miss Campbell?"

Lily threw a quick glance back to the lemonade table. Abby followed her gaze to find Raine handing a glass of the tart beverage to Jenna.

"It is now," Lily said, her voice cracking and she placed a practiced smile on her face as she took the reverend's hand.

"I trust I will see all of you for services tomorrow." Mr. Harris looked quite attractive in his denims and new, crisp black cotton shirt that appeared, at least for the moment, free of sweat.

After a few nods from Abby and the others, he returned his attentions to Lily with a broad grin highlighting his already handsome features. He seemed delighted with her acceptance to dance and Abby was drawn to the deep indentations in his cheeks. Dimples added a youthful, playful sense to his already charming appearance. His white collar was barely visible beneath the heavy black material.

I didn't know preachers were allowed to wear denims, she thought, since she'd never seen one do it.

"Your drink, Mrs. Redbourne."

Abby looked down at the glass extended to her and turned to meet the man's eyes who offered it to her. The mischievous smirk on Cole's most handsome face pulled Abby's thoughts away from the preacher's clothing choices. She took the lemonade, grateful for relief from a parched throat.

The sun was beginning to set and a low layer of non-threatening clouds blanketed the sky in a display of brilliant color. Abby saw several lanterns hung at strategic points of the platform, offering light to the dancing patrons, some even lighting portions of the yard.

Although the night air held a bit of a chill, Abby was grateful there was no sign of rain tonight. She'd had her fill in the last couple of days. Her purple shawl was a lot thinner than

she'd have liked, but still she pulled it up around her shoulders
and hugged her arms into her chest.

"Your comb looks stunning, dear. Just like I knew it
would."

Abby spun to see Mrs. Hutchison with her own glass of
the refreshing liquid.

"Cole," Abby placed a hand on her husband's forearm and
turned him to face the woman who had rescued her on her
wedding day and given her some most sage advice. "This is
Mrs. Hutchinson. She lives in the little hat shop in town. She's
the one who gave me my comb to wear at the wedding." She
smiled at the woman, who now eyed her speculatively. "Not
that anyone would have been able to tell I was wearing it,"
Abby added.

Cole bent over in a curt bow. "It's a pleasure to meet you
ma'am."

"Isn't the comb beautiful on your bride, Mr. Redbourne?"
She stared at Cole, an odd expression in her eyes.

"Oh, yes, Cole. Mrs. Hutchinson knows your—"

"You two should be dancing," Mrs. Hutchinson cut her
short. "It is your wedding party after all."

Abby furrowed her brows together. *That was odd.*

Cole set both glasses down on the edge of the railing and
took her hand, but before he could pull her onto the floor for
another reel, her father stepped between them.

"May I dance with the bride?" Abby was thrilled her father
was taking the news of her marriage so well and he had
accepted Cole as his new son-in-law. They were getting on
wonderfully and Abby decided that the evening was turning out
better than she had anticipated.

"Norah," Clay nodded to Mrs. Hutchinson before
whisking his daughter away in a delightful swinging motion.
Before she knew it he had swept her across the floor. Abby
didn't remember a time, since her mother had died, when her
father seemed so...alive. She'd missed it.

"I jes wanna see Abby." Jeremiah's voice carried over the
music and Abby saw him pushing at Cole as he tried to get up

the stairs. Raine was standing next to Cole within moments and the two brothers escorted Jeremiah away from the crowd.

"You ken't do this to me. You'll be sawry," she heard him screaming as they dragged him away.

And I would have married him? she thought with disgust.

"It'll be nice to have a foreman again." Her father stated simply, pulling her thoughts back to him.

"About that papa," she raised her head to look at him, "I was hoping Cole could be the new foreman."

Clay looked surprised. He opened his mouth to speak, but she kept talking. She really wanted Cole to feel like he had a place on the ranch and she didn't want to hear her father's excuses why it wouldn't work.

"I know you have already hired some fancy hired hand who's supposed to be the perfect rancher, but I hoped since Cole is now my...my husband, you would..."

She stopped when she realized he was laughing at her.

"Honey, Cole *is* the new foreman."

"Oh, papa, thank you."

"No, what I mean to say is that, Cole is the fancy hired hand who's coming to the SilverHawk as foreman."

Abby just stared at her father, attempting to digest the meaning behind his words.

"What do you mean, you hired Cole?" The idea was still not registering with her.

"Cole is who I sent away for. He would have been the new foreman even if you hadn't married him first."

"You mean, the reason Cole is here in Silver Falls, is because you sent for him? To be our foreman?"

"Yes, Abby. Cole is the new foreman."

Her lips pursed together and her frame stiffened. "He lied," she whispered. *He'd said he had unfinished business here in town. His own land. That he'd come to start his own ranch.* "He lied."

"Three of them have guns under their coats." Raine assessed aloud the group that had promised to escort Jeremiah home.

Cole had been watching Abby dance with her father and all of his original misgivings about Clay McCallister were beginning to clear. Raine's words pulled him from his musings and he turned to watch the small band of boys accompanying his new adversary as they disappeared into the darkening night.

"You gentlemen don't plan on leavin' too, do you?" It was Jenna. She was adorned in a fitted red dress that hung very low on her neck and exposed the majority of her shoulders and bosom.

"I'd hate to say I left the party without so much as a dance with the groom." She moved between the two men and linked her arms into both of theirs.

The two men exchanged glances.

Cole caught Abby's glare as she passed in a twirl with Clay. The steel in her eyes was molten hot and it unsettled him. She had been very soft and warm in his arms as they danced and he realized as he glanced down at the dark beauty who had taken his arm, that Abby felt threatened enough by Jenna to that her entire demeanor had changed in an instant. He removed Jenna's arm from his own and with a courteous bow of his head excused himself to go and check the stock of firewood for the two large pits.

The wood piles were nearly depleted. Raine and some of the other men had spent the better part of the afternoon chopping wood and stacking it behind the barn. They had also created two fairly large piles on either side of the dancing platform for easy access. Cole strode to the other side of the barn to retrieve more.

Although some families had already started to leave, Cole knew from experience with five older brothers and a sister who'd gotten married, that the festivities would probably last a few more hours. As he neared the edge of the building he heard voices through the darkness and stopped. Moving closer to the side of the barn he peered around the corner.

In the dim light, it was hard to make out the faces of those who were talking. He leaned his head forward a few inches more.

"He jes' thinks he can waltz in 'ere and take what's mine? Well, I'll show 'im."

The voice belonged to Jeremiah, and Cole guessed his small band of friends were with him.

The splintering sound of a cocking gun echoed in his ear. A cold barrel nudged his back prodding him forward.

"Hey, boys. Look here what I found."

Light from a newly lit torch cast shadows on Cole's surroundings. The man with the gun shoved him forward and onto the ground, his knee catching the majority of the fall. He looked up to see five drunken faces, bruised green by the firelight, staring back at him.

Cole slowly stretched himself until he reached his full height. He watched their eyes widen at the size of him, all being shorter than his six feet two inches. A look of fear flickered in each set of their glass-like eyes.

Jeremiah stepped forward, a toothy grin distorting his normally well-structured features.

"You, Redbourne, have taken what's mine and I want it back."

"Abby is not a thing to be had or taken." Cole eyed the man, disdain lacing every word.

"Do you really think I'm talking 'bout Abby." His speech was very slurred and he took a bumbling step toward Cole. "Yer a fool if that's what yer thinkin'. She was jes the easiest way to gettin' what I want. Timing was jes off a bit."

Cole brushed his elbow against his side. The angled butt of his colt protruded reassuringly from his belt. He assessed the group. Even when he'd been in England at school he'd not taken on five men alone. *I could sure use Raine's flawless sense of timing at a time like this,* he thought to himself.

"These odds seem a little uneven, don't you think gentlemen? And I use the term, gentlemen, lightly."

A familiar voice taunted Cole from just a few feet away. It

wasn't Raine. Cole squinted and could see the outline of a man leaning up against the side of the barn, hat low and head bent.

"I'd hate to have you mess up my little brother's pretty face, just after he took a new bride and all. Then, I'd have to return the favor. And, honestly, I am a little busy right now trying to catch a man who makes you all look like spoiled little boys."

A torch lit. Cole saw a rakish grin spread across the man's face.

"Rafe?"

Cole hadn't seen his brother in over a year. He was sure glad to see him now. His timing had always been as good as Raine's or better. He'd just proved that. He looked like he was doing well in his fancy duster and spit-shined boots. Cole had never seen anyone best Rafe in a fight, not even his brother William, who was a well-respected fighter in England. Cole was grateful to Rafe for evening out the odds a little.

All eyes had turned to the stranger, except for Jeremiah's who tried to take advantage of the distraction by taking a swing at Cole. It didn't take long for a brawl to break out. One of Jeremiah's cohorts went after Rafe. Poor fellow.

A white hot pain seared the back of Cole's head. The blow had come from behind. Someone had hit him with, what he guessed was, one of the long logs that had been cut for firewood. He fell forward.

For a moment, everything moved with an exaggeratedly slow speed. His vision blurred somewhat, but he looked up to see Abby start running toward him. He was sure he'd only imagined the look of sheer panic daunting her expression as she met his gaze.

"Raine," Abby screamed his brother's name. He watched through half closed lids as the world around him seemed to slow its motion even more. Abby twisted around while still moving slowly toward him, leaving colorful, blurred streaks in her wake.

"Papa," she screamed this time and Cole moved his head just enough to see both his oldest brother and her father making their way toward him. He couldn't hold his head up any longer and he collapsed to one knee. Reaching out to her from his half kneeling position on the ground, he closed his eyes, fighting to clear his head of the fog that engulfed him. He pushed off his bent leg and attempted to pull himself up from the ground.

Abby was directly in front of him now and he lifted a hand to her. A man's arm reached out from behind her and grabbed Abby, pulling her up short before she could reach him.

Cole blinked. He willed his eyes to focus on Abby's attacker. He took a step toward the man who struggled to keep a hold of Abby as she flailed and kicked at him.

His head finally started to clear, but before he could completely reclaim his senses, a rock hard fist connected with his gut and he hunched over again in unexpected pain, repentant for his stray in focus. William would not be impressed.

Another fist flew toward him. It belonged to Jeremiah Carson.

Grateful to his brother William for daily boxing lessons while at school, Cole pulled his arm in, tight to his body to protect his torso, and blocked his attacker from any more easy punches. His eyes finally regained their focus and he returned a jab to Jeremiah's already swelling jaw in a sharp upper cut. The man went sprawling backward. He landed with a thud and didn't get up. He appeared out cold.

Two more assailants grabbed him by the arms and a third began punching him in the gut. Cole tested the strength of those holding him back. He let his body fall limp for a moment. Satisfied they would support him, he jumped up and kicked the man in front square in the chest, sending him stumbling backward into a large hay stack.

Cole bent forward throwing the two men who held him to fall off balance. He used their slight confusion to his advantage, hitting each of them in the face with the backs of his clenched fists. Rafe had the largest of the men on his knees, his hands tied in back of him. Cole whirled around frantically looking for

Abby and her attacker.

Her scream sounded more angry than fearful.

"Let me go, Earl Spencer, right this instant or I will tell your pa you've all been paying the Simpson boys to do your chores."

Cole stood there, mouth gaping, as the man twice Abby's size released her with an unintentional shove and turned, running into the darkness.

"Sorry, Abby," he yelled as he ran, fading in the distance.

Abby ran her hands down the front of her dress and reached up to replace a tendril that had fallen onto her forehead during her brief struggle. She met Cole's eyes.

She ran to him, her hand's reaching up to his chest as if to brace him. "Are you all right?" she asked. "They didn't hurt you, did they?"

Cole laughed irreverently. Abby was so much more than she let on. "Are you?" he asked, his arm reaching around her and pulling her into him.

"They're all pretty scared of their pa. Brothers, all of them." She pulled back and looked around him at the two fallen men. "Except Jeremiah, of course." She straightened and met Cole's eyes with a smile. "I'm glad you're...not hurt."

"Hey, Charcoal...I thought Raine was with you." Rafe was pulling his charge from his knees.

"I am."

Cole craned his neck to see Raine pulling the two fallen brothers off the ground by the napes of their necks.

"You always did have good timing," Raine directed his comment to Rafe. Cole wasn't surprised they'd had the same thought.

Raine looked down at the two boys he had by the shirt collars. "Haven't I seen you two before?" He studied their faces. "Ah, yes. I broke up your scrap yesterday. You boys really need to find a better hobby." He walked them over to a large wood log and sat them both down.

"Nice of you to join us." Cole smirked at his oldest brother who now rested one foot on the log, stopping any hope they may have had for retreat.

"There were just five little ones. I thought you could handle it on your own." Raine's mouth broke into a wide grin.

"Six," Rafe corrected. Joining Raine on the lodge pole, he pointed at Abby's father.

"Here's the other one." Clay had a hold of the man, who'd run away from Abby, by the back of the shirt. He hauled him over to the others and pushed him onto the log.

"It's so good to see you, Rafe. How've you been?" Cole took the few steps between them in an instant and pulled his brother into a tight bear-like hug.

"Great. Another Redbourne. Just how many of you are there?"

Cole looked down at the Spencer boy who asked the question.

"Seven brothers. Eight all together. Even our baby sister could whoop the likes of you," Cole answered. All three brothers looked at each other and then together, all laughed in agreement.

"You smell smoke?" Raine's eyes widened even as he asked the question. Clouds of black smoke rose from behind a now illuminated hay stack.

"Where's Carson?" Cole suddenly scanned the area where Jeremiah had fallen. He was gone.

CHAPTER FOURTEEN

The acrid scent of smoke filled Cole's nostrils. Flames from the burning haystack licked the dry ground with vigor, searching for anything consumable.

"Caleb, go pull the water wagon around from the bunkhouse." Clay's command was obeyed in an instant.

Taggert had always provided a water wagon for his ranch hands to wash up and to use for drinking. He was glad to see it was not just his brother who was prepared with forward thinking. Cole was extra grateful at this moment for Clay's insight in having the water wagon close to the buildings. He didn't think they would be able to extract the water from the well fast enough or in large enough quantities to thwart the damage.

The small creek and falls were not far off the property, but to haul the water back to the ranch in large amounts would be time consuming and potentially fatal.

A handful of buckets were retrieved from the barn before the flames broke through. All the animals had been taken to the corral where the fire had already been extinguished.

Two lines were formed, one beginning at the house where water could be pumped and the other at the water wagon. Both lines ended in the vicinity of the barn. Each line was made up of eight to ten men with buckets of water being filled, passed, and thrown onto the fires.

Most of the townsfolk and ranchers had already gone home for the evening. Normally, Cole was irritated by stragglers, but tonight he was grateful for the extra hands. The women had retreated inside. However, Cole was not surprised to see Abby, at the front of a line, hauling water to the fiery blaze. Her face, streaked with ash and sweat, wore a determined expression and Cole was awed at her resolve.

"There's someone inside!" a gangly red-headed boy, toward the front of the line, called out. He looked oddly familiar, but Cole couldn't place him.

The kid couldn't be a day over seventeen and his arm was in a sling, yet here he was doing what he could to help. Cole followed his gaze to the barn. The flames were slowing their pace under the constant influx of water, but they still licked at the dry log walls, creating a smoky inferno.

Through the open doors of the smoldering barn, Cole saw something move. He stepped a little closer. The heat created a contorted veil that blurred the air in front of him, but through the haze, Cole saw a flash of color stammer to the side wall. Cole recognized the face of the man who'd attacked him earlier tonight. Jeremiah Carson was caught inside the sweltering death trap.

Cole's conscience fought with his anger. It didn't take long for his conscience to arise the victor, and after pouring a bucket full of water over his head to help protect him, he plunged through the flames into the section of the barn he'd last seen movement.

The fire had not reached the center of the building and the back wall had not yet been touched, but the smoke was becoming so thick that he didn't know how much longer he would be able to see.

A support timber had collapsed behind him and fire lapped at the now fallen beam, effectively blocking the solitary exit. Cole twisted his head from one direction to the other, looking for the man whom he suspected had started the blaze.

After a few moments, he found Jeremiah collapsed on the ground, near passed out. He leaned down, crooked his arms under the man's armpits, and dragged him toward the unburned section of the barn at the back. The smoke was heavy and Cole was finding it more difficult to breathe.

"No," Jeremiah scratched out of his throat, "Leave me alone. I didn't mean no harm, please don't hurt me." He patted Cole on the side of his face.

The stale stench of cheap alcohol on the man's breath was pungent enough for Cole to turn away momentarily. The fool was either insane or too drunk to realize they were in serious trouble and unless they found another way out, they were both about to meet their maker.

"Can you stand?" Cole asked as he pulled one of Jeremiah's arms over his shoulder and lifted.

"I said, don't touch me!" Jeremiah yelled with a slur. He threw his arms in the air to free himself and caught an unsuspecting Cole in the chin with his elbow, sending him sprawling backward into a newly kindled fire start.

A slightly stunned Cole shoved himself away from the burning timbers quickly, but some of the flames had already jumped onto his shirt sleeve. Cole beat at the flames with his free arm. The hole in the garment still smoldered, burning the sensitive flesh beneath it. Cole grabbed the hem of his shirt, pulled it up over his head, and threw it to the ground where he stomped it, effectively extinguishing the small blaze.

He looked up to see a portion of the roof burning now, dropping pieces of fiery wood into the straw laden floor at the center of the barn. The barn was gone. There was nothing more they could do to save it. He picked up his shirt and shook it open, laying it atop the small fire that had just started there and stomped it out with his feet.

"I should just let you die, *Mr. Carson*," he tried to scream at the nearly unconscious man who'd fallen back down to the ground, but the burning in his throat from all the smoke strained his voice. *Why am I saving him again?* he asked himself, knowing full well the answer.

Cole moved to the edge of the room and kicked at the wooden planks making up the barn wall, his muscles had been pushed too far and his strength was failing him. With one last kick, his boot finally broke through the wood.

"Over here," he heard someone shout from the other side.

"Stand back, Charcoal, we're coming through."

Cole moved away from the hole he'd created. Within moments Raine and Rafe both busted through the wall, splintering the wood into a gap big enough for them to escape. Cole closed his eyes in momentary relief. Then, worried that the barn may collapse on top of them, he picked up an unconscious Jeremiah, flung his new rival over his shoulders, and stumbled to freedom.

Rafe took the load from his shoulders and carried the man toward the house. Cole staggered back to the front of the barn and was glad to see the surrounding fires had been extinguished. The barn was the only structure still burning.

He dropped to the ground and rolled over onto his back, lying flat, trying to catch his breath and fill his lungs with air instead of smoke. Cole closed his eyes and breathed deeply, instigating a short series of coughs to force their way out.

The cool dirt felt nice against his bare back.

"What in Hell's name were you thinking?"

Cole opened one eye to Raine looming over him. He propped himself up onto his elbows and opened the other eye. His brother reached down for his hand and pulled him to his feet and into a hug. He gripped him a little tighter than was comfortable before pushing him away.

"Let me see."

"It's nothing," Cole lied, even as his arm throbbed with searing pain.

Raine inspected Cole's arm. "You should have Rafe take a look at that."

"It's nothing," Cole repeated and he pulled his arm from Raine's grasp.

It appeared that Clay had told those working the lines to stop their tireless efforts as it was to no avail. Cole looked over the smudged faces of a dozen or so men who had worked so hard to stop the inevitable, all staring dismally at the blazing fire.

"You should find your wife," Raine said. "I'll go grab Rafe, so he can take a look at your arm." He walked toward the house.

Cole turned around and spotted the man Clay had introduced as Doc Knight. The doc was covered in grime from his assistance in the line. He removed his jacket and picked up his doctorin' bag before leading Rafe, who was still carrying Carson, inside the house. Cole had only met the man briefly, between jigs, but was impressed now by his dedication to his profession.

It seemed the bunkhouse had sustained minimal damage and appeared mostly intact, if not for the scorched boardwalk and railings. Looking around the yard it appeared as though the barn had taken the brunt of the damage.

Cole scanned the dying crowd for Abby. He found her sitting on the steps at the back of the house, elbows on her knees with her clenched fists supporting her chin. Her faced was smudged and her hair was covered in black soot.

Cole pulled himself up and walked toward her. Her hair was in total disarray and as he got closer he saw that some of the falling strands had been singed at the end. Another of her dresses sacrificed, she sat silently, staring at the destruction before her, a single tear rolling down her soot stained cheek.

Before Cole could reach her, Rafe walked straight toward him and pulled him into a firm embrace. "You are a fool if I ever saw one, Charcoal." Rafe pushed him away. "I'm glad you walked out of there or I would have had to come in and get ya."

"How's Carson?"

"Pretty bad. We'll know more in the morning. The doc is with him now. Speaking of which, let me see that arm."

Damn Raine.

"It's nothing."

"Quit being such a baby and let me have a look," his older brother taunted.

Rafe turned him toward the light from the lanterns still lit above the dancing platform and pulled his arm up for inspection. Angry blisters had appeared and the reddened skin still felt like it was on fire.

"Found it." Raine came from around the front of the house and handed Rafe a jar of salve, but held the roll of stripped cloth until Rafe needed it.

Rafe opened the jar, which smelled of balsam pine, and spread a healthy amount of the sticky poultice over the burned area of Cole's arm. Then, he took the rolled bandage from Raine and wrapped it over the wound.

Within just a few seconds, the sting of his burns started to soothe.

"Guess all that training from med school comes in handy, after all," Raine teased.

When Rafe was left at the altar a few years back, he left Harvard Medical School to become a Bounty Hunter and between his experience with the Pawnee and Raine's tutelage with a gun, he'd become the most sought after in the western territories.

"Naw, just something I learned from the Indians," Rafe countered.

They all laughed.

Cole looked at his brothers and realized, for the first time in a very long time, that his family meant everything to him. He had been blessed growing up in a house filled with continuous noise and laughter. He and his siblings had all been very close and had always been there for each other. Tonight was no different. He pulled Rafe into a firm embrace. Raine joined them.

"Levi and Tag will be upset they missed all the fun." Rafe's white teeth contrasted starkly with the black smudges covering his lips and face. Cole and Raine both laughed. The twins had been fascinated with fire since they were little and had caused more than their fair share of incidents needing water buckets and lines of men to help.

Cole missed having his whole family together. He'd missed the last Christmas at the Redbourne Ranch when William had visited from England with his new baby. He hadn't wanted to see the disappointment in everyone's faces or the pity he'd been sure he'd see. So, he'd stayed away.

He looked back at the steps. Abby was gone.

"Thank you for your help, gentlemen." Clay worked his way through everyone who'd labored so hard, shaking each of their hands. When he reached Cole and his brothers, he extended his hand to Rafe.

"I don't believe we've met, but by the build of you, you must be related to these boys."

"Rafe Redbourne, sir." Rafe took his hand with a solid grip.

"Ah, the Bounty Hunter," Clay surmised, grasping Rafe's hand heartily.

Rafe glanced at Cole and Raine with a disconcerted look on his face.

"Levi," Raine said matter-of-factly.

That was enough. Rafe relaxed.

"I'm Clay McCallister. You and Raine here are both welcome to stay in the bunkhouse if you'd like for as long as you need. The fire only just reached the porch and we got it out pretty quick. There are some extra bunks in there and Martha makes a great breakfast."

"Thank you, sir," Rafe said and then as an afterthought added, "I'm sorry about the barn."

"Me, too! Aw, well, everyone is safe and the animals all got out in time. But, maybe if I have you boys staying around for a while, we can get it rebuilt quickly." Clay winked at Cole.

Cole found a new appreciation for Clay. In the midst of so much destruction, he didn't let them take away his humor

"Clay, have you found any...little black cloths lying around?" Raine asked.

"Not yet. It's too dark outside to see anything now. We'll probably find it in the morning."

"Black cloth?" Rafe queried.

Clay opened his mouth to begin explaining, but Raine stepped in.

"I'll tell you all about it little brother. Come with me." Raine nodded his goodnight and put a guiding hand on Rafe's back and led him toward the bunkhouse.

They turned around. "See you in the morning, Charcoal." Rafe's voice was higher than usual and the words were annunciated just so. When another grin broke through and Raine threw his head back and laughed, Cole suspected that their sudden whimsical mockery had something to do with the fact that this was, for all intents and purposes, his belated wedding night. He groaned.

"Goodnight." Every muscle in Cole's body ached. He was exhausted, but his mind would not stop racing. What would Abby expect of him tonight?

Why am I staying away from her again?

Cole sat down on the step Abby had occupied not minutes before and rested his forearms on his thighs. He had seen many wonderful and productive marriages in his family—his mother and father, Raine and Sarah, Ethan and Grace. All of his married siblings were happy with their mates and very much in love. Not to say they hadn't had their fair share of troubles, heartbreak, and adventure. But, somehow, they'd made a life together that rivaled the best of them.

Cole didn't want to screw it up. He felt alive for the first time in a long time and it was all because of the little spitfire who'd given him a new thirst for life. Abby. He couldn't lose her. He'd discovered in a very short time that she was unique. Special. And he wanted to do right by her. He'd been lost for so long and had hurt a lot of people. He wanted to earn her trust and her love before consummating what God already recognized.

Don't blow it, Redbourne.

"Just how many of you are there?" Jenna pulled him from his thoughts. She had appeared out of nowhere, every hair in place and not a smudge on her. However, the bottom of her dress was muddy and a piece of straw protruded from the hem.

"Seven. Why does everyone keep asking that?"

"Because more of you keep showing up." She laughed and took a step closer to him.

He looked at the window to the room he would share with

Abby. A light was burning. Shadows flickered across the curtains. Abby was already inside. His pulse quickened. He told himself it was just a physical response to the events of the day and the thought of lying his tired body down on a nice comfortable bed.

"Goodnight, Miss Jenna." He tipped his hat and walked toward the house, Abby consuming his thoughts. He reminded himself he wasn't worthy to have any emotional connection with her. Not yet. He hadn't courted her or earned her trust. They knew nothing of one another and he would not start his life with her with resentment or regrets.

He walked into the house and down the short corridor to their bedroom. His hand rested on the knob for a moment before nudging the door open.

Abby had wanted to jump from the stairs and rush into Cole's arms the moment she'd seen that he was all right, but when he'd stopped to talk to his brothers, she'd lost her nerve and had retreated into the house. To their bedroom.

Abby had been kissed before. Twice. But why she was thinking about it now, in the midst of what they'd just lost, astounded her. She sat on her hope chest, legs crossed, leaning backward heavily into the footboard of the bed.

"Fire's out," Abby heard a man yell from across the yard.

Cole would be coming in at any moment. Her body protested when she jumped up and grabbed the large pitcher from the table. Cool water would feel nice against her heated skin and maybe she could remove some of the grime from her face before he came in to retire for the night.

Pumping the water from the kitchen sink brought vivid, but distant memories to her recollection. She and Alaric had been no more than children when they'd fallen in love—if that's what it had been. Five years seemed another lifetime, but she would never forget the sweet sensation his first kiss had imprinted on her heart. It was hard to believe he was gone.

Jeremiah Carson had kissed her too, but it hadn't been the same. He'd crushed her against a large maple tree just outside of town and had greedily bruised her mouth with violent kisses. It hadn't been enjoyable in the least and she had been thankful when the Spencer boys had seen them and Benjamin pulled him away.

Thoughts of Cole invaded her memories. She raised her hand to her mouth, her fingers caressing the exact spot where his lips had brushed across hers at their wedding. They still tingled at the thought. Looking through the kitchen window, she smiled at the lock of hair that fell across his forehead as he walked toward the house. Kissing Cole would definitely be different. Anticipation fluttered in her belly like fireflies in the night.

She hurried back to their room, spilling a little water on the floor, and placed the pitcher back on the table next to the empty basin. Her fingers had just curled around the drying cloth hanging from a post in the wall, when the click of her door knob sent her spinning and she whirled around to face her future.

All at once their bedroom closed in around her. Cole's presence was everywhere all at once. The slow creaking sound of the wood on rusting hinges heightened her anticipation and when the door opened completely, he took his first step inside the room. Abby felt her knees go weak.

Cole's large masculine form framed the doorway. The only sounds she could hear now were the echo of his worn leather boots on the hard wooden floor and the delicious pounding of her heart. His face, soot stained and weary, had been carved to perfection with deep contours and planes that defined his chiseled features. The browned bare skin of his chest glimmered with sweat in the lantern's light.

She'd almost forgotten he had lied to her about his reasons for coming to Silver Falls. Almost.

He tossed his hat onto the bed and started toward her. He ran his fingers through his still damp hair, stopping mere inches

away. Abby could all but taste the sweat emanating from his
taut body.

"Fire's out," he rasped, his voice husky and dry as he
reached up to touch her face. "You look tired."

The feel of his fingers along her jawline sent tingles to the
pit of her belly. She looked up at him and could see the
exhaustion in his eyes. This stranger, now very much a part of
her life, had worked hard to help extinguish the fire that had
threatened the barn, the bunkhouse, and the corral. She was
grateful to him and his brothers.

"So do you."

He smiled and dropped his hand to his side, but did not
take his eyes off of her.

Now, she decided, would not be the best time to bring up
her concerns about his reasons for being in Silver Falls.

"Thank you," she said in its place, "for helping with the
fire. We've had a busy couple of days." She turned her back to
him and grasped ahold of the handle on the water pitcher. She
hoped he couldn't see how her hands shook as she poured him
a tall glass.

"Thank you."

His eyes crinkled at the edges in an attempted smile and his
normally dark brown eyes melted into black. Her eyes were
drawn to the bandages encompassing a good portion of his left
arm and hand. She was grateful he'd walked out of that barn
alive. She hadn't known he'd gone inside until Doc Knight had
passed her as he ran to retrieve his bag from his carriage. She'd
sat on the steps, staring at what she'd lost, grateful for what she
hadn't.

When Cole caught her stare, he moved to the far side of
the bedroom and sat down in the oversized chair her father had
moved to their room, and removed his boots. He pulled his
legs onto the footstool with some effort, then leaned back and
closed his eyes.

"You should get out of that dress," he spoke, his lids
remaining closed. "I won't watch. I promise." His tone was
even, but Abby saw the corners of his mouth twitch and self-

consciously she looked down at her purple dress, wet and ruined.

Covered in soot and laced with mud, she knew she didn't exactly look the part of a new bride. Maybe she never would. She just wasn't fit to be a lady. Pants were more practical and comfortable, especially for the kind of work she did every day.

Wearing nice dresses and pretty things had never been important to her, but she realized that when Cole had agreed to this marriage, he'd had no idea just how far from a lady she really was.

At the last thought, she snorted.

Her fingers shook as she reached for the fastenings at the back of the new dress. Another reason she hated women's clothing. Frustrated that she was unable to reach all of the fancy buttons, she thought of calling Martha, but quickly decided against it. She dropped her hands in exasperation and sat on the edge of the bed with her back toward Cole.

"Cole?" she inquired.

"Hmmm?" was his tired response.

She hated to bother him, but she did not want to sleep in the filthy and uncomfortable dress. "Would you mind helping me? Please?" she added for good measure.

Abby looked over her shoulder to see Cole open one eye first and then the other. He didn't move. She waited.

In one swift movement Cole joined her on the bed, sitting behind her. The touch of his fingertips against the back of her neck sent shivers dancing through her body.

She'd lost hope a long time ago of ever getting married. But here she was, in her bedroom, inches away from her husband. She bit her lip. Her mother and father had been so happy together. Clay McCallister had loved Clara *because* of her differences and as Cole touched her, his breath hot against her skin, she realized her hope for sharing her life with a man who would love *her* had returned.

Tonight, however, she wasn't sure what to expect.

Fool girl, she thought to herself. *Cole married you for the ranch, not out of some silly notion of love at first sight.*

The idea pained her a little, but she hoped that could change, with time.

"Where are your brothers?" she asked, forcing herself to focus.

"They're staying in the bunkhouse tonight." His voice cracked.

Abby leaned forward and reached for the empty glass he'd returned to the washstand. Her dress slid off her shoulders a little, taking the strap of her chemise with it. She caught the material at her bosom, and clasped it tight in front of her before it exposed anything more.

One moment Cole was next to her on the bed and the next he was stumbling over his boots, scrambling for his footing.

Amused, Abby handed him a newly filled glass.

"Thank you," he croaked.

The heat in his eyes enveloped her and she managed a slight smile. He drank the contents of the glass without a breath and handed it back to her.

"You should get some sleep." Abby pointed to the bed and felt the blush creep into her cheeks.

Cole nodded, but returned to the chair, pulling his feet back up onto the footstool.

Abby didn't know whether to feel relieved or rejected.

Time.

That was what they both needed. She walked over to the old Victorian wardrobe that had graced this room since she was a child, and opened the cabinet doors, hiding herself behind them. She removed the dress and allowed it to fall to the floor, kicking it aside.

Abby opened the top drawer to the right of the closet. Lying on top of her old, very plain and unappealing underthings was a thin white night shift with pink rosebuds adorning the severely scooped neckline. The flimsy robe that matched it hung on the open door of the closet. She smiled. *Martha.*

Once she donned the simple garment, she peeked around the door separating them. Somehow, the emptiness she thought she'd feel without her hope of seeing Alaric again, of being *his* bride, didn't emerge and she stole a quick look at the man resting in the chair. His uninjured arm dangled over the side and his body slouched awkwardly. His even breathing told her sleep had finally claimed him.

Cole shifted his position. A chair was no place for a man to sleep on what should be his wedding night. She padded her way to the side of the bed next to the chair and boldly raised her hand toward his face. She gingerly caressed his swollen and bruised jaw, her finger outlining the chiseled flesh of his features. A twinge of guilt swept through her as she recalled slapping him across the face yesterday.

It seemed like such a long time ago. It was hard to believe he had only been a part of her life for little more than a day. She liked having him around, enjoyed his company. She knew there must be some explanation to why he'd lied to her about coming here to start a ranch, but decided her questions could wait until morning. For now, after the night they'd had, he deserved some sleep.

The room was chilly. She reached for the spare blanket on the end of the bed and draped it up and over her husband's sleeping form, then turned back to the bed. She caught a glimpse of herself in the small intricately carved mirror just above the washstand. She stood back and looked at her reflection.

She had never worn anything so exquisite as the dainty night shift and the thin material felt heavenly against her bare skin. Just before she blew out the lantern and slipped into the large oak bed, she thought she heard a low groan come from the chair.

"Goodnight," she whispered into the darkness and pulled the heavy patchwork quilt up over her.

CHAPTER FIFTEEN

The tinny clank of metal beating against metal rang in Abby's ears and she awoke with a start and bolted upright, pulling the quilt up just under her chin. Cole was already standing at the window, looking out at the commotion. The moonlight played with the shadows on his bare back and shoulders and Abby watched in fascination as the light danced with his muscles as they moved.

Without turning to look at her, Cole motioned for her to join him at the window. How he'd known she was awake, she didn't know.

"It's a shivaree," he stated with a smile.

Abby looked out the window and saw a collection of ranch hands, townsfolk, and family all banging pots and pans together and singing. Raine, Rafe, and her father were at the forefront of the crowd, smiling and laughing while they sang.

"What's a shivaree?" she asked, her eyes widening in apprehension.

"What's a...? Don't tell me you've never..." Cole's voice trailed and he stared at her with an amused smirk lining his moonlit face. "It's just a bunch of friends and family wishing us well in our marriage. It's tradition." He tilted his head, his eyes meeting hers.

They locked.

Abby's breath caught in her chest and her knees threatened to give way.

"Are you ready to greet them? Although," Cole hesitated as

he glanced over her appraisingly. "You may want to put on something a little more...appropriate for company," he said with an appreciative nod, meeting her eyes again with gentle teasing.

Greet them? Abby snapped her head back to the window, her eyes searching the crowd that had gathered there. A strange feeling washed over her and somehow she knew Cole was watching her. She turned to him, eyes wide. The smile that danced in his eyes gave her courage and Abby slipped on her house slippers and donned her father's old coat.

"Will this do?" She asked, pulling the coat tightly around her.

Cole cleared his throat before bending in a gentlemanly bow. "For me, absolutely, but for them you might consider pants."

Heat rose once again to her face and she quickly pulled on her favorite riding trousers.

Cole extended his hand to her, his eyes never leaving hers. His dimpled smile weakened her already wobbly knees. "Come, wife. Let's go finish this party."

Together, hand in hand, they ran to the front door. Cole hesitated, but only for a moment before he tugged it open wide.

Whoops and hollers sounded from all over the yard as the well-wishing group moved around front to meet them. A dozen or so women were interspersed between the men and as Abby looked over their faces, she realized that despite the turmoil and devastation that had taken place tonight, family and friends could not be deterred from celebrating the wondrous gift of life and new beginnings.

Abby hugged the coat a little closer around her and leaned back into Cole. His hand rested at the small of her back and together they walked down the porch steps.

When they reached the bottom of the stairs, Cole moved into a group of men and received a hearty clap on the back by each of his brothers, her father, and several of the ranch hands.

Abby was ushered into a sparse group of women, all of them bidding her well and offering advice. Martha stepped into the middle and hugged her tight. Then, she turned, expecting to see Lily any moment, but she was not among the well-wishers. Abby thought it odd. She'd been so excited and so taken with Raine, she'd have thought Lily would have been on the front line alongside the others.

Abby tried to remember the last time she'd seen her tonight. She'd been with the new reverend. She hoped her friend was okay and that her dad was not having another episode. Worried a little, she peeked between the heads of several women to see Cole's tired, but smiling face staring back at her.

Abby couldn't sleep. She'd changed positions several times in the last few minutes, but could not seem to get comfortable. With her arm coiled around her pillow and her legs bent slightly at the knee, she lay on her side and watched Cole as he slept in her bed. *Our bed,* she corrected in her mind. He was so close to the far edge she was sure he would fall off at the slightest movement.

When they had finally returned to their room in the wee hours of the morning, after all their friends had departed, he'd closed the door behind them and stepped toward her. The harsh pounding of her heart, even now, echoed in her ears. His hand had cupped her cheek, his thumb brushing the area just below her eye.

"Goodnight, my little spitfire," he'd said before dropping his warm hand from her face.

She'd been inexplicably pleased when he'd forgone the chair and had climbed into the bed, under her patchwork quilt. She hadn't dared breathe as she'd climbed in next to him.

Abby was exhausted, but could not stop her mind from turning as it raced with questions. She propped herself up onto one elbow. This man who shared her bed was still a stranger to her. Unwittingly, she reached a hand toward him, stopping mere inches from his face.

She was drawn to him without doubt. However, she was wary to give her heart to a man who may never return her love. Why had Cole agreed to marry her? What brought him into her life? What secrets kept him distant? Why did he lie about coming to Silver Falls to start his own ranch?

Accepting she would not get her answers tonight, she quietly folded the blankets away from her and slipped off the bed, careful not to wake Cole. She glanced at his sleeping form, illuminated in the moonlight. Her limbs quivered at the sight of him. Her breath came up short and her stomach tightened when a soft moan escaped him. His features were more relaxed than she had ever seen them and she was taken in by his extraordinarily handsome face and sculpted arms.

There was a lot of work to do on the ranch tomorrow, especially now as they would have to consider the best way to go about rebuilding. She knew she should get some sleep, but it eluded her.

After the excitement of the shivaree, Abby had half expected Cole to lie down next to her and pull her into his arms. The disappointment she'd felt, still surprised her. She was quite inexperienced in such matters and wondered how her feelings of wanting to be close to him, to touch him, had grown so quickly.

The deal was to share the ranch, not your heart, she reminded herself. Being the best had always been important to her. She could ride and shoot better than any man she'd ever met...including her father, but when it came to female things with all the frills and feelings and such, she was at a loss. She didn't like how it felt one bit.

Shaking her head, she grabbed her new riding trousers from the floor next to the bed and rummaged through her wardrobe looking for a shirt.

Cole moved. She froze.

After a few moments she turned, squinting into the moonlight. His eyes were closed and his breaths still moved his chest in even rhythm. She exhaled long and slow. As she turned back toward the wardrobe, she caught glimpse of one of Cole's shirts lying across the chest across the room. She grabbed it, stealing one last look at her sleeping husband, and sneaked from the room.

Cole guessed Abby couldn't sleep any better than he could. She had been tossing and turning for quite some time, until now.

She quietly pulled the covers from her feet and swung her legs around the opposite side of the bed. Cole watched her through heavy lidded lashes as she pulled her jacket from the wardrobe. He was curious as to where she would be going in the middle of the night.

When Abby grabbed his shirt from the chest across the room before leaving, he could not stop the corners of his mouth from turning upward. Once the sound of her boots scuffing the floor had faded completely, he arose.

Restlessness had been his constant companion throughout the night and the thought of the woman in the bed next to him, with her long fiery blond tresses and full inviting lips, had made him more uncomfortable than he'd been in a long time. It hadn't helped that she was his wife, legally anyway. "Not yet, Redbourne," he'd told himself firmly.

Cole donned his boots and picked up the short leather coat he'd flung across the oversized chair and shoved his arms into it as he left the room.

Crisp cool air danced around Cole's face as he stepped onto the front porch. When Abby emerged from the stables astride a horse, Cole moved with surprising stealth over the rocky terrain to where Maverick had been tethered. He slid onto the horse's bare back and freed the leather straps. The stallion nickered quietly in approval.

"Where's she off to, boy?" Cole asked as he hunkered down near the horse's neck.

Being the youngest of seven brothers, Cole had learned the importance of knowing when and how to stay out of sight. He looked up into the darkened sky. The moon would allow ample light for his pursuit, yet the shadows of the night would still obscure him from her sight. He hoped.

"Okay, Mrs. Redbourne, let's see what you're up to."

A cold chill blew through Abby's hair, but she was determined and focused on riding. She wanted to feel the wind on her face and hoped the exercise would rid her of the thoughts of self-doubt and indecision that refused to yield.

The stable was quiet. Abby was grateful her tack had not been in the barn when it went up in flames. The idea of breaking in a new saddle was not a pleasurable thought.

"Who's there?" Marty, one of Cole's drovers, must have been lucky enough to take early watch. He held his rifle shoulder high ready to shoot.

"It's just me, Marty. Abby." She'd met the man earlier, when she'd stopped by to look over the new herd before dressing for the party.

He lowered his gun. "Abby? What are you doing up so early?"

"Couldn't sleep. Just wanted to go for a little ride."

"I don't know if that's such a good idea, with all that trouble last night. Are you sure you don't want to just head to the kitchen for a warm cup of milk or something?" His head cocked slightly to the side, one eye nearly closed.

Abby laughed. "I'll be fine, Marty. Back before you know it."

"I don't know ma'am. The boss'll have my hide."

She ignored his last statement and climbed the corral fence.

As Abby looked out over the horses, she realized how much she missed Bella. The thought of choosing another horse pulled at her as if she were betraying an old friend. She walked into the stable and down the row of stalls, full to capacity.

Chester nudged her arm with his nose.

"You're not ready yet, my new friend." She rubbed his nose and laid her face against his.

She lit a small lantern and through the small square window on the opposite side of the stable, she could see Old Jack, an aging grey Arabian, who nickered quietly in the paddock he now reluctantly shared with two paint geldings. Abby grabbed her tack and walked out to the paddock gate.

"Come on, Jack. Wanna go for a ride?" Abby knew her father would never approve. She draped her tack over the fence.

Jack had been one of his most prized studs. He had been a part of the SilverHawk's first season of breeding, but had recently been kicked in the face by a reluctant mare, which had made him a little skittish of mounting. Clay was planning to reintroduce him slowly. Abby felt sorry for the stallion. He had not been allowed out for quite some time and she thought he could use the exercise.

Abby looked at the healed skin on the Arabian's nose. She rubbed his neck and muzzle. "You look great Jack." She set down the lantern and picked up her tack.

The wind was a welcome companion as it caressed Abby's skin. Her hair wrestled with the breeze, flowing carelessly behind her. The moon had perched itself high in the sky, offering light to her path. She placed a low brimmed hat on her head, tucking her hair underneath, and bundled herself closer into the woolen jacket she'd brought with her.

Astride the horse and moving slowly through the meadow, Abby allowed her tortuous thoughts to re-emerge. She'd done it, all right. She'd won the wager with her father and the right to stay on the ranch, but at what cost? She married a man she just met, but she hadn't counted on the sight of him turning her insides to mush or his touch to ignite foreign flames within her.

Abby was so caught up in her thoughts she barely noticed that she had crossed onto the Johansson property. She'd ridden here many times with Alaric and recognized the area, even in the darkness. A small dell dipped into a beautifully hidden meadow just beyond the jutted rock at the brim of a cluster of trees.

Tall pines and aspens, normally black against the horizon, were now illuminated in rich orange and yellow hues from a fire. Men's voices and raucous laughter carried on the wind. She was very curious about her new neighbors. No one seemed to know anything about them and she wondered what they were doing at this time of night. She urged Jack forward.

Abby darted a glance behind her, unable to shake the feeling she was being watched. Squinting into the blackness of the direction she came, she waited. Silence. She looked forward again, inching Old Jack toward the glowing valley.

What am I doing? The thought crossed Abby's mind with a start. She was alone and it was the middle of the night. Pulling Old Jack's reins about, she turned for home. When the Redbourne name carried on the wind to her ears, she froze. Quietly, as if not to disturb even the breeze, Abby twisted in her seat back toward the voices. Her choices battled within her mind as she decided between turning home and soothing her curiosity.

Curiosity won.

Abby dismounted near one of the larger trees at the front of a dense copse. She tied the aging grey stallion to a lower hanging branch. Satisfied Old Jack was out of sight, she tugged on the lead to make sure he would not get loose. She crouched down, inching her way across the slope that would soon dip into the fire-lit camp.

This girl is trouble, Cole thought as he watched Abby moving closer to a mangy group of cowpokes sitting around a fire on *his* land. Most ranchers would be sleeping at this hour and a group of men laughing and drinking around a fire on land they didn't own could only mean trouble. Off to the right of the camp Cole spotted a temporary corral filled with a dozen or more horses.

Rustlers. Cole had seen his share of horse thieves to know these men were up to no good. From their lack of concealment, he guessed they were not aware anyone had claimed the property.

He had ridden along the ridge of a rocky hillside, keeping Abby in sight as he'd followed her. At this angle he could see straight down into the rowdy camp. But Abby would have no idea what she'd stumbled into until it was too late. Her curiosity would be the death of him.

A heavily mustached man lazily sat guard with a rifle resting at his feet just a few feet from Abby. She hadn't seen him and was moving closer to the crest of the malevolent encampment.

"Trouble all right," he grumbled aloud under his breath.

When they'd crossed over onto his land he had been amused at her apparent familiarity with the property. Now, his amusement was gone. There were vagrants trespassing on his property and Abby had dismounted and was heading straight for them on foot.

Cole was irritated he'd left his gun belt at the house. His brothers would be disappointed he had not been prepared for such a situation, especially at night in unfamiliar territory. He cursed himself as he dismounted and paced his way down the hillside toward an unsuspecting Abby.

Thinking only of her safety, Cole was determined to get back to the ranch undetected, with Abby in tow. He would talk with his brothers and together the three of them would return to check out the band of men who'd gathered here. He edged his way toward the grassy knoll where Abby crouched, hidden from the group.

He had a clear view of the men in the camp. There was

something about one of them, something vaguely familiar, that stopped his progress. Cole couldn't quite place it.

He rested down on his haunches, his arms leaning on his thighs as he scanned the camp more closely. This time he made sure to get a good look at each of the men. There were five. However, the one he wanted to see most eluded him. He was shorter than the rest. Smaller. It was difficult to see the man's face. His hat rode down about his eyes and his heavy woolen jacket was pulled up tight around his neck. There was almost something feminine about the way he moved. Cole thought maybe he would recognize his voice, but from this distance he could not make out what they were saying.

Cole fixed his eyes on the guard who had now seen Abby and was slowly moving toward her. He maneuvered through a small coppice of aspens. By the time the guard reached out for Abby's neck, Cole stood directly behind him.

"Not before I've had the chance to strangle her, friend," Cole whispered near the man's ear. He turned a surprised look at Cole who planted a determined fist into the large oaf's face. The man's eyes rolled back into his head.

One punch, Cole thought with pride. *Now William would be proud of that.*

Cole grabbed the man's arm to stop him from falling openly into Abby. She would scream for sure, alerting the others that something was amiss. He took the man's weight against his own and gently laid him on the soft covering the new spring grass provided.

As he turned back for Abby, Cole noted how the moonlight reflected against her hair, providing an almost halo like effect, while the fire enflamed her face with its display of scorching colors.

An angel with a devil's knack for trouble.

Voices carried to him from the camp below.

"Once McCallister sells out and our other little *problem* has been taken care of, it will all be ours." The voice was raspy and full of anticipation.

"What about Redbourne?" This voice was much higher.

Cole leaned a little closer at the mention of his name. He had only been in town for a few days. How did they know him? He didn't have long to ponder the question. He spotted a scrawny kid pacing back and forth on the other side of the ravine and returned to his purpose. By the determined look on the kid's face, he was fresh, taking his job at standing watch seriously. Cole did not want to test the boy's desire to fit in with the group by letting Abby get caught or worse, shot.

He approached Abby with the same stealth and precision with which he had apprehended the first guardsman. He reached out and clamped a hand over her mouth. She struggled, kicking against the hill. Her elbow connected with his ribs and while a low groan escaped his lips, his hold on her tightened. His balance thwarted, the couple tumbled sideways from their crouched position. Small granite pebbles fell in a sliding cascade below them.

Damn.

Abby, still within the confines of his arms, twisted and thrashed against his body. Without taking his hand from her mouth he pulled her head gently around so she could see him. Cole thought that once she'd seen his face she would be relieved, but the fear he saw in her eyes quickly turned to anger, then accusation.

At that moment Cole realized Abby had associated him with these strangers, these ruffians, these rustlers, and his patience left him.

Someone had to have heard them. He lifted his head enough to see the camp through an overgrown bush growing along the edge of the small valley. It was the only protection they would have from the ruffian's sights. Cole scanned the opposite side of the dell for the kid keeping watch, but could not see him. Abby kicked at him, causing a few stones to loosen and fall down the side of the cliff.

At once, Cole slammed his body over the top of hers until they were almost flush with the hill. Cole peered through the bush, assessing the damage the small noise had done. One of the men, with food dripping off his unkempt beard, had stopped and perked his head toward the sound. He wiped the pooling residue from his drink away from his chin with the whole of his arm and waved his other arm as if to silence the rest.

Cole didn't breathe. His hand remained steadfast over Abby's mouth. After a moment, she ceased her struggle and he looked down at her pressed beneath him. She was livid.

After a few minutes, the man returned to his food. Cole pulled back from Abby enough to allow her to breathe. He hoped the warning in his eyes would be enough to keep her quiet.

Realizing his hand still held her beautiful mouth captive, he retracted it as quickly as if he'd been seared with a white iron. Still, he placed a finger over his lips in a hushing gesture for good measure. She nodded. Satisfied she would not scream, he took her hand in his and started back down the incline.

Abby gasped, throwing a hand over her mouth at the sound. Cole followed Abby's eyes. The guard with the thick moustache was stirring. Cole squeezed her hand before releasing it. He lifted the man by his shirt collar and punched him in the face for good measure. Out cold.

"Go get your horse. I'll be right there," he whispered, almost inaudibly, as he headed up the mountain to retrieve Maverick.

CHAPTER SIXTEEN

A gun shot pierced the stillness of the night, leaving an eerie silence in its wake. Abby jerked her head toward the sound. Jack reared and snorted.

"Calm, boy," she soothed as she ran a hand over his shoulder. She unlatched her rifle from Jack's side and pulled it under her arm.

Where is he? She demanded in her mind as she quickly untied Jack from the tree branch, searching for some sign of Cole. Men's voices in the distance and the sound of restless horses carried on the wind. Still, she waited.

She twisted the riding glove she'd pulled from Jack's saddle bag and swatted it against her hand. Stomping her foot, she turned to mount the old stud when a lone rider charged down the mountain toward her. She took a step away to get a better look.

It was Cole.

He reached down as he passed and scooped her up onto his horse behind him, not breaking stride. Another shot echoed in the trees around her. A thin wiry branch splintered away from its base very close to her head. She looked up to see two men on foot, running in their direction, guns in hand.

Jack.

The horse was one of her father's most prized studs. She'd seen the collection of horses the men had corralled into the small round-up. These heavies were horse rustlers and now they would have Jack too.

Papa's gonna kill me.

She pulled her rifle into her hand and wrapped her arms securely around Cole's waist. "Turn around," she yelled to him.

"No," he shot back at her.

"We need to get Jack," she bellowed, gripping him even tighter as he picked up the pace.

Cole didn't say anything else, but pushed the horse back toward home.

Once they crossed onto McCallister land, Cole slowed his pace some, but still kept the horse at a good even tempo.

The excitement of the day was taking its toll on Abby and with little sleep, she was finding it difficult to keep herself upright on the horse without a saddle. She scooted herself forward on the horse's back, closed her eyes, and laid her face against the smooth angles of Cole's back and shoulders.

Cole finally stopped, but it was too soon to be home just yet.

"What's wrong?" Abby asked, shifting her weight forward again.

Despite Abby's weak attempts at protest, Cole grabbed a hold of her by the underarm and swung her in front of him. Her legs hung off the side of the horse. Both of his arms locked around her, cradling her, as he gathered and held fast to Maverick's reins.

Abby, too tired to be angry right now, rested her rifle on her lap and leaned into his shoulder. The safety she found in Cole's arms counteracted the intense emotions that had heightened her senses and she nestled a little closer into his fortified embrace. She closed her eyes, her head burrowing into the nook created by Cole's arm and shoulder. She fit perfectly.

Her reasons for being upset with her husband were becoming less clear.

Abby awoke to her name being called. Reluctantly, she

opened her eyes. Snuggled into the warmth Cole's chest provided, she was acutely aware of the sensations his nearness stirred within her. She tried to shove away from him, but the muscles in her arms would not cooperate. How she drifted off at the pace they'd been traveling escaped her.

They were home. Cole dismounted with her still in his arms. She closed her eyes once again and rested her head against the curve of his neck. He smelled of cedar and spice and a soft moan escaped her throat of its own accord.

He carried her into the house and into their bedroom. Abby tried to open her eyes, but they would not obey. She felt the warmth of the bed quilt being tucked all around her.

"We have to tell my father, Cole." Abby tried to focus on her words. She was so tired she was sure her words slurred. "Rustlers."

"I will," was his only reply.

Her eyes fluttered open briefly and closed again. He brushed a stray strand of hair from her forehead and tucked it behind her ear. She smiled. When she felt his weight leave her side, she felt an inexplicable void. She took a deep breath and all went quiet as she mused aloud, "I'm falling in love with my husband."

She smiled as sleep overtook her.

There was no time to ponder Abby's sleep induced confession. It was time for Cole to decide whether or not he trusted Clay McCallister. He'd already woken his brothers and they were at the stables prepping their horses. Nearly a quarter hour had passed while he'd stood in front of Clay's door, debating his next move. In his gut, he knew Clay was a good man, but his head still bickered for caution.

Rafe cawed. He had to hurry.

Cole knocked on Clay's door and was surprised when it opened immediately.

"I was wondering how long you was gonna stand out there." Clay scrubbed his jaw line with the back of his fingers. "Something on yer mind, son?"

"Rustlers, sir. Just over your property line a mile or so. With the Texas herd and all the new horses, I thought we best be cautious. My brothers are waiting outside for me now. We figure there's no need to wait for them to come to us. We're going to them."

"They comin' here?"

"Don't know."

"I'd ask how you know, but I'm afraid I wouldn't like the answer." Clay grabbed a rifle from the inside wall of his bedroom. "Well, let's go."

"Um, Mr. McCallister." Cole looked down at Clay in his dingy red winter underwear.

Clay followed his eyes. "Aw. What? You ain't never seen a man in his nothins before?"

He backed into his room, grumbling. After grabbing a pair of trousers from the large pile on the floor at the foot of his bed, he motioned for Cole to go on ahead.

"I just have to find my blamed hat."

Cole nodded and ran out the door. When he reached the corral, Raine handed him a lantern, already lit.

Rafe threw Maverick's reins at Cole. "Ready yet?" he asked with a raised eyebrow.

Cole mounted. He'd hitched Maverick with a saddle this time. Chasing rustlers was no time to ride bareback. The front door slammed open and a fully dressed Clay appeared, rifle in hand.

"While you boys are going after them, I'll get word out to the other ranches. If we know they're comin', they'll have a heck of a fight." Clay ran past them and into the bunkhouse where lights were already lit and ranch hands scrambling to get dressed.

Raine, Rafe, and Cole rode side by side through the darkness toward the marauder's camp. Rafe's Remington rifle sat easily in a holster across his back. Raine's Winchester rested at his side. All men carried two revolvers, one in each side strap, and Cole carried a double barreled shotgun across his lap.

Since Rafe was the closest thing to a lawman in town, Cole figured it was up to the Redbourne brothers to catch the small band of thieves. This would not be the first time they'd captured outlaws or recovered stolen horses together. It irked Cole that rustlers had set up camp on his land. He was sure that wouldn't go over very well when Clay found out.

The moment they reached Redbourne land, the men separated enough to cover both high and low ground. Rafe took the mountainside trail Cole had used when he'd followed Abby. Cole stayed on the main trail and Raine rode west of the area to scan the open meadows and glade areas. Each carried a lantern hooked to the metal loop at the front hitching of their saddle tack.

Cole was the first to arrive at the ridge. He looked down into an empty camp and closed his eyes in frustration. He looked up and spotted Rafe's lantern flashing a dull yellow glow through the mountainous wooded area. Before long, a small bouncing shimmer of light appeared to the west.

When the three of them pulled alongside one another, they sat on their horses at the top of the edge that overlooked the small dell where the rustler's camp had been.

"They knew we'd come back." Cole broke the silence.

Rafe pulled his horse to the right, Cole guessed in search of best trail down to the site. When he located the path on the far side, the other two followed.

Rafe was already poking at the ash and coals left behind from the fire when Cole dismounted.

"Can't track them 'til mornin'," Rafe said, throwing his poker stick on the ground.

"It's time to tell Clay the truth, Charcoal." Raine, still on horseback, pulled up next to his two brothers.

"He needs to know."

Cole's gut tightened.

"I was hoping to gain Clay's trust before telling him we own the land."

"*You* own the land," Raine corrected. "Maybe that will be a good selling point for his new son-in-law." Raine always tried to see a bright side.

"Were any of McCallister's herd taken? Cattle? Horses?" Rafe pulled himself back up onto his mount.

"There's no way to tell, tonight. Marty was standing guard at the corral, but most of the horses were taken out to the west pasture with the cattle."

Cole hadn't even thought about Clay's stock. He'd been so caught up in getting the thieves off his land he hadn't considered where the horses in the round pen had come from.

"There's not much we can do here until daylight. We should ride back and see if any others have been hit," Raine suggested.

On the ground, something flashed in the moonlight. Cole reached into the dirt and pulled out a long chain attached to a small oval, silver pendant. Cole brushed the dust off and turned it over. A one word inscription was carved onto the back.

"Querida," Cole whispered aloud.

It would be at least another hour before the sun peaked over the far mountain top. Cole needed to speak with Clay and he didn't think it should wait. After extensively searching the grounds, Cole could only guess he'd not returned yet from the other ranches. He led Maverick to the stable and hung the lantern on a low cross beam.

His mind filled with excuses for why he shouldn't be here. He removed the tack from the horse and, in a low grumble under his breath, rehearsed his next conversation with Clay.

"I own the Gnarled Oak and all the Johansson and Deardon lands. I only hired on here 'cause I thought you might be my best friend's killer." Cole laughed out loud. "That should go over well." He picked up his grooming kit and brushed Mav's coat.

"Alaric loved your daughter, sir" he continued his practice, "and while he was lying at the bottom of a ravine, near death, he made me swear to him that I would protect her." Cole shook his head. "I didn't know what he meant until tonight."

He lifted his head upward as if hoping for inspiration from above. He couldn't exactly tell Clay the whole truth. What would the man think if Cole admitted that in addition to his promise to keep her safe he'd had his own selfish reasons for marrying the man's daughter and they didn't involve running the SilverHawk?

It's different now, Cole thought to himself. He cleared his throat.

"Mr. McCallister," he began again, speaking into the air. "Clay, your daughter makes me feel more alive than I have in a year and I find myself a changed man. For the first time in a very long time, I want to be there for someone else." He stopped brushing for a moment and rested his hand against Maverick's back. "She makes me feel ten feet tall when I'm with her and I want you to know I have the means to take care of her, to provide her with a good life. In fact, I own--"

"Personally, I like that one."

Cole whipped his head around to see Raine standing with his back against the stall door, his arms folded across his chest and his hat riding low over his eyes. How had he not heard Raine come in?

"How long have you been standing there?" Cole groaned irritably.

"Long enough, little brother. Long enough."

Cole put down the brush and moved to Maverick's front hooves. He picked up one foot and began pulling the mud out from inside the shoe.

"What do you want Raine? What?" He threw down Mav's foot and moved to the other.

"You know what this will look like." Raine spoke calmly,

but his serious undertones were laced with sincere concern.

"I know." Cole threw a large clump of mud to the floor. "Clay will wonder why it is that someone wealthy enough to own the Johansson estate would work on his ranch for a foreman's wage. He'll think we were trying to sabotage him." He dropped Maverick's foot.

"That's just it, Charcoal. First, the wagon, then the fire, and now horse thieves? This is no coincidence. There's more going on here than just trying to rustle horses or cattle from McCallister's land."

"It's the land. Somebody wants it real bad." Cole grunted the words, scraping another clump of mud and straw from Maverick's hoof.

"Why do they want it?" Raine's leg perched on the bottom board of the stall. "I don't think it's the silver mine they're after. They wouldn't need McCallister's land to get there."

"I don't know." Cole dropped Mavericks foot. "Don't you think I have been asking myself the same questions all night?" He pulled off his gloves and shoved them into his saddle pack along with the hoof brush and pick.

"Okay, now don't go gettin' all riled up."

"They shot at Abby, Raine. At my wife."

"We need to talk to Clay. There has to be more he's not telling us," Raine suggested.

Cole checked the water trough in Mav's stall. It was full. "I don't think he's back yet."

"Then, we'll wait."

Early Sunday Morning

The front door squeaked on its hinges as Cole gently pushed it open. The last thing he wanted to do was to wake Abby or Martha or anyone else who may be living in the house. Since he was unfamiliar with the staff, he decided to be discrete.

He took a step inside.

Clomp.

In the quiet of the morning, his heavy boots echoed and each step was distinctly pronounced. He stopped and lifted his foot to remove the boot. With a firm tug, it came loose in his hand. Then, the other. This was the first time he could remember his boots coming off so easily.

Triumphant, he started again for their bedroom, but his sock covered foot caught the edge of the rug and his entire six-foot-two frame came crashing to the ground in a loud thud. He lifted his head in attempt to assess the damage, but when nothing stirred, he dropped his head back to the floor and laid there for a while, closing his eyes.

When he opened them again he was staring down the barrels of a shotgun.

"Stand up slowly and state your business here." The woman's voice was much older than Abby's and woven with apprehension.

Cole shifted to his side to glimpse the woman. The gun cocked. He could not make out her face as the only light in the room was coming from the kitchen, making her a silhouette in the darkness.

"Cole Redbourne, ma'am."

"Everything okay, Martha?" Clay came running from the kitchen with a lantern. "We thought we heard somethin'."

The woman pulled her head away from the gun site and lowered the gun to her hip. She took the lantern with the other hand and held it up close to Cole, who shifted uncomfortably.

"Well, what ya doin' on the floor out here?" Martha spoke, apprehension dripping with each word. He'd met her only briefly between dances last night, but had liked her right away.

He sat up and took hold of Clay's extended hand.

"Stand yerself up there and come into the kitchen so I can get a better look at ya," Martha coerced.

"Yes, ma'am."

He looked toward his bedroom door. A sliver of light from the kitchen spilled across the hallway.

"She'll be up soon enough," Clay told him. The older man placed a reaffirming hand on Cole's shoulder and led him to the kitchen.

The fragrant smell of sausage wafted through the air and Cole's stomach grumbled. He stepped into the fire-lit kitchen where Rafe, Raine, and Caleb already sat at the food covered table.

"Where did ya'll come from? I left my kitchen just moments ago, huntin' me an intruder, and here I come back and got three more of 'em sitting at my table." Martha grinned. She handed Cole a plate.

Eggs, sausage, flapjacks, corn muffins, and preserves all greeted him. Cole wondered if every morning would welcome him with such a delectable meal or if it was only reserved for Sundays.

The sun filtered in through the small window just above the sink and added light to the lantern lit room. The older woman was clearly visible now. Her graying hair was pulled tightly into a bun at the top of her head and her plain blue dress was covered by a work apron with thick rectangular pockets on the front. She set the shotgun in a rack at the corner of the kitchen and turned back around, holding a large plate of skillet fried potatoes.

Cole set his boots on the floor near the kitchen door and removed his hat. His hair fell lightly onto his forehead and he pushed the strands back away from his face with a short, concise sweep of the hand.

Martha smiled. Her eyes roamed the length of him. Cole felt heat rise in his neck at her appraisal.

"I'd bet you and your brothers here would be fearsome in a barn raisin'."

"Yes, ma'am. We've been known to win a few."

"Especially with all seven of us," Raine piped in between bites.

"Martha, let the boy alone." While Clay's voice came out hard, Cole was taken aback when his new father-in-law winked at her. "We have business to discuss." There was something playful in Clay's tone. If Cole hadn't been staring at the man, he would have missed the exchange between the two.

Martha blushed.

"Thank you for breakfast, Mrs. McCallister," Cole said, not seeing the resemblance between Abby and the woman.

Clay nearly choked on the mouthful of eggs he'd just put into his mouth. Cole looked from him to Martha, who dipped her head and brought her fist up to her mouth in attempt to hide her sudden giggle.

"She's not the missus." Caleb spoke for the first time since Cole had entered the kitchen. His tone mocking. "She's the help."

Martha's smile fell.

"Yes, well, speaking of that, I'd better go collect the eggs. Those chickens get a might sore if I don't get 'em early." She wiped her hands on her apron and excused herself to the barn.

"Caleb," Clay said, turning a hard look on the hired-hand, "I didn't get out to the Carson place yet this morning. Rustlers aren't going to try anything with daylight coming. Why don't you ride out and tell Zed what's happened. And you can tell him to come retrieve his boy too." It looked as if he were working really hard to keep himself composed.

"But—" Caleb started, his mouth full of food.

"Now!" Clay boomed, all playfulness gone from his voice.

Caleb stood and grabbed a handful of bacon and a slice of cornbread before begrudgingly pushing away from the table.

The door slammed shut behind him and Clay turned back to those at the table.

"I'm sorry. I just assumed that..." Cole didn't know what to say. He'd seen his own parents playful teasing and meaningful glances and assumed the simple exchange implied they were together.

"Don't fret yourself over it son. Martha is a good woman. She's been here since before my Clara passed on."

"I'm sorry," Cole repeated.

"Goin' on six years now we've been without her. 'Fraid that's why Abby's been so bent on sticking around here. She's just like her mother. Clara loved this place and those horses. Bella, the mare you boys put down, was her favorite."

That certainly explained a lot.

Cole sat down next to Rafe and started to fill his plate with the wonderful delights covering the table. Nothing was better than home cooking.

"Max Grayson and Henry Campbell want to call a town council meeting," Clay informed those at the table.

"I'm not so sure involving the whole town is wise just yet." Although the thought had struck Cole, it was Rafe who was the first to voice it.

"Go on," Clay encouraged.

"We need to devise a plan that will allow us to involve the town when the time is right. If we let on too soon what we're planning, we may just tip off the wrong people and we'll never catch them."

"Caleb told us you almost sold the ranch a few years back," Raine said.

Cole hadn't heard about that and leaned in a little closer.

"Ah, yes. When Abby's mother died I felt like a part of me had gone with her. I was ready to sell the place." A fleeting sadness appeared in Clay's voice. "Offers came from all over, but the two most prominent were the Carson's and the Grayson's. If it weren't for Abby's determination to keep the place and her…persuasiveness, the SilverHawk would no longer be ours."

"Clay," Raine asked, "who would stand to gain the most if you did sell?"

"I guess that would depend on who I sold it to." The older man rubbed the graying stubble on his chin and stood. Cole remembered how large the man had seemed, blocking the doorway at the church after the wedding, and realized now that although Clay was probably twice his age, he was still in good form.

"What aren't you telling us, Clay?"

"What makes you think I'm not telling you something?" Clay narrowed his eyes.

"My gut," Cole stated matter-of-factly.

Clay studied Cole for a while before responding. "Levi did warn me about your gut. Remember when I told you about the man who came to my door wanting to buy the SilverHawk a few weeks back?"

Cole nodded.

"I wasn't the only ranch he visited. A while back I got wind of some... government construction that would be coming through my land. I imagine there'll be a mighty big profit from the sale of that parcel to the—"

"Railroad," Cole finished for him.

Clay nodded in affirmation. "Anyone who knew about the railroad coming in would stand to gain a lot by purchasing my ranch and the surrounding properties."

This shed a whole new light on things. It had to be the railroad. Cole doubted that there were many left in this town that even knew about the silver mine Alaric's grandfather had kept secret for so long, let alone believed the legends surrounding it. So, what else could it be? Something just didn't sit right.

"Rumor has it that whoever bought the Gnarled Oak Ranch is behind it all, trying to push everybody out." Clay spooned a large heap of eggs onto his plate.

Raine and Rafe exchanged glances. Then, both looked at Cole.

"The Gnarled Oak?" Cole asked, ignoring his brothers.

"The land just to the north of us is the largest spread in the northern territory. Every ranch and property around here used to be a part of either the Johansson spread or the Deardon's."

A sinking pit formed in Cole's belly. It was time to tell Clay the truth.

"When Friedrich Johansson passed on, we thought young Alaric would take over, but nobody's seen or heard from him. Didn't even make it to the funeral."

Cole remembered when Alaric had received the telegram about his grandfather's passing. He'd said he wasn't ready for the responsibility of his name. Now, Cole understood why. It was all *his* responsibility.

"Clay, I—"

"Haven't met the new owner yet. Don't know that I care to. Goons with guns started showing up at folkses homes, demanding payment in full for their mortgage notes."

"Wait. What?" Cole was stunned.

"Most of the smaller ranches sold out. Some got loans from the bank." Clay took a drink of his milk. "Well, after a little pressure most of them sold out. After having their houses broken into, tools come up missing, unexplained accidents. Hell, the Lawson's had their entire herd poisoned." Clay leaned back against the large chair. "Although, I think they bought their land from Bill Deardon," he added as an afterthought. "Can't imagine any of Bill's kin resortin' to downright thievery."

"Because they wouldn't," Rafe announced and then both he and Raine turned to look at Cole, eyebrows raised.

He couldn't wait any longer.

Clay narrowed his eyes at Rafe and then followed the stares to Cole's face.

"Clay," Cole started, but everything he'd rehearsed in the stable flew out the window. "It's me. *I* own the Gnarled Oak *and* all the Deardon land."

"Hell. I didn't see that one comin'."

CHAPTER SEVENTEEN

Sunday

Abby awoke to the morning light filtering into her room, the rays warming her face. She knew it wasn't much past dawn and though she couldn't have had more than a couple of hours of sleep, she lay there, staring out her bedroom window, unable to close her eyes. She watched how the vibrant colors of the morning perched on the clouds along the horizon and tried to clear the sleep from her eyes.

She sat up and stretched her arms above her head. The heavy patchwork quilt, that had provided ample warmth throughout the night, fell off her shoulders in a heap in her lap. The added weight on her legs was heavy and constricting. She reached both hands beneath the thick material and tossed the blanket away from her, toward the bottom of the large four-poster bed. Taking a deep breath, she draped her legs over the edge and sat there, waiting, thinking. She glanced at the crumpled indentation on the other side of the bed.

A sudden recollection of all the night's events made Abby jump from the bed. "Rustlers," she muttered aloud.

On her way out the door, Abby caught her ruffled reflection in the washstand mirror and wished she hadn't. But this couldn't wait. As she shimmied into some blue denims and a white linen blouse, she cursed herself for falling asleep. Cole had probably already told her father everything. How would Clay McCallister ever believe she could take care of the ranch if she couldn't stay awake through the ordeal?

She pulled on her riding boots, which she realized Cole must have removed while she'd slept, and blushed at the thought of his hands against her bare skin. He was a distraction that was beginning to cost more than her good judgment. There was something going on at the ranch and until she could figure it out, it would be best to stay clear of Cole Redbourne and his beautiful dimples.

On the landing at the foot of the stairs she stopped. Voices were coming from the kitchen. It had been a long time since she'd slept past dawn and wondered who else she'd find at the breakfast table this morning. Standing just outside the door she listened as those inside engaged deep in conversation. She dared a peek inside and saw Cole first, his back to her, followed by the two of his brothers and her father, who sat in his seat at the head of the table.

Breakfast at the McCallister ranch was usually served right at six and Sundays were no different. Although it was the Sabbath, there were still chores to do, cattle and horses to feed, and meals to be made before heading into town for church.

With a glance at her great-grandmother's grandfather clock she saw it was nearly six thirty and hurriedly walked across the living area. The doors to the kitchen had been propped open and Abby stopped just short of the entry. Nervous, she ran her hands down her clothing and pinched her cheeks for some added color. She let out a slow breath before she stepped into the kitchen, where a brilliant ray of morning light shone through the window, warming her face.

"Hell. I didn't see that one comin'," her father said before all eyes turned to look at her.

She was immediately greeted by three of the most handsome men she had ever seen. One she recognized as another of Cole's brothers who'd joined them last night, but to whom she had not yet been introduced. It seemed Redbournes all came from good stock.

"Good mornin', ma'am," they said in unison, their presence striking, filling the entire room as they stood.

"Didn't see what coming?" Abby asked to no one in particular.

"You must be the woman who finally caught our little brother." She almost choked at the word 'little', but smiled instead. The man stepped away from the table and walked toward her. He placed his hands on her forearms and leaned down to place a kiss on her cheek. "I'm Rafe."

His voice was like warm honey and Abby felt herself melting in his presence. She felt sorry for girl who had to fight away the bees to get some of him.

"Welcome to the family," he said as he stepped away from her.

Abby was sure she was blushing from head to toe. "Good morning, Rafe. I'm Abby." She'd never been introduced like that in all her life and she stumbled over her words, unsure what she should say. "It is such a...a pleasure to meet you."

Cole pulled out the chair next to him. Clay was on the other side and leaned over to kiss Abby's forehead before re-taking his seat. "Good morning, sweetheart."

There was tension in the air. She could feel it in the room like a heavy cloud of emotion. Awkwardness took over as all conversation halted. Finally, Raine broke the silent discomfort.

"So, what brings the infamous Rafe Redbourne out here to Colorado?"

"Oh, right." Rafe seemed a bit startled by the question. "A bounty. Kidnapping," he said, picking up another slice of warm cornbread. "He took a young, soon-to-be wife of a British Duke and brought her west. His trail led me here."

"He was in town when talk of a Redbourne wedding party made him curious," Cole leaned over and whispered to Abby.

"Good thing I did too or Charcoal here may not have such a perty mug this morning." Rafe grasped Cole by the cheeks and squeezed.

Abby giggled.

"Very funny." Cole didn't seem amused, but some of the tension in the room lifted.

"Harrison Beckett is sly, all right," Rafe said loudly. "Ladies seem to think he's a real charmer. I have his sketch out in my saddle pouch." He took a long drink of his fresh buttermilk and then turned to Cole, his face serious. "I wish you'd sketched it. Whoever did this one... well, let's just say they lacked your talent."

Abby looked at Cole. He was an artist? There were so many things about him she didn't know. Watching the color rise in his face, the thought of her marrying a complete stranger finally sunk in. She knew nothing about him, but the more she learned, the more she wanted to.

"You draw?" she asked, still bewildered at the thought.

"I scribble." He picked at his food without looking up.

"Aw, don't let him fool ya. He's real good." Raine jabbed him in the side.

The awkwardness returned. She looked around at all four men in the room. They were unusually quiet.

"So, have we learned yet who owns the Gnarled Oak?"

Four pairs of eyes darted in her direction.

"Look, I know there is something going on around here, Papa, and I want to know what it is." She placed her hand over his much larger, clenched hand on the table. "What are we going to do about these rustlers?"

"Cole," Clay said as he continued to stare at Abby, his jaw flexed tightly before he slowly turned his glare to his new son-in-law, "why don't you tell me exactly what happened last night that my daughter, who you've sworn to me you would protect, is aware there were rustlers in the area."

Cole shifted uncomfortably in his seat. He looked up from his food, first at Abby, then at her father.

The door banged open and an angry Martha stood in the frame, her apron folded with a dozen or so eggs.

"Who's the cutup that locked me in the coop?" Strands of hair had come loose from her bun and her face was smudged with dirt. "If it weren't for Jack gettin' loose, I'd still be out there. Jim saw the blasted horse and heard me hollerin' when he passed the pen on his way to the stable."

"Jack?" Abby whispered and jumped to her feet.

"Martha," Clay stood from his chair and walked over to the woman, "are you all right?" He held her arms and scrunched down and tilted his head to look at her face.

Clay's jaw hardened again. "I want to know who's doing this, but if you boys have anything to do with it." The meaning in his words was unmistakable. He turned back to look at Martha, his hands still on her arms.

"I'm fine, Clay." Martha's voice softened. "Really," she added when it looked as if Clay would not believe her.

"Why would Cole or his brothers have anything to do with it?" Abby inquired, confused.

When all those at the table exchanged glances with one another, but avoided looking at her, Abby turned to her father and as she watched the tender way he moved his hands up to Martha's face and the concern etched deep in his brow, she realized for the first time that he was sweet on her.

Clay dropped his hands, a worried smile still plaguing his face, and cleared his throat returning to his place at the table.

Martha's chin lowered nearly to her chest and she brushed past him to the counter where she unloaded the eggs from her apron. When she turned back to Clay, her faced was fixed with determination.

"Whoever it was," Martha spoke with only the smallest of quivers in her voice, "tied the door shut with this." She held up a crumpled black rag, clutched firmly in her hand.

Abby's brows furrowed together. There was obviously meaning to the cloth. She'd found one just like it the other day in the barn after her run-in with the rattlesnake. Her father looked hard at her husband, then at each of his brothers. The friction in the air sizzled.

"Will someone please tell me what's going on here?" Abby demanded. Her hands balled into fists on the table.

"Clay." Cole's eyes did not move from her father, but held some sort of warning. And pleading.

Clay adjusted his focus on Abby. He picked up her hand from the table and nestled it warmly between the two of his.

"I guess it's time you heard the truth, at least what I know of it." He spoke softly, as if not to alarm her.

Her apprehension grew faster and more intense the longer he waited.

"What is it, papa?"

"I've tried to protect you. Even arranged for you to go to Denver, where you would be safe." He looked down at their hands. "But you are even more stubborn than your mother."

"Safe from what, papa? Does this have anything to do with those men Cole and I spotted on the Johansson's land?"

Abby searched her father's eyes.

"Truth is, I'm not sure what or who we're up against, but we'll take care of it. I think maybe you should go and stay with Lily for a few days."

"That's not fair, papa. I can ride and shoot just as well as anybody else and you know it. Better even. I could help."

"*That* is not the point. They are not my only daughter. Now, that's the end of it."

"Now, ya'll remember. It is the Sabbath today and church starts at ten. Whatever yer a plannin' on doin' best wait 'til after services." Martha wiped her hands in her apron after setting another plate of biscuits on the table.

All the men, nearly in unison responded, "Yes, ma'am."

"With all due respect, sir," Cole cleared his throat, "I would rather Abby stay here," he paused just long enough for Abby to see a flicker of indecision, "with me," he finished, his eyes now boring into her.

Abby thought her heart was going to lurch indiscriminately from her chest. She bit down on the edge of her lower lip. Her eyes roamed the length of him. There was no question in her mind she would be safe as long as he was with her. The sanctuary she'd found wrapped in the confines of his arms last night flooded back into her memory. Yes, Cole Redbourne was every inch a protector. And a distraction. She had to focus.

Clay scratched at his stubbled chin with his knuckles. After a long moment he conceded. "Okay." Then, he turned to Abby, "Don't you go gettin' any ideas, young lady. You may be a married woman now, but I'm still your father and I'm telling you to let us handle it."

Abby forced herself to smile graciously. She shifted her glance toward Cole. He picked up his hat from the table and winked at her just before he put it on.

You're not doing this without me. Her demure smile, still frozen on her lips, hid the audacious grin that threatened. She turned back toward her bedroom. *I'll just have to go about it a little differently.*

"How's Carson doing this morning? I'll bet he can tell us what happened," Cole asked, sarcasm edging every syllable. He tossed aside a large, scorched plank blocking his way into what was left of the barn.

"He was drunk," Raine said flatly. "I doubt he remembers a thing." Raine stepped over some fragments of rope and metal. He picked up a shovel head, the handle burned clean off.

"Doc said the Carson boy breathed in a lot of smoke and burned his throat pretty good." Clay hunched down next to what was left of a saddle. "He's coughin' somethin' fierce and has been slippin' in and out of consciousness, but Doc says he should live."

Shaking his head, Clay pitched the damaged riding seat to the outer edge of the burnt and falling frame. "That boy ought to be mighty grateful to Cole here for pulling him out of this mess."

Flags of smoke still rose from the debris all around them. The sweet aroma of freshly burned pine mixed with the springy scent of wildflowers brought out by the last few days of rain. They'd been lucky that, because of the moisture, the damage hadn't spread to the homestead or the stable.

"I'd still like to know what Carson was doing in the barn. If he'd started the fire, wouldn't he have been long gone before it became ablaze?" Cole looked down at the bandages wrapped around his forearm, covering the angry blisters he'd gotten from pulling the fool out harm's way.

He inadvertently thought of Abby.

The way she'd looked in their bedroom last night as she'd pulled a blanket up over him would be forever engraved in his mind. The thin material of her night shift had concealed little and when one of her sleeves had fallen off her shoulder and down her arm when she crawled into the large oak bed, he'd groaned. The battle between his desire for his new wife and his need to keep her safe had grown particularly fierce within the last twelve hours.

"You can go ask him yourself. He's still asleep in Abby's old bedroom upstairs." Clay pointed to a window on the second floor.

"Carson is…" Cole started, "in Abby's room?" An iron weight settled at the pit of his stomach. He recalled Clay telling Caleb this morning to have the kid's father come to retrieve him, but the idea of having him in Abby's room irked him. He kicked at a worn piece of wood that he guessed had been a hitching post and started toward the house.

"Her *old* room," Clay reiterated, calling after him.

When he passed Raine, he was accosted by the arm. "You heard Clay, Charcoal." Raine spun him around. "The man's throat is burned from the smoke. He won't be able to tell you anything, at least not right now."

The two men looked hard at each other until Cole shook Raine's hand off his arm and he twisted his neck to stretch the muscles that had tightened so forcefully moments before.

Abby joined them, dressed in her usual ranching attire, but this time her hair was pulled back with a ribbon, the same yellow color as her shirt, tied at her nape.

Cole pulled his eyes off her and addressed the others. "Has Rafe been able to get anything out of those Spencer boys?"

"They're still here?" Abby asked incredulously. "Papa. I thought you were gonna let Ben and his brothers go home last night." She placed her hand on her father's forearm and looked up at him.

If she didn't know much about being a woman, she was

sure learning fast.

"And let them cause more trouble? I don't think so," Raine chimed in. "It's time there was a little order in this town."

"They'll be all right, Abby," Clay responded, patting her hand. "Davey took them some of Martha's cooking to eat before these boys here cart 'em down to the town jail."

"Their pa's gonna be mighty angry. Besides, without a sheriff in town, what good will it do to lock them up?" Abby protested. "There's no one in town who'll watch them. I don't even think those cells have keys anymore."

"We'll think of something."

Raine and Rafe exchanged glances that contained some sort of hidden message. Both men smirked and by the look on Abby's face Cole thought she might just up and slug the both of them.

"We know it wasn't those boys, Abs," Clay said, putting his hands on his hips and looking around with disgust. "They're just a bunch of town bullies causin' a ruckus. Just like their father. Always have been. But if they know who started that fire, I want to know about it."

Cole's eyes traced the once protective walls that had been reduced to nothing but blackened frames, open and vulnerable. Whoever was taunting Clay was playing for keeps. Had the bunkhouse or any of the other buildings caught fire, the whole ranch could have been lost. Cole was missing something. He could feel it.

"Clay," Davey yelled, riding into the quad at a gallop. Jerking hard on the rein's he pulled his horse to a stop in front of the rubble. "There's a fence down on the north pasture and I reckon we're missing more than a dozen head."

"Any sign how it happened?"

"Just this." Davey handed a small piece of black fabric to Clay. "It was tied around one of the fence posts."

Clay slammed his fist into a scorched wall frame and it collapsed instantly. He kicked an empty milk pail across the length of the barn and shoved a burnt cross beam away from him and onto the ashen floor as he made his way toward the house. A small cloud of ash floated upward and then quietly settled back around the fallen debris.

"Who is doing this?" Clay spat through gritted teeth.

"You don't actually think someone burned down the barn on purpose?" Abby looked from one brother's face to the next until she landed on her father's. "Why?" she asked with a shrug.

At that moment Cole's head confirmed what his heart already knew. Abby had nothing to do with Alaric's death and neither did her father. Cole had seen enough loss, enough pain to last him a lifetime, and then some. Clay and Abby were a part of his family now. These vicious attacks had to stop and he and his brothers had become the best chance anyone had at stopping them. He hoped finding the culprit behind all the trouble would lead to some answers of his own.

"That's what we intend to find out," Cole assured her.

Abby didn't look assuaged. Her jaw tightened and her eyelids tapered. Cole had been told that she wouldn't take too kindly to being told to stay out of it, but for her sake, and his, he hoped she would listen.

"Come on, son. Best be getting' ready for church. We can talk to Henry Campbell and Zed Carson in town. We'll catch them after Sunday services." Clay put his hand on Cole's shoulder and squeezed.

"Carson?" Cole asked, looking to the second level window.

"The boy's father. They live just to the south of us. I can introduce you boys after the service and hopefully we can all sit down and figure out our next move. Although, Max Grayson won't be there."

"And young Carson?" Raine asked, lifting his foot to rest on a fallen stall door. "Mr. Carson isn't coming to get him?"

"Doc said not to move him for a couple of days. He'll be fine where he's at until then. Best to keep him close." Clay winked at a disconcerted Cole.

Cole raised an eyebrow.

"All the same, I'll have Marty keep an eye on him," Cole said with finality, heat rising under his collar.

Clay chuckled.

Raine and Rafe headed into the bunkhouse and Abby to the main house.

Clay walked past Cole to the charred debris in the corner of the ruins where a large support beam had fallen across a surrey. It now looked like a mound of splinters with charcoal wheels.

"Good thing we had more'n one of these buckboards. Just bought two more wagons to add to those we already had. This one was used mostly for trips to town on Sunday and such."

Clay looked around at the devastation at his feet. "We're lucky," he said, "we got all the livestock out before the roof collapsed and no one was seriously hurt." Clay stood there, his head making a circle his body followed. Piles of singed rubble met them all around. "This time," he added.

"I'm sorry about the barn, Clay," Cole offered.

"Yeah, me too. Horse tack, feed, a wagon, and a few breeding supplies, all lost to the flames. There's not much left." Clay clapped his gloved hands together releasing clouds of newly accumulated dust. "I'll get some of the boys to get out here and clean up this mess after church. There's no sense pinin' over what's lost."

"Mr. Patterson agreed to open the mercantile long enough today to pick up some grain and feed for the animals," Cole told Clay. "We'll have to drive back into town tomorrow to pick up timbers from the mill and the rest of the building supplies—tools, nails, and any other materials we'll need."

"Caleb and I made a supply list this morning before ya'll got back." Clay scratched his whiskered chin. "Come to think of it, I haven't seen Caleb since he left for the Campbell's this mornin'. Ah, well. He'll turn up. Always does."

CHAPTER EIGHTEEN

Abby's laugh was unmistakable and Cole attuned his ears to the refreshing sound. He perked up in time to see Abby walk out of the homestead on Rafe's arm. She had changed into a high-waisted topaz dress, lined in a sheer overhang, an older style without the bustle. Her hair was pulled back away from her face with sporadic tendrils wrestling free from the entanglement. She looked like a vision with the morning light behind her, illuminating her golden tresses and pulling henna undertones from the wisps of hair that framed her face.

Cole stood up straight. Watching her smile up at his brother so easily brought a scowl to his face and his insides glowered with envy. With keen awareness he watched them approach.

"Your wife is quite delightful, Charcoal," Rafe flashed one of those smiles he'd always bragged could capture the heart of any woman. "She was just telling me all about my little brother jumping in the mud on his wedding day."

Cole grimaced.

"Raine, you ready?" Rafe called loudly, turning his focus to their oldest brother, who was saddling his horse.

When Raine didn't acknowledge him, Rafe took Abby's hand from the crook of his arm and kissed the back of it. "Ma'am," he said with a tip of his hat before climbing over a few scorched boards toward the corral.

Cole kicked at an imaginary rock in the dirt. He pushed his hands even farther into the already snug pockets of his trousers.

The low neckline of Abby's dress revealed a cluster of freckles just below her collarbone that diverted him from all relevant thought.

"I think we're in for another stormy day," he said aloud.

The weather?

She was distracting him more than he cared to admit. With horse thieves, saboteurs, and killers on the loose in Silver Falls, he didn't have time for childish jealousies.

"Abby?" Raine led his horse over to where they stood and walked up behind them, surprise in his voice. A long, low whistle fell off his lips. "I had no idea you'd married so well, Charcoal."

Raine nudged Cole from behind as he removed his hat and bent forward in an exaggerated bow. "I have never seen any girl of Cole's quite so lovely as you, ma'am."

When Raine was upright again, Cole jerked his elbow backward into his brother's ribs, who hunched over in another bow, laughing and groaning at the same time.

Abby blushed. "Why, thank you, Raine," she spoke in a breathy sweet voice, very unlike her own. Her thick lashes lowered onto her cheek.

When she looked up, the expression on her face quickly changed.

"Davey," she yelled across the yard.

A gangly red-headed ranch hand was dumping a bucket of oats into the stable feeding trough.

"Why's Chester out in the yard?"

She pushed past them and marched over to where the young stallion was grazing on some tall grass in next to the stable in front of the corral.

That was more like the Abby he was getting to know, headstrong and willful. He had to stop thinking about her. About the way her hips swayed when she walked or the small indentation just below her right eye when she smiled. How she kept her chin high, even when it quivered some.

Stop, Cole screamed inside his head.

Abby grabbed a hold of the rust colored Morgan's reins

and led him back into the stable.

"It's about time the girl wore a dress to church. Maybe gettin' married has knocked some female sense into her." Clay looked admiringly toward the corral.

Abby emerged wearing the oversized green coat she'd worn the first time they'd met.

Cole's eyes narrowed. Clay had warned him that Abby usually attended church in trousers and sat on the very back row—if she wasn't standing in the back. So, he'd been unprepared for the vision that flaunted before him. Now, with her father's coat bunched up all around her and the look of satisfaction on her face, Cole could only surmise one thing. She was definitely up to something.

From what Cole had already learned about his wife, she was not about to sit back and let the men take care of things. There was a reason she was so anxious to go into town today, all gussied up, and Cole intended to find out exactly what that reason was.

Anxious to learn more about the man she'd married, and with nearly two hours before Sunday services would begin, Abby thought the ride to church would provide the perfect opportunity to talk with his brothers and get to know more about their family. And just maybe she could get some information from Ben Spencer and his brothers. They might know more than they were letting on.

"You are not riding into town in the wagon with my brothers and those hooligans. We've only been married two days, woman, and you want to make a fool of me already?" He stood on the top porch step and looked down at her, standing between Raine and Rafe.

"Since when do you care about appearances, Charcoal?" Raine asked playfully, casually placing his arm around Abby's shoulder.

"And since when do *you* decide with whom I may ride to church?" Abby asked. The defiance in her stare did not falter. Why did this stubborn man have to be so handsome?

"Since the day *I* became your husband." Cole shot Raine a look that promised hot spears.

Raine dropped his arm from around her.

"Friday, to be precise." Cole's jaw clenched and he raised a brow as if daring her to challenge him. She was sure his eyes darkened a shade.

Looking around at the others, who were all now looking at some miniscule speck in the dirt, she determined she would not be embarrassed. Now was the best time to establish the fact that, husband or not, attractive or not, she would not be ordered about like a little servant girl. She was a grown woman and it was time everyone around her noticed.

"Don't you want me to get to know your brothers, Cole?"

"If you wanted to get to know *them*, why on earth did you marry me?"

Was that hurt in his voice?

"You asked."

"I asked?" He nodded a few times. "I asked you. Well, Mrs. Redbourne, you're riding with me."

A split second of indecision was smothered before it could take root. She looked up briefly at her two very large brothers-in-law who stood on either side of her. They were *his* brothers. Of course they would side with him.

Well she needed answers and talking with Benjamin Spencer may be the only way to get them. She turned on her heel and darted backward, breaking into a dead run toward the west pasture beyond the corral where she'd seen three stock horses grazing. If Cole wasn't going to let her ride with them, she'd just have to ride alongside them.

Booming laughter trailed her on the breeze. She glanced back. Raine and Rafe both stood at the bottom of the steps watching her, laughing, while Cole remained stoic, his eyes following her every move. She smiled to herself.

The billowing skirt of the outdated dress offered Abby a

stronger sense of freedom as she ran. There were too many layers to most women's clothing and she found the bustles and corsets unsuitable for even the simplest of tasks to be done around the ranch.

Abby's hair floated in disarray around her as she moved quickly to the opposite side of the fenced corral. Her chest heaving, she placed a hand on the fence, attempting to unlatch the gate into the west pasture.

The lock was being more difficult than usual. She checked behind her. To her horror, Cole's six foot plus form jumped all four porch steps in one motion. When his feet hit the ground he was running full force in her direction. Exhilaration mingled with fear at the sight of him and for a fraction of a moment she simply admired his strong physique and agility.

Her eyes flitted to his face. The resolve in his features was enough to incite her to action. The lock simply wouldn't budge, so she darted to the area behind the small square training paddock that had been temporarily set up after the fire. She positioned herself where she could see him through the sparse wooden fence planks.

"Abby."

While she could not read the tone in his voice, her heart nearly stopped when he said her name.

"I'm riding with them." Her voice sounded breathless, but she wasn't at all sure it was from running.

She darted to the left and he mimicked her actions. She ran to the right and again he countered the move.

She glanced around. There was nowhere to run except into the field behind her and the fence blocked the way. Why had she chosen to wear a dress today? Catching his eye, it was her turn to raise an eyebrow. Cole started after her. Abby ran to the pasture fence, grabbed a hold of the top plank, pulled herself up and rolled over into the field. Relieved her dress hadn't gotten caught, she ran straight and hard toward the saddled brown and white Appaloosa.

Why is there a fully saddled horse out in the pasture? she wondered, but kept running.

The crunching sound of gravel being ground underfoot made Abby dare another glance backward. She turned to see Cole slide on the tiny bits of rock around the paddock. He bent forward to catch himself from falling. His hand barely touched the ground before he corrected his footings.

Abby watched in awe as Cole simply jumped the paddock fence and mounted one of the stock horses bareback. He rode the brown and white paint around the perimeter of the makeshift corral before he broke the horse into a run straight toward the enclosure wall. He cleared the first fence, then the second and once again Cole was after her.

The whoops and hollers of the others pushed her forward. More ranch hands had now collected in the yard, watching. Abby whipped around at a run. The Appaloosa had romped off back toward the corral. She looked ahead, focusing on a large rock formation jutting out of the ground and was determined to make it there before surrendering. Cole was gaining on her. She could feel it.

Being on foot would give her the advantage when rounding the rock. She would gain some time if she could just make it there before him. Laughter bubbled inside of her. Whether it was from her newfound liberation or the thrill of having a very handsome cowboy chasing after her, she was uncertain.

The grassy hay field had been cut recently, but tiny wildflowers of yellow, blue, and violet peeked through the blunt green blades. Specks of cotton flowers danced in the air and swirled about her as she whisked by. The sun, still very low in the sky, cast a warm glow around the meadow.

One moment she was a few steps from her intended destination and in the next a muscular arm reached out to her, grasping her around the waist just beneath her breasts, and hauled her through the air. The earth swirled around her.

With a thump, Abby landed on the stock horse's bare back facing a breathless Cole. His arm, still wrapped around her, pulled her close into his solid chest. The white linen shirt he wore was open slightly at the collar and Abby saw the beads of sweat formulated at the fascinating indent where his neck met his shoulder.

Cole led the horse in a broad circle, still at a gallop.

"You are riding next to me," he said as he leaned into her, his breath tickling her ear with the whisper. Though his words were stern, she noted the slight upturn at the edges of Cole's beautiful mouth when he pulled back and sat up straight. His arms kept her captive as he held the horse's mane.

Abby's witty retort caught in her throat as he brought the gelding to a halt. With a grin plastered on his incredibly handsome face, he slowly descended his head toward her. His strong arms encircled her, and she fought the urge to stare at his mouth. Her heart raced. She wet her lips with her tongue and closed her eyes in sweet expectation.

Nothing happened. She opened one eye to find him staring at something behind her, in the same direction of the old boulder.

Feeling foolish, she pushed against him.

He didn't move. He ignored her, his arms a rock vice around her. She tried to twist around to see what had carried him away, but she couldn't move.

"What is it?" Abby couldn't have missed the drastic change in his demeanor. All humor was gone from his face.

Cole's lips pursed and his eyes narrowed. Determination etched every line of his face. He relaxed his hold around her, if only a little, and pulled the horse about face. With little effort he had the gelding once again at a gallop. Abby lurched backward and his arm tightened around her. She instinctively wrapped her arms around his waist and leaned into his chest.

When they reached the edge of the meadow, Cole lifted her down with ease from the horse.

"Go in the house, my little spitfire, and do not come out until I come back." There was no hint of playfulness in his voice now.

"Come on, Charcoal," Rafe bantered.

She stared back at him out of defiance and held her ground.

"What could it hurt?" Rafe asked.

"Come on, little brother, we'll keep her outta trouble." Raine joined the teasing.

"Go." Cole's eyes had become black as iron, his tone leaving no room for discussion.

"What is it, Cole?" The smile faded from Raine's expression and his eyebrows furrowed into genuine concern.

Shivers made their way up and down Abby's arms. Cole had seen something out there that had frightened him. She knew this place better than anybody and if her ranch needed defending, she wanted to be on the front lines.

She nodded and headed for the house. The pistol hidden in her boot may not be sufficient.

Where's my rifle?

CHAPTER NINETEEN

"It's Caleb. He's dead." Clay knelt next to the lifeless body of the old ranch hand.

Splotches of blood glistened on the large rock and pooled around the man's head. Cole kicked the earth. He did not like this one bit. It was too close.

"Looks like his horse threw him." Rafe sifted through the upturned dirt at the base of the rock.

"An accident?" Cole stared skeptically at his brother. "You're telling me *this* was an accident?"

"I'm telling you it was meant to look like an accident." Rafe stood up and threw the remaining dust from his hand. "There were at least three horses right here as recently as this morning," he told them. "I'd imagine that saddled Appaloosa over there is one of them, but as for the others," he shook his head, "there are too many fresh tracks to tell for sure."

"How does he know all that?" Clay leaned into Cole and whispered.

"Experience," Cole replied through the side of his mouth.

Rafe had been taught how to track by the Pawnee Indians. He was the best Cole had ever seen.

"Impressive. Does he always get it right?"

"Usually." Cole moved back over to the body and looked at Raine. "Here help me get him wrapped up and onto my horse. We'll need to take him back with us."

Clay stood, his fists balled tight and his jaw clenched.

"I'm sorry about this, Clay," Cole said in a whisper. He

knew what it was like.

"He had no family to speak of. Caleb was the kind of man to keep mostly to himself. Still, we were friends."

"Found this in the middle of all that tall grass." Rafe held up a wooden plank and rotated it. The edge was dented in and still sticky with blood.

"How did this happen?"

"Someone hit Caleb over the head and threw him over by the rock to make it look like and accident," Rafe detailed.

"That's not exactly what I meant." Cole threw a sardonic smile at his brother. "How could we let this happen, right under our noses? What if that had been Abby?" Cole shuddered at the thought.

Raine helped Cole lift the rolled blanket with Caleb's body inside over the saddle on Raine's stock horse.

"Hey, Clay, didn't you say that when your foreman was killed he was holding the black handkerchief in his hand?"

"Yes."

Raine pointed to the arm visible from the edge of the blanket. A small torn piece of paper protruded from his stiff, closed fist. He wiggled it free and held it up, crinkled and dirty.

"There's no black cloth, just this." Raine smoothed the wrinkles and handed the note to Clay who squinted as he tried to make out the letters that had been scratched onto the yellowing paper.

"It's not a complete message. It only says, 'Sorry, I didn'. That's it." He passed it to Cole.

"What would Caleb have to be sorry about?" Raine asked.

Clay shrugged. "I didn't even know he could write."

"What's this?" Cole leaned toward Rafe, holding out the note and pointing to a small character at the edge of the torn piece.

"Looks like the number nine and W. Do you think he was trying to tell us something?" Rafe asked.

"Could be," Cole responded and then showed the marking to both Clay and Raine.

Clay took the paper from him. "That's not a nine." He

rotated the paper and pointed to the written letters. "See? It's a G. MG. Max Grayson."

"I shoulda known Jenna Grayson would be involved."

Cole looked up at Abby, astride Old Jack, carrying her rifle across her lap. He dropped his head in defeat.

"Does she ever listen?" he asked Clay.

"Nope."

How the hell was he supposed to protect her if she wouldn't listen?

"Let's get him back to the house." Cole lifted his chin toward Caleb's lifeless body. "I'd like to pay Mr. Grayson a visit after church." Cole folded the paper and tucked it neatly into his back pocket.

Abby opened her mouth to speak.

"And no, you're not coming."

Cole stared at the fresh mound where they'd buried Caleb's body. Frustrated at the answers that eluded him, he grabbed his shirt from the fence post and walked toward the house, where the others had already gathered.

"Maybe after church we can convince Reverend Harris to come out and provide a eulogy over the grave." Martha was suggesting to those sitting at the table as he walked through the kitchen.

Raine snorted. When Martha stared at him through narrowed eyes, he sat up straight in his chair. "Excuse me, ma'am. He's just new to the parsonage and needs a little...a...convincing. I'll be surprised if he's giving a sermon today." Raine's voice carried into the living room as Cole passed through.

Cole walked into his new bedroom and tossed his shirt onto the bed. He moved to the washstand, leaned down, and rested his elbow on either side of the basin, his hands in his hair. His reflection mirrored the dark circles that had formed under his eyes.

So many things had happened over the last couple of days, and trying to function on the hour or so of sleep he'd gotten last night was not boding well for his mood. He scooped some of the cool water from the basin into his hands and splashed his face. Through the drips of water coming off his eyelashes, he spotted the nail ring sitting on the far corner of the washstand and he picked it up.

"Were you close?"

Cole shot up to find Abby standing in the doorway to their room. He set down the ring, reached up and pulled the cloth down from the edge of the mirror, and patted his face and neck dry.

"You and Alaric, I mean."

Cole did not want to talk about Alaric right now. He picked up his shirt from the bed and threw it over his shoulders, neglecting the buttons.

Abby took a step into the room. He longed to reach out to her, to touch her face. To offer some sort of comfort or reassurance. He didn't. He couldn't.

"They're waiting on us." Abby reached down and took a hold of his hand. "May I ride alongside you?"

He brought her hand to his mouth and placed a firm, but gentle kiss on her closed fingers. The ride would give him time to talk to her. To make her understand that it was his duty to protect her. That he *needed* to protect her.

She smiled and released him.

Cole followed her into the kitchen, where everyone sat at the dining table.

"Well, let's go," Cole urged.

Apparently, they'd all been waiting for him. The scraping of chairs across the floor was deafening for an instant while everyone jumped to their feet and headed for the door.

They were getting closer and he hoped that today would provide some answers. Cole could almost taste the bittersweet resolution on his tongue as he reached for his hat.

Rafe was the first to the door with Raine at his heels. When they opened the door, his brothers stopped so abruptly that Abby slammed into Raine from behind and fell backward into Cole's arms.

"What the..."

She blushed. Cole liked that color in her cheeks. He set her upright behind him and looked to see what had caused the commotion.

Abby's friend, Lily Campbell, stood in the open doorway, tears streaming down her face. She spanned her head up Rafe's six-foot-three inch frame. Her eyes grew wide and she took a step back. Cole imagined any of his brothers would cause that reaction.

"Lily? What's wrong?" Raine rushed forward, pushing himself in front Rafe.

Cole thought the catch in Raine's voice unusual for him. When she turned her face to look up at his brother, he saw it. A small cut just below her eye and deep scratches that extended across her face toward her ear. The small cut had caused the surrounding skin and eyelid to turn a deep bluish purple at the edges.

Lily looked wildly from one brother to the other. Raine reached his hand to cradle her face in his palm. She fell into his arms and started to cry. For the first time Cole could remember, it looked as if Raine didn't know what to do. He stood there with a bewildered look on his face and shrugged. He placed his hand at her crown and caressed her long dark hair, soothing her. At the sound of a soft hiccup, he hugged her closer.

Abby, finally able to push through the men blocking the door, took one look at her friend and her soft features darkened with concern. "Lily," she demanded, "what's happened?"

Lily lifted her head from the crevice at Raine's shoulder. The tears had stopped. She pushed away from him with downcast eyes and took a step backward as if she were breeching some code of propriety. Turning to Abby, she opened her mouth to speak.

"Lily," Abby exclaimed, pulling her into the circle of her arm.

Cole knew Abby had just seen the cut below Lily's eye.

"What on earth has happened to you?" She reached up to touch Lily's cheek. Abby ushered her friend to a chair at the table.

"Papa, go get the doctorin' kit from the washroom," Abby ordered Clay. "Cole," she turned her beautiful green eyes on him, "go get the wash basin from our room." She smiled before returning her attentions to Lily's cut cheek.

Cole shook his head. *Our room.* It was still so hard to believe. He covered the area to their bedroom in moments.

The bed sheets were crumpled and a bunched blanket lay at the foot of the chair. *Not much of a wedding night,* he thought. *Patience, Redbourne.*

The wash basin was nearly empty. He picked up the porcelain pitcher still half full, grabbed a clean washcloth from the stack on the vanity, and headed back to the kitchen.

"It's my pa," Lily was saying when he returned. "He's decided to send me away to work."

Cole handed the washcloth and pitcher to Abby who took it, meeting his eyes for a solitary moment. Her brief smile warmed him and he watched as she drew Lily's long dark hair away from her face and turned her toward the light coming through the uncovered window.

"What?" Abby asked incredulously, returning her focus to her patient. "Where?"

Abby dipped the rag into the water and dabbed at Lily's cheek. Cole mused at how tough Abby was. Alaric had asked him to protect her, but Abby was capable. She had a strength others drew upon. He wasn't sure she needed protecting. At least in the way he'd expected.

"He would be so angry if he learned I had told you, but he's lost most of our money," Lily dropped her head to her chest, "on liquor and gambling. Now, we are being forced to sell our property."

Raine's jaw flexed, his eyes on fire. "So, he wants to sell

you to pay his debts." It was a statement rather than a question. Raine's voice dripped with disdain.

"Well, not exactly. He's just—"

"Where is he sending you?" Abby asked.

Lily sucked in a breath causing Abby to pull the rag away from the wound on her cheek.

"Montana territory."

Abby placed the washcloth back into the water basin and sat down across from her friend and sighed.

"It really doesn't hurt that bad." Lily touched her face, just below the cut and then quickly put her hand back in her lap.

"Did your father do this to you?" Raine asked, barely concealed anger tainting his voice.

Cole had heard that tone many times over the course of his twenty-six years and for Lily's father's sake, he hoped Henry Campbell had not hit his daughter.

"Rafe," Raine said as he nudged his head toward Lily.

Cole felt her uneasiness as he was sure did the rest of the room.

"Hi, Lily." Rafe stepped forward and placed his hands on either side of her face to look more closely at the blunt discoloration of her cheek. "I am Cole and Raine's brother Rafe. I am just going to take a look at that cut, okay?"

"Another one?" Lily lifted a hand to her eye and a small self-conscious laugh choked out her throat. "Wow." She tossed a fleeting glance up at Raine and then lowered her eyes instantly.

"Really, it's nothing. I... I just tripped over a log... last night in the woods, that's all."

Cole couldn't help but wonder what she was hiding from them.

"I wasn't...by myself," she added with a fleeting glance at Raine.

Raine's eyebrow lifted, but he said nothing and waited for Lily to continue.

"I was with Mr. Harris..." her voice trailed as she looked at Raine again. "I mean, the reverend asked if he could...oh, it doesn't matter anyway. I tripped and went face first into a low hanging tree branch."

Raine's eyes narrowed, but he said nothing.

"The revered tried to stop the bleeding with one of his handkerchiefs. We were on our way back to the house when we came across a bay roan tethered to the fence near the back of the barn. She was magnificent. I don't think I've ever seen a mare that large."

"Sounds like Rafe's she-devil of a horse." Cole spoke as he turned to Rafe. "You ridin' Lexa?" He'd always loved Rafe's high-spirited strawberry roan with the thick white highlights in her mane.

"It was the strangest thing. Mr. Harris saw something on the saddle. When I looked back at him, his face had drained of all color. He went as white as the streaks in the roan's mane, almost like he'd seen a ghost," she mused as if remembering the moment. "He wasn't awed by her, he was scared. It was a cool evening and even in the moonlight I could see him start to sweat."

"What did he see on the saddle?" Rafe demanded, ignoring Cole's question and leaning closer toward Lily. His ears had perked up and he was now concentrating even more intently on Lily's face. He cleared his throat and stood up straight when Lily looked him in the face, her wits suddenly clear about her.

"Is she," Lily hiccupped, "yours?" she asked, her bravado returning.

"Yes, ma'am. Now, please," the word ground through his teeth, "what did he see on that saddle?" Rafe's eyes had not moved from hers and the intensity of his stance was magnified by the stubborn set to his jaw.

Lily's eyebrows lifted in surprise as she looked at Cole and then at Raine.

Cole reached over and clapped Rafe on the shoulders and squeezed hard. "He's our brother, Miss Campbell. He won't hurt you." He shot Rafe a quelling look.

"Forgive me if I startled you, ma'am," Rafe said in a voice laced with honey. When he flashed his 'I'm disarmingly charming' smile at Lily, she warmed to him again.

Cole's eyes nearly rolled into the back of his head. He had always been disgusted by how easily each of his brothers could win over the ladies, even after acting the part of a dolt. All of the Redbournes seemed to have this effect on women the second they opened their mouths. It wasn't arrogance, it just was. For Cole it hadn't done him much good, but to attract fortune hunters and society snobs like MaryBeth Hutchinson.

Rafe lifted a booted foot to rest on an empty chair. He leaned an arm onto his thigh as he spoke. "Now, think ma'am, what was it he saw on the horse?"

Cole wondered at Rafe's sudden interest in her story.

"I don't know. He just looked at the saddle and then backed away."

Rafe shifted his body to look at Cole. "Who is this Mr. Harris? Is he British?"

"He's the new preacher in town, and yeah, how did you know?"

"Hunch."

"Raine and I just met him. He lives in the old church up the hill on the edge of town." Cole pointed with his head in the direction of Silver Falls. "Come to think of it, I didn't see him after the fire started."

"Why the interest?" Raine asked.

"Fire? Here?" The stricken look on Lily's face registered true surprise. "Is everyone okay?"

"Jeremiah Carson has a burned throat. He won't be talkin' for a while. No one else was seriously hurt, but we lost the barn and feed for the animals," Abby informed her.

Lily gasped. "I'm so sorry I wasn't here, Abby. When Mr. Harris," Lily threw a brief glance toward Raine, "I mean, when *I* got back from my walk, the Patterson's were just leaving and since my place is on their way, they offered to give me a ride. I knew I looked a sight and didn't want to cause a stir, so I went home. I'm sorry I didn't say goodbye."

She turned a weak smile on Abby. "Serves Jeremiah right, though, for all the things he said about you the other day."

Cole agreed with Lily whole-heartedly about Carson.

"Didn't Mrs. Patterson ask questions about your cuts?" Raine asked.

"I didn't want you all to see me, so I wrapped my shawl around my neck and face and told Mrs. Patterson the cold air was getting to me. I just wanted to go home."

"There is nothing you could have done. Honestly, had it not been for these Redbourne boys I'm now related to, and a few of the cowhands and lingering guests, there would not be a bunkhouse, corral, or fence left in the yard." Abby pushed a stray wisp of hair from Lily's cheek.

"What happened? How did it start?" Lily shook her head

"We're not sure yet, but we'll find out soon enough," Cole responded.

"I'll just bet it's that new landowner," she said and then looked over her shoulder at Clay. "Be careful, Mr. McCallister."

All eyes focused on Clay, who had leaned back against the counter top, one booted heel resting in the curve of his other foot, listening quietly to the entire interchange.

Cole had almost forgotten his new father-in-law had been there.

"My pa says whoever the man is that bought the Johansson place has a lot of money and influence and will stop at nothing to get his hands on *all* our lands."

"Will everyone stop saying that?" Cole screamed.

Lily stopped short, shock registering on her face.

"We're wasting time sitting around here. Come on, Charcoal, let's go." Rafe patted Cole's shoulder. "I don't want to miss any more of the sermon than we already will. I am more than anxious to meet this preacher, Mr. Harris." Rafe pulled on Raine's arm and walked out the door.

"Where's your pa, now?" Clay asked.

"When I left the house, he was sitting in his study with a bottle of his favorite bourbon."

"You can stay here as long as you like young lady, but your pa is going to know where ya are." Clay did not leave any room for argument.

"Thanks, Mr. McCallister, but I have to be getting home after church today. Folks have been delivering their pies and confections to my ranch all morning. We're hosting this Sunday's tea."

"Ah, well. We'll discuss this sending away business later," Clay said with a smile. "Church may just prove to be real interestin' today," he said, ushering the ladies out the door.

"The Lord. Is. Our. Rock," the new preacher shouted out to the congregation as he pounded his fist on the pulpit. "He is our refuge. Who saves us. From our enemies."

Reverend Harris raised his arms, his face upturned, and praised God. More than a few heads turned when the string of late comers filed into the back of the chapel.

"Where's Raine?" Lily asked Abby in quiet tones.

"He and Rafe wanted to get a few of his outlaw depictions up before church was over. They'll be here soon." Abby squeezed Lily's hand with understanding.

The last bench, at the very back of the church, had a few patrons sitting interspersed along the row, with Mrs. Hutchinson sitting on the end. Clay stood at the edge of the pew, bent over, and whispered something in Mrs. Hutchinson's ear. She turned around in her seat and when she locked eyes with Abby, she stood up and motioned all of them to join her on the bench.

Most of the pews were full for today's sermon and Abby guessed it was because the preacher was new to these parts and folks wanted a look. The entire front row comprised young ladies of marriageable age, vying for his attention.

When the preacher looked down over the congregation and saw the small entourage that came with her, his face went white and his confident, even theatrical demeanor abandoned him. His voice cracked.

"Mrs. Patterson will now lead us in singing *Rock of Ages*," he said, gathering the papers and bible from the podium and then he stepped down to sit on the front row.

The robust woman stood up, her husband giving her a little push off the seat, and turned around to face the parishioners.

"Rock of Ages, cleft for me," the familiar words filled the chapel.

A rich deep voice resonated next to her. Cole's voice rang clear as he sang. "Let me hide myself in thee."

Abby smiled and sat up taller in her seat. She was used to her father's singing, but if not for the words, it was often difficult to make out the tune.

Cole reached over and tucked his fingers into Abby's closed palm.

Raine and Rafe slid on the bench next to them at the beginning of the second verse and Cole's voice was joined by two more, equally as strong. Abby'd never heard harmony blend quite like it before. Half the congregation quit singing and twisted in their seats to look at the men seated next to her. It was clear the Redbourne men were accustomed to singing together. Even Mrs. Patterson barely mouthed the words.

When they finished the last verse, the chapel was silent. Then, a whisper. Then, two. Within moments, the entire group was a buzz and moving about.

Abby glanced up to see Mrs. Patterson making her way toward the back bench. She groaned inwardly. Abby really couldn't stand the overbearing, busybody of a woman who was waving at her, but she plastered on a fake smile and waved back.

"Abby," Mrs. Patterson took her by the arm, her ample bosom pushed up against Abby's shoulder. Abby fingered the pistol she still had hidden in her skirts.

"Abby dear, we'd love for you to join us for tea." She squeezed Abby's arm and turned to walk away. Then, as if in afterthought added, "And bring all of your handsome guests. You must introduce them to all of us."

As soon as the woman had gone, Abby's smile turned flat. What a difference wearing a dress and showing up with a group of fine-looking men made. She'd never even been acknowledged at church before, let alone invited to tea. She had to admit, it was what she'd hoped for when she'd put on the dress that morning. Getting to that party was vital.

The men had planned to head out to the Grayson place for a meeting and she hoped she could get them to drop her off at Lily's on the way. She'd worry about getting home later.

With her trusty little pistol hidden in her dress, what could go wrong?

"The good reverend is gone. Have you seen him?" Rafe scanned the remnants of the congregation.

"He's probably already headed up the hill. You really think—"

"Mr. Harris is my bounty. Harrison Beckett," Rafe affirmed.

"Let me see that sketch again," Cole asked.

Rafe pulled the drawing out of his pocket and handed it to Cole.

He studied it for a moment, unconvinced. He imagined the man with shorter hair and a bead of sweat dripping off his forehead. His eyes opened wide. "It is him."

They exchanged looks.

Rafe grabbed the paper from Cole's hands. "Which way?"

Cole pointed his brother up the mountain.

"Wait, Rafe." Cole gripped his brother's arm. "If Mr. Harris isn't the preacher, then..."

"We'll worry about that after I catch him." Rafe left.

Cole glanced over at Abby who was in deep conversation with her father. He smiled. The topaz dress suited her. He walked toward them.

"Abby, you haven't been to a tea since—"

"I know papa," she cut him off. "And I think it's about time. Don't you?"

Clay looked to Cole in silent exchange. Cole scrunched his eyebrows, not understanding what Clay needed from him.

"Papa, this is ridiculous."

"It's not my call anymore, Abs. You should talk to your husband."

Cole cleared his throat.

Slowly, she pivoted on one foot until she stared Cole in the face. She tilted her head and smiled, taking one step closer. She reached out a hand to play with one of the buttons on the front of Cole's shirt. She looked up at him with a coy look on her face. "Please?" She bit her bottom lip.

Boy, she'd been practicing.

After a long, uncomfortable silence, Cole narrowed his eyes at her, searching. She was definitely up to something, but what?

"No." He wasn't even sure what he was saying no to.

The smile fell from her face and a glower replaced it. "Since when has it been dangerous to attend a Sunday afternoon tea?" she retorted.

Ah, the tea.

"Since *you* started attending them. You have quite the knack for finding trouble, my dear."

"Papa?" she questioned impatiently, looking back at her father.

"You made your bed, little girl..." he responded.

She mumbled something under her breath. Her head shot up, her eyes alight.

"Mr. Campbell will be there. Mr. Carson too. Didn't you want to speak with them as well as Mr. Grayson about the rustlers?"

She'd resorted to logic. Smart move. He should really tell her about what they'd just learned about Mr. Harris.

It can wait, he decided.

Cole flexed his jaw. "Very well."

CHAPTER TWENTY

"It's time to finish this once and for all." A cold, scratchy voice came from the corner of the room. Aging fingers played with the black curtains hanging over the dusty windows behind a large captain's desk. "It couldn't have come together any better than this. I knew that getting rid of that Johansson boy would bring Cole Redbourne here to Silver Falls. It took longer than I'd expected, but he's here."

The only sliver of light coming into the room cast a yellow outline around the woman seated in the high back chair facing the south wall, her face and body nothing but shadows in the darkness.

"What about Abby?" the question came from the darkness.

"A minor detail that will work itself out," she dismissed with a wave of her hand. "I have collected more than a dozen deeds and with yours and Zed's, I will have enough of a dowry no Redbourne man would balk at. I've sent for my daughter. Once she arrives, Cole Redbourne will forget all about his new bride. I will not let that little chit take away from my MaryBeth what Leah Deardon took from me." Bitterness laced her words as she spat out the last woman's name.

Then, silence.

His eyes finally started to adjust to the darkness.

Voices in the hallway carried in through the study doors. People had begun to arrive for Sunday tea.

"Is everything in place?" The woman asked, dropping the curtain.

"Yes, madam." Henry Campbell stepped forward, the light cracking across his sunken features.

"And Spencer?"

"Awaiting our signal."

"Very well." She waved her hand dismissively. "Come here, boy. Step into the light and let me look at you." She directed her attention to where he sat on the edge of an overstuffed fainting couch on the opposite side of the room.

He stepped forward.

"Have they begun to suspect you yet, boy?" He still was having trouble making out her face.

"I don't think so." His voice cracked. "They've already found and buried Caleb."

"A fool and his conscience," she snorted. "He never should have tried to go back on our agreement. Threatened to tell Clay everything. I couldn't very well let that happen now, could I? It would have ruined all that I've worked for. That we've worked for," she corrected.

While some part of the youth was grateful to her for getting him out of the Colorado Institution for Boys, she scared him. More than a little. She'd offered him more money than he'd ever see in his lifetime, in return for his services.

At first, his tasks had been easy—get a job on the SilverHawk, let the horses out, cut some ropes. He hadn't expected Caleb to catch him dumping the wagonload of supplies, and had been surprised that the old hand was working with her too. Even though his conscience had told him otherwise, he'd convinced himself these little things were harmless in the long run and weren't really hurting anybody. But when he'd discovered that the boss had arranged for McCallister's foreman to be killed, it had already been too late.

Lately, her errands had become more involved, menacing. He'd not expected Jeremiah Carson to wander into the barn while he was lighting the fire and when the nitwit had passed out in a drunken stupor, he hadn't known what else to do, so he'd run. Once the fire had roared to life, he told Mr. Redbourne he'd seen someone inside and had been relieved when they both had emerged from the flames, alive.

I just want out, he thought to himself. *But how?* He'd seen what she'd done to Caleb when he'd turned his back to her. She wasn't as old as she led people to believe.

"There's just one final thing I need you to do for me." Her voice was full of anticipation. "Make sure you take Abby McCallister home. And go through the ravine."

Simple enough.

"And then my debt to you, ma'am?"

"Gone."

"Thank you." He turned to exit and bumped into Mr. Campbell. "Sir," he said and nodded good day before opening the study doors and stepping out into the bright foyer.

The light hurt his eyes at first. He leaned back against the closed doors and took a deep breath. *Driving Abby home, that's not too bad,* he thought. He didn't want to think about what might happen on that drive.

Lily Campbell walked around the corner, nearly bumping into him.

"Davey, you scared me. Is everything all right?" She smiled at him, her hand touching his forearm.

He stood up straight, pushing away from the closed study doors. "Fine," he squeaked. Clearing his throat, he tried again, "Fine," he said in a much lower voice.

He could feel the flush rise into his cheeks at her question. Lily truly was the most beautiful woman he had ever seen and he turned away from her, hoping she would not notice the black and blue evidence of his indiscretions on his face. However, he noticed a small cut just below Lily's eye and a fire lit in his belly. He could only imagine how she'd gotten hers and it tore him up inside.

"Are you joining us for tea?" she asked. A curled strand of her ebony hair fell across her face, concealing her wound cleverly.

"A man's gotta eat," he responded with false merriment. The idea of someone hurting her made his blood boil and he glanced back at the room he'd just left.

Lily smiled and pointed to the hall.

Her kindness warmed him.

"Food's in there. Are Clay and the others with you? Raine?" she asked, hopeful.

Was she actually blushing? Of course, she liked Cole's brother. He determined that when he came back to collect his last payment, he would kiss Lily smack on the mouth and then walk out the door, never turning to look back on Silver Falls, Colorado.

"I think Clay's in the barn, speaking with Mr. Carson. I'm not sure where Raine or any of the others got off to."

"Martha brought her crumb cake. You should try it," Lily said as she turned toward the patio. "Oh, and Davey...I'm so glad you could come." She smiled, then disappeared through the side door.

Davey scrunched up his face with resolve. "Let's do this."

"Stay alert and be careful on your way back today. You should probably avoid the ravine. It will leave you too vulnerable, closed in. Nothing can happen to Abby, do you hear me?" Cole clapped the gangly red-headed cowhand on the back and squeezed his arm firmly. "We can't be too careful with all the trouble that's been going on."

"Yes, sir," Davey responded, but didn't quite meet Cole's eyes.

Trouble was brewing in the air. Cole could feel it. Everyone had seemed eager to attend the Sunday tea at the Branded H. Cole figured they needed a bit of diversion after all the recent strains that had been put on the folks in town, but realized it would create the perfect opportunity for someone to make mischief. He wondered why Max Grayson hadn't come or his daughter, Jenna, and now wanted to pay them a visit even more than he had before.

"Davey," Cole said loudly. The kid finally looked up and

locked Cole's stare. "Keep her safe."

Davey dipped his head in acknowledgement.

A rider approached. Cole shaded his face against the sun. Clouds of dust kicked up behind the strawberry roan that Cole immediately recognized as Rafe's horse, Lexa. Why was his brother in such a hurry?

He grabbed a hold of Mav's reins and mounted his black steed.

"Remember," he said, turning to Davey, "don't make me regret trusting you."

Cole turned the horse about and darted toward his brother at a gallop.

Rafe pulled Lexa in a circle to face up with Cole so they could talk.

"Preacher's gone!" Rafe stated between breaths. "Found this."

He handed a small piece of burned parchment to Cole. The last few letters of the scribbled name had been torn away. Jenna Gra— appeared in faded ink.

"Guess you're comin' with us to the Graysons?" Cole tucked the paper into his vest pocket.

"Let's go."

Cole whistled to Raine. Within a few moments, both Raine and Clay were ready to ride.

"We in a hurry?" Raine called out to his brothers, a hint of mockery in his strained voice.

"What's the matter big brother? Getting too old to keep up?" Rafe laughed as he pulled ahead of the others, Raine right on his tail.

As Cole started forward, a strange knot formed in his gut. He was unsure if it was anticipation or trepidation, but he couldn't shake the feeling he'd missed something.

"That's far enough." A formidable looking man in denims

and spurred boots met Cole and the others at the Grayson property line with a rifle slung menacingly across his lap.

Three men accompanied him on either side, each of them with guns within easy reach.

Max Grayson.

Cole let his hand fall casually to the butt of his sheathed Winchester.

"We'd like a word with you, Max." Clay's voice was steady, his eyes focused on the man they'd come to see.

"Why, Clay? You want my land so bad, you'll have to come and get it."

Cole didn't know what he'd anticipated the rancher would say, but it certainly wasn't an accusation.

"Want your... Now, why on earth would I want *your* land? I have my own spread to worry about." Clay appeared just as taken aback as Cole felt.

"I have to admit I never suspected you, McCallister. All your talk of sticking together and helping each other."

"Suspected me of what?" Clay's voice elevated a notch, in barely concealed warning.

Cole did not like the direction this conversation was heading. Something had obviously set Mr. Grayson on edge. Cole assessed each of the men in front of him. If this went badly, someone was going to get killed.

"My foreman is in the bunkhouse right now with Doc Knight. He was ambushed last night. Nearly killed."

"Ambushed? By who?" The surprise in Clay's voice was sincere.

"As if you don't know." Mr. Grayson spit into the dirt. The burly man to the right of him nudged his horse forward a step, the tight clench to his jaw and the flared nostrils showed scarcely restrained aggression. His lip curled and his eyes appeared sunken in from lack of sleep.

"Max, listen to me." Clay's voice was calm and steady. The only indication he was not as composed as he appeared was that his hands were gripping his reins so tight they shook. "We've been friends a long time, you and me—"

"I woulda thought that stood for somethin', but not after this."

"Mr. Grayson?" Cole urged Maverick forward. He stopped short when his action was greeted by five rifles barrels aimed directly at him.

One clicking noise sounded to his right and another immediately to his left. His brothers, especially Raine and Rafe, had always been very protective of him and Cole had no doubt their cocked guns pointed at those who threatened him. He didn't turn around, but patted at the air to tell Raine and Rafe to lower their munitions.

"Mr. Grayson," he began again, "there've been a lot of strange accidents over at the SilverHawk over the last couple of weeks. Just last night, we lost the barn in a fire. Considerin' how wet it's been, don't you think that's a little odd."

"You come out here to accuse me, son?" Max Grayson's face turned a purpled red behind his thick white mustache.

"Of course not." Cole paused. He needed to know why Mr. Grayson was so quick to assume they were the one's causing trouble and in order to do that he would have to gain the man's trust. "You had anything out of the ordinary happen 'round here?" he asked.

"Who are these men, Clay? I don't recognize a single one of 'em." Mr. Grayson shifted uncomfortably in his saddle. "Hiring new thugs, or are they the rustlers you came to tell me about this morning?" His voice still held accusation, but this time it shook with uncertainty.

"Max, this is Cole Redbourne. He is my new son-in-law and these here," he said pointing to the others, "are his brothers, Raine and Rafe. They have a lot of experience in these matters, Max. Let 'em help us."

"Redbournes, huh?" Max scratched his chin. "Any relation to Levi?"

"Brothers." Clay nodded.

The man seemed to ponder the idea for a moment. Then, without another word, signaled for the others to lower their guns. A scrawny, unshaven cowpoke circled around in back of them in escort fashion.

Cole should have been surprised Max Grayson knew Levi, but somehow wasn't.

"Come," Mr. Grayson commanded, turning his own horse around and heading for the main house.

Clay urged his dapple forward. The Redbournes followed.

Afternoon tea was nothing like what Abby had expected.

"Watercolors," Mitchell Patterson, the storekeeper's oldest son called out.

Lily placed a finger on her nose and sat down next to Abby with a gleeful smile on her face. The young man switched her places and drew a word from the little purple velvet satchel on the lamp table. He threw his hands up in the air and started waving them around.

It was clear to Abby she would not find out any gossip today. It appeared as if even the older women were enjoying the break from their daily lives. Mrs. Hutchinson sat in the corner with her fashionable hat and smiled in observation.

"Too bad your husband and his brothers couldn't stay. They would have been quite entertaining, I'm sure." Lily slouched against the back of the chair for only a moment before returning to her most lady-like posture. Abby hadn't missed the way her friend had allowed her ringlet curls to fall over the discolored portion of her face.

"This has been..." Abby struggled for the right word, "lovely, Lily. I had no idea people loved to play games so. But I really must be going."

"You can't fool me, Abby McCallister, um, Redbourne," she corrected. "I know you are bored out of your mind and just want to get home and help the menfolk find out what's going on around here," she whispered.

"Windmill," a deep voice sounded just behind Abby from the doorway.

A tall man, with grey speckles in his hair, stepped forward. He wore black trousers and a black shirt adorned in a crisp white collar. "Glad to see you all are still having your Sunday tea. I'd meant to be back in time for services this morning, but alas, the good Lord just didn't see fit I guess."

"Reverend Daniels," Lily immediately stood up and walked around the high backed couch to greet him. "Welcome back. You're here just in time to take a turn."

"Did you bring Reverend Harris with you?" One of the young Simpson girls asked with a giggle, hope evident in her big, bright blue eyes.

The preacher stared at her, a clouded expression crossing his features. "I'm sorry, Miss Natalie, but who?"

The girl's face fell. Abby stood up and looked at the man who'd baptized her.

"The new reverend, of course. You know..." Abby encouraged. "The one who took your place while you were away."

"Abby?" The reverend laughed softly in disbelief. "I hardly recognized you. You look lovely."

Unaccustomed to others paying notice to her appearance, Abby averted her eyes and rubbed her neck. "Thank you."

It only took a moment for Reverend Daniels to recover. "Now, I don't know what's going on here, but no one was sent to take my place. I'm the only pastor that I know of in more than a hundred miles."

Abby's head whipped back toward the man and she stared for several moments. "So, if Mr. Harris wasn't the preacher, then..."

Her mind raced.

"Then, how'd he marry us?" she asked, deflated.

The reverend choked. "You're married?"

She glanced at Lily.

"I've got to get home."

Lily took a step toward her, nodding her head with understanding.

"Has anyone seen Davey?"

She pinched at the skirt material near her knees and lifted as she ran down the hallway and outside toward the garden. She'd seen Davey hitch the wagon to the fence in front of Mr. Campbell's roses.

If Mr. Harris wasn't a preacher...

Her head jerked from side to side, looking for any sign of the freckled cowhand who could drive her home. She wished she'd ridden the new stallion, Chester. Patience had never been one of her strong points and her sense of urgency to get to her father and Cole with information about Mr. Harris only increased her unease.

When she at last found him walking around the back of the house, she grabbed his arm and pulled him along the stone pathway to the wagon.

"We have to go. Now." She lifted one foot to the metal rise.

"What's yer hurry, Abby? I haven't had a chance to get somethin' to eat yet."

Abby whirled around to face him, her dress falling back down around her feet. An angry purple and blue bruise encased his swollen left eye. Add that to his injured arm from the wagon accident and he looked a sight.

"Davey, what in heaven's name happened to you?"

The slim redhead pushed past her and began untying the reins from the garden fence.

"It's nothin', Abby. Just a misunderstandin' over a game a cards is all."

Abby hated asking for his help.

"Davey, I think I know who's behind all these *accidents*."

He stopped. "What do you mean *accidents*?" He imitated her inflection of the word, his eyes narrowing in on her with scrutiny.

"Davey, please. We must hurry," Abby said with an impatient edge to her voice. She turned away from him and lifted herself up onto the wagon seat.

"All right, all right. Don't get all bent, Abby." He walked around the front of the buckboard and pulled himself up. "It shore is mighty strange seein' ya'll gussied up.'"

Abby looked away. If people didn't stop mentioning her new look, she would have to use one of them for target practice.

"Let's go then. But from now on," his steely gaze moved upward, overshooting her eyes to an unknown location behind her, "the name is David." His voice seemed distant somehow. Hollow. A haunted expression fell over his features, overpowering his typically childlike appearance.

Abby lifted her eyebrows and dipped her chin to the right in attempt to hide the smile that threatened.

Davey focused on her, his voice softening. "Okay?" he added in a boyish plea.

"Thank you," Abby leaned over, placed her hand on his unbandaged forearm and squeezed, "David."

She glanced into the back of the buckboard. The sight of her Winchester rifle mounted to the side of the wagon bed reassured her. No one would be at the SilverHawk this afternoon because of the tea and she would not let anything else happen to the ranch. After Davey dropped her at home with her gun in hand, he could ride out to the Grayson's and get her father. And Cole. She had to get word to them before it was too late.

She'd think about the repercussions of not being officially married later. If they could just find Reverend Harris, or whoever he was, he could lead them to the new owner of the Gnarled Oak and they could put an end to all this mystery and mayhem once and for all.

Something wasn't right. Cole could feel it in his gut. He scanned his immediate surroundings before following the others through the homestead and into Max Grayson's study. The ranch appeared just like any other—cows in the pasture, horses in the corral, ranch hands fixing fences—nothing was visibly amiss, but Cole could not rid himself of the feeling that something was terribly wrong.

He glanced about the room. Except for the lack of books against the walls, it reminded Cole of his father's study. Framed drawings and paintings hung throughout the dark, musty room. With the curtains drawn, the sun touched the back wall, illuminating a collection of maps and landscape drawings.

Cole was fascinated with the intricacy of the maps. The detail was extraordinary and the technique awe inspiring. He walked the length of the room, stopping in front of each frame.

"Who's the artist?" Cole turned his head over his shoulder and asked Mr. Grayson.

"Not sure. Just initials scribbled at the bottom. See there?" Max pointed to the lower left corner of one of the pictures. PBH.

"I have some just like it in my office. Johansson gave a set to each of us when it all started," Clay offered.

Max Grayson's eyebrows lifted in surprise as he moved behind a mahogany desk that consumed nearly half the room. He reached into a large cabinet, pulling out a bottle and five small glasses. The honey colored liquid was poured into the first glass and he slid it across the desk to Clay. When he offered the second glass to Cole, Cole shook his head. He'd learned a long ago the ill effects drinking had on his reflexes and had determined to never touch the stuff. He couldn't afford to.

"No, thank you," he declined.

Each of his brothers in turn refused the glass. Mr. Grayson shrugged his shoulders and downed the brew in one swallow. He set the glass back on the table, refilled it, then leaned back in his chair, one hand still on the tumbler and the other resting on his midsection.

"Have a seat, gentlemen," Mr. Grayson invited, tilting his head toward the chairs at the outer edge of the wall.

Raine sat in the chair next to Clay, but Cole and Rafe remained standing.

"What is so important, Clay, you had to bring along all of

Levi's brothers?"

"Oh, this isn't all of us, Mr. Grayson. We are seven brothers total." Raine smiled easily as he spoke.

Mr. Grayson's mouth opened and he stared blankly at Raine.

The sunlight glinted off the glass of the farthest framed map on the wall. Something about the drawing pulled Cole closer and he lifted it off its nail. Upon inspection, he was even more awed by its sophistication.

"Max, is this the only map of Silver Falls in your collection?"

The white haired man nodded. "But there are five others similar to it. One for each of us who own a part of the original mountain spread."

"Mine's hangin' in my study," Clay pointed out. "And I think Henry and Zed still have theirs too."

"I'm not sure where the map for Deardon's place is or Johansson's for that matter," Max offered.

"Each of our individual maps are recreated portions from a master drawing of Johansson's original spread. If you're looking for that, you'll want to find Freidrich's grandson or the man he sold the property to," Clay said.

"Alaric Johansson is dead." Cole spoke in a low voice. He took a small weathered note from the inside pocket of his vest and handed it to Clay.

Clay scanned the message and looked up at Cole. His eyebrows formed a solid crease across his forehead. "Where did you get this, son?" Clay's tone held a touch of accusation.

Cole knew he'd kept his secret too long.

A loud pounding on the door captured the attention of all the men in the room.

"It's Weston, Mr. Grayson." Doc Knight pushed the door open and stood, dark circles lining his eyes. "He has awoken."

Max pulled himself up out of his chair in a hurry and grabbed his hat from the rack at the entry.

"Wes is my foreman," he said over his shoulder before disappearing out the door with the doctor.

Cole followed. As they climbed the stairs to the bedroom, the doctor mumbled a few words to Mr. Grayson Cole couldn't hear.

When the door opened, the pungent aroma of liniment smacked Cole in the face. He could see the injured man, bandaged around the head and arm, and one of his eyes looked puffy and swollen beneath the black and purple bruising.

Mr. Grayson sat down in a chair at the edge of the bed and removed his Stetson. He leaned forward onto his knees, fidgeting with the brim of the hat.

"Glad you're still with us, Wes." Mr. Grayson dropped his head as he spoke. Only when he said the man's name did he look at him. "Who did this to ya, son?"

Wes stared at the ceiling, but his shoulders scrunched into a half-hearted shrug, evoking a grimace from his parched lips. He started to choke. Doc Knight filled a glass with water and moved to the side of the bed. He lifted Wes's head enough that he could gently ease the cup to his mouth. It was then Cole noticed the unfocused expression in his eyes. The man was blind.

"He hasn't spoken a word since he opened his eyes." Once the doc was satisfied Wes'd had enough to drink, he nodded to Mr. Grayson who leaned in a little closer.

"We're going to find out who did this to you," Grayson said. "Do you hear me?"

The man's eyes closed and a single, fat tear trailed his tightly clenched jaw. When he opened them again, his lips pursed and Cole sensed the fear of a horrible truth beginning to sink in.

He felt sorry for the man. He didn't know the physical reality of losing his sight, but he'd experienced the blinding effects of self-pity, self-loathing, and the heavy despair of loss. He wouldn't wish that kind of heartache on any man.

The chair scratched against the floor when Mr. Grayson slid it backward to stand up. "We'll find him."

the many layers that made up the nonsensical dress she wore, she gripped the back of the seat and pushed herself up and over, just as another shot sounded. Her skirt caught on one of the seat planks and she flew forward, tumbling onto her stomach on the flat boards lining the wagon bed. The buckboard squealed in protest. The wood near the axel cracked.

Another shot.

The horses reared and anxiously started prancing backward. One blew hard through his nose and the other snorted.

Looking to her left, she spotted her Winchester rifle secured to the side of the buckboard with two latches and reached for it. Her fingers slowly slid down the length of the cool steel of the barrel until she reached the first latch. She had to stretch another inch before she could release the lock.

Once the gun was freed, she pulled it close to her and closed her eyes with a silent prayer of thanks. When she opened her eyes, she relaxed her grip on the gun enough to open the barrel and check for ammunition. Eleven.

Assured the rifle was loaded, she used her elbows to crawl forward until she reached the side railing and could see through the slats of wood. The horses still retreated backward and had almost reached the spot Davey had fallen. Thick red pools of blood spread rapidly across his chest.

"Whoa," she yelled. They seemed to recognize her voice and did as she commanded.

Abby couldn't get to Davey without exposing herself, but she had to do something. While she hated to admit it, Cole had been right. She had a knack for finding trouble all right.

Whoever was after the ranch had to be getting desperate. This was certainly no accident. She rolled onto her back, her gun cocked and ready to shoot.

Cole's handsome face fixed in her mind. *Oh, Lord,* Abby pleaded in silent prayer. *Don't let this be the end. Cole needs to know him. I need to tell him.*

Abby kicked at the back wagon door and was surprised it broke open on the first kick. She slid off the back and

CHAPTER TWENTY-ONE

The pass was unnaturally quiet and Abby found herself scanning the trees for any sign of trouble. A slight blur of color caught her eye. Davey had been oddly quiet on the drive and she wondered if he sensed it too.

"Davey?"

He shot her a quelling look before returning to focus on the road ahead.

"David," she corrected. "Can we go a little faster? Something is not right."

"I'm..." Davey paused. "I'm sorry, Abby," he said.

The boy's head dropped and he turned to face her, something perplexing prowling about his young features. A pained expression crossed his face, his eyes squinted. Then after taking an extraordinarily long, deep breath, he turned focus back to the team of horses and belted, "Hi-yah!"

The buckboard shot forward.

Abby grabbed a hold of the bottom of her seat to b herself for the sudden flight.

"Listen, Abby," he yelled over the noise and jostlir wagon, "stay down," he warned.

Crack. A shot rang out and Abby watched in horr Davey's body flung from the seat over the side of the and onto the hard rutted road. Abby's instincts took grabbed a hold of the reins and tried to reach for th just behind her in the wagon. It was too far back.

Abby pulled the wagon to a hard stop. Forget'

behind the rear wheel. Holding the gun close to her chest, she chanced a quick scan of the horizon. Nothing.

She took a deep breath and stood, pulling the gun into shooting position on her shoulder. In one quick movement she had thrust herself from behind the wagon and began to fire in the direction from where the shots had come, making her way toward Davey. The team of horses pranced about, but did not bolt.

When she reached Davey's body she turned back to the trees and fired two more shots before grabbing a hold of the kid's booted foot and pulling him back toward the buckboard. She tugged hard, but with the gun tucked under her arm, he was just too heavy to move to a safer position.

A moan, barely audible, reached Abby's ears. He *was* still alive. Another shot flew past her ear and she launched herself behind wagon for cover. If she couldn't get Davey behind the wagon, maybe she could move the wagon to cover him. She slowly made her way to the horses. Abby managed three more shots before she reached the skittish horse's head. She grabbed his reins and coaxed the team backward, hopefully blocking them from their assailant's view.

The sound of her heart in her ears was deafening.

She glanced at Davey and for the first time since he'd been a part of the ranch, thought about his family. He was so young. He must have a ma missing him somewhere. Abby set her Winchester on a protruding wooden ledge just above the wagon wheel and crawled back to Davey. She placed her arms beneath his shoulders and dragged him to the front wheel.

She grabbed her gun and reached over the wagon bed, frantically feeling for a fresh canteen. It took a moment, but finally she found the strap and yanked. Looking behind her with squinted eyes, she unscrewed the canteen lid.

Satisfied her attacker was still to her north, she crouched down and poured some cool water into Davey's mouth. It burbled up and dripped down the side of his face, tinged with swirling bouts of red.

"We'll get you to the doc, David," she reassured him. "Just

hang on a little while longer."

Abby closed the canteen and set it next to Davey's head. She grabbed the butt of the rifle and started to stand, but was stopped by a weak hand on her forearm.

"I'm so...sor-ry, Abby," Davey's breaths were coming in ragged heaves, every syllable strained. He opened his hand. A black rag fell open and onto her dress. She stared at it, trying to reconcile its meaning in her mind.

"Shhh." Abby placed a finger over his lips. "Just rest for a minute, David. I'll be right back."

His grip tightened around her forearm. "Just call me...Davey," he gasped with an awkward lift to his lips.

"Davey," she smiled back.

He closed his eyes and the tension in his neck relaxed instantly.

Abby dropped her head, one small tear squeezing from her tightly closed eyes. *What did you get yerself mixed up in, Davey?* Indignation swelled within her and in one fluid motion, she reached for her gun, pulling it instantly into position and screamed. She whipped her body into a standing position and aimed for the hills.

"I wouldn't do that if I were you."

The chilling voice behind her was familiar and the cocking of a gun unmistakable.

She shifted her rifle to one hand as she raised both arms into the air. Slowly, she turned around to face Davey's killer.

"You?" was all she could manage. Shock and fear both vying for control. "Why?"

"No need for answers where you're goin', missy. It's time to say goodbye, Abby McCallister."

She closed her eyes and the whistle of a shot rang through the otherwise still afternoon.

"At least two men are dead, another blinded. Cattle and

horses are missing. Clay's barn is burned to ash. Who else is going to get hurt before we find the man responsible for this mess?" Cole ran his fingers through his hair as he paced Mr. Grayson's study, the apprehension in his gut growing stronger by the moment.

"You wearin' holes in the floor won't get us any closer, Charcoal." Raine's easy manner irked Cole, mostly because he was already brimming with impatience.

The study door opened. Cole's head jerked up to see Mr. Grayson as he entered the room.

"What happened last night, Mr. Grayson?" Cole assailed him, moving to the entrance with quick precision. "What happened to Wes?"

"Set yourself down, son. I want answers as badly as you. Wes is like a son to me." Mr. Grayson sidestepped Cole and walked back to his desk. "And call me Max."

Cole reluctantly sat down in the chair opposite Max's desk. He leaned forward onto his knees and stared at the white haired man as he took a seat behind the desk.

The door opened again.

"Gentlemen, this here's Charlie." He nodded to the burly man who'd greeted them at the gate. "And this...well, I'd like you to meet my daughter."

Cole stood up with a start when the door pushed open a little farther to reveal his new acquaintance. His brothers joined him and the three of them stood there and stared.

Jenna, adorned in a crimson blouse and brown riding britches, walked through the door. Her lips, nearly the color of her shirt, were a striking contrast against the backdrop of her ebony mane. Her beauty was remarkable certainly, but Cole had known his share of beautiful women and he knew better than to turn his back to a vixen.

Max pulled Jenna into a one-armed embrace and placed a kiss on her forehead. "Hello, my querida," he spoke softly.

Cole lifted an eyebrow. He reached into his pocket and rubbed the silver pendant there between his fingers.

Jenna stepped forward away from her father and extended

her hand to Cole.

"It's nice to see you again, Miss Grayson," Cole said with a slight nod, taking a hold of her hand, his politeness feigned.

"Why, how lucky are we to have all three of y'all right here in our home." She did not take her dark brown eyes from Cole's face and she held fast to his hand.

Fiery green eyes overshadowed Cole's thoughts and he realized this brazen temptress could never compare to Abby, the beauty who already bore his name. Well...almost. The thought of her twisted his gut until he realized it was Abby who haunted him, Abby who was in danger. It had pricked at his gut for the better part of an hour. He disengaged himself from Jenna and turned to her father.

"Time's run out. I need to know what happened to Wes, Max." Cole spoke slowly, his words more deliberate this time. "Now."

He knew the moment Raine and Rafe reached either side of him. From the look on Max's face, Cole guessed the three of them together posed a very intimidating picture. *Good.*

With a breath of resignation, Max motioned for all of them to sit down.

"Drovers and ranch hands from all the ranches around here gather together on Wednesday nights for a weekly poker game," Max started. "Last night was no different. Charlie here said that after a heated discussion between one of your ranch hands and Wes, the two of them stepped outside to handle it." He looked up at Clay.

Cole scooted forward in his chair.

"Charlie kept the rest of them inside, while Wes took care of the kid. When Wes didn't return after a few minutes, Charlie went outside and found him lying face down in the mud, his head covered in blood. He thought Wes was dead for sure. That's why I was so sure you'd been the one causing all the trouble." Max jutted his chin toward Clay. "It was one of yours who done this to Wes."

"Who was it?" Cole demanded. "Who did this?"

"Don't know the boy's name. But with that bright red hair

and freckle spots all over his face, I reckon you'll know him. Charlie said they all just call him Kid."

Clay scratched his chin and looked up at Cole without lifting his head all the way. "Davey," he said flatly.

The boy couldn't be more than seventeen.

Clay stared at him, his eyebrows scrunched together.

"It's Davey."

"We just said that."

"No. Think about it. Every time there has been an accident, he was there. He was at the bar when your foreman was killed. He was the one who told Caleb the horse had gotten out. He was the one who was hurt in the wagon incident, and even when Martha was trapped inside the chicken coop..."

"It was Davey who got her out." Clay's face lit with comprehension.

Again, a gnawing sensation bit at Cole's insides. He ran through the brief interactions he'd had with the young cow hand. He felt the blood drain from his face.

"He's driving Abby home from the Campbell's. He'll have her alone." Cole burst out of his chair. He could not sit any longer.

He strode toward the door, but stopped at the threshold. "Ma'am. Gentlemen," Cole nodded his head toward Jenna, then Max and Charlie.

"Wait. I may also be able to help." Jenna stopped him.

Cole eyed her with apprehension.

She looked at her father and then to each of the men around the room before she fixed her gaze back on Cole.

"I'm...a Pinkerton."

Cole's jaw dropped and he worked quickly to pick it back up again and he raised a single eyebrow. He'd never heard of a female Pinkerton before and when he looked over at his brothers, he noticed she'd caught the interest and undivided attention of both of them.

"I'm back here on assignment, but will help where I can."

Cole reached into his pocket and pulled out the small locket he'd found on his property.

"I believe this belongs to you." Cole stared at her hard. "Querida," he finished with a contrived smile. He closed her fingers around the metal chain and hastened to the door with his brother and father-in-law at his heels. He had to find Abby.

"Where did you get this?" Jenna yelled after him.

He ignored her question and had almost reached the stable. "Charcoal?"

Cole turned around when Rafe called his name from the Grayson's doorway.

"I'll be right behind ya. I need to have a little chat with the lady first about a certain non-preacher," Rafe said.

Cole nodded and turned back toward his horse.

Low clouds had suddenly turned a darkened gray. Another storm front was setting in. He had to find Abby. Now.

"Martha." Clay's voice was frantic. "Martha."

"I'm here," she said as she walked out of the kitchen. "What's all yer yellin' about, Clay honey?" When the woman noticed Cole standing at the door, she blushed, looked down, and wiped her hands on her apron.

"Have you seen Abby? Has she made it home from the Campbell's yet?"

"Come to think of it, no. She left in quite a hurry after Reverend Daniels showed up. I didn't have a chance to talk to her. Bert and Jim drove me home." Martha looked back and forth between the two men standing in front of her. "Clay, what's wrong?"

Worry lines etched into the woman's face as she waited a reply.

The two men exchanged glances. If this Davey kid was mixed up in all the trouble, Abby wouldn't be safe. Cole didn't hear Clay's response. He was already out the door. Raine and Rafe both met him near the corral.

"She's not here," he called back as he mounted his horse.

Clay ran out of the house just as he pulled Maverick around.

"Ya!" Cole yelled and kicked Maverick into a run. He heard the others pull up behind him, but did not pause long enough to look.

He'd told the young ranch hand not to take Abby home through the ravine, but he would bet his horse that is exactly where he'd taken her. If this Davey kid did anything to hurt Abby or had anything to do with Alaric's death, the boy wouldn't be safe around him.

The air had turned crisp. It bit into Cole's face as he raced toward town. He prayed Davey had stayed on the main path and had not diverted on the way home. He was closer than ever to finding the truth about Alaric, yet it was something else that drove him forward. Fear, he realized. Fear of losing the one thing he'd once believed he could live without. Love. He loved Abby.

He pushed Maverick harder. He had to reach her before something happened. Before he lost her.

Gun shots. The pounding in his chest nearly knocked him from his mount, but he pressed forward. When the wagon came into view at the south end of the pass, Cole pulled Maverick to a stop. Something was terribly wrong.

He scanned the confines of the pass and up into the hills. A glint of steel flashed from the cluster of trees at the top of the ridge. From his position, he could see Abby hunched behind her wagon, rifle in hand, and Davey lying lifeless at her feet. There was no time to waste.

He dismounted, a Remington in each hand. Raine was right behind him. Cole glanced up to Rafe and motioned for him and Clay to climb the ridge. They would find the shooter and stop him.

Movement drew his eye to some huddled foliage at the base of the ravine behind Abby. Cole hunched lower. When a man appeared out of the brush, Cole aimed. He was too far out of range and wouldn't be able to get off a clear shot.

A few yards away, he spotted a massive angular rock

protruding from the side of the hill. If he could make it that far undetected, he would be within shooting range. He glanced to the ridge line and saw that Rafe and Clay had managed to reach the rim undetected. They'd dismounted and had already made their way to the cluster of trees on foot.

Cole crouched as low as he could to the ground and rushed to the rock. Raine joined him.

"She'll be all right, Charcoal. We'll get her."

Cole couldn't respond for fear his emotions would betray him. He lifted his gun and rested the barrel along a small crevice in the rock. Though the clouds were low and the temperature had dropped dramatically in the last half an hour, the air was eerily still.

Fear gripped him the moment Abby left the base of the wagon and stood, rifle in hand. She'd not seen the man approaching her from behind. However, she stopped, hands in the air, and turned around.

From this distance, Cole could barely make out the look of recognition as she faced her attacker. She knew the man.

The boorish gunman raised his pistol, level to Abby's head. Cole had to do something. And now. He aimed. He didn't have a good angle to the man's heart, but one shot in the head would do it.

His finger started to bend against the trigger, but before he could complete the action, another shot echoed through the small canyon.

He held his breath. He'd hesitated too long. Dread gripped his gut. Like waking from a bad dream he watched as Abby's attacker fell in one long, drawn out motion to the ground. Abby had not been hit. She was alive.

Cole pushed himself away from the rock, running. He swiftly swung a leg over Maverick's back, dug his heels into the horse's flanks, and rushed toward the wagon.

CHAPTER TWENTY-TWO

Abby waited for the pain. It didn't come. She took a deep breath, fresh air filling her lungs. She was alive.

Her eyes opened to Jefferson Spencer lying in a lifeless heap just feet away from her. She blinked hard. An incessant drumming filled her ears and she tried to shake it from her head. As the pounding got louder, she looked up. The sound came from a quickly approaching rider on horseback.

Cole. Her heart leapt at the sight of him. Had he done this? Had he saved her once again?

One instant Cole was on his horse and the next he was making his way toward her. She wasn't sure he had even dismounted, the movement had been so fluid. Then she felt his hands on her face, tilting her chin upward to meet his kiss. The familiar fluttering in her stomach was replaced by the thundering of a herd of horses dancing on her insides.

Is this really happening?

His mouth crushed against hers and instead of pulling away she yearned to be closer. Needed him to be closer. Her lips parted ever so slightly. Tingles started in her mouth and worked their way through her body, down to her toes. He felt good. She was safe. This felt right.

Cole's hands tightened on her jaw, pulling her into him. It was not enough. The connection she felt to him at this moment was more intense, more fulfilling than anything she had ever experienced. She slid her arms up his chest and over his shoulders. Her fists closed around locks of hair at his nape and she pulled him closer.

Cole's fingers traced over her hair and down her body to her waist.

Abby collapsed against him, responding to his every touch. For her, they were alone in the middle of a dream, working together to shove away the reality of the horror she'd just experienced. She was acutely aware of his hands, entwined in the fabric at the back of her dress, pulling her even tighter into his embrace.

When a deep seated groan escaped him, he withdrew his lips from hers and looked down with eyes that reflected a full blown storm. With Abby still cradled in his arm, he brought a hand up to caress her jawline, his thumb rubbing over her lips. After a few moments of silence, he bent his head toward her, moving closer until his lips were mere inches from hers. The wait, torturous.

Please.

His mouth connected in soft surrender, capturing her lower lip between his.

Finally, she breathed, almost audibly.

Cole buried his face in her neck. "I thought I was going to lose you." He placed a light kiss just above her collar bone. "When I'd only just found you." His breathless admission both surprised and delighted her.

Never before had a man infuriated her so, yet never before had one evoked such emotions. She loved him. She knew it now without question. Tightening her own arms around his neck, she cradled her head into his neck.

Someone behind them cleared his throat.

Abby opened her eyes when Cole lifted his head away from her.

Raine motioned his head toward the dead Mr. Spencer.

A vacant feeling overcame her at the loss of Cole's warmth from her face. He didn't let go and seemed reluctant to pull away. His eyes fixed once again on hers and he bent his head forward, dropping one last kiss firmly on her mouth. However, his touch never left completely.

He stepped back, sliding a hand down her arm until it found and clasped her fingers. Turning back to Raine, he pulled her gently along behind him as he walked to the body.

Abby was breathless. She rubbed her unencumbered fingers across her lips and smiled.

Dear heavens.

Cole suddenly went rigid, pulling Abby back into the moment.

"I know him," Cole said, a look of bent anger steeling his features. "His name is Mason Gregory. I met him in Kansas a week or so before Alaric died."

Abby looked from Cole to the dead man lying at their feet, her brows furrowing in confusion.

"Cole, you must be mistaken. That," she pointed to the dead man, "is Jefferson Spencer."

"You know him?" Raine asked.

Abby took another step forward, her fingers still hooked with Cole's. She nodded. "All my life."

"Spencer? As in, related to all those boys we carted into town, Spencer?" Cole asked as he squeezed her hand.

She nodded.

His jaw tightened.

Cole met her stare, a different kind of storm brewing in their depths. His walnut brown eyes changed into a shade nearing black.

At the clacking sound of hoof beats behind her, Abby tore her gaze from her husband to see Rafe and her father approaching on horseback. Rafe dismounted first and tossed an unconscious Earl Spencer onto his shoulder from the horse's rump.

"Now, how'd he get out?" Raine asked with disgust.

"Davey." Abby spoke, sadness lining her voice as she looked over at the inert redheaded youth. "He knew something was going to happen. He told me he was..." she paused briefly before whispering the last word, "sorry."

Rafe tugged Earl's limp body from his shoulder and laid him on the ground in front of the others.

"What is going on?" Abby's voice quieted, but with firm resolve.

Clay joined them, another Spencer brother in tow.

"Let's just ask *him*." Clay, who'd obviously heard their conversation, had a hold of the eldest Spencer boy by the nape and shoved the mussed young man forward into the small group.

A deep growl rolling in Cole's throat took Abby by surprise. She tightened her grip on his hand, something telling her not to let him go.

"Tell me what *he* was doing in Kansas." Cole nearly shouted at him, pointing at his father.

Benjamin Spencer's eyes grew wide as he scanned the faces of each of the men looming over him.

"Kansas?" Cole asked again, this time through gritted teeth. His stare grew cold as he waited for an answer. His brows furrowed and his stance became more rigid. Abby grabbed a hold of his wrist with her other hand and held tight.

Benjamin stared at him in confusion, his eyes now the size of silver dollars.

"Ben," she coaxed in a soft voice.

The man veered his gaze away from his intimidators and found her.

"Abby, we never meant for nobody to get hurt." Benjamin focused his attentions on her, the lone woman in the group, surely hoping to gain sympathy. He rushed toward her, a plea in his voice.

Cole stepped protectively in front of Abby, her hand still held tightly in his grasp.

Ben stopped short.

A flash of amusement touched Rafe's face and Abby realized he had just seen her hand entwined in Cole's. She smiled back, despite her knowledge that the danger to the Spencer boys amplified with every moment that passed.

"He was gonna kill you, Abby." Ben's eyes met hers with fierce intensity. "I couldn't let that happen."

"*You* shot him?" Abby asked in disbelief.

The meaning of his actions sunk deeper and her gratitude for his sacrifice swelled. Abby pulled her hand from Cole's and took a step toward the tormented young man who'd just taken the life of his own father to save her.

His head dropped into his hands and for the first time in her life, Abby saw a Spencer shed tears. Without apparent regard for the consequences, Ben threw his arms around Abby's neck and shoulders and hugged her, a little too tight for comfort, but Abby didn't let go.

"Thank you, Ben. Thank you for saving my life."

"And mine." Earl lifted his head and pushed himself up onto his hands. His voice was low and hoarse. The younger of the two Spencer brothers sat up and with a wary look at Rafe, who stood directly above him, he dragged himself along the ground toward Abby and his brother. When he reached Benjamin's feet he repeated, "And mine, big brother."

Ben let go of Abby and reached down to help Earl into a standing position. Together they limped over to a semi hollow log and sat down.

Abby shot a surprised look to Rafe.

"Wasn't me," he said with his palms up. "He was out cold when we found him."

"Pa was angry they got the better of us last night." Earl rubbed the side of his neck. "But we didn't start that fire."

Cole snorted, throwing his hands through his hair in visible frustration. Abby ignored him.

"Why'd your pa kill Davey?" Abby asked point blank.

"We was just supposed to scare you is all. I had no idea he was gonna shoot the redhead kid," Ben responded.

"Why scare Abby?" Raine placed his booted foot on the log where Earl sat.

"Somebody was gonna give us enough silver to pay off the farm if we could make a few problems go away."

"What problems?" Cole asked as he took an intimidating step forward, his eyes scrunching speculatively toward the young brothers. "And what was your father doing in Kansas?"

Earl slowly lifted his head to meet Cole's intense stare. "Pa went to Kansas to find Alaric Johansson and persuade him to sell the Gnarled Oak."

"Alaric? What does he have to do with any of this?" Abby demanded.

Cole obviously knew more than he'd let on and she wanted answers.

"And do you know what happened to him? My closest friend?" Cole yelled.

Earl looked away.

A snarl found residence on Cole's face just before he lunged. Rafe and Raine both reached out, each grabbing a side, holding him from reaching his target.

Ben moved between them and Earl.

From the fierceness in Cole's stance and the tightness of his fists, Abby realized that his brothers were the only barrier to an ill fate for Earl.

"Alaric deserves justice!" Cole nearly screamed the last word. His hands balled into fists while his insides tightened, then burned as if they'd been torn apart all together. He pounded his fists against the kitchen table. The dark recesses of his mind had tormented him with guilt for so long that Spencer's death still had not brought him any nearer to finding closure.

"Isn't death justice enough?" Raine asked.

Cole felt cheated. Someone else had done his job. He cursed inwardly. Determination all but consumed him. More than ever, he needed to find the malefactor who'd paid to see Alaric dead. Even if it meant sacrificing everything.

A loud banging sounded from the front door.

"Who's callin' at this time of night? And on Sunday," Martha muttered as she lifted her shotgun from the wall and walked out of the kitchen.

"Cole," Rafe broke through his thoughts, "you have got to

stop allowing anger to cloud your judgment. Alaric is gone. Nothing we do will bring him back."

Guilt transmogrified into anger and the fire Cole felt inside fought to consume him. His fingers tugged at his hair in frustration.

"Don't patronize me. You have no idea what it's like to lose your best frien—"

Without warning, Rafe's fist connected fiercely with Cole's already tender jaw.

"You think you're the only one who's ever been hurt, little brother," Rafe said, rubbing his knuckles and shaking his lead hand, "well, wake up."

As Cole picked himself up from the floor, regret swept over him. He looked around at all the people standing in the room, knowing what each of them had lost, and knew he'd gone too far.

Cole flexed his aching jaw and locked eyes with his brother.

"Rafe," Raine said.

The hardness left his expression at the mention of his name.

"You're not alone, Charcoal." Rafe patted Cole firmly on the face in the same place his fist had planted its mark. "You never have been." Rafe wrapped his arm over Cole's shoulder and pulled him into a quick embrace. "You never will."

When he let go, Cole rubbed his face gingerly and glanced up to find Abby watching him. Flashes of the last few days passed through his mind. An imprint of Abby, smiling up at him as they'd danced at the wedding celebration, skittered through his thoughts. The soft, melon-like scent of her hair had engrained itself in his nostrils and he longed to twine his hands in the luscious fullness of her fiery tresses, to pull her close to him. The memory of her kiss seared his thoughts with fervor as he recalled her eager response to his desperate loving.

No. Rafe was right. It was time to wake up. He couldn't allow the bitterness and need for vengeance to control him. There was too much at stake now. Cole studied his wife, holding her gaze. Abby's fire blond locks fell in disarray across her forehead and down her back. She was beautiful. He'd thought he could sacrifice everything, but looking at her now, knowing what he would be giving up, everything was just too high a price.

Still, he had to know. Silver Falls was his home now and he intended to protect it. The walls of the rustic kitchen closed in around Cole as he paced the room with heavy steps. Silence met him from the lamp lit table. It seemed no one dared speak.

Cole's jaw clenched even tighter, but his eyes remained on Abby.

"Alaric was my best friend," he confessed, "and someone killed him for his land." Cole wasn't asking for absolution, but he hoped she'd understand.

Visions of Alaric, riding just a few paces ahead of him around the bend, and the sight of him lying in the bottom of the gorge, broken and dying, had tormented Cole for more than a year. His fingertips pressed at his temples, willing the memories to stop. "I need to know who that someone is and stop him from doing any more harm."

"Well, we know all the calamities around here lately and Alaric's accident are connected," Raine surmised. "Now, we just have to figure out how."

"The railroad," Clay said in a hoarse voice. He cleared his throat. "Levi sent papers to me, Max, and Friedrich, just before he passed away, depicting the railroad proposal. I'm guessing he sent something like that to the Deardons as well." Clay pushed his chair away from the table and moved toward the door.

"Clay." Cole wanted to tell him everything. "Wait. What did you say? The railroad is going to pass through Silver Falls? Where exactly?"

"Allow me to answer that."

Everyone looked up. Standing against the kitchen doorframe with his riding duster folded over his arm, was Levi, dressed in denims and a crimson button down shirt. Cole couldn't remember the last time he'd seen this brother without a suit. By the shadows on the man's face, Cole guessed he'd not slept much in the last few days.

Raine and Rafe both pushed out of their chairs and launched themselves at him. Levi's face broke into a huge grin. In turn they clapped each other on the back in a bear-like hug. Cole watched.

"Come on, Charcoal."

It had been a long time since he'd seen Levi. Although, it had only been a short while since he'd seen his brother's spitting image in Texas, when he'd picked up the cattle and horses from Taggert, Levi's twin. Cole's emotions clashed together like thunder striking out at a clear sky. He couldn't decide which feeling was stronger—anger at Levi's involvement in his current situation or appreciation for it.

Appreciation won. Cole moved forward and joined in the playful reunion.

"What are you doing here?"

"When Mother told me you thought McCallister here might have had something to do with Alaric's death, and that you'd headed out here to find the truth, I knew I needed to help." Levi reached a hand out to Clay. "I'm sorry for calling at such a late hour, my friend."

Clay stood halfway from his chair and shook his hand. "It's good to see you, Levi."

"To answer your question, Charcoal, the railroad would like to purchase sections of your land, McCallister's, and Grayson's."

Cole closed his eyes.

"Cole's land?" Abby stepped forward from the shadows and asked, befuddled.

Oh, no. Please don't say it. Not now. Not before I can explain. She won't understand.

Levi looked up at Cole, who made the slightest shake with his head. It went unnoticed.

"Cole has always been the modest one. Did my youngest brother forget to mention he owns the Gnarled Oak and the entire town of Silver Falls?" Levi nodded his head. "Yes, the Johansson and Deardon lands...all his."

"Levi." Cole's voice held strict warning.

"And he had all that *before* marrying into his substantial inheritance."

Cole closed his eyes briefly and shook his head. Why hadn't he just told her the truth?

Abby glanced at him, as if for confirmation. He held her eyes, but she turned away.

"Abby," he reached out for her arm, but she shook him off.

"Don't."

She pushed past Levi and Raine, then to the front door. It banged shut.

She was gone.

Abby needed air.

While the others had sat at the table in deep discussion over the events of the past few days, she'd backed away and listened.

Before marrying for his substantial inheritance, Levi'd said. What did that mean, exactly?

She couldn't breathe. It felt like all her wind had been sucked from her chest and she had to concentrate on every inhale, every exhale.

Cole had come to Silver Falls to avenge Alaric. He'd believed her father had something to do with his friend's death and Abby realized he'd had multiple reasons for marrying her and none had to do with her.

How could I have been so stupid?

He lied about everything. He lied about coming here to start his own place. He lied about needing the job with her father. He lied about his reasons for marrying her. The last lie hurt most of all. She'd been fooling herself to think he could love her. That he'd want her. She could have accepted it had she known from the beginning. But now it was too late. She'd given away her heart and there was no turning back.

Abby pressed her eyes shut against the pain. One fat tear squeezed from beneath her thick lashes. She rubbed her hands vigorously over her bare arms, hoping to fight the evening chill. Using the back of her hand she wiped the lone tear from her cheek and looked down at the topaz dress she'd worn to church. She lifted a handful of the material and dropped it again. As much as she'd wanted to believe it, a fancy dress could not make her into something she wasn't. A lady.

Cole Redbourne came from money. He didn't need her or the ranch. She wondered if he'd known all along Mr. Harris wasn't a real preacher. Without warning she bent over and burst into sobs. She thrust her hands to her face, hoping to bury her weakness.

When she finally caught her breath and the tears stopped flowing, she straightened. Maybe her father had been right all along. It was time for her to visit her aunt Iris in Denver. He wouldn't sell the SilverHawk now. She was sure of it.

Cole would discover soon enough she'd learned about Mr. Harris. She would save him the grief and herself the embarrassment. A stage would be in town in the morning. She would be on it. Surely, Aunt Iris would understand if she arrived on her doorstep unannounced.

Abby opened the door very quietly and tiptoed across the wooden floors of her empty bedroom. She sat down on the bed and whispered into the darkness.

"I miss you, Mama."

Without changing out of her dress, she snuggled beneath the covers and pulled them up to her chin. "Please, God, let me be strong."

CHAPTER TWENTY-THREE

Monday

Cole had been outside their bedroom door for the better half of the morning, sitting in the chair, standing by the fireplace, waiting for Abby to emerge. He didn't want to wake her, but she hadn't come out for breakfast and he needed to talk to her, to tell her the truth.

He lifted his fist to knock at the door.

"She's gone, son."

Cole whirled around to see Clay standing with his back leaned up against the pole at the base of the stairs.

He dropped his hand to his side. "Gone where?" he asked.

He'd gone to the bunkhouse last night with his brothers, knowing Abby would be waiting in their bedroom with questions he wasn't prepared to answer. So, he'd stayed away.

"She left this for you." Clay threw a folded piece of parchment across the long table behind the couch.

Cole eyed Clay, whose expression appeared grim. Gingerly he opened the note.

Dearest Cole,

As I am sure you have already learned, Mr. Harris was not Reverend Daniel's replacement, but an imposter. We are not husband and wife as we believed and I relieve you of any sense of duty to come after me. My aunt will see to it that I am provided for. I assure you I have no illusions that what we shared was real, but I do want you to know I will

*always carry a place in my heart for the man who rolled in the mud for me.
I wish you luck in your life, Mr. Redbourne. I am afraid I am too
weak and could not bear to hear your reasons for leaving me. So, I will say
goodbye here. Know you have made an impression on me I am not soon to
forget. Thank you for even pretending to marry a tomboy like me.*

Abigail McCallister

Cole looked up from the note. "Pretending?"

Who was pretending?

Clay watched him with squinted eyes.

"Where would she go?" Cole asked his would-be father-in-law.

"Let her go, son." Clay pushed off from the pole he leaned against.

"I can't." His voice cracked, but Cole didn't care. He couldn't lose her now. He would not let her go. "I love her," he whispered.

"Well, why ya standin' here tellin' me, son? The stage leaves in half an hour."

Cole darted from the house to the stable. Town was at least an hour's ride from the SilverHawk in the buckboard. He could make it in half that if he pushed Maverick hard.

"Get it all squared away, Charcoal?" Levi jumped off the wooden plank porch of the bunkhouse and followed him into the stable.

"She's not here," Cole answered while pulling his tack from a hook on the wall. "She's leaving on the stage for Denver. Levi, I have to stop her."

Levi nodded, grabbed his work coat off a chair in the stable, and headed for the bunkhouse. "We're right behind you," he yelled back over his shoulder.

Cole pulled the last strap with a firm grip and hauled himself up onto Maverick's back. He ducked his head as he passed through the stable doors, and with only a slight nudge, Maverick seemed to feel his urgency. As if the signal had sounded from the starting line at the track, the steed broke into a dead run toward town.

Dust swirled around the stagecoach as it trampled down the only road into town. Abby had been waiting on the wooden bench in front of the post office since sunup. She knew Gus, the driver, would probably want to catch some breakfast at the hotel before heading on to Denver, but she was prepared just in case he didn't.

Abby had awoken in the early morning to find that Cole had not retired to their room for the night. She'd moved to her vanity desk, avoiding the unruly reflection that would have been sure to greet her, and had penned a short note.

It will be better this way. Cole deserves a lady, she reassured.

Abby reached for the sugarcane handles of her large carpetbag and pulled. The handle came unlatched. Rather than fidget with it, she stood up and tucked the bag under her arm, then ambled down the two steps to the street.

Not needing much for the trip, she'd shoved three of the dresses Martha had hung in her closet into the travel case at her side, along with a few personal items. Aunt Iris would certainly not approve of her current attire, but Abby had not wanted to make the bumpy ride into Denver a disheveled mess and uncomfortable. Her trousers and clean shirt would have to do.

Her hair was pulled away from her face with a plain brown ribbon. No need to fuss over her appearance this morning. This is what she'd looked like every day before the Redbournes came into town.

The stage was coming in at break-neck speed and immediately Abby reached for the gun tucked into her belt. She dropped her bag and dashed toward the approaching transport, but could not see what or who was causing the rush.

"Whoa," Gus yelled and his horse team obeyed, sliding a few feet before coming to a stop.

"What in—" she stopped short.

A woman's scream bounced off the confined space of the stage and out through its windows. Abby looked up at Gus who wiped a streak of sweat from his brow. The stage door sprung open and an older woman, about the age her mother would have been, stepped down off the coach and to the ground.

"Where's the doctor in town, please?" the woman asked over her shoulder as she reached her hand up to another female passenger on the stage.

When no one responded, the woman looked directly at Abby. "The doctor, dear?"

Abby was taken aback by the swell of the second woman's abdomen and leapt forward with an extended hand to help her down from the metal stepping plate.

"He's just down on the corner. I'll take you there." She turned to the younger woman. "Can you make it that far?"

The young woman nodded through strong, exaggerated breaths. She stood up straighter and smiled at Abby, her face damp with perspiration.

"It has passed for the moment..." she said, looking at Abby expectantly.

"Abby," she offered her name and smiled.

The young woman pulled her tighter into her arm. "Abby," she repeated with a grin.

"Go," Abby yelled to Mrs. Patterson who had just crossed the street from the mercantile, "tell Doc we're comin'."

The bustled woman opened her mouth in surprise and then closed it when the young woman let out another scream of agonizing pain and hunched forward. Mrs. Patterson scuttled down the boardwalk toward the doctor's office.

The sound of an approaching horse tore Abby's attention upward. A single horse emerged through the dust, at a full gallop, carrying two riders. One of them jumped from the horse and landed running toward them. When he reached them, Abby backed out of the way and he swept the expectant mother into his arms. Her pain seemed to have subsided again momentarily.

"I'm sorry, my love. I would've been here sooner, but my horse threw a shoe. We should never have made this trip in your condition."

Abby turned away as if intruding on a special moment between husband and wife.

"It's all right, Eli." The young woman placed her hand on his face. "This is Abby," she said as she looked over the man's shoulder.

"Cole's Abby?" he asked. His eyes opened wide and his eyebrows lifted.

Abby stared at them, dumbfounded.

Cole's Abby, she repeated in her mind.

When another scream sounded, Abby motioned toward the doctor's office. "This way," she called and ran ahead of them.

Doc Knight stood in the open doorway and ushered them inside. He motioned for Eli to put his young wife down on a table behind an old worn curtain and disappeared.

Eli reemerged and began to pace the small quarters of the waiting room.

Abby didn't know what to do. She turned to leave, but the older woman took a hold of her arm. "Thank you, Abby. I'm afraid my daughter has a will of her own and refused to stay home. I guess she comes by it naturally." She smiled.

They sat down on the window seat, the woman's arm still linked with hers.

"The train wasn't bad, but I don't think any of us realized how rough the road between Denver and Silver Falls would be by stage."

The look on Abby's face must have betrayed her puzzlement.

"We couldn't wait to meet my son's bride. This is Jameson," the woman said, pointing to a rather large, familiar looking man Abby had not even seen enter the office. "And I'm Leah," she lifted her arm around Abby's shoulders and squeezed. "Cole's mother."

Cole fixed his eyes on the immobile stagecoach in front of the telegraph office. No driver in sight. He scanned the boardwalks for any sign of Abby, to no avail. A small crowd had gathered near the mercantile. He dismounted, tied Maverick to the hitching post in front of the sheriff's office and crossed the street with a hurried step.

"And lawsy sakes," he heard Mrs. Patterson saying, "riding on a stage in her condition, why it's just not—"

"Excuse me, ladies. Have any of you seen my wife?"

The woman in the peacock hat pointed at Doc Knight's office and Cole's heart lurched from his chest. He swiveled around, his legs pounding hard against the dusty street.

He nearly ran over the short, finely dressed woman who stepped around the stagecoach in his path.

"Cole, dear," Mrs. Hutchinson reached out and placed her hand on her forearm. "Have you met my daughter?" she asked. "She just arrived on this morning's stage."

"Excuse me, ma'am, but Abby—"

"Oh, but, I insist," Mrs. Hutchinson interrupted, her eyes cool and her grip on his arm a lot stronger than he would have guessed her capable.

His eyes followed the woman's extended hand.

"MaryBeth?"

She was the last person he'd expected to see in Silver Falls. The last person he wanted to see. *I hope it's not permanent.*

"Cole!" MaryBeth squealed. She reached down to gather the layers of her skirt and rushed to his side, her face upturned toward him.

Cole rolled his eyes heavenward. When MaryBeth had come to Kansas to live with her cousins, everyone had assumed her parents were deceased. The fact Mrs. Hutchinson was her mother begged many questions, but Cole had more pressing things on his mind and the likes of MaryBeth Hutchinson would just have to wait.

He took a deep breath and attempted to remove the woman's hand whose grip had become vice-like on his arm. "Mrs. Hutchinson, please."

She let go, but MaryBeth moved to block his way.

"Aren't you glad to see me, Cole?" MaryBeth placed her hand on his chest and jutted out her lower lip, like she always did when she wanted something.

"Not now, MaryBeth." Cole took a hold of her hand to remove it from his person. He didn't want to think about the reasons she'd come to Silver Falls, he just wanted to get to his wife. To make sure she was safe. *Why would Abby be in the doc's office?*

Abby stepped out onto the boardwalk. Her eyes flitted between him and MaryBeth. Cole could only guess what must be going through her mind and he threw MaryBeth's hand away from him as if it had burned.

He took a step toward the doctor's office. "Abby," he called out, a plea in his voice.

When his father appeared in the doorway behind Abby, followed by Eli, he froze. Hannah wouldn't have made the trip to Silver Falls so close to her time. *Oh, yes, she would,* a voice inside his head insisted. That would explain the doctor's office, but not why Abby was standing there with his family.

He knew the moment his father's gaze fixed on him. Jameson Redbourne broke into a huge grin and stepped off the boardwalk toward him.

"Hannah's having her baby. Doc says everything is going to be just fine."

"Hello, Jameson." Mrs. Hutchinson's voice turned low and sultry.

Cole jerked his chin forward, his mouth open, his eyebrows scrunched together. *What? How?*

Jameson turned to the woman, his face losing all expression when he saw her face. "Norah Marcusen?" he asked in disbelief.

"It's been a long time, stranger," she said, moving a little closer. "It's Hutchinson, now."

Cole watched with trepidation as the older woman seemed to regain some of her youth when she looked at his father.

"Norah," Jameson reached a hand up to Cole's shoulder

and squeezed, "I see you've met my son."

An unkempt man stumbled onto the street toward them and started to yell. "I'm not gonna do it anymore, Norah." He brought the large bottle in his hand up to his mouth and took a drink before continuing. "The people in this town've lost enough 'cause a you."

"Why, yes." Mrs. Hutchinson cleared her throat and ignored the drunkard's display. "He's a lot like his father, this one." She smiled in answer to Jameson's question, but appeared visibly distracted.

"Ya gonna kill me too?" The man tripped over his own foot and fell forward into Mrs. Hutchinson, spilling some of his drink down the back of her olive dress.

"How dare you, sir."

"How dare *you*, madam."

Cole's father reached out a hand, grabbed a handful of the cheap twill material of the man's jacket, and righted him. "Best sleep it off, man, and leave the lady alone."

"Lady?" he snorted. "She ain't no lady."

Without warning his father landed a punch directly in the inebriated man's face.

He fell backward and landed with a thud near the wheel of the stagecoach. The man shook his head and rubbed his jaw. "Jes ask 'er." He took another swig of his rot gut. "Got told Spencer is dead and the boy too." He pushed off the ground in attempt to stand, but his legs didn't hold and he tumbled sideways.

"You jes get rid of us when ya don't need us no more? Well, I'm done. Not gonna do it no more." He pulled himself up to the stage wheel and leaned against it. "I don't care how much land ya says ya gonna give me."

"Shut up, Henry!" Mrs. Hutchinson spoke, though her mouth barely moved. Her cheeks flushed. She took in a deep breath and closed her eyes.

When her focus returned to Jameson, she laughed nervously. "Now, where were we? Oh, yes. I believe you accompanied my daughter on the stage."

Cole didn't hear the rest of the exchange with his father, but moved closer to Mr. Campbell who looked as if he may pass out at any moment. Henry? It had to be. This drunkard was Lily's father. Cole had only seen the man at a distance at the Sunday tea.

"Mr. Campbell?" Cole knelt down next to the inebriated man.

Red, glassy eyes turned to him, squinting in a visible attempt to focus.

"Yer Abby's fella, ain't ya?" Mr. Campbell propped himself up with one arm on the ground to the side of him.

"Best be careful, son. She'll stop at nothin' to git what she wants."

"And what does she want?" Cole looked up at the woman in question. Her eyes darted anxiously between his father and Mr. Campbell. When she caught Cole's stare, she scurried toward them.

"Cole dear, don't you pay him no nevermind. He's intoxicated and speaking nonsense."

"Ask that Jez-e-bel 'bout yer friend," Mr. Campbell's head started to fall, "in Kans—" he didn't finish his last word before he passed out cold.

Cole's mind raced.

Alaric. The man knew about Alaric.

He grabbed Henry Campbell by the front of his shirt collar and pulled him up so their noses nearly met. "Wake up." He shook the man. "What about Alaric?"

"Cole."

Only Abby's voice could have penetrated the darkness that had overcome him.

"Cole," she coaxed.

He closed his eyes and then opened them again. His hands were balled into fists around the unconscious man's shirt collar and Abby's hands covered them, persuading him to let go. His fingers released their grasp and he pulled back, away from the drunkard.

Cole whipped his head up to look at Mrs. Hutchinson,

whose face had turned stone-like. Her eyes darted from one side to the other.

"What do you know of Alaric?" Cole demanded quietly. He reached down to take Abby's hand. He needed her. He could scarcely breathe.

A composed smile settled on the older woman's face and she responded with calm. "Do you mean Friedrich Johansson's grandson. Such a shame what happened to him."

"Mr. Campbell said to ask you about my friend. In Kansas." Cole stood to his full height, a good foot taller than the woman in front of him. "Why would he say that?"

Mrs. Hutchinson took a step backward and nervously reached up to fiddle with the wisps of hair that had come loose from her coiffeur at the base of her neck.

"Why, he's speaking of MaryBeth dear. You *are* friends with my daughter, are you not?" The quiver in her voice was slight, but it was there.

Doc Knight's office door opened and Cole tore his gaze from Mrs. Hutchinson.

Leah Redbourne stepped out onto the boardwalk.

"It's a girl," she yelled. "Everyone is fine."

Eli, the proud father, whooped loudly. He picked up his mother-in-law and spun her around before disappearing again into the grey painted building.

Jameson took off his hat and hit it against his thigh. His grin carved excitement into his face. This was the first of eight grandchildren to be a girl.

In two long strides, Cole's father made it up onto the boardwalk and grabbed his wife around her waist, pulling her tightly into him. Cole had watched his parent's affectionate behavior his entire life and had always hoped to find that kind of love with his own wife. He squeezed Abby's hand. They may not be married, but he planned to rectify that as soon as possible.

"Not this time," Mrs. Hutchinson whispered. She reached into her handbag and pulled out a small, ivory handled derringer.

"Look out!" Abby screamed at his parents.

Before Cole could react, Abby had let go of his hand and had lunged forward. She pushed against Mrs. Hutchinson's extended arm, thwarting her shot.

The older woman moved quickly, with more precision than Cole could have expected. She reached out and caught Abby by the hair.

Abby grunted. She moved her hand slowly toward the pistol sticking out from her belt.

"I wouldn't, dear." Mrs. Hutchinson said next to Abby's ear, loud enough for Cole to hear.

"You're just like her," the older woman jutted her chin toward Cole's mother, "stealing away what doesn't belong to you. What could the likes of you possibly have to offer Jameson's son? A rancher," she said the word with disdain. "Who's ever heard of a woman rancher? It's downright immoral. My MaryBeth is a lady fit to be a Redbourne, and she's beautiful." Mrs. Hutchinson pulled Abby close to her and held the derringer tightly against her chin.

"Mother!" MaryBeth's voice almost reached hysteria. "What are you doing?" She stomped her foot in the middle of the street. A small cloud of dust kicked up beneath her.

"Getting for you what I failed to get for myself." She pushed the gun harder into Abby's jaw.

Abby scowled.

Cole's jaw clenched and he immediately regretted the action. He opened his mouth to flex the throbbing muscles in his face.

"Norah."

Mrs. Hutchinson snapped her head toward Cole's mother.

"Norah, let the girl go." Leah put her hands up in front of her and took a step forward. "Someone's going to get hurt."

"*Going* to get hurt? Do you have any idea what you did to me that day?" Mrs. Hutchinson moved the gun away from Abby's face and pointed it toward Cole's mother.

Jameson stepped in front of Leah.

Riders approached the north end of town. It had to be his

brothers. They had only been a few minutes behind him. He closed his eyes. *Please, God, let it be my brothers.*

"Look around you, Norah. There is no way out of this unless you put down the gun and let Abby go." Jameson attempted to reason with her.

Maverick snorted. Cole glanced over at the sheriff's office where his horse had been hitched. If he could just make the few paces without being seen, his rifle would be within easy reach. He took a slow sideways step.

"Don't even try it, handsome." Mrs. Hutchinson's eyes were like steel and they pierced Cole when she looked at him. She pulled harder on Abby's hair, still clutched within her grasp.

Abby winced in pain.

Cole breathed a little easier at the sound of multiple cocking guns.

Mrs. Hutchinson pulled Abby around with her to face three dismounted Redbourne brothers, all with rifles pointed directly at her. She returned the derringer to rest just below Abby's ear.

"Such strapping young men," she said appreciatively. "So nice of you to join us. You've got until the count of three to lower your weapons." She stood up straighter, her voice gaining confidence.

"Do it," Cole yelled to his brothers in a tone that left no room for argument.

Each, in turn, laid their guns at their feet.

"What's going on here, Charcoal?" Levi asked as he begrudgingly set down his Winchester rifle, his hands straightening in from of him, palms out for the woman to see. He slowly stood from his crouched position.

Mrs. Hutchinson laughed.

"These could have been *our* boys, Jameson. It may have been a long time ago, but we *were* betrothed." She paused for a moment, turning her gaze to Cole's father. "You loved me once, but I understand. I was a poor miner's daughter and so it was easy for Leah to lure you away from me with a plentiful dowry and promises of land."

"Is that what you think? That I married Leah for money?" Jameson stepped off the boardwalk, his head tilted.

"Well, I was not going to allow the same thing to happen to my daughter." Her reverie had been short-lived. She turned to MaryBeth. "Your father was a weak man, child. He didn't understand how important it was for you to have property and a rich dowry to offer a husband. But I do. I know all too well what it costs to be lacking. And I wasn't about to let that happen to you."

"Mother, what are you saying?" MaryBeth stepped out from behind the stagecoach.

"That she killed 'im."

A dozen heads snapped in the direction of the weak words.

Henry Campbell sat himself upright with a grimace and wiped at the drool hanging from the corner of his mouth. "It was her that got that Johansson boy killed and she was the one done told Spencer ta get rid o' the freckled kid. I reckon I was next since I helped 'er find the rustlers'n such."

Mrs. Hutchinson turned the gun on Mr. Campbell.

"Henry," she spat, "you couldn't just keep your mouth shut."

Abby pitched her elbow into Mrs. Hutchinson's side and stomped on her foot. The woman released her grasp on Abby's hair, who stumbled breathless toward his parents.

Cole watched in horror as the assailant's focus and double-handed aim returned to the spirited woman he loved. Without further thought he rushed forward. His life would mean nothing without Abby by his side. He had to protect her...at all costs. He jumped.

The gun fired.

Pain ripped through Cole's side. His entire weight fell against Abby, thrusting her to the earthen street. Screams faded into the distance as darkness consumed him.

Lord, please let him be alive.

Abby couldn't breathe beneath Cole's heavy, motionless form. She pushed against his shoulder with her arm and, with the help of her hip, rolled him off of her. She sat up, allowing air to fill her lungs. She reached out and hooked her hands under Cole's arms and pulled his body up until his head rested in her lap. Blood seeped heavily from the wound in his side and had begun to spread up to his chest.

This can't be happening.

Abby gently raked the hair out of his face. She caressed his forehead and temple.

"Abby?" Cole croaked in a low voice. His eyes flitted open.

She wiped the tears from her cheeks and managed a smile. "Look. I'm still here, Cole. No running away. I'm right here."

His eyes closed again and his head sank deeper into her lap, he was no longer conscious.

Within moments Raine was next to her. He bent down and lifted his brother's limp body into his arms and nodded to her. He pushed past the group that had collected around them and with determined step reached the doctor's office in just a few short paces.

Levi reached down and brought her to her feet. He didn't release her hand, but pulled her along with him to the doctor's door.

Abby paused at the entryway. Levi let go and she turned to see Rafe binding Mrs. Hutchinson's hands, none too gently, behind her. She didn't envy the woman. The hard look on Rafe's face and tight clench to his jaw showed barely concealed restraint.

She lowered her head and pushed against from the doorframe. Cole had come to her rescue again. He'd sacrificed himself for her and she realized that she may have been wrong to believe he hadn't felt what she felt. Love.

Is it possible?

She rushed to the curtain, but Jameson stood in her way.

"The doctor is working on him, Abby. He gave strict instructions that no one was to be let inside."

"How is he?" she whispered.

"We won't know for a while."

When Jameson reached out to pull his wife into his arms, Abby darted around him and pushed her way into the room with her husband.

"Abby," Doc Knight chided. "You need to go outside."

"I won't leave him," she said as she stepped to the side of the bed across from where the doctor was working and picked up Cole's hand.

Don't you leave me, Cole Redbourne. Not now. Not ever.

CHAPTER TWENTY-FOUR

One Week Later

"It's not your mother's wedding dress, Abby, but you did manage to find some man to marry you." Lily lifted one of Abby's golden curls which sprung back into place when she let go.

"You are beautiful," Martha added, "a true vision."

Abby looked into the vanity mirror and smiled at her reflection. She pinched her cheeks and was pleased with the color that appeared there. It had been a long time since she'd been this happy.

"I still feel like me. Just with a fancy dress."

Cole had been adamant they not wait to be married again and so his mother had commissioned the most beautiful snow white dress to be made for the special day. It was amazing how money could make things happen so quickly.

Abby believed it impractical, but Leah Redbourne had insisted.

Cole's wound was healing with no sign of infection. After Doc Knight had removed the bullet, he told Abby that he was a lucky man that it had hit him where it had. Nothing vital had been damaged and he expected Cole to make a full recovery. However, he emphasized the need to make Cole take it easy.

An impossible task. Stubborn man.

A knock sounded on the door and then it cracked a little.

"May I come in?" Abby's soon-to-be mother-in-law poked

her head into the room.

Abby stood up and self-consciously smoothed the skirt of her dress.

"Yes, please."

"We'll just be downstairs." Martha put her hand at Lily's back and smiled at Abby. She turned and nodded to Leah before leaving the room.

Abby had been moved back into her old bedroom while Cole recuperated and until they could be properly wed. It seemed very empty without many of her personal effects. She looked around at the barren walls before fixing her eyes on Leah, who stood just inside the closed doorway.

"My son is a very lucky man."

Abby felt heat rise in her face at the appraisal and she was unsure how to respond. She cleared her throat and looked down at the floor.

Leah laughed. She curled her finger under Abby's chin and lifted her head.

"My dear, you are lovely. Everyone is waiting, but I wondered if you would like to wear these." Leah held out three wild-flowered hair pins in her hand. "I wore them on my wedding day, as have each of my new daughters."

Abby smiled.

Leah put them in her hair and tilted the mirror upward so that Abby could see herself. The flowers rested on her crown just in front of the line of her veil.

"They are beautiful. Thank you."

Leah put her arms around Abby's shoulders and squeezed as they both looked into the mirror. "Are you ready?"

Abby nodded.

Leah turned from her and left the room.

Abby walked toward the door. Music had begun to play. She reached down to the beautiful flower bouquet that Martha had gathered for her.

She exhaled and stepped out onto the landing. She'd run down these steps a thousand times, but right now, in this dress, it seemed all new to her.

She glanced down over the balcony and found her father, waiting at the bottom of the stairs. She took her first step. Then the next until her father reached out and linked her arm with his.

By the fireplace at the far end of the living area, Cole waited. He stood tall, his shoulders back, his hands linked in front of him. A short grimace touched his face, the only indication he was still in pain. However, when he looked up at her, his eyes the color of charred coal, the pain left his face, and was replaced by a smile that lit Abby's heart on fire.

He was the most beautiful man she'd ever laid eyes on and she turned to her father in a whisper. "Pinch me, please."

He smiled down at her with a twinkle in his eye and cupped his hand over hers on his arm.

Abby wasn't prepared when her father let go, but as she took a hold of Cole's extended hand, she felt...home. Though his lips were now relaxed, the smile in his eyes sent a wave of warm tingles down through her body and to her toes.

This time the wedding meant something much different to her. The man she married was the man she loved and she could not wait to start building her life with him.

"You may now kiss the bride," Reverend Daniels announced.

She turned to face her husband, her stomach suddenly a flutter.

His head bent toward her, his lips parted. When his mouth claimed hers, she melted against him. He broke their kiss and pulled her in tight.

"I love you, Abby," he whispered.

She didn't care that the whole town and their families all watched their exchange. The only thing she knew was that she was where she belonged. In the arms of the man she loved.

Abby stood in front of the window, moonlight spilling all

about her. The sheer-like material of her nightshift flowed behind her in the breeze from the open casement. Her dark silhouette contrasted against her immediate surroundings.

"You are beautiful," he whispered. Without taking his eyes of the apparition before him, Cole closed their bedroom door.

She remained still, staring out into the night.

He stepped toward her and cringed at the pain that still accompanied all movement. The moon cast a luminous sheen around her entire form. He ached to touch her, to prove this vision standing in front of him was real.

Cole reached his hand up and slid the thin fabric from her shoulder. The warm glow of light from his lantern caressed her skin and he bent forward to kiss the exposed area.

Her head tilted backward against him. He pulled her closer, cursing the sharp pain that seared through his side.

She circled slowly around to face him, placing her hand on the side of his face and smiled. Her fingers slid down his cheek and rested on the top button of his shirt. He held his breath as she undid the small knob and moved to the next.

When his chest was fully exposed, she moved her hand to rest over the bandage encasing his abdomen.

"Thank you," she spoke softly, staring up him with wide trusting eyes, "for saving my life."

He lifted a hand to her chin and caressed her lips with his thumb. He didn't want to think about what his life would have been like without her. She was his rescuer, his salvation, and he loved her.

His other hand moved to the back of her neck and he held her face close.

"Thank *you*, Mrs. Redbourne, "for saving *me*." Cole leaned his head down to join his lips with hers in a kiss that promised all the hope, love, and happiness that only forever could bring.

ABOUT THE AUTHOR

KELLI ANN MORGAN recognized a passion for writing at a very young age and since that time has devoted herself to creativity of all sorts. Being a wife and mother are two of her most important and favorite roles, while being a writer is in her blood. She also moonlights as a Creative Designer – creating covers and more for other authors, photographer, jewelry designer, painter, and motivational speaker.

Kelli Ann is a long-time member of the Romance Writers of America and was president of her local chapter in 2009. Her love of and talent for writing have opened many doors for her and she continues to look for new and exciting opportunities and calls to adventure. She loves to hear from her readers.

www.kelliannmorgan.com

WATCH FOR

the Bounty Hunter

REDBOURNE SERIES BOOK TWO
RAFE'S STORY

COMING LATE 2012

CPSIA information can be obtained at www.ICGtesting.com
Printed in the USA
LVOW10s1742101014

408244LV00003B/123/P